"YOU'RE ALMOST
TOO REAL."

Jacob's warmth enwrapped her. "Too exciting...." He spoke thickly, as if drunk on strong wine. Searching his amber eyes in the moonlight, Camille knew the greatest impetuous thirst and the greatest misgiving.

"I'm real, all right." Her nails dug into his wrist. "Please let go."

He kept her dangerously close, his other hand sliding to the firm swell of her breast. She gasped, and was silent.

"You see how it is with us?" Jacob sighed at the hardening of the tip under his sensitive caress. "How can you pretend we're strangers? What can we do about how we feel?"

Camille didn't answer. She longed to make mad love to him here on the sand. In some respects, he was her perfect mate—but the very mystery of the man mocked her. Maybe Jacob was a bastard, and she a fool.

Books by Christine Hella Cott

SUPERROMANCES

These books may be available at your local bookseller.

For a free catalog listing all titles currently available, send your name and address to:

Harlequin Reader Service
P.O. Box 52040, Phoenix, AZ 85072-2040
Canadian address: Stratford, Ontario N5A 6W2

Christine Hella Cott
PERFUME AND LACE

A SUPERROMANCE FROM
W🌐RLDWIDE

TORONTO · NEW YORK · LONDON · PARIS
AMSTERDAM · STOCKHOLM · HAMBURG
ATHENS · MILAN · TOKYO · SYDNEY

Published February 1984

First printing December 1983

ISBN 0-373-70098-9

Printed in Canada

CHAPTER ONE

CAMILLE PULLED THE KEY RING out of her pocket. From the many assembled she chose the largest, a three-inch-long brass key. It gleamed dull gold in the fading blue wash of beginning twilight—and she realized she had lingered too long. She fitted the key into the door. Twisting the tarnished brass knob to be certain the lock was secure, she turned. Flicking up the collar of her yellow rain slicker so the brim of her hat would send the rain down her back instead of her neck, she left the shelter of the veranda. Puddles had formed on the stairs, slabs of Nootka marble, gray-and-white stone worn in depressions from many years' use. Her yellow rubber galoshes sent the water flying as she ran down into the garden.

The grass was sodden underfoot, the trees bare and stark against the pale golden shimmer of the western sky. It was too overcast to detect a sunset, and the Olympic Mountains, southwest across the Strait of Juan de Fuca, were shrouded in a watery veil. South, the open stretch of the strait melted into the sky without horizon. East, in the dim afternoon and the pelting rain, the lights of the city of Victoria twinkled like earthbound stars past the jut of Albert Head. Clouds in every possible shade of powder blue tumbled and rolled and billowed in their eastward hurry toward mainland Canada. When she was across the lawn and halfway down another flight of marble stairs leading to the beach in a long shallow curve, she turned suddenly to look back at the house she had just left.

Its dark and lonely windows tugged at her heart-strings. A wistful sigh escaped through lips that were full and as pink as the deep blush of a damask rose. The misty light, however, was kind to the old house, for the shell-pink paint didn't look nearly so worn as it had when she'd arrived in the cold brightness of an early December noon. Why, in the imperceptible deepening of twilight, the house didn't look shabby at all but graceful and elegant—quite in keeping with its whimsical Queen Anne style.

The foundations were sturdy granite, built into the rock of the low headland. The variation of thin weatherboard and patterned shingle soared up three floors. Gingerbread decorated the many gables; bay windows large and small decorated the walls. Veranda columns rose to fancy millwork, supporting a smaller sun deck above. The tower stood to the right of the door—no Queen Anne house was complete without a tower or two. The veranda bellied out around it on the main floor, and the deck's dainty balustrade encircled it on the second. From the third story, the view was superlative. Camille knew this vista by heart, as she knew everything else she associated with the house.

It was small compared to other mansions of the Victorian era, but to her, with its surround of Gary oaks and pines and red-trunked arbutus trees, it was perfect. When the house was built in 1890, the prevailing fashion was to name one's abode. In this case, the brass plaque hanging from the millwork above the marble stairs bore the legend, Damask.

Camille smiled to herself as she stood contemplating the house. Then her coffee-brown eyes reflected annoyance as she remembered that, once again, she had forgotten to prune the roses that rambled over the granite foundation and, in the summer, clambered up the trellises to shade the veranda. Closing her eyes for a moment, she could imagine the popular, garden-variety roses as they looked in summer, with the golden yellow of Alchemist twining among huge trusses of exotic cinnabar-red Illusion, the pure white and powerfully fragrant Aimee Vibert, the clove-scented Champney's Pink Cluster and—

But she'd spent too much time indoors, changing the furnace filter, lighting the seven fireplaces, dusting, cleaning and checking for mildew. Afterward, quite irresponsibly, she'd taken the dustcover off the armchair in the tower room and, with the fire crackling heartily nearby, had curled up to gaze dreamfully out the window...wondering at some far-off day in the hazy future when she would be living here with some as-yet-unknown lover...a husband? For when she married the house would be hers, her mother had promised her—more than it already was.

A dash of cold rain against her cheek brought her smartly to the realization that she'd better hurry home, or Robbie would be annoyed. Tonight she had supper to prepare, as well. Camille ran down the last of the stairs, gaining the narrow strip of beach. Her galoshes crunched on the wet round stones as she hurried toward the last pale shimmer of sunset's suggestion. From long habit she scanned the strait for the bold black-and-white of killer whales out there among the seals and the sea lions. Last night she had heard the sea lions, returned to their winter feeding grounds, barking on the beach. . . .

A few seals stayed all year out on Rice Rocks, past the western tip of William Head, so their comings and goings didn't bat a local eyelash. And since the sea lions came on the beach at times, often at night when one could hear their sociable grunting, they were regarded as commonplace soon after arrival. But the whales never became commonplace, no matter how often one saw them. Everybody in the vicinity regarded them with a proprietary air.

The community, composed of small farms, was only twenty minutes from downtown Victoria, on Vancouver Island. It was known as Metchosin, Metchosin being a native name for "big smelly fish," since a whale had once been beached right on this strip of sand and shingle.

The light was growing too dim for sightings now. The rain began to fall in curtains. Shivering, Camille scrambled over and around the maze of beached logs to eventually find herself at the foot of the path home. A gust tip-tilted her fisherman's hat, sent it splat against the trunk of a wind-bent pine. Hastily retrieving it before it was off, helter-skelter, she anchored it firmly over her riot of equally wayward short blond curls.

Dashing up the path through rose beds neatly mulched and pruned for winter evoked another flicker of guilt at the task she'd avoided at the house. When she was only a hundred paces up and away from the beach, the gale didn't seem quite so potent, although the remaining light was suddenly steeped in blue. Up and up through the wide stretch of lawn she raced, rueful about how late she really was.

Home was ablaze with light, smoke was curling out of the chimney, and mother was probably upstairs, getting ready to go out. She was having dinner that evening with Rachael, a friend of hers from school days. Because Rachael was up on architecture, Camille knew this undignified but pretty house—which could use a new coat of paint, as well—was a combination of Ontario Cottage and Saltbox. The former influence, Rachael had told Camille, was evident in the encircling porch and the row of dormer windows in the slant of the roof, the latter, in the house itself, two stories high in the front, only one in the back. Rachael was rather on Camille's mind today—or more particularly, her mother's invitation to dinner was.

She sped around to the rear of the cottage, reached the worn tarmac of the drive, slipped through the small gate in the yew hedge and ran the several remaining yards to the workshop. It was a huge, long brick building—which Rachael was at pains to pigeonhole in architectural terms—and which housed the warehouse, the distillery and the laboratory. The rest of the workshop was in darkness, but the glazed windows of the lab shone light patterns onto the wet concrete pad out front. Camille invaded the quiet in a flurry of rain and cold and wind.

Robbie, wearing a white lab coat, the low heels of his galoshes hooked over the rungs of his stool, sat by the foot of the long, T-shaped stainless-steel counter that divided the lab. The top of the T ran almost the entire length of the inside wall, one end stopping to accommodate a filing cabinet, the other to make room for a floor-to-ceiling bookshelf filled with heavy perfumery tomes. Her brother swiveled immediately, scowling.

"You're late! Where were you? Since you're the Nose in the family, the least you could do is be here when you're needed!"

"Oh, I know, and I'm ever so sorry!" she exclaimed, smiling winsomely. Taking off her hat, she shook out her curls, which really wasn't necessary, for they automatically sprang out in joyous release. She added, before her brother could continue, "What are you doing?" Shedding the slicker, she advanced into the meticulously tidy, relentlessly clean laboratory with its pervasive perfume scent. She looked at the little flagon in his hand, all but hidden within the quick curl of his fingers.

"Nothing," he replied airily. Then, "Where were you?"

"Damask."

"Oh." She could see he almost forgave her, just as she would almost have forgiven him had he lingered in his greenhouse when he was required elsewhere. "Here." He pushed over a small glass tray with four strips of paper on it. They were sniffing blotters, or as they were called in the perfume industry, *mouillettes*. One end was dipped in a perfume sample and left to dry before it was sniffed. Every time Robbie concocted a master batch of one of their perfumes, Camille checked it before the next step—dilution in prepared perfumers'-grade alcohol.

Camille lifted the blotters one by one, inhaling each fragrance, a deliberate action requiring concentration. Just as a wine taster would stand absorbed with a sampling swirling around his mouth, so was she absorbed.

"Mmm." She opened her eyes. "That waft of orange blossom in Island Rose is pure magic, isn't it?"

"If you say so. I could have gone ahead, but you remember as well as I do what happened with the second batch of Woodsmoke. That rotten musk!"

"Adulterated musk, Robbie," Camille corrected automatically. Did she remember! It had been painfully embarrassing when that batch of Woodsmoke, her own creation and a men's perfume, had quickly soured. Robbie hadn't thought it smelled that bad, but to Camille's sensitive and tender nose it had reeked. Rachael, who had bought a bottle for her husband, Wilson, had asked Camille the next day whether she really thought men should smell like that. Luckily Rachael had pointed out the failure, for if it had been one of the stores they supplied . . . !

Ever since then, Camille checked each master batch before dilution. If that was perfect, there was little chance anything could go wrong. Nevertheless, every week she double-checked the lightproof, water-

and airtight vats in which the finished perfume was stored, and, of course, sampled the essence again before the final step, bottling. The Beesley perfumery had a reputation to uphold, and if it was lost the results could be fatal. A small family-owned-and-operated business that emphasized quality, not quantity, made heavy demands on all of them. The perfumery was their livelihood, yet not all that romantic, as people tended to think.

"How sweet!" a tourist had said, visiting the perfumery's small store. "It's just too, too quaint, isn't it? And this tiny shop, smothered in roses! So cute and old-fashioned! And don't you fit the whole idea of perfume, dear! Don't tell me—is that your mother? The family resemblance. . . . Oh, you must have fantastic fun, *making* perfume! What a lovely spot. I'm so glad we came! I must say Victoria is one of the prettiest little cities we ever saw, and your place here by the sea is enchanting! Why, when we were driving past those rows and rows of rose bushes, the smell was pure heaven—and so romantic!"

And Camille, who had known her brother was out in those rose fields surrounding their home and Damask, spreading unromantic manure, had simply smiled. But she had been able to reply truthfully that the whole family loved making perfume.

Indeed, she wouldn't dream of doing anything else. Robbie, too, who preferred live roses, especially over the tedious laboratory work, would be bereft without one to bury his nose in. Even in the wintertime, the shop and the house were burgeoning with blooms from his greenhouse. He didn't think there was anything effeminate about the culture of roses. Nobody seeing him thought so, either. The younger feminine tourists would often ask, "Who was that blond guy in the fields?" They would glance at her hair. "Your brother...? Could we go for a walk out there?"

Camille, leaning over the counter to look at their footwear, would suggest with a sparkle of amusement and a charming smile, that there was a garden just outside the shop door for their pleasure—but if they were intent on the fields, to go ahead. And they were welcome to pick a rose or two, but please, only those that were full blown. Rosebuds were needed for distillation into essential oil, so since it took some two hundred fifty pounds of rose petals to produce an ounce of essential oil, every bud was precious.

Three out of the four perfumes the Beesleys manufactured were older than Camille. Their main line, Island Rose, was quite ancient, for her great-great-grandmother had brought the formula with her from France. It was she who had made the first perfume on this property, and it was her husband who had built Damask. For five generations the Beesleys of Beesley Farm had faithfully produced Island Rose. Camille and Robbie's father, a chemist, had made one careful alteration to the original recipe. Then, between the births of his two offspring, he had created Island Violet and Lavender Mist.

Woodsmoke was new, a rather brash departure from tradition—it was for men! But Camille sensed her father would have approved, were he still alive, for he hadn't been one to hold back the times. He would also have delighted to know there was really, truly, another Nose in the family. There wasn't a hope of creating a new perfume if someone involved didn't have that fundamental asset. Robbie had a good nose, but not a Nose, and neither did mother.

"As far as I'm concerned, you can go ahead!" Camille concluded and saw, when she replaced the last blotter, that Robbie was staring abstractedly at the flagon in his hand. Another *mouillette*, its dipped end dark, lay on the counter just past his hand. Reaching beyond him before he could prevent her, she snatched it up and wafted it to and fro in front of her nose. "What's this?" she asked quickly, then sniffed and sniffed again. "What is it!"

"You mean you don't recognize it?" he asked with careful indifference.

"Well, I know it's rose, an essential oil, no additives. But it's not from Grasse...no, and it's not Bulgarian, either...not rose geranium, not tuberose.... Oh, it's lovely! So warm!"

"You think so?" His eyes, a dark coffee brown like hers, shone up at her with subdued excitement.

Camille opened her eyes, considering her brother over the slender strip of paper. She grinned suddenly, delightedly, then said, with appropriate reverence, "It's yours, isn't it? It's your new rose. The oil you would never let me near. Oh, Robbie! You mean you've been keeping this under your hat since summer?"

"I wanted it to age properly. I wanted to make all the tests first, and you know I'm not too swift around the lab. Is it...really different from our stock rose?''

She could see her answer was of such immense importance that she felt a little frightened in case she disappointed him. Again she inhaled the scent, with the utmost attention to its quality, its depth. "Of course it's similar, owing to our temperate climate and the soil. It has strains of Rosa Centifolia and Rosa Damascena for parents—but it *is* different. Oh, Robbie!" Camille was overcome. She knew the attention her brother had lavished on his as-yet-unnamed strain of rose. Two years ago the parcel of land they referred to as "the back sixty" had been planted with it. This year the first crop, albeit a small one, had come off, and Robbie had been very secretive about the result of distillation.

He sat there beaming at her like a ray of sunshine the day had previously lacked.

"How can you just sit there?" Camille cried in excited protest. "You should be dancing! Don't you realize what you've done?"

But all he said was, "Do you think you could make a new perfume out of it?" while his eyes did the dancing for him. He brushed a hand through his hair, a wavy cornsilk mass rather more relaxed than Camille's irrepressible mop.

"Could I!" she exclaimed, taking a few impromptu twirling steps around the counter. "Have you a name yet? You'd better not call it Beesley! Your rose needs a really special name, and maybe we'll call the new perfume by the same."

"Well, you'll have to study the scent first to get

some idea of what kind of perfume it would suit. Maybe the name will come from that. You're better at that sort of thing, anyway." He gave her the flagon.

"Let's go out tonight to celebrate!" she announced over her shoulder, going to her own area in the lab on the right side of the top of the T, next to the filing cabinet. "Mom's going over to Rachael and Wilson's tonight for dinner, so she's already busy."

"Oh. Does that mean you're cooking supper?" He pulled a face. "What are we having?" he added with obvious misgiving, putting jars of various chemicals he had been using back into place in the glass-fronted cupboards above the counter.

"Hamburger hash," Camille threatened, labeling the flagon he had given her with "Robbie." Surrounding her counter beneath the cupboards was what was known in the trade as an organ, and this was where she composed perfume. The organ basically consisted of a semicircle of shelves—five in all—each just deep enough and high enough to accommodate more of the same bottles. There were some six hundred little brown bottles gathered there. Labels of different essential oils from around the world were attached to the bottles, as well as quite a few of the modern synthetic names. As she made space on the bottom shelf and inserted Robbie's flagon, a faint shadow passed over her face. "Do you realize this is the third dinner mom's been invited to in two months?"

"So? She's always going over there. And you

know Rachael is a piece of furniture around here, so what's unusual about a dinner?''

"Nothing... only—only it's the third *dress-up* dinner. And guess who's completing the foursome for the third time. Charles! You know, Charles Darby, Wilson's brother,'' she added a shade impatiently when Robbie looked vacant.

"I fail to catch your drift. Why shouldn't Rachael and Wilson have his brother and her best friend over for dinner? Camille, you have a way of making a mystery out of—of a clam shell!'' Robbie dismissed witheringly.

"You missed the fine print. It's a formal dinner, dress-up and all that. Candles and champagne cocktails! And if I must dot the *t*'s, Mr. Charles Darby, retired businessman from Toronto—wealthy, healthy and fit—just happens to be a widower. And mother's a widow. You see....''

"You cross *t*'s. You don't dot them! You're crazy! Anyway, nobody likes him, so I don't suppose mom does, either. She's probably just being neighborly, since nobody else is. The man lives right next door to us!'' Next door was a mile away down the beach past Damask.

"But the candles, Robbie—the champagne!''

"Mom? No, not mom! You see a mosquito and expect a plague! There's no way mom would, not after dad.... I know it's been five years but— When,'' he challenged, "has she ever gone out on a date? She wouldn't even think of it!''

"And maybe we would never think of it! Comfortable old mom. Well, open your eyes! Maybe she is forty-four, but she happens to be a very attractive forty-four. She's beautiful, Robbie. We're so used to her we don't notice. And besides that, she's everything else, too. You know how dad felt about her. Why not somebody else? Now that I think of it, I can see all kinds of men falling hopelessly in love with her!''

"You sound like one of those schmaltzy novelettes. Really, Camille!''

"It's possible!'' she insisted doggedly. "And, well, I want mom to be happy more than anything—but not Charles Darby!'' Her light voice was tinged with revulsion.

"Mmm, I know. Never met anyone colder and haughtier in my life. So I don't think we have anything to worry about.''

"Maybe not,'' Camille sighed, remembering Mr. Darby's curiously flat gray eyes. She shivered. "Phyllis says, for all his money he's really tight—to the point of meanness.''

"Phyllis is a gossip— Oh, she said to tell you we had a good day in the store, the start of the Christmas rush. Steady trickle all day.'' Minding the shop was one of mother's chores, and since it was open seven days a week, Phyllis, who lived nearby, came Fridays, Saturdays and Sundays to relieve her. Occasionally Camille helped out.

"Anyway,'' Robbie continued, "Wilson's pretty tight, too. You know Elaine's always complaining about her allowance. According to Rachael, he's disappointed in their daughter's spend-happy ways. Now that they've spoiled her rotten, they want to complain. Which reminds me, I wish you wouldn't take Elaine's castoffs. She's so gracious about giving you her old clothes, it makes me sick.''

"Since you and Elaine sucked thumbs together in the cradle, you should be used to her by now,'' Camille replied mildly. "And where else would I get a silver fox fur jacket? I don't care if it's secondhand when it's brand-new to me! But Robbie...if these dinners aren't romantic, it could be something just as bad...."

He groaned at her ominous tone. "Now what are you talking about?''

"Well...." What she was about to say was so dreadful a thought, she hadn't even wanted to complete it in her mind. But her worry was eating away at her, and she had to get it out in the open if only to be assured that she *was* crazy. "Elaine said yesterday her Uncle Charles was already bored after just eight months of retirement. He's begun to look around for a small business to buy. She said his modus operandi was to take over companies that were, well, in trouble, buy in cheap and take over. That's apparently how he made his millions.

"Look, Robbie, mom keeps the books, always has done, so we never see that side of things. We don't really know our financial position. Have you also noticed our standard of living has gone down since dad died? Have you noticed the whole place needs paint, not only Damask? I know you've seen all the holes in the drive! And mom's really been economizing lately.''

"What do you mean?''

"I caught her trying to resurrect a dress that's years out of date instead of just buying a good one for tonight. When I gave her our last order she asked if we could buy synthetic ambergris, because it's so much cheaper than the real thing. And just this morning she asked me to trim her hair, when you know she always goes to the hairdresser!"

"Maybe she didn't feel like—"

"Then, when Rachael invited her to go to Vancouver with them next weekend she refused—that's twice now. She keeps putting off getting the boiler fixed, too."

"So you're thinking that maybe money-magnate Charles is behind these candlelit dinners, instead of Cupid Rachael?" Camille nodded slowly. Her brother frowned rather fiercely all of a sudden. "When that land came up for sale on the other side of Damask, I hoped we could buy it. We need more land. But while mom was hemming and hawing, Mr. Darby swooped down and picked it off!" He stared over at her. "But if we are in trouble, wouldn't mom tell us first before she told anyone else, especially Charles Darby? Oh, but wait a minute! You're infecting me with your instant calamities! Why should we be in trouble?"

"You're always stuck in a rose—you don't see much else! Our biggest sales are to the stores in Victoria. Sure, our own little shop does well in the summer, but you know last summer was bad for all stores, what with the ferries' striking and tourists afraid of being stuck on the Island!" Vancouver Island was referred to as "the Island," as if there could be no other, by those who lived there. "Since dad died— We don't really know how to manage a business, and none of us has ever looked after the selling-to-stores aspect. We've skated by for five years on dad's work, but haven't you noticed our orders are getting smaller? Some of the stores, when they change managers or owners, don't buy from us anymore. Robbie—" a note of urgency crept into her voice "—when were you last in the warehouse? You make batches as usual, and the warehouse is full— when it should be half-empty!"

For the first time in their argument Robbie began to look genuinely uneasy. "I hadn't noticed," he finally admitted quietly.

"I think one of us has to go out and sell." Robbie was obviously horrified. "And I think I'm the logical choice," she continued stoically. "Mom would hate being away from home. She already has enough to do, anyway. You're needed here. As it is I'm the odd-jobber, so I'm expendable. I wish I had thought of this before the Christmas buying season, but it took a while for things to sink in. Damn. The clincher is, mom let Trudy go this morning!" Trudy came in once a week to do the heavier cleaning chores around the house.

"But I thought Trudy was away visiting her daughter!"

"She was. But today's Friday, her usual day, and when she came mom told her she wasn't needed anymore. For a while there I thought both of them would burst into tears! I didn't want to worry you, Robbie, but now I think we'd better both worry, for our own good. And I'm not hitting the panic button. I've assimilated all the facts with due care and attention.''

"Okay, okay, don't rub it in. Come on. Let's get these formulas back under lock and key. Once the safe's open, we'll check the bank balance. I don't suppose you looked at it?'' Robbie's eyebrows rose.

"No, it...sort of felt like trespassing, sneaking around by myself. But with both of us, and I'm sure mom won't really mind...."

Although the lab, the distillery and the warehouse were all under the same roof, the lab wasn't connected with the rest. Donning rain gear, they left its clinical white and hurried along the length of the building. Next to the lab was the extensive distillery; next to it, the warehouse. The small office was tacked on to the warehouse end. A covered walkway connected the office to the store, which was adjacent to a public road that allowed access to the beach. When customers or visitors alike came, they had to use this road. The first driveway they came upon was labeled, Beesley Perfumery, the second, Beesley Farm, and this second driveway led in between the house and the perfumery compound to form a loop around the garage. The first driveway only led to the shop and its little garden enclosed in a yew hedge.

Another hedge completely surrounded the perfumery compound. Inside was the big brick workshop. The garden shed was to its left, and Robbie's vast greenhouse ran along the rear of both. The store inside the rose garden was for customers. Only friends came inside the home territory—only staff and family inside the compound. In fact, a high, stout wire fence was totally hidden within the compound's lovely yew hedge, and a locked door in the walkway separated the shop garden from the perfumery. People couldn't just walk around inside this enclosure, what with the dangers of the lab and the distillery, not to mention the threat to the family's precious secret perfume formulas.

A pair of hefty standard poodles, Boogaloo and Razzmattaz, were part of the security measures of Beesley Farm. To friends, the dogs were bouncy and lovable; to nosy strangers, adamant. *They must be in the house having supper,* Camille thought, for otherwise there would have been four shadows flitting into the office.

Three different combinations opened the office safe, as well as a trick switch that would defy anyone unfamiliar with the arrangement. The security precautions of the farm were justified, Camille believed, even though it was situated in sleepy little Metchosin on peaceful Vancouver Island, an island that never quite lost its holiday-resort aura, even in winter. After all, the formulas were their bread and butter—no formulas, no perfume, and therefore, no income. And in their own way, the Beesley scents were quietly famous. Camille knew of two cosmetic conglomerates that desired the rights to their primary lines, had offered to pay handsomely for them. But the Beesleys would as soon have sold Damask, or the farm, or themselves.

Robbie never spared a thought for the precautions. He took them for granted, just as he took for granted that the safe's combinations were nowhere on paper, only locked in the minds of the three remaining Beesleys. The neighbors hadn't the slightest inkling that any security precautions were in force. As far as they were concerned, the dogs were pets, all hedges mere windbreaks necessary for delicate roses. And a secret safe? What safe, when everybody knew shop proceeds and petty cash were kept in a strong box in plain view in the house.

Robbie opened the latch of what appeared to be a small antique medicine chest hanging on the office wall. From long habit, he scarcely had to look at the dial of the exposed safe as he spun the knob first one way, then the other. With two combinations completed and the switch activated, the first door swung open. Seconds later, after the third combination was finished, the second door slid upward to reveal the interior. He tossed the four neatly printed formulas, encased in clear plastic sheaths, in their customary place on the top shelf. The paper that bore Island Rose was yellow with age under its protective covering.

Camille, standing behind him with her hands in the pockets of her jeans, said, "We should make copies of those formulas. If anything ever happened to them we'd be sunk. I know you have a good memory, but I doubt you know by heart the sixty-nine ingredients for Rose, the seventy-eight for Violet, the ninety-seven for Lavender and the ninety-nine for Woodsmoke!"

"And then we'd have eight pieces of paper to worry about rather than four!" Robbie scoffed.

"What could happen? Why do you always expect something to happen? Calamity Camille!" His hand hovered for an instant over the ledgers on the next shelf. Then with a determined sigh he lifted them out. "I don't like to do this."

"We have to, before it's too late."

"There you go again!" Nevertheless, he seated himself behind the old desk and spread the first book of accounts wide. Camille bent over his shoulder.

"I can't make heads or tails of this," he muttered after a moment, a perplexed frown creasing his wide brow.

"Let's see.... Lord, what sort of a system does mom have? Oh, I know, this is the lavender farm." Their lavender fields were farther inland, about ten miles away. They grew only roses and lavender. All other ingredients were ordered in. "There must be one book for an overall view. Open that black one."

Leafing through the black ledger, Robbie said slowly after a while, "I didn't know this place was so expensive to run!"

"And the fancy perfume bottles—they've gone up in price again. So has everything else, it seems."

"Look at this freight bill. We'd better start delivering our product ourselves."

"If I'm going to be selling, I'll do that. But where, where, where is our bank balance?"

"Could this be it?" Two blond heads bent over the row upon row of figures.

"You're right, that's it," Camille breathed in relief. The total sum seemed blessedly large. "And these must be the outstanding bills...." Reaching into a drawer, she took out a calculator and quickly added up the debit, subtracted it from the balance and saw that not too big a dent had been made.

"What do you say now, Calamity?" Robbie joked, grinning broadly.

"Well, just think, Robbie. This has to get us through to next spring. We don't make much money in the winter months—it's summer and the tourist trade that keeps us afloat. And look—" she flipped several pages back "—in September it cost us around six thousand to operate, in October the same, November likewise. So figure how much to stay in business till next March, add another month for the accounts receivable to come in, and what do we have left? What about emergencies? What about the boiler? You want a new tractor, too. Then in the spring and summer our operating costs practically double, with all the extra staff we need."

Robbie's eyes, fixed on hers, grew worried again. "We're a little skinny, huh?" It was a rhetorical question. "If we let one gardener go...."

"We can't. We've only two. Harry helps out as it is now and he's our handyman. Besides, if we lay off a gardener plus Trudy, people will start to talk. Nobody's going to talk if I make a few calls on stores. We can't risk gossip, with or without Charles Darby looming behind us with his millions. You know the old saying, 'like rats deserting a sinking ship.' If people figure we're in trouble, they'll assume it's because our perfume isn't as good as it used to be. They'll stop buying, and that'll really fix things.

"Monday morning I'm going to load the truck

with samples—try my luck in Victoria. We might be able to catch some of the Christmas season. The stores will have already bought their supplies, but we can promise immediate delivery. Dad used to go out and get orders," she said firmly when Robbie began to look doubtful. "Why shouldn't I?"

"Listen, I'm behind you all the way! But mom won't like it—we'll have to talk her around. Why don't you take the car and I'll take the truck, and we'll both scour the countryside Monday morning?"

"No, Robbie. We can't spare both of us. And even if we have hit the panic button, we don't want to look as if we have. No, no. We have to be calm, cool and collected about this."

"Aye, aye, cap'n!" He smiled at the large-sized determination in his small-sized sister. She was fragile in comparison to his tall sturdy build, and in looks took after their mother, while his sharper, more rugged features had their father's stamp. But in their hair and their temperaments it was the other way around. Robbie had mother's waves along with her even nature, while Camille had her father's wild unruly locks and dark eyes sparkling with volatile spirit. He went on musingly, "While you're off I'll man the ship here. I'll see if we can't tighten our belts a bit. We've been living as if we found the magic porridge pot of our fairy tale days, although why anyone would want a never-ending supply of porridge I can't imagine!"

She smiled, feeling immensely cheered by her brother's apparently unshakable good humor, not to mention his equally indestructible good faith. Here she had been upset and frightened, taking things much too seriously, as usual. Not that the situation wasn't serious, but her tendency to fret only made matters worse.

"Should we tell mom we looked at the books?" she asked, as her brother replaced the ledgers and locked the safe, locking the medicine cabinet on it.

"No," he said after a moment's reflection. "We don't want her to think we're worried, or she'd worry more. Let's just try Plan A for all it's worth and see what happens."

Locking the office behind them, they went out into the stormy night. "You don't think there's anything to these candlelit dinners, then?" she asked, just before they parted.

"It's probably just Rachael trying to impress the high and mighty from back East—you know, showing Charles we can do things up right at this end of the country. Wilson may be worth a lot, but beside his brother he's a mere monetary shadow—" a quick grin flashed across his face "—and so Rachael's likely putting on the dog, in this case, the brother-in-law. Now that you've suggested it, though, I see what you mean about mom. But not Charles Darby. Not in a million years!" He turned toward the lab and flung, "I'm starving!" over his shoulder.

Once in the house Camille headed upstairs. The two apricot poodles raced up in front of her.

"Oh, there you are, dear. Were you at Damask? Robbie was looking for you." Her mother was fitting pearl studs into her ears. The resurrected dress, in soft blue wool, looked stunning on her trim figure, much more curvaceous than her daughter's slender shape. She had added a lace collar and cuffs and narrowed the skirt.

"I've just seen him. Mom, you look terrific!"

"Why, thank you!" Fern Beesley smiled as she turned from the dressing-table mirror. "What are you two doing tonight?"

"Oh, we...." Camille wondered whether she should say anything about Robbie's rose, then decided he should be the one to reveal the good news. "We might go down to the pub, or maybe to that St. Nicholas dance in the hall down the street."

"Good. You both work too hard, you know. Sometimes I worry.... I do wish you'd go out more."

Camille, abstractedly pondering her mother, wondered whether Charles would find her as attractive as she appeared in that instant. The lamp enhanced gold threads in the pale cream shoulder-length waves of her hair, the dress emphasized the softness of her large velvety brown eyes. Her skin glowed with health, and other than a few lines of maturity at the corners of her eyes and mouth, it was smooth and youthful. There was no mark of bitterness or regret for a dissatisfied life on her heart-shaped face. Occasionally Camille surprised a look of lonesome sadness there, but at present her mother seemed almost merry. The reassurance Robbie had given her began to melt away as a sense of foreboding crept over her.

"But we got out a lot!" Camille protested hastily. "Really, mom, I'm twenty-three! Don't you start finding dates for me again—or else! Robbie's three years older than I am, so I doubt he'd appreciate any meddling in his love life, either.''

"That's just it," Fern pointed out. "You don't have any."

"Now, mom. All in good time."

"You sound older than I am when you talk like that!" Fern replied tartly.

Camille quickly decided to abandon this old point of contention. "It's cold out. D'you want me to start the car for you?"

"No, that's all right." Fern dabbed on some Island Rose. "Charles is picking me up."

She stared at her mother, aghast. "Charles is?"

"Yes, dear. Since he lives right next door, why should we take two cars into Victoria?"

Camille's anxiety increased. "Oh, of course," she murmured lamely, feeling enormously affronted that some stranger from Toronto, whom nobody liked, was carrying her mother off with him in his car. That made this dinner much more like a date. She watched in silence as Fern smoothed a barely noticeable gloss of lipstick over the full rounded mouth so much like her own.

Camille was in the kitchen putting together a ham-and-cheese omelet when a sleek little dream of a sports car, a Mercedes she saw after a second's surprise, came to a quiet precise stop beneath the grape arbor attached to the back porch. Hadn't her mother said Charles drove a Cadillac? Somehow it seemed most improper that a man in his fifties should drive a dashing sports car, an intimate two-seater. This dinner out was sizing up to more and more of a date every moment!

Shushing the dogs, she called, "He's here, mom!" But there was nothing she could do to stop the surge of antagonism she felt toward the man who stepped out of the car and bounded up the porch steps. He had slowed to a more decorous pace by the time he arrived at the door.

Camille pretended she didn't hear his first knock. "Oh, good evening, Mr. Darby," she said pleasantly a few seconds later. She noticed how Boogaloo and Razzmattaz eyed him in unconcealed distrust. "Do come in. Mother will be down soon." Looking quickly away from cold, granite-gray eyes, she was suddenly nervously aware of how she must appear, windblown and rumpled in her housecleaning clothes, a plaid flannel shirt and jeans. Since she had her mother's dark lashes and brows, she seldom wore makeup except when going out. Altogether she must look a sight, while Charles Darby looked absolutely impeccable and correct in a dark suit and crisp white shirt. Not a hair was out of place, not a whisper of flamboyance about him anywhere. Her cheeks were tinged with pink as she resumed chopping ham. "Would you prefer to wait in the living room, Mr. Darby?" She tendered a smile to him.

"I'll be comfortable here," he returned curtly, seating himself on a small couch under the windows, unsmiling and indefinably disapproving.

"May I get you a drink, Mr. Darby?"

"No." His voice was as glacial as the piercing gaze.

Absently chopping the ham to a fine mush, Camille racked her mind for something else to say. Luckily her mother came down the stairs very soon. Camille's radar was alert for the slightest hint of romance, but although Fern and Charles called each other by their given names, nothing more noteworthy came to light. He was stiff and austere; Fern, reserved. Camille was breathing a little more easily when they both went out the door.

"Have a good time tonight, both of you," Fern put in at the last minute. "I think you should go to the dance. Sounds like more fun. Don't wait up for me. Cheerio!"

ROBBIE WAS HOME from the dance by the time Camille walked into the living room shortly after 1:00 A.M. He had the television on but was immersed in a huge volume on the propagation of roses. The first thing she said was, "Mom's not home yet?"

"No—"

The dogs started barking out in the yard, and Camille hastily secreted herself on one side of the living-room doorway to peer around it. She could see down the hall to the kitchen and the back door. For an awful moment it looked as though Charles might come in with their mother, but then he turned and went back down the porch steps. Camille released a sigh.

"He didn't kiss her good-night," she whispered as she quickly sat down and picked up a magazine.

"Why is it that you two always wait up for me, although I never do for you anymore?" Fern asked, coming into the room.

Robbie shrugged innocently. "I'm only reading."

"And I just got home," Camille added. "I, er, got a ride with a friend," she tacked on lightly, knowing her mother would ask.

"A friend? Who? Not Greyson?" Fern queried, smiling with faint curiosity at her daughter, and Camille knew she'd given herself away. She should have named somebody, she thought, wincing inwardly. Robbie was now looking at her with interest, too.

"Well, yes, it was Greyson," she said in a most offhand way. "How was your evening, mom?"

"Lovely. Rachael quite outdid herself over dinner, then we chatted. It probably sounds very boring to you young folk. How was the dance?"

"Okay," Robbie answered.

"The Christmas decorations were lavish—put me right in the spirit," Camille added. "How about a nightcap?"

"What's this about Greyson?" Robbie interjected, and she could have kicked him. "Ever since Elaine put a stick in the works, you haven't gone near him!"

"Elaine did not put a stick in the works. She just happened to mention there was Another Woman, for which I was very grateful. It was no big deal that Greyson gave me a lift home. We can be friends, can't we, even though there's no chance that we'd ever get together. Elaine may be snobby, but she's not one to bad-mouth!"

"Okay...but I wonder. I suppose it didn't occur to you she could be jealous?"

"Of Greyson?" Camille teased.

"No, of you," her brother persisted. "She gets such nasty pleasure giving you her castoffs."

"Now why on earth would she be jealous of me? She has everything she wants! What do you want, mom, brandy?"

"But money can't buy friends, only hangers-on."

"Now, Robbie," Fern remonstrated gently, "don't be unkind."

"I'm not. I'm being honest. And she wasn't all too pleased tonight when the band dragged you onstage to sing 'Jingle Bells.' "

"Did they really drag her?" Fern asked.

"Of course not, mom," Camille inserted, "it's just that I didn't—"

"And if you hadn't been so busy dancing, you would have noticed that she spent most of her time smoking cigarettes—alone."

"Oh. Did she?" Camille's brow creased. "I wish I'd noticed. She's put herself on such a high horse that sometimes she needs a bit of coaxing to come down to earth with the rest of us, that's all."

"Um hm," their mother put in. "She does seem to create her own problems. In her case, her fat pocketbook has done her nothing but harm, I'd say. Oh, that reminds me, I have some news!" She instantly had her children's undivided attention. "Charles's son is coming home tomorrow!"

Robbie looked blank; Camille felt disappointed and relieved at the same time. That was hardly newsworthy as far as she was concerned!

"Don't you remember, Camille? I told you Charles had a son in his early thirties."

"No, I—I don't remember."

"No? You never listen to me, dear! His name is Jake. He's been abroad for several years—in Paris most recently, gathering research. He's writing a book."

"Oh, really?" Camille hardly sounded interested. "How nice."

"Yes, and Jake might even be staying home this time. Charles is so pleased!" Camille couldn't imagine Charles Darby being pleased about anything. "Jake is a professor of archaeology," Fern continued happily.

"I didn't know there were archaeological digs in Paris," Camille observed with faint sarcasm.

"He was studying ancient documents, I think Charles said. I'm curious to meet him. Aren't you?"

"Me?" Camille looked astonished.

"Oh oh." Robbie grinned. "Watch out, kid. Looks like mom and Rachael have their bows and arrows out!"

Fern shook her head emphatically. "Nonsense, Robbie!"

"Mother!" Camille cried, "don't you dare invite Jake over here to meet me!"

"Well, darling, Charles said Jake would probably enjoy seeing our setup, since his field is unguents and ointments and antique remedies... or something like that. A very specialized branch of archaeology. And Charles would like to see our workshop himself. Your greenhouse, too, Robbie. I told him all about your experiments. He was very impressed!"

While their mother observed them both with a

great deal of fond pride, Camille and her brother shared a speaking glance.

"Oh—" Camille shrugged, pretending a trace of boredom "—I don't suppose our backwater perfumery can be of gripping interest to either of them. Anyway, if this Jake was in Paris, why didn't he go to Grasse, the most famous perfume district in the world? Oh, let's change the subject. Mom, Robbie has some news, too! Some great news!"

Robbie's announcement prompted the popping of a bottle of Christmas champagne in celebration. At one point Camille stopped herself just in time from saying, "This new rose could be the break we need!" She and Robbie glanced at each other again. She knew it was what they were both thinking. If she could create a worthwhile perfume, that might be just the impetus, with a bit of judicious publicity, to send the farm's sales sky high. But the development of a brand-new perfume took time, plenty of time— months, a year.... Well, Camille decided, she wouldn't rest until she had done it. She had been itching to get back to her organ, supplied with hundreds of exotic materials—and now she had all the inspiration one could wish for!

THE FOLLOWING DAY Camille restocked the store, bringing Phyllis trays of bottled shampoo, cologne and talcum powder and armloads of the pretty boxes so that Phyllis could package in between customers. With Robbie's help, Camille completed the weekly cleaning of the laboratory and took an exact inventory of the rolling library shelves in the lab, which were filled with aluminum-sheathed glass jugs of essences, tinctures and oils from faraway places. Then she reviewed the warehouse supplies to determine how much stock she had available to sell. She began to select products to go in the truck for Monday morning.

Each different fragrance had its satellites—the soaps, the toilet waters, the body oils. The truck was jammed to capacity by the time she was finished. It made her optimistic to be so well supplied, for, if the truth were known, the thought of boldly knocking on doors peddling her wares made her nervous. She and Robbie had decided to say nothing to mother about Plan A. If she didn't know about it she couldn't object, and once her daughter brought home an emptied truck, how could she possibly object?

No sooner had Camille sat down at her organ, when Elaine rang through from the shop to say she'd come to buy her Christmas presents and couldn't Camille wait on her?

"What's the matter?" Robbie scowled. "Isn't Phyllis good enough for her?"

"She probably just wants to talk," Camille replied patiently, pulling on her rain slicker to protect herself en route to the shop.

The Beesley products weren't inexpensive. While Elaine was contentedly choosing ensembles for her various friends, Camille was happily aiding her.

Elaine put the conversation on a more personal level. "I've just been to welcome the prodigal home." She grimaced. "My dear cousin Jake! Honestly, I swear Uncle Charles almost seemed warm today. He makes me nervous—always has.''

Camille nodded in agreement. ''Does Jake make you nervous, too?''

''No, just half mad and half bored. We never did get along, but then we're not what you would call a close family. They never came to visit us, and I think we only went to Toronto three or four times. I saw him when I went to Paris last year, though.''

''He's writing a book?'' Camille asked, just for something to say.

''Ha! Jake's been writing a book for the past seven years! You'd think, with all his university degrees, he would want to do something useful. But teaching is apparently not his cup of tea, so he sits around on his duff, either taking more courses or writing that book of his. Personally, *I* think Uncle Charles thinks it's time Jake started paying his own meal ticket. When I dropped in I got the impression he was trying to convince sonny to go into business with him.'' Elaine sniffed loftily—as if she spent her time devoted to worthy causes instead of finding new ways to spend her father's money, Camille said to herself, then regretted the unkind thought.

''But what sort of business would a professor of archaeology be likely to be interested in?'' Camille asked doubtfully.

''I don't know, but Uncle Charles has sure been asking a lot of questions about your mother, you two and this place in general. Don't you see, a present-day perfumery is vaguely in Jake's line of interest. I mean, he knows all about what Cleopatra painted her face with, so it would be a merging of the past and the present.''

Camille stopped herself from saying there would be no merging of any sort! Instead she responded casually, ''Oh, we don't want any business partners. Your Uncle Charles is out of luck if he's looking in our direction.''

''Well, maybe he figures capital backing would come in handy. Wasn't Robbie on the lookout for more land?'' The last question was put somewhat slyly as Elaine's eyebrows rose.

''We haven't found a suitable piece. The type of soil is crucial, you know. And we don't need financial help.'' Camille smiled sunnily.

Elaine tucked a strand of her dark hair behind an ear and sighed. ''Oh, well, since you let Trudy go....''

''Mom thought she was getting a little frail for such heavy work.'' Camille lied glibly, wondering at the ease with which the lies came.

''Personally, I think it stinks—daddy buying sonny his own company to play with! Especially when Jake is nothing but a perpetual schoolboy! Research in Paris, eh? Do chickens have teeth?''

Camille laughed, and Elaine, obviously finding the sound irresistible, started laughing, too. ''All right, so I don't appreciate my cousin Jake.'' She shrugged.

FOR THE NEXT TWO WEEKS Camille spent practically every day on the road, traveling from store to store and from town to town all over the island. Robbie, who added her odd jobs to his own work load, was surprised at the many odd jobs there were to be done. Their mother, who was presented with a fait accompli when Camille arrived home the first night with an almost empty truck, had to give in to the new state of affairs, although she sighed that her children already had too little time for fun. If running the perfumery didn't allow for any, then something would have to be done—a suggestion that inspired Robbie and Camille to work with even greater diligence. Not for anything did they want a couple of strangers messing around their home.

"Why didn't we think of selling before?" Camille wailed to her brother. "Look at that bank balance! We have another month's operating costs taken care of now!"

The truth was that store owners discovered—at the same time Camille did—that she had quite a persuasive manner. They found it most difficult to shut the door in her face, and once she had their ear, they found themselves pitted against such earnestness, such pride of product, such eagerness that they felt like Scrooges when they attempted a no. When they said no, Camille asked why. She might not be aggressive, but she was tenacious.

In the evenings she studied Robbie's essential oil for its individual qualities, as well as the various chemicals that went into its makeup. Then she had to decide what kind of a perfume to develop, a spring, summer, fall, or winter type of fragrance? A harmonious bouquet, with many intermingled scents, or one dominant sensation? A sensuous musky aroma, a vibrant spice, or a delicate flowery waft? The creation of perfume was often likened to composing music, for it was both an art and a science. Camille spent very many happy hours at the organ.

"I do wish you'd come to the party tonight!" Fern urged one morning close to Christmas. "Even Robbie's coming!"

Camille, who knew Charles and Jake were planning to be at Rachael and Wilson's party, felt no inclination to go. Despite her mother's denial, both she and Rachael had tried several ingenious ways to bring daughter and nephew together. The more they tried, the more Camille resisted. If she never set eyes on Jake, that was fine with her.

"I think I'm coming down with a cold," she quickly replied, faking a sneeze.

"See? You're working too hard! You need to relax. I'm getting the notion you're purposely avoiding Jake."

"Now why would I do that?"

"You don't seem to be interested in men!"

"Oh, I like them well enough." Camille grinned, her eyes twinkling merrily despite her mother's aggrieved frown. "I have a date tomorrow night, and I want to be sure I'm not sick, so I'd better stay home tonight. Give Rachael, Wilson and Elaine my love."

"A date? With whom? Greyson?"

"No, the owner of that gift shop I was telling you about, that one near the Crystal Gardens."

"Oh, but Camille, I'm sure you'd like Jake. He's such a nice boy!"

She wrinkled her nose. "But mom—I don't like nice boys!"

CHAPTER TWO

BEFORE CHRISTMAS was actually upon them, Camille had to resort to some ingenious methods herself to avoid Charles Darby's wonderful son. For some obscure reason Rachael and Fern had become fixed on the notion that they would make an ideal couple. But as Jake, too, seemed markedly reluctant to meet Camille, the ladies' efforts met with no success. When there was no possible way for Camille to get out of going to some festivity, Jake managed to extricate himself instead. One or the other would be present, but never both. In fact, Jake's obvious avoidance suggested he probably thought she was in on the matchmaking, which made her blood boil. She almost wanted to meet him then, just to administer an unmistakable snub.

All further encounters with Jake's father only convinced her to dislike and distrust Darby the Elder more. He was a cold fish, Charles. Never once did she see a look of delight or pleasure, or really any emotion whatsoever in his pale gray eyes. He was always correct, always haughtily courteous and quiet-spoken. But it was his curt, precise, measured tone that irked and annoyed her, made her want to drop an ice cube down his neck just to see what happened. Robbie, who shuddered with her when discussing their neighbor, hadn't much to say about the son.

"Well," he reflected, "he doesn't talk much, keeps to himself. Stares off into space, looks right through people as if they weren't there. I saw old Mrs. Plumtree chatting him up, oozing Christmas cheer, and he walked away right in the middle of her monologue!"

Camille laughed. "I've often wanted to but I've never had the nerve."

"I don't think he even realized what he was doing. He just sauntered off like a somnambulist."

"What can mom see in Jake?"

"I don't know. Maybe it's the fact that none of the village belles have made the slightest impression on His Eligible Bachelorship. All the mamas have been doing their best."

"Our mama included!" Camille had gone to Robbie for information on their newest next-door neighbor, since she had closed her ears to Fern's praise of him. She didn't dare show any interest or curiosity for fear of being launched into a blind date. She could only wish her mother hadn't this Cupid-like flaw in her character. "Is he good-looking?"

"Well, he's not the Hunchback of Notre Dame," Robbie offered. "Okay, I guess, if you like—" The arrival of their mother at the breakfast table put an abrupt halt to the conversation.

Fortunately, Charles Darby and son removed themselves to the Bahamas for Christmas and New Year's and, as it turned out, most of January. Christ-

mas dinner at the farm, with the remainder of the
Darby family and a good many other friends and
neighbors, was a merry affair, noisy and spontane-
ous—nobody walked away from anybody in the middle of anything. No cold codfish eye put a damper on
the fun or promoted nervousness, and Elaine, having
been jiggled from her high horse, was seen giggling
with handyman Harry. With a ceiling-high Christmas
tree all aglitter, no one minded the absence of either
sun or snow; the blustering rainstorm without made
the atmosphere within that much cozier. The Ontario
Cottage-cum-Saltbox, exceedingly homey and comfortable if not sumptuous, fairly rocked with good
cheer. Any well-wishers who came knocking at the
door went in and didn't come out again. The
spacious house all but burst at the seams.

And so Christmas passed into history and New
Year's was spent visiting the visitors. By the middle
of an icy January, Camille and Robbie were plotting
Plan B.

She was seated in a white lab coat at the organ, the
results of her research on Robbie's essential oil on a
pad of paper before her. She now had to determine
what type of perfume she wanted to conjure, then to
set about concocting it by mixing perhaps a hundred
different elements in varying amounts to end up with
a product that was the reality of her inner vision, or
her inner dream aroma. Each perfume had its top
note, the first refreshing tang perceived upon opening the bottle; a middle note, the full-bodied character of the fragrance in question; and the bass note,
the long-lasting impression. Just as a song isn't

played one note at a time, but in harmonizing chords, so did these notes have to harmonize to produce one cohesive theme, Camille realized. While she had no official schooling in chemistry, she had been painstakingly tutored by her father. The job before her put a gleam in her eye more than anything else could.

Robbie, in white coat, also, was stirring a ten-gallon vat of cold cream. The subtle smell of almond oil hung deliciously in the air.

"Your Christmas sales were all very fine and good, but...." He paused as he brought the five-foot-long paddle full circle in the vat.

"They're a flash in the pan if we don't keep it up," she agreed. "But I've restocked all the stores since Christmas, and there's nothing doing until the March buying season."

"We can't tighten belts any more than we have, either. If only those bottles we use weren't so damned expensive!"

"But they're especially made for us, always have been, and they're really lovely, Robbie. They're synonymous with our perfume." The bottles were locally made, of opaque milk glass with swirls of delicate pink through the white for the Island Rose, violet swirls for the Island Violet, a mauve gray for the Lavender Mist. Woodsmoke had a plain, elegant white bottle. The vessels combined beauty with practicality because light, as well as water and air, was injurious to fine perfume. "Besides, the way our costs are rising, the bottles are only a thin slice of the pie."

"Your taking over our deliveries has helped, but still, it's all not enough—not enough to regain our former status and not enough to expand. I know we've got good-quality equipment, but even good quality wears out—the boiler, for instance. Also, the bottling machine went on the fritz again yesterday in the middle of the shampoo. You should have seen the mess!'' Robbie shook his head, bringing the paddle around full circle again. It was heavy work, stirring ten gallons of semisolidified cold cream.

"I'm glad I didn't see it! But the fact of the matter is, Robbie, that the Island simply isn't a big enough market for us anymore. And if the ferries go on strike again next summer, it won't be only the tourists that scream and tear out their hair!''

"There ought to be a law. Well, you know, we do have a month's leeway now. What if you took that money and used it for a sales trip?''

"Like to Vancouver?''

"Uh-huh. And Calgary. And Saskatoon. Winnipeg....''

"Toronto, Montreal, and so on and so forth? Egad! And I was nervous about touring Victoria!''

"What else do you suggest, whiz kid? The only way we can keep up is to sell more. Either that or slowly but surely go bankrupt. As you said, the Island isn't big enough.''

"If I can do it here, I suppose I can do it there.'' Camille took a deep breath. "I agree. It has to be done. Since March is the buying season, I should make the trip then. It will probably take me the whole month, so I'll have to get the orders here processed by the end of February. Most stores here I can sell to on the telephone, now that they know me.''

Camille was frowning in concentration, scribbling furiously on a sheet of paper.

"But don't forget," Robbie warned. "There's mom. We'll have to convince her."

"We will. We're swimming in stock...."

"And by March I can have tons more made...."

"It's worth a try."

"What have we got to lose?"

"Only that one month's leeway. As Charles says, it takes money to make money. If we don't try Plan B, we'll have everything to lose!"

"Not to mention Charles breathing down our necks."

"That alone is enough to send me off like a rocket!"

"All right!" Robbie stopped stirring, pulled a stool up to the counter. They began to work out the finer points of Plan B, as well as just how to present it to their mother.

"Not too soon," Robbie said, "or she'll have too much time to protest."

"Not too late, because we have to organize, set up appointments beforehand—all that sort of thing."

They decided to spend another two weeks honing their plan. At the end of January, Fern would be cornered with a perfected scheme to put the perfumery firmly back on an upward trend.

Robbie frowned. "I wish we knew more about business."

"We'll learn!" Camille asserted with more confidence than she felt, thrusting out her chin like the bow of a tiny battleship.

THE DAY THEY HAD SELECTED to confront their parent dawned, and Camille, conscious of wanting her in the best possible mood, elected to prepare supper. Therefore it was with considerable surprise that she learned Fern wouldn't be there to enjoy it. She was going out. That in itself wouldn't have been alarming, except for the fact that she didn't inform Camille where she was going or with whom. This was unprecedented. More alarming than anything, the Darbys next door had returned from the Bahamas. Camille brooded all through their dinner. Even Robbie's calm acceptance that the unveiling of Plan B would have to wait until tomorrow did nothing to ease her sense of doom.

"I'll bet you anything she's with Charles right this minute!" she cried, frustrated. "She knows we're not really keen on him—that's why she said nothing!" Pushing her plate aside, she rose to pace the kitchen floor. "And you've heard how she's been talking lately—that idea we're tied down here and don't have time to enjoy ourselves. Yet she knows our financial position even better than we do." Robbie continued eating. "Maybe, right this second, she's asking Charles's advice. The businessman par excellence! Oh, how can you stuff yourself at a time like this?"

"For Pete's sake! She could be down the street playing bingo!"

Camille snorted in a most unladylike way. "Mom doesn't play bingo! She's out with a man. I know it!"

Sure enough, that night a sleek little Mercedes

sports car brought Fern Beesley home. It was small consolation that there was no good-night kiss to be seen by spying.

"I told you so!" Camille flashed.

"Breakfast tomorrow," Robbie said through gritted teeth. "Countdown. And I'll make the bacon and eggs!"

"I WILL NOT have my daughter out on the road like—like any common salesman!" Fern cried, gesturing with her hand in abhorrence. "I've heard about the dirty jokes! No. What would your father think? Anything could happen, anything at all—strange hotel rooms, no one to turn to."

"Mother! Be reasonable!" Camille pleaded.

"I will be no such thing! Reasonable! Why should I be reasonable? You're the only daughter I have!"

Robbie explained, Camille argued, Robbie urged, Camille begged.

"This is a fine thing! Both of you shouting at your mother!"

"Don't you see? Of course it will mean more work and longer hours for Robbie and me, but if we sell more we earn more, which means we can hire more staff, which means less work and shorter hours in the long run." Camille had to stop for breath.

"Camille's got a level head if I do say so myself. She's not about to get involved with any amorous adventurers, mom!"

Camille added, "I won't have the time to look at men!"

"It's not your looking I'm worried about. If only

you would. There's Jake, right next door, one of the nicest young men I've ever met, and you want to go away! You haven't had the time to be young and carefree, and now you want to take even more on your shoulders. Your father— What we need here is some clear-sighted management. Heaven knows I don't know the ins and outs of business and—''

''We've always been a family business,'' Robbie interrupted, ''and Camille and I would prefer to keep it that way. I don't want a bunch of strangers mucking around. I don't even want to talk about it! If we pull together....''

All their mother would say was that she would think about it. When they discussed it again a few days later, Fern murmured with a shake of her head, ''Even Charles doesn't like the idea.'' Camille choked on her coffee. ''He pointed out that you might not be up to a grueling sales trip.''

''Charles! What has Charles to do with it?'' Camille sputtered, incensed that he should have the gall to stick his nose in where it wasn't wanted. Who did he think he was? ''This is between us! It's our company, our life. Please, mom? I'll call home every day if I have to! You'd think I was a baby!''

''You're my baby.''

''Oh, mother!'' she groaned, sinking her head into her hands. Then, brightening suddenly, Camille exclaimed, ''I'll go out on a date with Jake if you'll let me take the sales trip!''

Shocked at the depth of her daughter's determination, Fern sat staring mutely at her. Later that day, she agreed to Plan B, but didn't hold Camille to her end of the bargain, though she insisted on making all the travel arrangements and setting the itinerary. She also took care of booking by telephone her daughter's appointments to the various department stores and specialty shops.

"At least," she affirmed, "I now have some idea of the sort of people you'll be dealing with."

"Okay, but please keep to the inexpensive hotels, mom. We can't afford anything plush at this stage."

"I have given my blessing, and you will kindly leave the rest to me. Sit down, dear. Now, every Friday I want you to call home, and...." The trip was set for the first three weeks of March; available funds would just manage to stretch that far.

CAMILLE SCARCELY KNEW where February went, it passed so quickly. Beesley Farm was in a vortex of activity. While she and Robbie prepared, bottled and packaged additional perfume, cologne, soaps and lotions, in addition to their regular work, they conversed darkly about Charles Darby's encroaching interest in the perfumery and their mother's continuing involvement with him. She took him to see the provincial museum in Victoria, a wonderful museum by all accounts, but Camille wished it would vanish off the face of the earth. He took her to a musical concert. Was Charles thinking romance or business? Or, the toad, was he using one to get the other?

Elaine, never one to tell untruths, aggravatingly snobbish though she might be, had overheard her Uncle Charles remarking to her father, Wilson, that he would never marry again. Charles hadn't stopped digging for information about the Beesleys, and now he was focusing on the sales trip. He had hired Trudy for his housekeeper, so what had she told him? How much had mother confided in him? Since Charles preferred to take over shaky establishments because they were cheap to buy into, perhaps that was why he disapproved of this sales trip. Rachael herself had said he was ruthless. It was fairly certain that Jake was staying home, that father and son might go into business together. What remained to be seen was what business? If his scholarly layabout son had been coerced into agreeing to work for his living, he was more likely to want a perfumery than a dairy farm or a shoe store.

Jake, apparently, was still bent on avoiding her, as she was him. All matchmaking efforts by Rachael and Fern, freshly implemented since his return from the Bahamas and her rash promise, were wasted. Yet perversely, more diligently Jake extricated himself from seemingly innocent meetings, the more Camille fumed, thinking his vanity insupportable. He should have realized by now she had no interest in him!

"I'm not asking you to date him, darling," Fern prompted. "Only to meet him. Where's the harm?"

"I don't like the sound of him."

"When you haven't heard *one* word I've said to you about him! Really, Camille. Sometimes you're as stubborn as your father used to be!"

But Camille was stubborn about her impending sales trip—not much else. She had once been to California and had visited Jasper and Banff, on the British Columbia–Alberta border, but no farther afield than that. Now here she was, setting out to go right across Canada, four thousand miles from home. But that was the least of her worries. The trip seemed to occupy every waking minute, haunting her dreams at night. So much rested on it. Never had she undertaken anything so weighted with responsibility. A cold sweat broke out on her brow, when she thought it just might end in disaster. She was prepared to blow all that money, yet what if no stores bought anything? Still, she had to go, and furthermore, make a success of it. Because if she didn't . . . .

"How would you like Charles Darby as your boss?" Robbie asked her. "Just remember that every time you get scared on your trip."

"He could fire us if he wanted to!" she agreed, adding, "And there'd be nothing we could do about it."

"He could sell our formulas."

"Sell our land."

"No more roses."

"No more Damask." Yes, Camille *was* stubborn.

"I'll take care of Damask while you're gone," her brother volunteered shortly before she was to step into the Twin Otter float plane. This was one of the links between the island and the mainland, the quickest link, since it traveled from harbor to harbor, downtown to downtown.

"Give me a kiss for good luck. C'mon, Robbie."

As he bent to plant a swift peck on her cheek, Fern surreptitiously wiped a tear. She was full of last-minute warnings.

"Yes, mom. No, mom. Yes, I'll call every Friday. Mom, I'll only be gone three weeks!"

"If you want to come home tomorrow, you come home!"

"I have to go, mom!"

On the plane Camille scarcely spared the time to observe the scattering of Gulf Islands below, set in the Strait of Georgia, a tossing silvery blue expanse of waves hurried by a brisk wind, the tantalizingly soft warmth of spring in its bluster. Instead she studied her daily reminder and the list of appointments ahead of her that day. In an hour, at nine forty-five, she would be meeting a Mrs. Trevor at the Hudson's Bay department store. At ten-thirty another appointment, another at twelve over lunch, another at two, another at three-thirty, the last at five. She had to be on her toes—she wouldn't have time to feel frightened!

Opening her purse and double-checking to be sure she had enough cash to take care of taxis, her credit card for lunch, running over her price list once more to be certain she had every item memorized, snapping wide her sample case just to verify nothing had been forgotten saw her through to touchdown in Vancouver's Coal Harbour. Flagging a taxi, she had to open her reminder book again to give the cabbie the name of her hotel.

"The Bayshore, please. How long will it take to get there?"

"About two minutes, miss. It's only a block and a half away."

"Wonderful!" Two minutes later she was saying,

"*This* is the Bayshore?" Even in her haste, even though her mind was occupied with Mrs. Trevor and exactly what she would say to the woman, Camille couldn't help but see that the Bayshore was nothing short of opulent. And she was booked in till Friday morning—four nights! At what cost? Her mother had obviously wanted her to stay in comfort in high-class hotels, but little did she know she was only making things more difficult. Now Camille would have to sell more just to pay for all this lavishness. She heaved a sigh, then went to check in and deposit her suitcases.

By six-thirty that evening, Camille had returned to the plush lobby of the Bayshore. She felt exhausted. Her sample case had grown impossibly heavy as the day wore on. She hadn't expected selling to be so tiring, but all she wanted to do now was to lie down somewhere and not say another word for the rest of the day.

But collecting her key from the front desk, she found herself saying to the clerk, "Will you please send up the biggest coldest gin and tonic you can lay your hands on?" before a bellhop came to relieve her of the sample case and usher her into an elevator.

Five minutes of lying flat out on her big double bed revived her somewhat. She drank in the utter peace and quiet, absorbed the fabulous view of nighttime Vancouver asparkle against a backdrop of royal blue, the water, mountains and sky. Camille was soon bouncing off the bed. Fetching her case, she climbed back on the bed and, with a frisson of excitement, opened her case. She took out her book of accounts, as yet unused, opened it to the first page where a sheaf of papers was inserted. Seizing the pile, she flung it up over her head with an unrestrained, "Yippeee!" Just then her gin and tonic arrived.

Gratefully sipping the drink, she became more businesslike and collected the scattered papers. They were order sheets. Only one store had turned her down—only one! She could scarcely believe it. Of course, Beesley Farm had been established for more than a century, and their product was of the highest caliber. She also had excellent references from satisfied stores back home, but all the same she was wildly delighted and completely surprised by her awesome success. The Bay alone had ordered fifty cases of Island Rose perfume, thirty cases each of the three others, plus colognes and toilet waters, powders and fancy soaps.

Camille wanted to phone home right that minute, but reconsidered that tomorrow she might not have such a good day, that it was too early to gloat over her stamina, which Charles had maligned. Besides, long-distance telephone calls were expensive, but if her first day was any sign, she and Robbie had been right about expanding their market. "It just goes to show," she said aloud to the view past her wide windows, "that ignoring the world beyond one's doorstep is not smart!"

Now she was hungry—famished, in fact—and wondering what to do about dinner. Eat in her room? Find the restaurant? But the prices in the dining room were most likely exorbitant. Maybe she should have a hamburger in the coffee shop instead.

A knock at the door interrupted her vision of a fat juicy steak with mushrooms on the side. Smiling to herself about her mother's admonitions regarding strangers, she went to see who it could be.

"Greyson!" She stared at him in astonishment. His dark blue eyes were twinkling happily back at her. Casually but well dressed in cords and sports jacket, he was as handsome as ever, his brown hair glossy under the hallway lights.

"Hi," he said with a grin. "You had dinner yet?"

"Uh, no," she murmured.

"Surprised to see me?"

"What are you doing here? Come on in—there's no point in standing in the hall!"

"In Vancouver, you mean? I had to pick up a shipment of parts." His father owned the closest service station to Beesley Farm. Greyson was in the process of taking over the operation. "Robbie came by this morning for gas and he told me you were here, so... here I am. I'm going back tomorrow morning, as soon as I have some gaskets and bushings I couldn't get tonight. I'm staying at my cousin's. You haven't had dinner yet, have you?"

"If I don't eat soon I'm going to faint!"

"Let's go!"

"Oh, but I should change."

"Why? You look...you look...."

"Yes?" She laughed. Normally Greyson wasn't caught short of words.

"It's just that I'm not used to seeing you looking so...sophisticated. That black suit really becomes you. Let's eat here at the hotel. I've only got the garage truck, and to put you inside a greasy, smelly, dirty old truck would be quite impossible. Now come along, Puff—and no, you don't have to comb your hair. Just put on your shoes. The maître d' won't let you in, no matter how wonderful you look, if you don't have shoes.''

Camille slipped into her black heels. ''Nobody's called me Puff in years!''

''Yeah, well, you stopped looking like a dandelion a long time ago. When you were ten, you were all skinny legs with knobby knees and a fluff of yellow hair.'' He didn't add that the legs weren't skinny and knobby anymore, although there was a great deal of them. ''Now what are you doing?''

''Patience, Grey. I'm only adding perfume!''

They came out of her hotel room, laughing together over some shared memories. Their laughter caused a fellow inserting his key in the door next to hers to glance up. As Greyson took her key to lock her door, she saw the man pull gold-rimmed glasses farther down his nose to stare sharply at her. For a startled second amber eyes bored into hers, then flickered over to her friend. The next instant Greyson took her arm, and they passed the other man, discussing her deficiency at baseball.

''You never could catch a ball but you always smelled nice while you fumbled. Perfume for baseball.'' He chuckled. ''Even clam digging. Perfume for everything. Now tell me about your day.''

''Oh, Grey.'' Stopping impulsively, Camille put her hand on his arm. ''I'm so glad you're here! I wasn't looking forward to a dinner all alone. I was bursting to talk to someone!''

He had stopped with her, and all of a sudden Camille was aware that she was enormously fond of him still but undecided about more. She sensed that he, too, was undecided... so they stood there in indecision holding hands.... Out of the corner of her eye she noticed the man down the hall still watching them. When she glanced curiously back, he disappeared into his room.

In the meantime the elevator had opened on their floor. No one came out; it appeared to be empty. She and Greyson raced to catch it and were mildly surprised to find a man in the corner next to the board of lighted buttons.

"Wrong floor," he muttered at their inquisitive glances, pushing the button for one floor down while Greyson pushed *L* for lobby. In a moment this rather uninteresting-looking person slid out, while Grey caught the door to hold it open for more people coming in. The door was open long enough for Camille to see the man dart into a stairwell, and before the fire-escape door closed behind him, head up the stairs. Why would he go up after he had just come down, she wondered, smiling at the vagaries of some people.

"So—" Greyson pulled her arm companionably through his "—just how many bottles of perfume did you sell today?" She needed no further coaxing. The remainder of the evening was spent with the indecision shelved for the present and their old friendship more firmly and happily reestablished.

Camille's second day on the job wasn't as rewarding as the first, but neither was it anything to cry over. Apart from her scheduled meetings, she'd managed to garner an appointment with the friend of a store owner, another buyer and so sold another twenty-five cases of mixed goods amid curried deep-fried prawns and steamed rice bread and egg rolls in Vancouver's famous Chinatown. She returned to her hotel room late, staying awake only long enough to have a soothing bath. Wednesday and Thursday slipped away in a flurry of meetings and running for taxicabs. Very early Friday morning she was on her way to the Vancouver International Airport, and Calgary.

On the plane she thought with satisfaction about calling home that night. She could thumb her nose at Charles Darby now. If the rest of her trip went as well, the Beesleys of Beesley Farm would have nothing to fear from obnoxious millionaires! Once their product was displayed on store shelves, she had no doubt it would sell, and stores had this wonderful habit of reordering goods when sold out.

Calgary's windy snowless streets were full of businessmen in black trenchcoats, hunched with collars up against the cold and briefcases at their sides, hurrying this way and that. She hurried, too, from one appointment to the next, her heavy sample case thumping against her knee, her nose cherry red above the collar of her silver fox jacket, the jacket Elaine had ever so graciously bestowed upon her.

The call home that evening was quite an event. Her brother actually got excited, and her mother, usually more voluble than Robbie, was calm, delighted by the sales and relieved that her daughter hadn't yet been kidnapped. After another heavy day of business on Saturday, even though she was tired, Camille chose to go to the hotel restaurant for dinner rather than to eat in total solitude in her room, as she had on the previous evening.

Once seated in the dimly lighted, luxurious room downstairs, she looked with interest at her fellow diners. After years of seeing mainly the same faces, she had glimpsed in the past week a thousand new ones without coming across the same face twice. It sounded silly, but she had never thought seriously about how many men there were in the world—untold thousands!

But then, as her eyes meandered over the throng, she thought she had seen one particular face before...but she couldn't remember where. She might even have sold the individual in question some cologne. Where and when would surely come back to her. He was smoking a pipe, reading a magazine or folder of some sort. He wore glasses with thin gold rims. Searching her mind brought no answer, so she gave up and continued to observe the other occupants unobtrusively. It was always fun to watch people eat; one could almost tell what they were like, based on such a simple action.

Her gaze kept straying back to the man with the pipe. If only she could remember. The more she looked at him, the more she realized he was very pleasant to look at. Not that his appearance hit one over the head. He wasn't one who made women gape or feel faint, but yet...oh, yes, she considered, returning her eyes to him once more, he *had* some-

thing. He won the prize for the most attractive man
in the room, hands down, with that wealth of tawny
hair and very angular face, wide at the forehead and
cheekbones and narrowing to the chin. If only he
would take those glasses off so she could get an unobstructed view.... As she watched, he took the
pipe from his mouth and, still reading, deposited it
in the ashtray. Then, still reading, he groped along
the tablecloth for his already buttered dinner roll.
Spellbound, Camille watched his absentminded
quest.

Ah, he'd found it. Automatically he raised half
and bit into it. He didn't wolf it. He didn't pick at it.
He seemed scarcely aware he was eating. Camille
dropped her chin into her hands and sighed, en-
grossed in this fine specimen of manhood. Perhaps
she'd seen him in her dreams. That might explain her
blank memory. She smiled at her definite case of
whimsy, and at that exact moment he looked up and
straight at her, as if her gaze had suddenly
penetrated. He didn't return her smile. Peering at her
over his glasses, he simply stared levelly back at her
for a time before resuming his reading.

Realizing he probably thought she was trying to
flirt with him, and that he'd pointedly turned her
down, she sighed again, wriggling in her seat and
wondering where her dinner was. She gazed past the
stranger then, ignoring him, but since he was reading, her effort at nonchalance was wasted. Vaguely
she noticed the man sitting directly behind him, and
to her surprise thought she recognized him, too. But
again, where and when evaded her. Could he be the

policeman who had given her the jaywalking ticket yesterday?

While the officer had been scribbling out her ticket, for which she had to pay a fine, she'd stood there furious and shivering. "Can't you write a little faster?" she'd snapped.

No, the second fellow wasn't the cop, for although she had been annoyed with him, he had still had a nice aspect. There wasn't anything particularly nice about this fellow. Shrugging, Camille decided to concentrate on the women in the room.

SHE SAW VERY LITTLE OF CALGARY, for on Sunday, her one free day, she had to inscribe the week's paperwork into the ledger. She understood then that she should have copied each day's business every night, for now it took her twice as long, trying to recall pertinent details beyond the bare business facts. The job kept her deskbound all day. Nevertheless, it was a joyous task when she added up all the money she'd made. She'd sold more than she'd ever expected to. Eighty percent of the store owners agreed with her that she had a most desirable product.

Out of her lofty hotel window she could see a barely undulating buff plain wherever high buildings didn't obscure the view. To the west, far, far away, a low blue ridge of mountains lay between the earth and sky. There was no warm chinook while she was there. The weather continued to be bitterly cold.

Monday night, some ten thousand feet up in the air on her way to Saskatoon, Saskatchewan, she listed

that day's sales and whatever else struck her as noteworthy in the ledger—she was learning the ropes as
she went. By the time she arrived in Saskatoon it was
almost eleven, but the prairie night was incredibly
bright with a full moon shining, endless stars sparkling and northern lights shimmering and dancing in
ghostly green and pink and white on a vast expanse
of pure glittering snow. The beauty of it caught her
unaware. She stood outside the airport terminal gazing, oblivious to the subzero temperature until a cabbie flagged her down with an offer of his rate into
town. Once more she was ensconced in one of the
city's most elegant hotels.

By the following night, she'd had several invitations to dinner, for drinks, for this that and the
other. She'd come to the conclusion that there were a
considerable number of presentable men in the
world. Traveling and selling perfume seemed a bona
fide way to meet them, from the cheeky young university student who rescued her from a patch of ice,
to the suave graying businessman who lent her his
calculator when hers ran out of steam. But although
she had a healthy interest in men despite her mother's
gloomy complaint, she turned all offers down, for
she was simply too busy. Her mind was too occupied
with facts and figures to permit her to socialize.
Besides, romance on the road was a complication she
didn't want.

Wednesday morning, in a pleated tartan skirt and
vest, with a bow at her throat and her fox fur over
her arm, Camille was ready to face a Saskatoon hidden in a veil of snow and a morning of appointments

before her noon flight to Winnipeg. Camille stepped into the elevator...then stood gaping at the man who shared it with her. He wasn't wearing glasses this time, and his pipe was unlighted in his hand. Now she remembered where she'd seen him before. He'd been in the hallway of the Bayshore, staring after her and Greyson. And in Calgary absently eating his roll. Now here! She wanted to reach out and touch him to make sure he wasn't an apparition.

He said nothing—he scarcely looked at her. Then she remembered that the fellow who had been sitting behind him in Calgary was the same person she'd glimpsed in the elevator in Vancouver. She marveled at her fabulous recall. Stealing a sidelong look at the stranger, she saw that he was gazing straight ahead at the elevator door. She wondered whether to start a conversation, something like the male line, "Haven't we met before?" He was standing right beneath the light, so his face was cast in sharp planes of light and shadow. Something about that pattern disturbed her, something familiar, as if she'd met him even before Vancouver...yet vague, as if it had been a long, long time ago.

But that was ridiculous, and if she wasn't so certain she would think the likelihood of seeing the same person in three different cities ridiculous, too. Nevertheless, here he was. And wasn't it ironic that of all the men she'd met, the one man whose attention she truly would have appreciated seemed not to notice she existed. But that was life, she sighed to herself. While he stared single-mindedly at the door, she peeped at him through her riot of curls.

He was tall without being Tall, possessed of a neat, slender, straight build, his shoulders nicely wider than his hips. A severe dark suit and a blinding white shirt fitted to perfection—indeed, everything about him, from the shiny tips of his shoes to the gold brown sweep of hair over his forehead was perfect without making him appear pampered. His face was lean, his skin a healthy bronze tone. His wide high cheekbones were well-defined, narrowing to a jutting chin, abrupt and square. His eyes, she knew, were a curious amber shade, deep-set. His mouth was his softest feature, and it was shaped in pure male poetry. All this was most attractive, but what exactly was it about him that was so intriguing?

Men, experience had taught her, were every bit as vain as women, yet this one seemed to have no awareness of his appeal. He seemed to live in a world apart. He *was* different, and that lack of concern about his appearance was part of the difference. There was a quietness, a complete calm about him, too. He didn't twitch or shuffle his feet or scratch his ear, waiting while the old-fashioned elevator made its long slow journey. Now that she looked more intently, she saw that his visage wasn't weathered or care-worn, yet he possessed a certain air of toughness. He wore no wedding band, and how she wished he would talk to her! But he didn't, so she took in his fine leather briefcase and the camel-hair overcoat slung over his shoulder. Where was he going? Why was he here? Who was he?

Summoning up her nerve and unconsciously lifting her chin, Camille ventured, "Hi."

In the confines of the elevator, cut off from the world for what seemed like hours when it was only a few minutes, she thought she'd stopped breathing when he turned his head, finally, to look at her. He seemed surprised to find he wasn't alone.

"Hello," he said gravely, then turned back to the door.

Camille was unaccountably disappointed—piqued and aggravated, too. Wasn't he the least curious as to why they should happen to be in three different cities at the same time? Wondering whether to remark on this, she considered that he was more than different; he was a trifle weird—peculiar might be the mot juste. Anyone else would have at least said, "Fancy meeting you here!" Even the policeman with the ticket had been friendly.

No more was said by either one, and the elevator opened on the lobby. Camille wished she had made any stupid remark as she watched him walking away, right out of her life.

At noon she was in the elevator again, going down as before, with her sampler and suitcases at her feet. The ledger was three order sheets thicker than it had been that morning. She felt content and excited—her stamina holding up just fine—and full of zest to tackle Winnipeg. The attractive laconic stranger couldn't have been further from her mind when the elevator stopped, and he came in.

When he said, "Hello" almost immediately, she took a startled step backward.

"H-hello." She gathered her wits.

After a moment he added, "You're leaving?"

Amazed at this verbosity, she replied after another moment, "Yes. I'm going to Winnipeg."

"I'm staying for another two days."

"Oh."

"How long will you be in Winnipeg?"

"Only till tomorrow night. My schedule is very tight." She was dazed. What a lot of talk all of a sudden—and he would have to have a pleasing voice as well as all his other assets. It was soft, deep and serene. She almost wished he squeaked or something, so that she might like him less. "Are you a salesman, too?"

"I'm on a lecture tour—the major universities."

"Lecturing on what?"

"The sociological implications of remedial and preventative naturopathy."

Her dark eyes had grown round. She hadn't a clue what it was he had just said. "Are you a...a doctor of some sort?"

"More of a professor."

"Oh?"

He saw her confusion, and the faintest of smiles lighted his intense tawny eyes. He elucidated, "A B.Sc., an M.A., and a Ph.D—not a medical doctor."

"Shouldn't you be older to have all that?"

For a second the sensitive mouth hinted at an upward curve. "I started early. Your sales must be doing well."

"How would you know?"

"Deductive reasoning. You asked me if I was a salesman, too. And you look on top of the world. What are you selling?"

Camille felt somewhat overwhelmed but gratified by his sudden curiosity. "Perfume."

Taking her in, he simply nodded and slowly said, "Yes."

"It's a family business." She swallowed, wondering about that yes. "It's terribly important that I do well."

She found his steady gaze, those incredibly intense eyes, downright unnerving. She felt as if she had swallowed at least a dozen butterflies. What was he doing—reading her like a book, piercing the deepest recesses of her mind? The tip of her tongue edged out to moisten her lips.

"I'm certain you could sell perfume to a lumber store," he commented with the same enchanting gravity. "Where to, after Winnipeg?"

"Toronto. I'm there for six days."

"Then we'll probably meet there," he said. At that moment the elevator door slid away to reveal the lobby. Before she could say another word he sauntered off, and a bellhop eager to assist with her luggage intervened, giving her no chance to call after him. How could they meet in Toronto when the professor didn't know where she was staying, when she didn't even know his name. Nor he hers. She stared after him, perplexed and astonished.

Peculiar? No, he *was* weird! Maybe all that studying at such an early age had adversely affected him. He must be dreadfully intelligent, she thought, remembering the burning vitality of his eyes. What on earth did the sociological implications of remedial and preventative naturopathy mean? She could scarcely say it, much less get a grasp on it. Why had the elevator ride been so short this time? Damn, damn, damn! Meet in Toronto! How? All the way to Winnipeg she thought of the professor rather than the schedule of appointments awaiting her on touchdown.

The city was in the midst of a minor blizzard. What would have totally incapacitated Victoria or Vancouver was hardly noticed here. Business continued as usual. Briskly Camille set about the work at hand—meeting buyers, shaking hands, smiling, explaining, demonstrating, writing up orders, shaking hands again, and on to the next on the list. In the back of her mind was always the impossible hope that somehow or other the professor's casually spoken words would come true. But he hadn't said they would meet; he had only said "probably." Finally she had to admit she was completely captivated by this stranger, this ship that had passed in the night.

Thursday evening, her ledger satisfactorily fatter with order sheets and her page-by-page listing of facts, Camille was high in the sky and on her way. Toronto.

In a city so huge, there had to be thousands of hotels. However would he find her? He wouldn't even know whom to ask for, even if he wanted to find her. He "probably" didn't want to—otherwise he would have ascertained a few facts for himself. Pleased though she was by her business success, she sighed dismally. The truth of the matter was, she shouldn't think about him at all. Becoming infatuated with itinerant strangers was pure foolishness. He hadn't shown more than a cursory interest in her. He couldn't be accused of encouraging her. Only civility had prompted him to talk to her. . . .

She knew it was stupid to ask the desk clerk at her sumptuous hotel whether there were any messages for her, but she couldn't resist. Of course there were none.

Making her promised call home the next day temporarily banished the professor from Camille's thoughts. Her news was still excellent. Robbie was ecstatic, and mother had relaxed enough to be thoroughly excited and unabashedly proud of her offspring—both of them. She had none of their financial acumen, she said. Glancing around her deluxe room, Camille tended to agree, though she hadn't the heart to agree aloud. When Fern asked how she'd been behaving, she replied with all honesty, "Like unto a nun." No amorous adventurers had accosted her—more the pity, she added to herself.

"Yes, mom. . . . No, mom. . . . Really, mom! Okay, bye. Oh, put Robbie on for a second, please?" Her parent signed off, and her brother came on. "What's been happening with you know who?"

Guardedly Robbie murmured, "I don't like the looks of things. They went dancing—yes, dancing— last Saturday night. She bought a new dress!"

"Uh-oh. Well, at least we've managed to put a spanner in his works as far as the perfumery is concerned."

"For now. *If* the stuff sells in the stores and *if* they reorder, we've climbed out of the ditch, but—"

"Yes, I know—it's too soon to start crowing. Well, we'll show the Darbys not to mess with us!"

"You bet! Keep up the good work, kid!"

Camille grinned. "Tell Charles I've never felt better, stamina-wise!"

After the telephone call, feeling suddenly very alone with the voices of home still ringing in her ears, Camille paced the floor, reviewing the situation. Charles and mom—dancing! Oh, no! Museums were one thing, dancing quite another. But if he wanted to buy the perfumery, there were ways of stopping him. Such as asking an impossible price. He was a penny pincher. All in all, she reflected, consoling herself, the future of Beesley Farm looked considerably brighter than it had just two weeks ago.

SATURDAY PASSED in a series of appointments. She was getting used to the hectic pace. Naturally, in Toronto orders were bound to be large, but they had exceeded her every expectation. It seemed buyers couldn't resist those beautiful little milk-glass bottles of exquisite perfume, especially and surprisingly since they were made in Canada, Canada not being known for its fragrances. "Tourists," the buyers told her again and again, "will go for this! It's the ideal souvenir to take back home! It's been a real pleasure meeting you, Miss Beesley." Some even went so far as to say, "I'll send recommendations for you on to our store in Montreal." Or Ottawa. Or Halifax.

Flushed with satisfaction, Camille returned to her hotel that night. She felt not in the least tired, but as if she wanted to sing, dance—and tonight, for the first time, she was rather lonely. Wandering around her room on the third floor, looking out on the bustling street below, alive with people celebrating Saturday night, she yearned for some company. Somebody to share her exuberant mood. Somebody to laugh with. Somebody to talk to about something other than perfume! She wanted to kick up her heels and paint the town magenta or something—anything! Anything but sitting alone in an impersonal if lovely hotel room.

Wouldn't it be smashing if her professor showed up out of the blue, she mused, wondering whether he was in town yet. But there was no point mourning his lack of interest in her, and going out by herself to some nightclub seemed a cold unrewarding solution. She might be many things yet she had never exactly been gregarious with strangers. Even though she didn't want to admit it, she felt hesitant and uncertain about tackling nighttime Toronto on her own.

Neither could she bear the thought of staring at these four walls all night. She'd already had dinner on the way to the hotel; she'd been too hungry to wait. The TV was boring when what she wanted was live, not canned, company. What to do?

Going to the desk provided, where she had already completed her day's accounts, she found the hotel's brochure. For entertainment it boasted a pub, a lounge, a nightclub, a disco, two restaurants, as well as a coffee shop, an indoor swimming pool, a sauna. Well, she didn't like to drink by herself, and she wasn't in the mood to go dancing without the professor. But what about the sauna? She had always loved them and perhaps she would find others basking in the heat. After changing into her voluminous bathrobe, she departed, her spirits restored, for the hotel basement.

The basement was as luxuriously appointed as the rest of the hotel. She found the sauna and the women's change room without delay. Putting her things in a locker and wrapping a bath towel around herself, she selected a few fragrant articles from her collection to take in with her, bundled them up in another towel and proceeded to the sauna. A blast of hot air, aromatic with cedar, met her as she opened the heavy door. The sauna was empty—except for the professor.

There he was, lying stretched out on the top bench. There he was in the flesh—really, for he hadn't a stitch on. Camille stood rooted to the spot, letting all the hot air escape past her.

"Close the door! Oh.... Well, come on in. We can share, can't we?" He sat up, and calmly picking up his towel, wrapped it around his hips.

Her heart was thudding high in her throat; she could feel every massive thump in every cell. Gulping, she automatically stepped into the dim, small, hot cave, pulling the door shut behind her. For a few incredulous seconds more she simply stared at him.

At last she found her tongue. "You! Where did *you* come from!"

"Winnipeg, same as you," he replied, not in the least surprised to see her, when she had to shut her mouth with an effort.

"Oh," she managed weakly. He moved over a bit so she could sit beside him on the top bench, where it was the hottest. As she sat down it occurred to her that neither of them had much on...and that she'd just seen this stranger in the nude. It was not the usual way to strike up an acquaintance!

"Why are you looking at me like that?"

"Why?" She couldn't stop staring at him. "Why! In the whole great big city of Toronto, we end up in the same sauna?" Her voice, she realized, was shaking.

"The odds against that aren't as great as you think, not when we're both staying in the same hotel."

She spread her hands. "But how did you know we would end up at the same hotel? Again?"

"I knew," he returned placidly.

"How?"

He smiled all of a sudden, a wide full smile, and inside her a host of butterflies fluttered up, twirling. That white grin held her suspended in space—it was devastating. When he did smile, the whole of him did, the eyes, too. She was mesmerized.

"I've been checking your forwarding address from hotel to hotel," he finally answered, deliberately holding her gaze. The very personal, direct contact must have sent her blood pressure up a notch.

"Oh. Deductive reasoning again. I wouldn't have thought of that."

"You're not used to traveling."

"Er, no. Then...you know my name, too?"

"Camille E. Beesley."

A faint husky sigh left her lips.

"What's the *E* for?"

"Elenora." So he *had* wanted to see her again! She gazed at him in sheer awakening delight.

"It's old-fashioned."

"My great-great-grandmother's name. I've been calling you the professor. What else do I call you?"

"Jacob Darleah."

Camille blinked. Had he said "darling"? Had he read her mind? She blushed pink under his steadfast intent gaze. "H-how do you spell that?" He told her, and she felt vastly relieved that his deductive reasoning didn't extend to her private thoughts. "Is there a middle name?" she asked, restored from panic. She was beginning to feel as though she was in the middle of the most wonderful evening of her life.

"Nathaniel. Were sales good today?"

Reaching inside her bundled towel, she withdrew a bottle of Island Rose moisturizing lotion. She had to do something with her hands—and her eyes—for if she kept on looking at him she would either drown in warm amber depths or reach out and touch him. "Yes."

"I thought so."

She stopped in the process of loosening the cork. "I wish I could tell as much about you as you can about me."

"You radiate happiness. I'm beginning to think you radiate as naturally as you breathe."

Camille wasn't sure what to make of this. She pushed some curls off her brow. He took the bottle from her, uncorked it, smelled the contents and handed it back. "I—I guess I'm pretty happy most of the time," she said a little blankly. "I haven't thought about it." Without realizing the allure of her actions, she poured some lotion into her hand and began to smooth it over a small shapely foot and ankle, progressing upward, first one leg, then the other. Delicate, true-to-life rose, the scent as heady as if the bottle were filled with rose petals, the sun and dew still upon them, began to fill the dim sauna. He had been silent for so long that she added, "You don't radiate much. I can't tell whether you're happy or not."

Looking up, she saw her comment had startled him, just as his had startled her. He had been, in his intent way, watching her ministrations. Immediately she felt wholly self-conscious, totally, physically aware of their mutual near nudity. The hot close air seemed to shimmer with that awareness. If anything, he was more attractive without clothes. His body was sleek and firm and well muscled...slicked with perspiration. He had a thick mat of dark gold hair across his chest, tapering down his stomach.... She took a deep steadying breath. Their sauna seemed the most intimate private place on the face of the earth.

He didn't answer. Slowly he took the bottle from her and as if it were the most natural thing in the world, poured some lotion into his cupped hand, put the bottle down, spread the lotion evenly over both palms. Softly and sensuously his hands moved down her throat. His touch couldn't have been more sensitive or gentle. Camille sat utterly still in shock. Should she be letting an almost complete stranger do this to her? But his hands continued, down her back to the towel, over her shoulders, softly, smoothly, lulling her with the pure heaven of tactile sensation. All the way down one arm he caressed her skin, unhurriedly, pausing only long enough to add more lotion. In a daze she turned slightly, and her eyes drifted closed as his fingers slid slowly, slowly down the other arm until her hand lay limp and trusting in both of his. For a long exquisite moment neither of them moved. Her eyes still dreamily closed, she had no notion he had moved until she felt his lips touch ever so lightly upon hers.

CHAPTER THREE

"OH...." CAMILLE WHISPERED FAINTLY, withdrawing a couple of inches and opening her eyes. She felt all shaken up inside.

"Mmm...." It was the barest sound in his throat. Fingertips feathered across her cheek.

"Jacob."

"Mmm?"

"I was just practicing the name. For a second I thought I'd forgotten it."

The fingertips slipped underneath her chin, and with a slight pressure, tipped it up and foreward. His movements were calm and easy, as if he thought she might shy away like a wild doe and he wanted to reassure, as if he thought the moment breakable, and her infinitely fragile, and both much too precious to bruise. She had never been treated in precisely this manner before, this careful lovemaking in exquisite slow motion. Fascinated by him, she didn't demur as he bent closer, once again settling his mouth on hers.

The second kiss was long and light, sweet, gently seductive, achingly warm; it made her dizzy. She wanted it to continue forever. But he lifted his lips away and looked at her, his eyes, many shades lighter than hers, running over her face and searching her eyes, lingering on the tempting full curve of her pink mouth. He seemed able, without saying a word, to communicate rather a lot.... Leaning against the wall, he slid an arm around her bare shoulders and brought her to lean against him, holding her close but not forcing in any way.

Nestled comfortably into his side, Camille spared a moment to wonder at the circumstances—mighty unusual—when the last time they'd met, in Saskatoon, they'd merely talked for a few minutes in an elevator. From that to this! Yet this didn't *feel* unusual, although her common sense told her it should. It felt right. It felt as though nothing else could possibly have happened other than that they should be cuddling at just this minute. She had known, even back in Calgary, she would like to get close to him. Now that she was, she was enveloped in previously unknown bliss.

In the dim light, in the bone-deep heat of the sauna, in a silent shimmering peace and contentment laced with the essence of a rose garden, nothing was said. The very atmosphere seemed saturated with sensual awareness. Time turned elastic and fluid, seconds hung forever, then tripped over each other like toppling dominoes toward the inevitable moment of change.

But when that moment came she wasn't sorry. His hand lifted her chin again, and as she turned and tilted her head, the arm around her shoulders tightened faintly. His mouth hovered over her parted lips, lowered with intent....

Rudely the sauna door was yanked open. A crowd

of toweled people burst in, chattering and giggling and carrying on—and sniggering about what they'd interrupted. Jacob's arm tightened more, as if he were trying to protect her from the sly looks and wisecracks now being tossed back and forth about what conveniences saunas were.

"You're all only jealous," he drawled softly with a contented smirk of his own. Instantly the group switched from laughing at to laughing with. The two were entreated to join the party.

Rising from her cozy seat beside the professor, Camille added, "We *were* having a party," eliciting more laughter. Holding on to her towel, she turned her head to say with a flashing smile, "Cheerio... Jacob," and disappeared.

She was running like a deer now. His parting glance had been particularly vivid, a level direct warning that they had only just begun. What *had* they started, Camille wondered, pressing her hands to her burning cheeks. She felt inside out and outside in, upside down and sky high all at the same time. The professor wasn't like any professor she had ever known! Not like any man, either....

When would she see him next? Tomorrow, or not until Montreal? Tomorrow was her free day, Sunday. But he might be leaving then. Suspended in a delicious shivery eager apprehension, she knew she couldn't wait to see him again.

STEPPING OUT OF THE TUB the following morning, wreathed in a subtle lavender mist, she hadn't even had time to dry herself properly before a knock on the door sent her flying into her bathrobe. She had telephoned room service for coffee. They were certainly prompt! Behind the steward was the professor, with a handful of tiny pink rosebuds clasped in a ruffle of paper lace.

Her heart skipped several beats. Momentarily gripped with astonished delight, she stood silently aside for the waiter to roll the trolley past her.

"Oh," she said. "Would you bring another cup?"

He vanished to fetch it, leaving them alone, and Camille turned to Jacob Nathaniel, feeling suddenly absurdly tongue-tied. But he was calmly contemplating the shadowy hint of cleavage between the lapels of her fluffy white terry-towel robe, so that she stopped in the act of rolling up her sleeves to slide her fingers up and pull a little more material across her breast. Catching her eye, he allowed the merest hint of a smile to touch his lips. He reached out to take her hand, laid his offering in her palm. "They reminded me so much of you, Camille." He closed her fingers around the lace-cushioned stems.

Then the efficient steward was back with a little glass vase, asking them if they would care for anything on the bottom shelf of the trolley—orange juice or fruit or Danish pastry? Jacob looked at her, and she shook her head. He said, "No, thank you. We're having breakfast out."

While Camille stood gazing with rapt pleasure at her flowers, the professor poured the coffee. Rising, he handed her a cup and saucer. As soon as his eyes again met hers, the feeling of numbness vanished as quickly as it had come. "Good morning!" she exclaimed, smiling radiantly, uninhibitedly at him.

"It is," he returned. Rather than flattering her with words, the intensity of his tawny eyes told her more plainly that she had aroused his male appreciation, that she was utterly beautiful, swathed from throat to toe in the robe. He wasn't looking the least distracted or absentminded. Her pulse was racing. She had already begun to realize he was a single-minded person—when he was thinking of one thing he concentrated on it to the exclusion of all else—and just as he'd been surprised to find her sharing the elevator with him in Saskatoon, now it seemed he would have been surprised to learn the earth was full of people besides her. "You're not working today, Camille?"

"No," she responded breathlessly.

"Have you ever been to Toronto before?"

"No."

"It's my hometown—let me show it to you."

"I wanted to go exploring today."

"Me, too." And his beguiling half smile made her wonder whether he was thinking of the same kind of exploring as she was.

Taking her coffee to the window, feeling afloat with elation, she gazed out on the quiet Sunday morning of the city, saw the sun glittering on a freshly fallen mantle of snow and happily asked, "Where do we start?"

"With breakfast." He joined her at the window. "And then—"

Suddenly she felt him stiffen beside her. Glancing

inquiringly at him, she saw he was staring at a fellow on the street below. There were few pedestrians out this early. She followed his absorbed gaze, only to see a very ordinary person on the sidewalk next to a newsstand, facing the hotel. She was just about to turn back to Jacob when she took a second closer look.

"It's him!"

"Who?"

"Why, don't you recognize him?"

"You've seen him before?"

"Of course I have. He was in the Bayshore elevator, standing in the corner, when Greyson and I stepped in." She explained the fellow's odd behavior, the reason for her having noticed him in the first place. "I don't suppose you'd have seen him from the hall. And then he was in Calgary, at dinner, sitting at the table behind you. Now here he is again!"

"You didn't see him in Saskatoon?"

After a moment's reflection she shook her head. "But what a fantastic coincidence. There he is again, right outside our hotel. He looks as if he's waiting for someone. Funny, if you hadn't noticed him I never would have. He blends right into the background, doesn't he? Hmm."

"What?"

"I...don't think I like him. I had lots of time to watch him eating his dinner. He ate furtively." She laughed at her own description. "He seemed to be afraid someone would snatch his plate away."

"Or perhaps that someone would snatch *him*

away," Jacob murmured with a faint smile. "More coffee?"

"I wish he would go away and quit lurking on the street like that. I'll bet you he's a private eye or a spy or something. I mean, if he were waiting for a friend, wouldn't it be much more comfortable to wait in the hotel lobby or in the coffee shop? Jacob!"

"Mmm?"

"Isn't it queer that he should show up wherever we go?"

His smile grew indulgent. "Are you smuggling something? Are you laundering money? Or carrying secret papers? Wait—I have it! You must have formulas you make your perfume from, and aren't such formulas usually highly secret?"

Her eyes dancing merrily, Camille agreed. "That's it. He's a spy after our secret formulas. And he's going to kidnap me, hold me ransom for them. Mom and Robbie will have a terrible fight over which of us to give up, me or the formulas!"

"It's totally a family business, then? Beesley Farm?" When she looked puzzled, he shrugged and said, "I read the label on your body lotion, which said, 'Made and bottled at Beesley Farm, Vancouver Island, British Columbia, Canada.'"

"Lord, you're observant!"

"Yes.... Go get dressed, Camille." A bare hint of pink washed over her cheeks. "If I'm going to show you Toronto all in one day, we have a lot of ground to cover. And if anybody's going to be doing any kidnapping...it'll be me."

It was the start of a truly wonderful day, a whirlwind of sight-seeing with Professor Darling—Darleah—pointing out the sights and answering all her many questions. Although snow had fallen during the night, the sun held a springlike warmth in its rays. Ice skaters were out on the frozen pool of Nathan Phillips Square. Behind them was the strikingly modern City Hall—government for more than two million citizens—which consisted of a clam shape between soaring semicircular towers. To the east of the square was the Old City Hall, a venerable stone edifice in Victorian Romanesque style. The beautifully restored building to the west, Jacob told her, was Osgoode Hall, headquarters of the Law Society of Upper Canada since 1832. The hall's elaborate wrought-iron fence and gates, he added, had once been used to keep out wandering cattle. Now the square was surrounded by the massive office towers of downtown Toronto.

They drove along the shore of Lake Ontario in a candy-apple red Jaguar Jacob said he'd borrowed from a professor at the University of Toronto. She saw Yonge Street, Bloor Street and Spadina; they lunched late one thousand one hundred feet above ground in the CN Tower. As their restaurant revolved full circle, revealing ever more city on one side and the vast expanse of Lake Ontario on the other, she exclaimed, "I can see forever!"

"Since it's a clear day, about seventy-five miles to be exact." While her eyes hung on the awesome view of a concrete jungle, his dwelt on her heart-shaped face. . . .

After lunch Jacob took her to Casa Loma. When

she first caught sight of it she said, stunned, "We've got a castle in Victoria, too, Craigdarroch Castle, but it's a miniature compared to this!"

Casa Loma had ninety-eight rooms. The ceiling of its Great Hall rose sixty feet high. An eight-hundred-foot-long underground passageway to the stables, a three-hundred-foot tower were just two of its features, and every room bespoke a fanciful opulence typefied by the gold-plated bathroom fixtures in the master bedroom. Cost had obviously not been a consideration—even the stable horses had dined from porcelain troughs!

After a refreshment stop, it was on to the Art Gallery of Ontario—Rachael had made her promise to visit it. There Camille's appreciative eye took in paintings by Canadian artists—Tom Thomson, Cornelius Krieghoff, Homer Watson and Emily Carr—with whom she was more familiar, for that lady had lived on the Island—as well as by Rubens, Pieter Brueghel the Younger, Degas, Gainsborough, Franz Hals, Rembrandt, Van Dyck....

"What do you want to do now, Camille?"

"Sit. I think I want to sit more than anything else. If I see one more thing I shall explode."

"What about dinner in a very nice place I know? If I see one thing more, I'll eat it, even if it's a Salvador Dali!"

Troy's was a tiny restaurant, cozily furnished with Canadian antiques. It was restful yet elegant, their little table very private. Every mouthful from appetizer to dessert was delectable. They were quite alone... more alone than they had been all day long....

It was much later that night when Jacob opened the door to her hotel room. As she slid out of her fur jacket, he switched on a lamp; he didn't remove his coat.

"I'm going on to Montreal tomorrow," he said, watching her every movement.

"Oh...." Camille was conscious of a crushing disappointment. "I—I'm not leaving to go there until Wednesday night."

"By that time I'll be in Quebec City."

"I'm not going there at all."

"Where to next?"

"Fredericton. We—mom, Robbie and I—decided it would be best to hit one major city in every province."

"Where are you staying in Fredericton?" After leafing through her daily reminder, she told him. "Not the same hotel," he continued. "What days?" She told him. "Then, Camille, we'll meet in Fredericton."

Her heart began to race as he slowly came closer. "In—in Fredericton," she agreed a little shakily. That was more than a week away, she thought in distress. "I—I've had a lovely day!" Her voice was almost a whisper, for now he was so close she didn't have to speak very loud, and she couldn't, anyway. "Thank you, Jacob."

"I didn't run you off your feet?" His eyes were sparkling down into hers, fixing her with a warm gaze that sent little tremors along her nerves.

"I'll sleep like a baby!" She smiled back, dropping her lashes, veiling her eyes, afraid he might read her too clearly, afraid to seem too eager....

His hand came up to lightly touch the side of her neck. Slowly his fingers tangled in the curls at her nape. "Camille...you will be careful? Don't...." He paused as if he didn't know how to express what he wanted to say.

"Don't play with strangers?" She laughed.

"Something like that."

"But you are a stranger."

"Not—" his fingers tightened "—anymore. Not after last night." His thumb trailed along the line of her jaw, and she shivered inside at the burn in his cat-like eyes. "Dammit, I hate to leave you alone!" he added abruptly.

At which Camille drew herself up to her full height, still a good deal less than his, and firmly thrust out her chin. "And don't you," she warned, "start talking like my mother!"

"I am ten years older than you."

"Oh, really, Jacob! I'll turn up in Fredericton just fine, you'll see! I am not—despite what some people might think—a nitwit. I have any amount of stamina, and furthermore—"

His hand at her nape continued its subtle insidious caresses, doing untold and untellable things to her equilibrium. "And furthermore, you're adorable. It would be the easiest thing in the world to ask you to come with me now."

"It's a tempting thought...."

"Don't encourage me," he murmured, then bent to kiss her. It was quite a different kiss from the ones before. It was definite, explicit...and tinged with hauntingly tender desire. "Fredericton, Miss Beesley, and don't get there late!" With that he was gone.

Camille stood looking at the closed door. Abstractedly she wandered to her bed, sat on the edge, then fell backward to stare at the ceiling. Fredericton seemed light-years away! She was mad, crazy about Professor Darling—Darleah. He had turned her whole world upside down in the space of a day, ever since last night. . . .

She *had* to be crazy to fall in love with somebody while traveling, but she was afraid she had done exactly that. She had never met anyone remotely like him before, and if he thought her adorable—she hugged the thought to herself—he was divine. She hadn't discovered anything about him she didn't like. She liked the way he smoked his pipe, the way he earnestly put on his glasses whenever he had to read something. She liked his tranquility. She liked his manner, which precluded playing games. When he said something, she believed him. He might not always be laughing but he wasn't a stick-in-the-mud, either. He wasn't an intellectual snob. He possessed an easy assurance that was part of him rather than a shield, a natural trait that didn't need any proving.

Expelling a long dreamy sigh, Camille rose from the covers to get ready for bed. What a pity Victoria and Toronto were so far apart. This trip would be over soon enough, and then what? In the course of the day, she and Jacob had discussed many things, mostly concerned with whatever it was they were viewing at the time. But over dinner at Troy's they had begun to talk about more personal matters. He hadn't any brothers or sisters, though he had a father somewhere. Now, Camille tried to dredge up what she'd actually learned about the man, she realized she didn't know much more about him than she had that morning.

He had said Toronto was his hometown, but hadn't mentioned where he was living at the moment. Most people had a permanent address somewhere, so she assumed his was Toronto. Other than this lecture tour, he appeared to be without any particular responsibilities—he wasn't actually employed anywhere, by anyone. And while he hadn't thrown money around that day, he certainly hadn't scrimped. Without permitting the slightest argument, he hadn't let her pay for anything. Altogether, now that she thought about it, he was puzzling. Although he had answered all her queries, she reflected that he hadn't, in answering, given many hard facts. But now at least she knew that naturopathy, loosely defined, referred to the study of natural medicinal substances. He was concerned with how this study had evolved with the evolution of man.

She had briefly sketched in her milieu back home, had told him about the perfumery and how the family ran it—but not, of course, about their financial worries or unpleasant next-door neighbors. Jacob had been very interested, which had been flattering. He had asked many questions of his own, among them, whether she was attached to anyone back home. After a faint hesitation, she had given him to understand there was no one, at which point he had casually mentioned he hadn't had much time to form attachments himself....

It was probably futile to continue such a relationship, she told herself again and again. It was probably for the best that he was far away for a few days. It gave her time to think. She missed Professor Darleah too much, but she couldn't guess if he missed her equally, or at all. After a week had passed, would he still remember her, or was she placing too much importance on a temporary acquaintance?

Monday, Tuesday, Wednesday passed much faster than Camille had expected. Being booked with appointments from morning till night, then having to record all the transactions, have dinner and study the next day's appointments left her just enough time for a soak in the tub before tumbling thankfully into bed. Yet in the drowsy moments before sleep overcame her, she considered Jacob and thought about Jacob and yearned for Fredericton.

WEDNESDAY NIGHT she was on her way to Montreal. She was looking forward to seeing that city. This coming Sunday, though, she would be out on her own exploring it.... In the meantime, she had work to do. A little worried about not being able to speak French, she nevertheless discovered her concern was unfounded. Business continued to be brisk—very brisk—and by Friday night, when she called home, she wished she knew where Jacob was so that she could call him, too, to tell him her good news.

"Any more dancing going on, Robbie?"

"No, but you know those local businessmen's-association dinners mom never goes to? Well, she went last Wednesday night—with Charles."

"Blast!"

"That's what I thought. All I can say is, thank heavens we talked her into this trip of yours. When I add up the take so far, it looks like you've robbed a bank!"

"It looks nice on paper, but don't forget that's all cash on delivery or thirty- and sixty-day receivables. Hang up, chatterbox!"

That Saturday night, with the previous Saturday night fresh in her mind, Camille felt very lonely and very far away from everyone who meant anything to her, hardly gung ho about doing the town. On the contrary, she was tired, worn out after the long week. But not tired enough to go straight to bed. She dialed room service, asked for a pot of coffee, a double brandy and brochures on what to do in Montreal. She would, she decided, watch a movie on TV and plan a solitary adventure for tomorrow.

A little more used to the prompt service by now, she was ready to answer the knock on her door a few minutes later. She wasn't ready for the professor.

"Jacob!" she cried faintly. Overcome, she went to fling her arms around his neck just as his closed around her and lifted her right off the floor. His mouth covered hers, a second's hard ravishment, before he settled her back to earth, closed the door behind him and drew her again into his arms. And then he was kissing her once more, his lips potently real on hers, hot and sweetly devouring, hungrily seeking her response, melting her into him without reserve or hesitation. Pressing her lissome body closer yet, he continued the kiss at greater leisure.

When at last he raised his head, he was laughing softly, making her realize he was as happy as she was. Anchoring one arm around her in case she had any idea about putting some distance between them, he threaded a hand through her wayward riot of curls. "Have I come too late to take you out on the town, Camille?"

"Oh, Jacob," she repeated, breathless and dizzy.

"I missed you, too," he replied in his deep soft voice.

"But—but aren't you supposed to be in Quebec City?"

"Well, yes, but I remembered you had a free day tomorrow."

She laughed at his easy straightforward explanation, her eyes shining up into his. "You're something else, Professor Darling!"

"I hoped you would say that."

"Actually, I meant 'Darleah,' only I keep getting the two mixed up." He was bending to kiss her again when there was another knock on the door.

"Just once you'd think they'd get orders mixed up or forget to come altogether!" she protested as he reluctantly released her. And to the steward, "Would you bring another cup, please? And another brandy?"

Her fatigue, she found, had vanished. Once again he was pouring the coffee, just as he'd done in Toronto. "Montreal never sleeps, Camille." He seemed to be fond of her name, judging by the lilt in his voice when he said it. "Would you like to see some of the night life?"

"The thick of it!"

"Then I know just the place."

"You've been here before your tour?"

"Many times."

"Oh. What should I wear?" As she saw his expression, she added hastily, "I'll figure it out." She had come to realize something more about the professor: he might be unconcerned about his own physical attributes, but that's where his curious naiveté ended. It was as if he'd spent most of his time involved in matters other than romance...but when he did focus on romance, he had no shortcomings that she could discover.

While searching the closet for suitable attire, she questioned him about the lectures he'd given since she'd last seen him, in Montreal at both the Université de Montréal and McGill, in Quebec City at Laval.

"I'm enjoying it, but it's brought home to me that teaching is not my forte. I couldn't do it every day. I'm much too...absentminded."

"You mean you forget what you're talking about?" Camille chuckled. "I think I'd like to sit in on a lecture, just to see what the sociological implications of remedial and preventative naturopathy is all about. What a mouthful!"

"It impresses the students—" he grinned "—and every bit helps."

Glancing at him over her shoulder, she commented breezily, "Were I a student I'd want to be taught by you—what fun, a professor who forgot what he was teaching."

"That...would be terrible!" Glancing at him askance, she saw he was serious. "Professors are not supposed to...er...with the students. It's frowned upon. And I want to very much with you." Camille stood motionless, her breath quite gone. "What have you been doing? Becoming the most successful saleslady of the year?"

"How do you always know things like that?"

"Like what?"

"Like how much I've sold. Which—" she beamed "—has been truckloads!"

"Your ledger on the desk. It won't shut anymore, it's so jammed with papers."

"I've been selling, selling and more selling. I've never shaken so many hands in my life! I swear somebody puts lead in my sample case when I'm not looking. I think it weighed two tons by the time I returned tonight." She was finally satisfied with her wardrobe selection. "But at lunch today I played hooky. I stumbled across a sale I couldn't resist, and anyway, I figured I deserved a treat. I was sick of everything I'd brought with me."

"I take it you bought dresses." He smiled, glancing at the damask pink dress in her hand, obviously not intended for business functions.

"Two! I went mad and bought a pair of shoes, as well! But I have to look good, don't I? Believe it or not, everything cost me less than two hundred dollars, so it wasn't an awful splurge. Montreal is fantastic for clothes! It was such fun. And I've learned all kinds of French, too—"

Going into the bathroom to change, she left the

door open a crack so she could still chatter away to him. It didn't matter what nonsense she had to tell him; the erudite professor seemed to enjoy it all. When she popped her head out the door because his voice sounded suspiciously close, she found him leaning on the wall next to the bathroom. He took the opportunity to kiss the tip of her nose. She was only in her slip by this point, so quickly retreated to emerge fully dressed a few minutes later.

The pink satin was simple and chic, the bodice fitting smoothly without frills or lace or buttons or any visible means of closure. The material flowed down to hug her slender waist and the curve of her hips, and ended at the kneecaps. The narrow skirt's two side slits allowed for ease of movement, the garment's only concession to extra detail. Its sole purpose was clearly to enhance what was beneath, which it did extremely well. The newly purchased shoes were a mere excuse for footwear, light and tiny and nude in color, only noticeable because they increased her height. Camille wore her mother's pearl stud earrings to match her necklace of pearls, her hair scooped up at the back with mother-of-pearl combs. Leaving her nape bare but for a few escaped curls, she had no other adornment except a touch of Island Rose.

"I'm ready," she announced. Swiveling away from the hotel's excellent view from the twenty-eighth floor, Jacob looked at her without comment. Only a small husky sigh escaped. She didn't think his appraisal could have missed an inch of her from head to toe, and she tingled with self-consciousness until he took his hands from his pockets to gather up her fur jacket. While he was helping her into the silver fox, Camille felt the heated brush of his lips against her nape. She was glad he didn't say anything. Words would have been prosaic after that glimpse of banked passion in his amber eyes. . . .

"We'll start, Camille—" even the way he said her name had her pulse racing deliciously "—with a few clubs, then round off the evening at Pierre's. It's one of the liveliest places in town. Good old Pierre wouldn't have it any other way."

"You know Pierre of Pierre's?"

"He's a friend from way back—Pierre Beauchamp. In fact, I've borrowed one of his cars, although I haven't actually seen him since I've been in town."

When the parking attendant brought "one of his cars" to a regal stop before the grand front entrance of her hotel, Camille murmured with wide eyes, "So what is it?"

"A Bugatti Type 50J, circa 1932." The vehicle was a long gleaming sweep of midnight blue, meticulously restored. "Pierre has many passions—one of them is old cars. This is the smallest and the least conspicuous of his collection." Attentively Jacob handed her into the passenger seat. "Do you like it?" he asked, as if she just might not. He slid behind the wheel, pushing and pulling buttons and switches from the mind-boggling assortment on the wooden dash.

"As long as it runs," she said with a laugh, just as the engine purred to life. She noticed as they drove away into the night that Jacob handled the car as if it were his own. She knew how to drive everything from tractors to her brother's finicky Fiat Spider, but she wouldn't have known where to start with this model. "Are you mechanically inclined?"

"My dad likes old cars, too, so I know a bit about them. Generally he loathes Pierre, but when they're discussing camshafts, they're the best of pals. You, I think, will like Pierre. I know he'll approve of you— probably too much!"

"Oh.... Are ladies one of his passions?"

"You might say that. He's been married and divorced six times. He likes them all."

"So he keeps his cars—and gets rid of his women."

Chuckling, he replied, "It's the women who get rid of him. As his third wife said—another friend of mine and my favorite of the bunch—'I adore Pierre, but one hour of him and I'm exhausted by all that sizzling energy!'"

"Does his nightclub sizzle, too?"

"It's a cabaret, and conservatively speaking, it sizzles!"

"Jacob...?"

"Mmm?"

"Did you really come all the way from Quebec City just to see me?" This might be an artless question, but she didn't care.

"Yes, I did. And it was the best idea I've ever had."

Jacob, it seemed, knew his way around metropolitan Montreal. He took her from one bar to another, each differing in decor and clientele, each showing a different face of the city. Most memorable was the bar shaped like a huge aquarium, with large clear Plexiglas tubing running along the walls, forming an extension to the watery playground. She loved every minute, was fascinated by everything—most of all by her enigmatic professor. A part of her kept hoping, halfheartedly, that he would do or say something to annoy her, so she wouldn't be quite so smitten, so hopelessly enthralled by him, floating inches off the ground again.

Pierre's was situated at the very top of an office tower, and that was only its first unexpected feature. The ceiling was very high, receding into nothing, its pinpoint lights giving the effect of the out-of-doors on a summer night. Lush greenery everywhere added to the midsummer night's dream; small lanterns on the tables glowed like captured fireflies. For those who preferred to be out of the mainstream, there were deep plush love seats on various levels. For those who enjoyed the thick of society, there were crowded tables on the main floor.

Although it was well after 1:00 A.M., the place was packed, the gathering as lively as if the night had only just begun. The latest fashions were commonplace, diamonds dripped, silk shimmered. There were a few startling hairstyles, more than a few casual blue jeans, some straitlaced business suits. The rich warmth of Edith Piaf's anguished voice came pouring out of hidden speakers, the music loud enough for people to talk without fear of being overheard, but not loud enough for them to have to shout. The room hummed with humanity.

"Where—" she looked up at Jacob "—are we going to find a place to sit?"

He paused for an instant, his gaze drifting absorbedly over her upturned face. "You really do radiate beautifully, Camille.... I've never met anyone with such a talent for simply being alive. Not even Pierre—"

At that moment they were pounced upon by Pierre, or rather, the professor was pounced upon by a devilishly handsome middle-aged gentleman, fairly dazzling in a Liberace-esque suit. The silvery wings in his black hair at either temple looked almost too perfect. Camille guessed this was their host. Despite his outrageous interpretation of glamour, Pierre managed to appear dignified and supremely arrogant. Voluable French was directed at Jacob.

The professor, elegant and calm, listened, grinned and attempted to squeeze in a word or two of his own. The men were, Camille could tell, very good friends of long standing, yet she couldn't help but wonder what two so diametrically opposed could have in common. Pierre looked decidedly worldly, slightly decadent, the type to be quickly bored where Jacob would be endlessly fascinated by people and events. Then she knew what it was: their vitality. In Pierre it oozed from every pore; in Jacob, it was all contained in the eyes.

"A woman?" Pierre suddenly expostulated in English, "*Non!* Me, yes, but you?" Then his eyes alighted on her, and slowly the expressive brows rose. "Ah," he said after a moment. "Yes!"

"Does that mean he's not going to throw me out?" Camille smiled, her big brown eyes dancing with interest.

"*Enchanté, mademoiselle*—and I mean that!" With thoroughbred panache Pierre Beauchamp touched his lips to the back of her hand.

"He does, Camille. Otherwise he would just have said, *'allô.'*"

"Eh, he mocks my accent, the boy genius. Little does he know you find it ravishing, yes?"

"It's very pleasant," she agreed, laughing back. Pierre was quite irresistible in his own way.

Gallantly he took her arm. "Come, *mes amis*, I have the best table in the house for you!" They proceeded, engaging in a rapid-fire conversation, to the highest bank of seats, where they could see everyone and everything without being in the limelight themselves. "Last night," the cabaret owner continued as Camille slid into the center of the circular couch, Jacob on one side of her, "I had a situation!" He slid in beside Camille. "Both the minister of finance and the external affairs representative wanted this spot. La, la, la!"

"So how did you sort it out?" Jacob queried, smiling faintly at Camille.

"Most delicate, as you can imagine!" Their waiter arrived, his service an art of professional yet warm hospitality as he took their orders for cocktails and recommended hors d'oeuvres. "But I tricked them both, so neither got it. Instead the grand-nephew of—" he lowered his voice "—of Saudi Arabia sat here, where you're sitting now, *mon enfant*."

"I'm honored, I'm sure," Camille laughed. "If I'm not mistaken, the seat's still warm."

"Where did you meet this young lady?" Pierre demanded of Jacob.

"Vancouver."

"Eh? On your tour? On the road?" Pierre had already railed at his friend for neglecting him, to which Jacob had replied that since he hadn't been in Canada for the past year, he could scarcely have done otherwise. "But 'ow *tragique*! 'ow *romantique*! In Vancouver you say the first words—"

"That wasn't until Saskatoon," Jacob interrupted.

"Not until Saskatoon? You waste much time! So in Saskatoon the passion flowered?"

"Nothing flowered until Toronto. You're too damn nosy, Pierre."

"Only taken by surprise. You—the brain, the misogynist, never the time for the ladies—you have the fortune to see Camille before I, who's always looking!"

"What," put in Camille, even though she had a pretty good idea, "is a misogynist?"

"A woman hater!"

"Pierre exaggerates," Jacob objected mildly.

"I never exaggerate! I don't believe in it!"

Camille was gazing at the professor in marked interest when he suddenly said in a non sequitur, "No pictures, eh, old chum?"

A conspiratorial look flashed across their host's

face. *"Mais non!"* Secret excitement animated him as he studied Jacob narrowly for a moment. Then he added to Camille, "Did you know his I.Q. is alarming?"

"Where did you meet?" Camille was brimful of curiosity.

"In Paris, years ago," Jacob told her before Pierre had the chance to answer. The mention of Paris in connection with him struck her as somehow significant, but she couldn't think why. "When you meet a Canadian in Paris, it's like old-home week!"

"You would charm Paris!" Pierre assured her.

"I think it would charm me, and I'm a little more interested in Grasse, actually." When her reason for this came out, Pierre gazed at her with even more flagrant admiration, taking in the soft carefree tousle of cornsilk hair with her peaches-and-cream complexion, the pale delicacy unexpectedly contrasted with dark brows and deep brown eyes.

"Perfume. . . . Of course. Yet you are rather unlike a rose yourself—not a hot-house bloom, but a fresh innocent wild flower, *mon enfant*!"

Such expansive flattery had her lips trembling with wry humor. "I'm hardly an innocent baby," she avowed.

"Me, I would not have waited until Toronto. I would have put you over my shoulder and carried you off to my cave!"

"I don't think it's done nowadays."

"See? You are so innocent!" Pierre had already taken her hand. Now his shrewd gaze, having lingered on her hair and the sweet youthfulness of her face, her rounded lips, her bare throat, sank farther to the luscious swell of breasts above the damask pink.

"If you will kindly remember, old chum, I did see her first," Jacob commented easily. "Keep your sticky fingers off."

"Ah...so?" returned the older man, suave and debonair. He smiled at Camille, then at Jacob, offering a quick rhyme in French, which he repeated for her benefit. "It rhymes in English, too, although the meaning changes a little: 'he would trust me with his life—but never with his wife!'"

"Just so." Smiling crookedly, Jacob turned in his seat, his eyes flickering over to her.

"And he is right, too, not to trust me with you, Camille." Before gracefully releasing her hand, Pierre brushed another kiss across the back of it.

"You, Pierre, are a rogue, evidently the first real-live rogue I've ever met. I thought they existed only in the dictionary."

It seemed she had complimented him, for he beamed back at her. He wanted to know more about the perfumery, more about Jacob's tour, and he was pleased to divulge interesting tidbits about his clientele, who was who and whom they were with. Just to keep things from getting dull, he said, he had hired out-of-work magicians as part of his staff. When people least expected it, their waiter would make their napkins dance across the table. One night, as the pièce de resistance, a waitress had neatly executed a somersault in the middle of a wineglass-juggling act.

"My guests, they never know what to expect. Here anything might happen, and they like it, for they come back! I would rather close the place down than become old hat!"

As the lilting flight of piano notes faded, baby grand and player vanished into the black shadows of the stage; there was a second's hush before the stage curtains started to ripple. The sound-and-sight-shattering excitement of a full-line cancan burst upon them. Camille's lips parted in astonishment and delight. The colors, the lights, the music, the split-second precision of the dancers whirling and twirling, skirts and petticoats airborne in high kicks—she had never seen anything like it live. Jacob watched her face, clearly satisfied. Pierre was, too—not that she noticed.

The second number followed directly on the first. A row of gold miners tapped and shuffled and high-stepped their way onstage, flung their respective belles into the air to catch them, flipped them down between their booted legs in a froth of lace. Another number featured a female lead singer among the flash and flitter, a male baritone providing balance. The next act was a solo, the stage in deepest shadow but for one spotlight trained on a well-known Canadian vocalist. The crowd stamped and cheered.

A few moments' pause, and the show was on to a burlesque act, silly, uproarious comedy, slapstick and good-natured. Some of the crowd spontaneously added lines when they saw fit, and Camille yearned to be able to understand the language. Jacob translated important snippets so she wouldn't lose the gist of the story. Pierre left for a while, bent on straightening out some minor problem that had arisen. When next Jacob explained a line, he finished it off with a slight nibble on her earlobe. . . .

"Use the key—you know where it is," Pierre instructed Jacob as they were leaving. "Whatever you do, don't wake up my new butler, Brandon, or he'll be giving me the evil eye tomorrow. Good butlers are hard to find these days. But are you certain you want to leave already?" Already was four-thirty in the morning.

Camille was tired, deliciously tired—drowsy, languid and content by the time they reached her hotel. She could, of course, have walked under her own steam, but it was ever so much nicer to rest against Jacob and let him escort her, with a strong arm around her waist, down the hall to her room. They conversed in whispers, for it was too late—early—for anything else.

Inside, he put her purse aside with the key and, turning her in his arms, slipped her coat off her shoulders, tossing it on the desk chair.

"What time would you like to get up tomorrow morning?" His voice was like velvet. His hands, moving lightly, slowly up her back, settled her in closer to him.

Sliding her hands up over his shoulders, nestling her head against him, she suggested dreamily, "Why don't you call me when you wake up?"

Held against the hard contours of his body, she absorbed the feel of him in sweet hazy yearning, utterly satisfied to remain like this with him, to have him this close always, to be close enough to enjoy the nuances of his individual male scent, to want to do all this and more....

His gentle careful touch simmered down her back...around and over the curve of her hip to follow the indent of her waist, up and up her back again until his hands rested on the bare flesh of her shoulders. She tipped her head to look into his eyes. Unclasping her fingers from behind his neck, she trailed the small pink tips down the concave line of his cheek, which was just beginning to feel faintly raspy. He turned his head to kiss the palm, his warm imprint there sending a frisson of sensual shock spiraling through her. Her fingers spread into his hair at the temples as her eyelids fluttered down and her lips parted. Folding her closer into his embrace, he captured the willing softness of her mouth. The hint of passion that had run like a thread through the evening smoldered into a sultry fire. His penetrating tongue, sliding along the inside of her bottom lip, provoked an exquisite trembling within her. A few seconds seduction more, and he ended the singeing contact when she very much wanted it to continue.... Camille wondered at his restraint.

HALF-AWAKE SUNDAY MORNING, lolling in her bed, too comfortable and warm and lazy to want to open her eyes yet, Camille was instantly mobile when her telephone rang.

"Good morning, Sleeping Beauty." Jacob's deep voice washed over her. "Are you still in bed?"

"Mmm, Professor Darling. Are you?"

There was a moment's silence. "Camille, you make me wish I was there with you.... Yes, I'm still in bed."

"What time is it?" Her voice was breathless.

"It's...it's about ten-thirty."

"How's Brandon this morning? You didn't wake him up, did you?"

He chuckled. "No. I tiptoed in shortly before the milkman arrived. Breakfast at noon, Camille?"

She turned onto her stomach, bunching up her pillow. "Yes, Professor—oh, yes—and whatever else you had in mind."

"Make that eleven-thirty. And you might not bother getting out of bed...."

"Oh.... Is that on your mind, so early in the morning?"

"It's not early; it's ten-thirty!"

"What on earth is Pierre thinking of, accusing you of being a bookworm?"

"He was just apprising you of all my bad points while trying to ingratiate himself—the scum!" He chuckled again.

"I might not be in bed when you get here."

"And I'm not answering for my actions if you are. Bundle up, angel. The radio has informed me an unexpected cold snap is settling in. To make sure you're all buttoned up before I get there, I won't come before noon."

Camille was still smiling five minutes after the phone call was over. His restraint of the night before was obviously nothing to worry about. Stretching luxuriously under their blankets, she contemplated the day before her. All day with Jacob. She kept thinking he couldn't make her any happier than she already was, yet he kept on surprising her. She'd never felt quite this way before.

Little had she known on her way to that first appointment with Hudson's Bay in Vancouver that her trip was going to turn out like this! Not only marvelous sales, but such an earth-shaking experience as Jacob. She understood what Pierre had meant last night when he'd said, " 'ow *tragique*!"

There was today, and after that, Fredericton... and after that? She hadn't asked Jacob what he meant to do once his tour was over. She was afraid to. She was afraid to hear he would be returning to Toronto, and sometime or other might come to visit her.... How tragic, indeed! It was stupid and foolish to form attachments while away on business, she'd decided very early on. But no tomorrows should interfere with today....

Regardless of her mother's warnings, or her brother's or her own common sense, Camille bounced out of bed and hurried over to the windows. Pulling the red velvet draperies wide, she saw to her amazement that it was snowing, snowing like the middle of winter when a tentative spring should be beginning to melt the ice. Luckily for her, Elaine's steady weight gain had assured her a sumptuous white cashmere sweater to snuggle into.

Camille and Jacob's sight-seeing that day was much more relaxed than the Toronto tour. Rather than walking side by side as they had in the Ontario city, they strolled with their arms linked, like the other lovers out enjoying the winter wonderland. By dinnertime Camille could order her own meal in French, and although their waiter grinned at her accent, at least it was a kindly grin.

Each got a little more background on the other. Jacob's father was his stepfather; his natural parent had died long ago. His stepfather was embittered by the loss of Jacob's mother, whom he had loved very much.

While Jacob already knew that her father, many years older than Fern, had died after a heart attack, he now learned that Mr. Beesley had been the creator of not only two perfumes but all the satellites. He had spent most of his waking hours in his laboratory, dedicated to it as Robbie was dedicated to his roses.

When Jacob asked her whether the lab was still in use, she replied that indeed it was. When he asked if the lab had changed in the past five years, she answered, oh, no, her father, should he suddenly come back to life, could step right into it without noticing any years had passed. No one but family had access to the laboratory, partly because of the confidential formulas that might be in plain view, partly because of potentially dangerous chemicals. She wasn't surprised by Jacob's avid interest in the Beesley perfume lab, for she'd discovered enough about him to know he was something of a chemist himself.

Since she still wanted to sit in on one of his lectures, he promised to arrange a student pass for her in Fredericton. As he would be there first, he would leave a message at her hotel, so that upon arrival she could get in touch with him immediately. All this pleased her, but still, all day long and into the evening, a tiny demon inside couldn't help wishing he were less of a gentleman, kept whispering to her that there was so little time left for them. Despite his clearly stated feelings, he didn't take advantage of the situation. He didn't kiss her once. While his eyes made love to her and his velvety voice caressed her, that was as far as he went, with the result that she was further puzzled by him. Jacob was a mystery to her, enigmatic and reticent, yet at the same time startlingly open where his intentions were concerned. She could only wonder when he meant to carry out those intentions.

But in the middle of his good-night kiss in her hotel room, she discovered he was holding back for some unexplained reason. His lips were oh so softly covering her mouth, yet his body grew taut with erotic tension until it was a powerhouse of male desire, robbing her of the will to remove herself from this dangerous excitement. Her heart madly hammering elemental signals through her veins, she kept utterly still in dizzy suspense. Then, entirely unpremeditated—she didn't know whether she dared spark the threatening conflagration—she sank her small white teeth into his bottom lip, an act intending no pain, only invitation. Suddenly it wasn't enough merely to sense his desire. She wanted to experience it with an almost overwhelming need.

His reply to that tantalizing bite was instantaneous. Before she knew what had happened, he had swept her slight form up into his arms and was carrying her over to the bed. For the first time she realized some of his strength as his arms held her against him, gauged the measure of his previous reserve as his lips forced hers apart to admit the deep exploring probe of his tongue, before he lowered her into the pillows. Just as he had swept her into his arms, so was she swept into the revelation of his naked desire.

With his hard sinewy length pressing her into the blankets, the clothes separating them seemed a useless obstruction. With his scorching urgent touch roaming down her throat and caressing the curved thrust of her breast, the clothes seemed an abomination. Through the white cashmere sweater, he had the tip of her breast rising high and taut beneath his sensitive fingers. A muscled thigh slid between the softness of hers, and his inflaming mouth warmed the damask pink of her lips into a deep blushing red. And then his hot, sweet, ravening kisses were coursing over her face, igniting her skin, burying themselves in her profusion of blond curls, teasing the shell of her ear before his lips halted on the pulse point just below her lobe. She was shivering in intense sensory delight. She clung to him in heady abandonment, his hand slid beneath her, down over the trim roundness of her derriere. He pressed her hips up to fit snuggly, perfectly against his. . . .

But just as rapturous pleasure was flooding through her, so was doubt. It was too soon and too immediate for her to completely accept the inevitable. She was stunned by him, deliciously stunned by this whole new side of him—wildly physical, profoundly sensuous. Now that it seemed he was about to fulfill her yearnings, every last one of them, she was the one holding back. A sigh caught in her throat, made him pause. Very slowly, with utmost care and exquisite tenderness, Jacob ended his kissing and caressing.

"Camille," he murmured huskily, his lips brushing across hers, "my love...." Her dark silky lashes drifted open to see a wry half smile appear. "It may have taken me a little longer than Pierre, but I was going to abduct you to my cave in, oh, about one second more. I think you've found my...inner man, the passionate one." He frowned.

"Don't you approve of him?" she murmured wonderingly, surprised by the frown, for she approved wholeheartedly.

He shifted his weight as he lay on the bed beside her, still holding her close with an arm around her waist. His next words reflected his tension. "I like him fine, considering I'm only just getting to know him. But, Camille, this is neither the place nor the time...." He was looking at her as if she were some rare species, as yet not fully discovered, and he could scarcely believe she was real.

"You...really are different, Jacob, darling." She laughed shakily, so in love she felt bathed in pure emotion.

"You're just as different to me. I've never been a monk, but it strikes me now that I've spent most of my life living inside my books rather than in the real world. Meeting you is a bit like meeting a volcano, only to have it erupt under my feet."

"Oh...." Her brow puckered.

"Volcanos are beautiful..." he assured her

gravely, with a sparkle in his exceptional burnished eyes. They were like cats' eyes, she thought dazedly, mesmerized by them. Tiger's eyes.... His hand at her waist sank down to curve around her hipbone. "Nature at its most powerful."

"But possibly destructive," she softly objected.

"Mmm...." He picked up one of her small hands in his strong, thin brown fingers. "Yes, very possibly." His gaze feasted on her, and unconsciously her fingers twined with his. Just when she hadn't thought she could love him more, she discovered she was still in the process of falling. When, she pondered, was the right time, and where, the right place?

CHAPTER FOUR

MONDAY NIGHT, a full day's work behind her, Camille was sitting in the quiet of her hotel room contemplating the vicissitudes of life when her telephone rang. She was delighted to hear the charming Pierre replying to her hello.

"Oh, Pierre, how nice to hear your voice!"

"And how delightful to hear yours! *Mon enfant*, Jacob asked me to take care of you while you were in Montreal. Do I understand you are leaving tomorrow? May I ask if you would dine with me tonight?"

"Oh. Oh, he did?" She shivered with joy. "Why, yes, that would be lovely!"

Jacob had been right about the midnight-blue Bugatti being the least overwhelming of Pierre's antique car collection. His friend arrived in state an hour later in a brilliant yellow Rolls-Royce about as long as a locomotive. Seeing it, Camille was doubly glad she'd worn her other new evening-type purchase, even though she'd been sentimentally hoping the professor would see it before anyone else. Still, having company for dinner was much better than being alone, with Jacob some six hundred miles away in Fredericton, and Pierre was a highly entertaining companion. He would have been her second choice in any case.

It was only when they were leaving one of Montreal's exclusive restaurants after dinner that Camille understood what Jacob had meant Saturday night about no pictures. Out of nowhere, she and Pierre were blinded by flashbulbs blazing in their faces. Pulling her hand from Pierre's to shield her eyes, she clutched him with the other and asked what in the world was going on.

"The press, Camille. I am not unknown in Montreal, and when I'm seen dining with an utterly enchanting *jeune femme* after a six-month abstinence, it makes for news!" He chuckled, well satisfied with his popularity. "Smile, *chérie*. Just smile, and I will answer all the questions!"

She wished she'd had the foresight to ask for no pictures, as well. Pierre, however, was enjoying himself. He chatted to several reporters as if no one could possibly be more interesting than he was—except, perhaps, his exquisite companion. He gestured toward her and talked away, but she had no idea what he was telling them, could only hope for the best. Tentatively she smiled but hung back, trying to shield herself behind Pierre, but this seemed to arouse greater curiosity. Finally Monsieur Beauchamp held up his hand in a positively royal gesture to indicate, "That's all, folks!" They escaped to the back seat of the Rolls, with the chauffeur bowing them in and the flashbulbs popping.

"Oh, Pierre!" she gulped, "that was awful!"

"You have never been in the news?" he asked, surprised.

"No! And I don't think I want to be, either!"

"Don't worry, little one. The reporters, they always try for the scoop, but the editor might not think me worthwhile news, and so probably nothing will appear," he soothed, sounding uncharacteristically modest. "Now, *chérie*, since we have lingered so long over dinner, and since I do not wish to annoy my dear friend Jacob, I will take you home before it turns midnight. Although. . . ."

"Oh, yes, Pierre, I should have an early night." Her eyes twinkled at his faint sigh of regret. "I had a lovely evening. Thank you."

The next morning Camille was packing her suitcases for the flight to Fredericton when her telephone rang. Not expecting a call, she was baffled to hear the voice of the Eaton's buyer, her first appointment in Montreal. Was he canceling his order? Had something gone wrong? But no, he wanted to order more.

"C'est magnifique!" he exclaimed.

"Er, what's *magnifique*?"

"Have you not seen the morning paper?"

She gasped. Embarrassed and chagrined, she replied, no, she hadn't yet had the opportunity.

"Ah, Mademoiselle Beesley, the results, the results! Since the doors open this morning, everybody wants your perfume!" He laughed richly. "I must have more immediately! Fortunately, I received the first shipment just last night. It was not yet on the shelves this morning when the demands started." He chuckled again. "You could not, *mademoiselle*, have done better! Already we phone the *Gazette* to acquire the photo for our own advertising. That was the best

picture. Would you be willing to sign a release
form?''

"Ah—" she gulped weakly "—yes. Send the
papers to my home address. Now, how much more of
what would you like?" Camille hastily snapped open
the sample case to retrieve the already packed ledger.
"The—the best picture? You mean there's more than
one?"

"But of course! In *Le Journal de Montréal*, too!"

Camille moaned quietly to herself. The next second she was scribbling down the buyer's reorder as
fast as he dictated it, and had to admit to being
pleased—it was a very large order. Robbie must be
outdoing himself to get the shipments delivered with
such speed, bless him.

After hanging up, she wondered whether any of
the other stores in the city would call, whether she
should delay her flight, just in case, when the telephone rang again. It was another buyer. Their shipment of perfume hadn't yet arrived, but they'd had
numerous requests for it this morning. When would
it get here? Could they order more immediately?

Camille could scarcely believe it. What in the
blazes was in the papers? In between calls she phoned
room service to ask them to deliver every paper in
Montreal to her room *tout de suite*. With an alarmed
look at her watch, she phoned the airline to switch
her flight to one leaving an hour later. She would
have to be on the run the moment she touched down
in Fredericton, but that couldn't be helped. The
phone calls kept coming in from every major department store she'd signed up, one after the other—

quite a few of the smaller stores, too. The news-
papers arrived, but she was too busy taking orders to
read them.

At last there was a lull. Opening Montreal's
English paper first, the *Gazette*, she searched
through its sections, to find herself splashed across
the top of a page. She couldn't prevent a little yelp of
dismay. Her very first thought was, *thank God Jacob
is some six hundred miles away!*

The friendly dinner out with Pierre looked far
more like a lovers' tryst in this picture. She was leaning a little backward, Pierre bent over, kissing the
palm of her right hand. She had her left hand up in
protest, as if she were a shy maiden overcome by the
romance of the moment, a fairy tale come true.

But it was when she read the type beneath the
photograph that she choked. Are wedding bells ringing for the seventh time? Who is the mystery woman?

The column beneath went on, "Pierre Beauchamp,
well-known man about town, confessed last night
that he's hoping to coax his shy young companion
into matrimony. 'If only she would say yes!' he
laments. The mystery woman is none other
than...."

Camille winced at being described as shy, then read
on to see herself further described as the perfume
princess—more of Pierre's rhetoric. The article
touched on Beesley Farm, overgrown with special
perfume roses in the faraway west, the unparalleled
poignancy of its fragrances—she was wearing Island
Rose when Pierre first met her—and the uniqueness
of such an industry in Canada. The story went on to

say why Camille Elenora Beesley was gracing Montreal with her presence, finishing with another of Pierre's flamboyant quotes.

In *Le Journal*, Montreal's largest French paper, a tabloid, was a collage of three pictures: one with her hand over her face, as if she and Pierre really were involved in a lovers' tryst and she didn't want to be recognized; another of Pierre kissing her palm; and another as they slipped into the Rolls-Royce. Of course she couldn't translate that caption or the story that went with it, but from the sensationalism of the pictures she could guess at the contents! She really had had no idea Pierre was such a celebrity.... Pierre!

"Chérie," he reproached her, a split second later, "please don't shout at me this early in the morning! You should know better than to telephone me at this hour."

"Pierre—" Camille took no notice "—how could you? How could you! 'Coax into matrimony! Perfume princess! Wedding bells ringing!' Have you gone berserk?"

"Now calm yourself, Camille, *chéric*. I did it in the best interests of business. Just think of the free advertising for my club! And have you not profited, too? Is not your perfume selling like...like hotcakes? What better advertising can there be? You and your brother, in your innocence, did not think of it, did you? But an ad in the paper is one thing. A marvelous story such as that—that opportunity comes only once! *Is* not the perfume selling like hotcakes?"

"Well, yes, but...." She paused, feeling helpless and overwhelmed by his smooth arguments.

"So?"

"But it's a lie, Pierre!"

"What is a lie? That I would marry you? I swear to you I would! Where is the lie?"

"But—but you're not!"

"And that is a pity! When, in a few weeks, the reporters want follow-up, I will tell them you turned me down. Then everyone will hurry to the club to see me eating my heart out for you. It was pure inspiration on my part, and you, *chérie*, should kiss me— not shout at me!"

Shaking her head, Camille gave up. What could she do—it had already been done!

Just before she left the hotel, she called home to give Robbie the new orders and tell him immediate shipment was necessary. For some reason, she said, the perfume was selling like hotcakes here in Montreal. He was suitably impressed with her work and went on to say he'd sent all previous shipments by courier express, as they wanted satisfied new customers. Camille congratulated him on his good sense. There was nothing new to relate regarding Fern and Charles, he told her, and since mom was in the shop at the moment, he would pass on the wonderful news. Before she hung up, Camille suggested when she arrived home, they really ought to consider an advertising campaign of some sort. Then, leaving instructions with the front-desk clerk to redirect orders to the farm, she ran to catch a taxi and the plane to Fredericton. And Jacob.

SHE FIRST STOPPED AT HER HOTEL in Fredericton to unload her suitcases; there was no message from the professor, either at the front desk or in her room. He had promised to leave one, and for the first time her faith in Jacob wavered. A cold little stab of fear struck through her heart. But it was still early in the day, just past one-thirty in the afternoon. Her first appointment was at two. She had no time to fret.

After freshening up, she set forth into the tree-lined streets—elms, the cabbie informed her, adding that she should see them in the summer when their glory did the city proud. The late cold snap apparently held the whole of eastern Canada in its grip. The temperature was far below zero, with blowing snow severely reducing visibility. It veiled the pretty, sedate little city on the banks of the St. John River, veiled the many stately buildings harking back to the days when Fredericton had been an elegant garrison town. Snuggling deeper into her silver fox, Camille turned from side to side, trying to see as much as she could while the cabbie's directing finger pointed here and there. She was also, even though she knew it was improbable, hoping to spot Jacob on some street corner.

Having eagerly hurried back to her hotel after her last meeting of the day, she was at first surprised not to find a message waiting for her. There was no hurry then, so she wandered disconsolately up to her room, wondering, puzzling, reflecting.

There wasn't a note slipped under her door, either. Perhaps the desk clerk had made a mistake. She telephoned down, but the same clerk had been on duty all afternoon, and was very sorry, miss, but there were no messages whatsoever.

Could the professor have got his days mixed up? He had never revealed the least absentmindedness where she was concerned. Pacing around her hotel room, a lovely, old-fashioned suite, she could scarcely appreciate its graceful comfort. She couldn't believe he'd forgotten. Any minute now he would call and she wouldn't have her day's bookkeeping finished, so she'd better get right at it. Calling for a pot of coffee, she opened her ledger.

When the coffee came, there was no Jacob behind the steward. The coffee was drunk, the business—satisfactory by all accounts—finished, and there was still no Jacob.

He should have arrived here yesterday. He knew she would be in town by noon today. The fact that she'd been an hour and a half late shouldn't be calamitous. Yet that appeared to be the case. In his message he was supposed to tell her what hotel he was staying in, which meant she couldn't even call him.

By nine o'clock that night Camille was practically in tears. She had been looking forward to seeing him so much that the sheer disappointment was crushing. Maybe something terrible had happened to him. Maybe he'd been held up. Then why hadn't he left a message, or better yet, called her from Quebec City? It wasn't as if he couldn't afford one long-distance call.

Inspiration dawned. She put a call through to the University of New Brunswick. Had Professor Jacob

Nathaniel Darleah lectured today? After various delays and instructions to call a different number, she finally learned the professor had indeed lectured earlier that day and was scheduled to again, tomorrow.

Well, at least she knew he was in town, and that he was well. But why didn't he call her? Didn't he want to?

She asked the floor steward to give her the names of Fredericton's best hotels. After several minutes he returned with a handwritten list. Camille set about dialing all three, politely asking whether the professor was in. The receptionist at the third hotel revealed that the professor couldn't be disturbed at the moment. Would she care to leave a message?

Camille replied no, slowly hanging up the receiver. Of all the hotels in the city, he'd picked the one right across the street from hers. She could see it from her room, all lighted up through a gently falling curtain of snow.

She fell to pacing again, reviewing that last day in Montreal, asking herself what could possibly have happened between Sunday night and Tuesday evening. Was it possible he had lost interest in her already? Had he met someone he liked more, a greater volcano? She was leaving tomorrow noon for Charlottetown. Beyond Fredericton she knew nothing of his plans, nor he hers. The uninterrupted silence of her room was slowly driving her mad. Willing the telephone to ring did absolutely no good.

Was it a case of don't call me, I'll call you? Were

the games starting at last? Perhaps he hadn't meant anything he'd said to her. But Pierre had called Jacob a misogynist, so surely the professor wouldn't cultivate clever lines to tumble ladies into his lap? Perhaps Jacob had come to the conclusion that a hasty romance on the road wasn't his style. Or what if he did just want a quick fling, even though he hadn't acted like that?

The unavoidable fact was he was right across the street, and he had bothered neither to send a message nor to call. He must *not* want to see her. There could be no other explanation.

Camille was numb. She couldn't accept the truth. Unable to stay in her dreadfully silent room and unable to decide whether to call him, she went out for a solitary dinner. To conserve funds, and since it was bitterly cold outside, she chose a plain little restaurant kitty-corner to her hotel.

Unfortunately, once she was seated facing the window, she realized she was right across from the brilliantly lighted front entrance of Jacob's hotel. Now she would have to sit there staring at it and wondering.... Maybe he'd decided women were not for him; his work was too important and took up too much of his time. Maybe he was afraid of getting hurt—no, he had too much grit and self-assurance to let that stop him. Biting into her lip, she sternly controlled the foolish desire to cry—she hadn't cried in years—and ordered a toasted bacon-and-tomato sandwich and fries. She pushed the chips around the plate once they came. She'd put far too much ketchup on, when she liked them with gravy, anyway. Taking another sip of coffee she lifted her eyes to the street. Through the falling snow, she saw the professor coming out of his hotel.

Motionless, she stared at him and his companion, a very attractive woman with long blond hair sweeping down either side of her face underneath a pert little hat. As they descended the stairs he took the woman's arm. She could see they were intent on their conversation.

Camille tore her eyes away from the dull shine of tawny hair, from the camel-hair coat with the turned-up collar. She'd been holding her breath and released it now in a long shuddering sigh. Obviously he was too busy to call her—but not busy with his books. An instant later her eyes were on them again.

Shortly after the first shock came a lesser one—another man was coming out of that hotel—none other than their spy! She was certain of it, snow or no snow. Jacob and the woman had crossed the intersection, were now in front of her hotel and proceeding onward. With a look in both directions, the spy—she didn't know what else to call him—followed them. Alert, Camille noticed another man sauntering a short distance behind the spy. Why would anyone stroll so casually on a night like this?

Just when she'd convinced herself her suspicions were unfounded, the spy ducked into the dark doorway of a boutique in her hotel. The second fellow, who had also crossed the intersection, veered down the side street in the same moment to duck into the side doorway leading into her hotel. Then she saw why—Jacob and the woman were coming back. They recrossed the street, gained the near side and continued through to the lobby. The spy slid inconspicuously out of the boutique doorway. He had barely reached the near street corner when the other fellow came out of hiding to tail them.

Now Camille was intrigued by this cat-and-mouse game. The spy entered the professor's hotel, and after a few seconds' pause, the second spy did, too. Who was following whom in this curious display? Five or so minutes later, the procession repeated itself as Camille sat staring in rapt attention. Out came Jacob and his companion, and after a decent interval the first spy, then the second. Jacob and the woman proceeded across the street as before. Their entourage crossed discreetly behind each other until everyone had disappeared from her range of vision down the street. For an absurd second Camille thought of following all of them in turn, but by the time she'd paid her bill and was out on the frosty, snow-shrouded street, all four were gone.

Then what she'd seen really didn't matter anymore. What mattered was that she knew there would be no message for her when she returned to her room, which was indeed the case. Her numbness had worn off. The sight of the woman excitedly talking and talking away to Jacob, as he attentively listened and nodded and then said something in return, confirmed her worst fears. He didn't want to see her.

Scalding tears ran down her cheeks when she was once more alone; she couldn't stop them. How glad she was that she hadn't called him! To be plunged so unexpectedly from the heights to the depths was unbearably cruel. Couldn't he at least have had the decency to say goodbye? She would probably never see him again, and that was the cruelest cut of all....

STIRRING HER MORNING COFFEE, her chin in her hand, watching the soft, steady, dreamy fall of snowflakes, Camille felt the dreadful rise of tears again. Determinedly munching through a slice of toast, she opened her daily reminder. Perhaps she should call him anyway—just to tell him about his two spies, of course. Was he in some kind of trouble? But he would probably think she'd made up the weird and wonderful story just to talk to him, and there was no way, no possible way she was going to force herself on him! That still left the matter of the spies....

Camille couldn't make up her mind whether to call Jacob. When her last appointment was over, she realized the morning had passed too quickly. Now she had to return to the hotel to pack her bags for the flight to Charlottetown. There might be a message awaiting her.... If so, this might prove that the woman last night was a colleague of Jacob's, a fellow professor, perhaps.

But in reply to her casual question, the desk clerk assured her there were no messages. No messages! He was letting her go. He hadn't kept his promise. He didn't want her at his lecture—he didn't want her at all. What she had thought was genuine had turned out to be spurious. Were her instincts so wide off the mark? Devastated, she began to hate Jacob a little— deliberately he had misled her, let her down. Pierre must have known all the time what his friend was

like. And she had known better than to fall in love
with a complete stranger; her copious common sense
had done her no good whatsoever. Well, fools had to
learn the hard way.

SHE DIDN'T FEEL quite so philosophical on the short
flight to Charlottetown—second by second she was
leaving him farther and farther behind. She began to
wish she'd written him a carefully emotionless note
concerning his two spies. She should at least have
warned him. But why would a professor be shadowed
by two men? It made no sense. Vancouver, Calgary,
Toronto, now Fredericton—the same man, con-
cealed in the corner of the elevator, sitting behind
Jacob at dinner, outside their hotel waiting on the
street below, now following him down the street.
Same city, same time, same hotel. Spy number one
was no coincidence. What about spy number two?

Just then Camille had her first glimpse of Prince
Edward Island, trapped in the sunshine glimmering
through the snow-cloud ceiling, the flakes temporarily suspended. The high red sandstone cliffs were encircled by a gray sea below and capped with white
above, a wide wintry pastoral landscape dotted with
miniature farmhouses. Before the passengers had dis-
embarked, it was snowing again.

Whisked by taxi through Charlottetown's streets
on her way to her first appointment—she was flying
out again that night, and so had left her suitcases in a
locker at the airport—she was struck by the thought
that this tiny city was very much like Victoria. The
charming old red brick facades and the gingerbread

on the wooden buildings, virtually unchanged by the passage of time, had a distinctly English Victorian air, just like home. How glad she would be to get home.... All the fun had gone out of her trip.

Although she had memorized the names of the Charlottetown buyers on the plane, she had to open her reminder once more—every time she thought of the professor he wiped out all else. The whole trouble with perfection was that it disappeared too soon. Reality set in. Her brief romance with Jacob had simply been too perfect to last.

THAT NIGHT Camille was on to Halifax, feeling weary and desolate. Tumbling gratefully into bed in her sumptuous room, she wondered where Jacob was now, what he was doing right this minute. And then she resented him more for robbing her of the sweet forgetfulness of sleep.

The following evening, she hadn't quite closed her room door behind her when the telephone started ringing. Her heart lurched uncomfortably. Jacob? What would she say to him? Should she be cool and distant?

"Oh, Camille!" and her mother burst into tears on the phone. "Who is this person? How can you— h-how can you...."

"Mom? Please—"

She heard Robbie say, "Let me talk to her!" The next instant he roared over the wire, "What the hell is going on?"

"Calm down, Robbie. What happened?"

"What happened! If you don't beat the living end!

I suppose you figured your family wasn't important enough to inform!''

"Inform?" she asked blankly. "About what?" she added cautiously a moment later.

"About what? About what?" he raged. "Mom's in tears, and you ask about what?"

"Stop grinding your teeth or you'll wear the porcelain down."

"Camille," Robbie continued in a dangerously quiet tone, "who is Pierre Beauchamp? For Pete's sake, he looks old enough to be your father! How could you get involved with a character like that? Don't you have any sense? Mom almost died when she saw that picture of you sitting on his lap in the back seat of that god-awful Rolls! What's he done to you? I'll kill him; I swear I'll kill him! That debauched—"

"Pierre is not debauched—and neither am I, thank you very much! I was not—do you hear me—not sitting on his lap! It just looked that way because of the angle of the picture!"

"But—"

"He's really very nice. He's a friend of a friend, who only took me out to dinner and straight back to my hotel afterward. That was all there was to it, but the papers blew it up into...into, well, you saw what into."

"But what about those ringing wedding bells?" Robbie demanded, slightly mollified.

"I didn't realize what he was saying at the time because, Robbie, in Montreal people speak French!" She went on to give him Pierre's explanation for the deed. "And it did work, after all, didn't it?"

"But you don't have any friends in Montreal! How can he be a friend of a friend? What *have* you been up to?"

"I, er, met this. . . person traveling and met Pierre through him. That's all. Boring, really."

"What person?"

"Just another fellow traveler. I am old enough to talk to strangers, Robbie. I can take care of myself—there's no one for you to kill. After all, don't I deserve an occasional night off? And, how the hell did *you* get hold of those pictures?"

Robbie sounded relieved. "Well, our paper picked up the scoop off the Canadian Pacific wire service—all of it! This morning *The Victoria Herald* phoned to ask if they could do a bit of a story on us, using those pictures, et cetera. Of course mom wanted to know what pictures. What a shock, to learn you were pasted all over the front page!" He spoke as if it was as embarrassing to be in the papers as it was to be to jail.

"It was hardly the front page!" she snapped.

"Now you're going to be in the *Herald*, too."

"It'll be good for sales," she replied grimly.

Robbie sighed. "I suppose so."

"Honestly, you'd think I'd committed a crime!"

"Dear? Camille?" Her mother came back on the line. "Thank heavens you're not getting married!"

"That's a switch for you, mom!"

"You know what I mean. If you say Pierre is nice, then—" she sighed "—he must be but. . . he doesn't give the impression of being a Sunday-school teacher. Naturally we were upset."

"You have some Sunday-school teacher lined up for me, do you— All right, I'm sorry, mom. Yes, mom. Of course not, mom. No, I'm fine. Sales are terrific. Yes, isn't it wonderful. See? Charles *was* wrong! No, I'm not really all that certain that he was concerned for me. What? What? Mom, you're not making sense! How can I have met Jake Darby when I'm here and he's there?"

"Not Jake Darby, dear. Jake Darleah—Jacob Darleah!"

Camille stared at the receiver in her hand. "Mom, I don't understand.... What are you talking about?"

Groaning at her daughter's dimness, Fern explained as if Camille were a child of three. "Jake, my dear, Jacob. Jacob is Charles's son, his stepson, and I told you that! If only you would listen to your mother!"

"He can't be!" Camille breathed, horror-struck.

"Well, of course he is. Jacob Darleah. Really, dear, sometimes I wonder about you!" Fern reproached her daughter. "The only reason I agreed to your trip was because I knew he was going on a lecture tour and you two would be in the same cities most of the time. I booked you into his hotels whenever I could so you'd have somebody close to turn to. I asked him to keep an eye on you, you know—"

Camille interrupted, trembling, "Mom—"

"And if it wasn't asking too much, to take you out to dinner once in a while so you wouldn't fall into the hands of, well, people like that Pierre fellow. Really, dear, do you think you should trust him? I know you said— But, now, you haven't met Jake? Haven't set eyes on him? Isn't that odd!"

"Mother. Mother, how could you! How could you do such a terrible thing? Please, please tell me you didn't!"

"Only to keep an eye on—"

"Mother!" Camille wailed, mortified. "How could you force me on a stranger like that? Yes, I met the professor, only I didn't realize he was Jake!"

"But how could you not? Camille—"

"I'd never set eyes on him. Why should I recognize him? Oh, mom!"

"Darling, you're not crying, are you? What's the matter? What have I done?"

Getting a grip on herself, Camille replied as steadily as she was able, "No, I'm not crying. You know I never cry. I'm just a little disappointed that you should think I need to be babysat. I...I'd better go. This is costing us a fortune."

"Oh, now I've upset you. I'm sorry. I didn't know you would take it like this. I didn't mean to— I only did it for the best, and...."

When the call was over, Camille hung up the receiver with a shaking hand. All of her was shaking, from the inside out. Shame and rage stormed within her. Jake. The snake! The *bastard*! She wished she had the professor in front of her. She would tear him up into a thousand bits and throw them into Halifax Harbour!

Not only had he misled, but he had also deceived! If mother only knew how he had "kept an eye on her!'' And what evil purpose could he have had for keeping his identity such a secret?

She realized now that she should have caught on. Jake and Jacob were both professors, both had grown up in Toronto, both had been abroad until recently, both had been in Paris. But surely more than one professor in this world came from Toronto! On the other hand, how was he to know she'd closed her ears every time her mother sang his praises? He must have thought she would realize he was her next-door neighbor as soon as he told her his name. He must have wondered when she didn't.... Well, maybe he'd wondered, but he hadn't bothered to enlighten her.

Groaning, Camille remembered how she'd thrown her arms around him when he'd turned up unexpectedly in Montreal. Following her mother's instructions, he'd taken her out, had kept her too busy to fall into the wrong hands. *Blast him off the face of the earth,* she fumed, curling her hands into fists. While he'd been performing his neighborly duties, he'd had a little fun of his own....

The reason he'd decided to keep his identity a secret was only too plain. Daddy Charles wanted to buy him a company, and Jacob must have chosen the perfumery. Only now did she link those sociological implications of his to archaelology, the evolution of natural medicinal substances to the ancient unguents and ointments Elaine had spoken so disparagingly of with reference to Jacob. Elaine didn't like him, either, small wonder. His cousin was his peer and therefore could see through him in a way the older folks couldn't.

All those flattering questions he'd asked about the laboratory! He wanted it for himself, for his own esoteric concoctions. Well, over her dead body! Like father, like son—both of them probably using romance to suit their ends. She fervently wished they would start their own company, rather than preying on a widow and her naive offspring. Did Charles see big bucks in the perfumery business? And hadn't she known she wouldn't like Jake, hadn't she just *known*?

Her rage wore her out, and so that night she fell asleep almost instantaneously. Feeling refreshed the next morning, but no happier, she hadn't much more appetite than she'd had the day before. It was Friday, and she would be flying to St. John's, Newfoundland, later that day. On Sunday she would be flying home from St. John's. Even the pleasure of getting home was dimmed, knowing *he* was living right next door!

The ringing of her telephone startled her. Swallowing a mouthful of toast, she forced it down with a hasty gulp of burning hot coffee. While uselessly fanning her mouth, she lifted the receiver.

"H-hello. Camille Beesley speaking."

"Camille? It's Jacob."

Of course she knew it was Jacob. No one had a voice quite like his. She said nothing.

"Camille?"

"Yes?" she managed, almost nonchalantly, as if she weren't surprised, as if he were merely a casual acquaintance. Thinking rapidly, she decided not to let on that she had all the facts, at long last.

"May I take you to lunch later?"

She noticed he sounded reserved, the way he'd been the first time she'd talked to him in Saskatoon. "You're here in Halifax?" she prevaricated coolly.

"The same hotel. One floor up."

Camille swallowed, perspiration beading her brow. Blindly she stared out at the whirling snowflakes beyond her windows. "Well, well. Oh, I should tell you I saw our spy in Fredericton—and he was following you, not me. There was somebody else following him, too. I wanted to tell you at the time, but I didn't know where to get hold of you," she lied. "And since you didn't seem too upset by him in Toronto, I assumed it probably wasn't all that important."

"You saw him? When?" Was his tone guarded?

"Let me see...." She pretended to hesitate. "I think it was Tuesday night—yes, that was it. I saw you leaving a hotel across the street from mine, and he followed you and so did the second man. Anyway, I'm glad you called, because I wanted to let you know. It did seem rather...bizarre." There was a long pause.

"May I see you at lunch?" Jacob's tone was constrained.

"Oh, I'm sorry, but I'm already engaged for lunch." Well, she was. She was going to be engaged in flying to St. John's. "But thanks for the thought, Jacob."

"Are you being sarcastic?" he demanded testily.

"Me? No. Why should I be sarcastic? I have to run, professor, or I'll be late for my first appointment. Goodbye."

Hanging up, Camille thought she'd done pretty well—not acting surprised that he hadn't left the promised message, not acting like anything at all, really. Just cool, offhand and casually friendly.... Certainly not as if she bore any grudge....

She didn't absorb much of Halifax and adjoining Dartmouth across the harbor, except that they were big cities: waterways and lakes everywhere, snowy expanses of park sandwiched between the modern and the remaining bits of history. Two massive suspension bridges spanned Halifax Harbour. Crossing over, Camille saw the sleek gray warships of the Canadian Forces Maritime Command far below, huge freighters coming and going from the busy container port.

Upon touchdown at St. John's airport, she couldn't help wondering whether Jacob was coming to Newfoundland, as well. What did it matter? There was an uncrossable distance between them, anyway.

Her hotel was close to the deep, U-shaped harbor in the heart of the downtown area; she could see the waterside activity from her windows. Pausing only long enough to comb her hair and add a touch of lipstick and perfume, she then dashed off to meet her first buyer. She had become used to talking to cabbies. They were quite informative, and most were friendly and liked to chat. This one told her that in St. John's, one either went straight up or straight down, and she found he was right. His accent was different, too—a little Irish, a little English, all soft and slurred together. When she asked him about it, he laughed and said she was the one who had the accent, even though she came from an island herself. "You, m'dear, speak like a mainlander!"

Everywhere she went she was offered tea, sometimes rum, and English biscuits sat on many an office desk. Folks were friendly, the pace more leisurely than in Halifax—not that she had time to sit and chat, much as she would have liked to. She even had an appointment over dinner in the evening.

Sitting in a comfortable, old-style restaurant on Water Street with a satisfied customer, she learned she was looking out on probably the oldest street in North America. The mere thought was thrilling. Camille was more then pleased to be so busy, to have every minute filled up, for thinking beyond the business at hand had become too painful a pastime.

Saturday flashed by. That evening she was booked for dinner with a friend of a store owner and early Sunday morning she was packing her bags for home. Although the day had just begun, she felt tired and run down. Now, instead of wanting to go home, she wished she were fabulously wealthy just so she could run away from everybody, leave everything behind.

But no. She loved her family and Beesley Farm. She loved the perfumery—Damask, too. She loved creating perfume and she had a new one to work on—Robbie's essence. Her sales had boosted their finances enormously, so really all was well on the home front. All she had to do was ignore her next-door neighbor. . . .

FROM ST. JOHN'S TO TORONTO, switch planes there, from Toronto to Vancouver, catch the Airporter bus into the city, catch a taxi to the Air B.C. terminal in Coal Harbour, wait ten minutes, catch the Twin Otter float plane back to the Inner Harbour and Victoria. Home at last. And there were Robbie and mom, already waiting for her.

After the flurry of greetings and hugs and kisses, Camille immediately peeled off the much-too-warm silver fox that had served so well in the colder eastern climate.

"How are you, darling?" her mother queried anxiously, as if Camille had been to war.

Laughing, she shook her head. "No limbs gone, Mom. I'm fine! Why shouldn't I be? But I am a little tired."

"You poor darling," Fern crooned, and for once Camille really didn't mind the babying. How could she have thought she didn't want to come home! Robbie caught her eye, grinning, and she grinned back and nodded. Dear mom.

A multitude of questions and answers ricocheted back and forth as she was bundled into the family station wagon. Boogaloo and Razzmattaz, in the back seat, were almost beside themselves, greeting her with great wet doggie kisses she kept trying to avoid. Talking a mile a minute, she gazed around at the elegance of the Parliament buildings, the equally charming and equally huge Empress Hotel—both faced the Inner Harbour—and the pretty blue lamp posts bedecked with hanging flower baskets spilling their bright blossoms. She stopped in midspeech to say, "St. John's is a little like this, and so is Charlottetown."

"You're a minor celebrity around home—you were in the weekend paper." Robbie was still grinning. "Oh, and the shop has been deluged yesterday and today. Poor Phyllis is having a fit!"

"Good Lord!" Camille exclaimed.

"What?" Fern and Robbie questioned in unison. Her mother added, "Did you forget something?"

"Yes. I forgot how green everything is here. Just look at all the flowers! Daffodils and pansies and tulips! Tulips! It was snowing when I left St. John's. In fact, for a while I thought they were going to delay my flight. The cherry trees are blooming, too. Isn't that forsythia? The magnolias are out. Oh, am I glad to be home!"

"You never did say how you liked Jake. Did you know he's already home?"

"No, I didn't. Jake?" She shrugged noncommitally. "He's...quite nice, I guess."

"Oh...." Her mother sounded disappointed.

Robbie caught her eye again, and when she grimaced he hastily cleared his throat and pretended he was concentrating on the traffic, all but nonexistent on a Sunday evening in peaceful little Victoria.

"I bought some clothes in Montreal—mom, you should see the boutiques there! And the prices!"

"What did you buy?" Fern was all interest.

"Clothes!" Robbie protested. "Clothes?"

Although Camille was tired, they stayed up until all hours talking about her trip, each city, the people she'd met, Pierre, of course...and exactly who it was who had introduced her to him. How much had been sold against how much the trip had cost, how many orders still had to be sent, how much more product had to be made now that their backlog of stock was depleted. Soon summer would be upon them, and with it the tourist trade. Fern and Robbie related that Elaine had gained several more pounds, Harry their handyman had almost broken his leg falling off the roof while reshingling, the bottling machine had failed again and how the field work was progressing. The roses had just begun to bloom.

As she was walking up the stairs with Robbie, both of them yawning, she asked, lowering her voice so their mother wouldn't hear, "And what about the codfish?"

"They went out for dinner last Saturday night, and not to Rachael and Wilson's! To the Empress, no less! Dancing afterward. I tell you, I don't like the look of it."

"I'm afraid I rather put my foot in it. When I met Jacob, I didn't realize he was *the* Jake, and when he asked questions about the perfumery I answered."

Robbie groaned. "You idiot!"

"Yes. But luckily I didn't divulge the state of our financial affairs, nor did I discuss obnoxious millionaires, so at least I spared myself that embarrassment...."

"No more's been said about getting outside help to manage, but I'm worried—what are we going to do about the encroaching codfish?"

"How should I know? What can we do? We can't

forbid mom to go out with him. Let's just hope she tires of him or they have a fight or something.''

After everyone else had gone to bed Camille was still up, sitting at her bedroom window, open to let in the wonderfully fresh night air. She could hear the soft sweep of breakers on the shore.... She was still dressed and, obeying a sudden impulse, tiptoed back downstairs. Pulling on the silver fox fur since it was handy and her yellow galoshes, she quietly let herself out the door. Down the cushiony lawn she walked, the wind tugging at her hair. The quiet and the freedom of the night soothed her troubled soul. Down to the beach, where her galoshes crunched on the stones, she wandered. How nice it felt not to have an appointment in X minutes.

At last she found herself at the marble stairway leading up to her house, Damask. Halfway up, she stopped to inspect her favorite tree, the weeping willow that stood in the bend of the stairs. When she was small she had lain beneath its boughs for hours— her secret hideaway. Now, even in the darkness of night, she could see it was feathered over with slender new leaves. She reached for a frond to run it through her fingers. The baby yellow green leaves were as soft as silk.

Drifting onto the lawn, she noticed it had already been mowed. The flower beds were bursting with daffodils, and the climbing roses were in full leaf. How pretty the house looked in the gloom. It would look so much nicer with a light shining from a window.... Oh, well. Maybe someday. She didn't want to think about someday now, not with the knowledge of Jacob burning in her mind. Because some day, when she married, mom would give her the house. Robbie didn't want to live here, and her father had built the cottage for Fern when they married, so she didn't want to live here, either. Camille wanted to share Damask with the man she loved. . . .

Camille didn't see a tallish figure falling back into the shadow of a side wall, but he had seen her. Her curls, glinting in creamy disarray in the moonlight, were gilded bright silver, as visible as a flag. She went up the second set of stairs to sit down on the top one. The dark figure had moved forward to the corner, where he stood motionless, obscured by the climbing roses. Moonlight sheened on his hair, turning some tawny threads to gold. His eyes were in deep shadow, yet they glowed mysteriously yellow like a tiger's.

Camille was crying before she realized it; a single tear fell onto her hand. Really, this was disgusting, this sentimentality. But she was saying goodbye to a lost dream. She didn't love Jacob anymore. This was the first and last cry she would allow herself. In five minutes she would never think of him again. No one must ever know. . . .

There wasn't a sound or a movement to betray that her solitude was shared. Only when she finally stirred to slip away down to the beach and vanish into the night did the shadow detach itself from the house, gliding away in the opposite direction.

THE PERFUMERY was abustle the following week. A lot had to be done in a relatively short space of time. Local shops in Victoria were calling for more product, since Camille's picture in the paper, coupled with the history of Beesley Farm, had prompted eager across-the-counter sales. Fern and Phyllis were kept hopping in the little shop. In between the customers, the curious and the beginning trickle of tourists, they had barely enough time to box fragrant goods and restock shelves. However, they ended work when the shop closed each day at five, while Robbie and Camille kept going. Not only did the warehouse have to be filled to see them through the spring and summer seasons, and the possibility of reorders from her trip, but the fields and fields of roses also had to be tended. Unwanted shoots had to be trimmed, the ground had to be mulched and fertilized, spraying against insect pests and plant diseases had to be done. Finally, there was the lavender farm to cultivate.

That Wednesday night, Fern tried to coax Robbie and Camille to join Charles, Jake and her at the premiere of the Cannes film festival winner in Victoria.

Robbie declined. "Oh, mom—you know I hate weepy love stories! And I never could stand trying to watch a movie and read subtitles at the same time. Count me out."

"Camille?"

"What?"

Sighing, Fern repeated her suggestion, adding that if Camille came along they would make a nice foursome. Since her daughter thought Jake was "quite nice," she had resumed her efforts at matchmaking.

"Er, no. I'll be at my organ tonight."

"Camille! You can't work all the time!"

"But it's fun, not work. Besides, I—I promised to see the film next week with Elaine."

Camille was already in the laboratory when Mr. Darby and son came to collect her mother in a big white Cadillac. Meeting Jake was unavoidable, she knew, but she was going to delay it as long as possible. It was obvious he was in favor of the budding romance between Charles and Fern—why wouldn't he be? Such a connection was sure to bring him and his father closer to their aim of annexing the perfumery.

Friday at lunch time Fern casually asked Robbie when he came into the kitchen, "Have you anything planned for Sunday evening?"

Camille, who was right behind her brother, didn't have time to warn him before he replied, "Don't think so. Why?"

"Charles has invited us all for dinner at their place." Their mother looked very innocent. "I've agreed for us."

Robbie's discomfort was nothing compared to Camille's. "But mom, I—I've a date Sunday night!"

"A date? Since when? Honestly, Camille, Charles is going to take another nonappearance as a snub. That's exactly what it is, too! What's got into you? You're usually so friendly—too friendly, if anything."

"This morning that gift-shop owner called, and I've already agreed to go out to dinner with him. At the Empress. I thought you'd be happy I had a date!"

"What gift-shop owner?"

"You know. I went out with him before my trip."

"Oh, him," Fern said, sounding unimpressed. "But you're coming, Robert Beesley!"

"Er, I suppose so." Robbie looked down at his plate.

"Where's Harry?" Camille changed the subject, feeling sorry for her brother. Harry generally joined them for lunch.

"He had his lunch early. He wanted to get to the lavender farm and took along the gardeners." She looked searchingly at her daughter. "What *is* the matter with you, dear?"

"With me?" Camille protested, eyes wide. "Why, what do you mean?"

"Oh, I don't know. You've been different ever since you came back. Aren't you well?"

"I'm perfectly fine."

"You're not yourself. You're usually so—so bouncy, happy. You're not happy now, are you?"

"Um. . . ." Camille cast around wildly for a good answer, smiled brilliantly at her mother and said, "Why shouldn't I be?"

"That's what I want to know," Fern persisted. "What's turned you silent and serious?"

"Just watch me tackle this stew!" she countered with a grin, ladling more onto her plate.

"You're not pulling the wool over my eyes, and don't think you are. Is it a man?"

Camille stared. "Man?"

"Yes—you know, the opposite sex! Is it Pierre?"

"Pierre is a darling, but the only thing that captivated me about him was the way he kissed my hand. I'm not . . . pining away for any man. The idea!''

"Then what? You've been overdoing it, working late every night this week, that's what! You should be happy about your sales—we all are—but you don't appear to be. You seem to feel it's all not enough. You, too, Robbie! If we can't manage alone, then we just can't, so there's no sense in knocking yourselves out trying to. I'm beginning to think we should take on a business partner. Somebody with some capital to invest, somebody who knows how to manage a small business properly. And don't look at your mother like that, you two. I'm not suggesting treason!''

CHAPTER FIVE

"INVESTORS? Like who?" Robbie demanded quietly.

"Well, like Charles, for instance." Fern's eyes darted brightly from one to the other.

"If he's got money to throw away, why doesn't he build his own laboratory rather than trying to hog ours!" Camille was too upset to be rational. "That's what Jacob wants—our lab! He asked a hundred questions about it on my trip, the sneak! If he's in, I'm out!"

"But dear, do think for a minute. What's the problem if Jake gets a corner of the lab? He won't be in your way. Besides, Charles does have some good ideas—that we should advertise, for instance."

Robbie and Camille had talked over just such a plan, but to have an outsider sticking his oar in where it didn't belong was too much.

"We can make the perfumery work if we're just given a chance!" Robbie objected.

"We'll sell one of our formulas before we'll sell a half interest in the farm!"

"Now Camille, don't overreact!" Robbie exclaimed. "We're not selling anything."

"Threatening us with a foreign invasion is only going to make us work harder to prevent it—don't you see that, mom?"

"You both hate the idea?" Fern sighed. "Or do you just dislike Charles?" There was an extended moment of great discomfort.

"We only want the chance to do it ourselves," Robbie explained, mindlessly shredding a slice of homemade bread. "So we don't do everything right—we're trying to learn. What chance will we have with Charles taking over? We'll be employees on our own turf. Nothing personal, but this place is our whole life. It's always been in the family, and Camille and I want to keep it that way!"

"Please, mom. Please don't sell us out—not yet. Things are looking much brighter already. Robbie and I have only just begun to make it work. Give us a chance!"

"When both of you gang up on me, *I* haven't a chance. Very well. Have it your way. If you want to work all day and all night, if you want to worry about every penny, then go ahead. But hear me now. I don't want you to get your hopes up too high." Her offspring looked at her askance.

"Your sales, Camille, were marvelous, but if our product doesn't sell well in the stores—if we don't get plenty of reorders—all could still be lost. We need a record summer, too. We need big improvement, and not only that, steady improvement. If we go bankrupt it's all over. If we bring in a partner now, we could still be saved."

"You've changed, too, mom," Camille said slowly. "You've always been optimistic. Now, all of a sudden, you're prophesying doom." She didn't like the change, either, not one bit.

"Charles has opened my eyes."

"What does he know about a perfumery!"

"Nothing. But he knows about business, and we are, first and foremost, a business!"

"You're even starting to talk like him!" Camille charged resentfully.

Shocked, Fern Beesley looked at her, then at Robbie. Slowly her eyes dropped.

Camille felt dreadful, and especially bitter toward Charles Darby. He had caused a rift in a family that had always stuck together. He had been the nub of trouble and quarrel. He had even caused their mother's faith in them to waver. Fern wasn't wholeheartedly backing their efforts. It was a bit of a blow.

After lunch, and because it was Friday, Camille set out to do her weekly chores at Damask. Today she escaped with an even greater need for its lovely peace and solitude. At least Charles and Jacob couldn't intrude here, as they did everywhere else. It didn't matter that she tried to forget Jacob, for her mother kept bringing him up—either him or Charles. She couldn't think of one without thinking of the other. Cold-blooded, the pair of them! If Charles really cared for Fern, would he be turning her against her own family?

Shuddering as if to physically dismiss the two men, she set immediately to her chores. She threw the doors and windows wide, carefully removed all the many dustcovers and carried them outside to snap them in the fresh sunny air. She cleaned out the seven fireplaces and laid new kindling and logs—oil heat was much too expensive to drive the damp from the house. She slid a dust mop from room to room. She washed all the downstairs windows, made of beautiful stained and beveled glass. A feather duster reached odd corners and mantelpieces and chandeliers. To prevent musty odors, she replaced the saucers of ammonia in every room and deposited newly made sachets of lavender flowers and lemon verbena in closets and drawers. A few drops of sassafras oil scattered around kept the flies out. A bit of cedarwood oil here and there stopped the moths from eating their way through the upholstery.

One unsavory job remained. The only place she didn't like in the house was the cellar. It was so perfectly creepy a place, huge and dark and dank with granite walls and granite floor—so cold! There were only two light fixtures to dispel the gloom. Camille only went down there four times a year, and it was time for her spring visit. Checking for leaks or flooding was a must. Harry's cat usually took care of the vermin. She wished she had the big orange animal with her now as she crept down the narrow stairs, flashlight in hand.

Everything was as usual: the rows of empty wine racks, grampa's dreadfully dusty wine-making equipment.... Her father had never dabbled in that hobby. He'd spent too much of his time in the laboratory, at work. Camille, flashing her spotlight here and there along the rows of old barrels, old trunks, the coal shute where she and Robbie had played as children, suddenly wondered why her father had been so immersed in his lab work.

She had never really puzzled over it before. She knew how long it could take to compose a perfume and its satellites, but still. . . . She couldn't remember his making much that was new after she was seven or eight, yet he had spent hours and hours locked away there. Of course, he'd spent some time teaching Robbie the technique for mixing batches, much time teaching her. What had he done when all alone?

She could remember nights, very late, when she couldn't sleep and would sit by her window, only to see the lab's lights go on. Blinds had blacked out the windows, but a thin sliver of light along the top edge of the clerestory would give her father away. Why, after mother went to sleep, did he get up and get dressed and go back there? Long ago, when she'd asked her mother why, the only reply she got was a pat on her curly head and, "There, there, dear. You know daddy likes to putter."

Funny how looking at the sooty coal shute brought back the memories. Sweeping her flashlight around again, she ascended the stairs, deciding to bring Harry's tomcat, his pride and joy, for a visit next Friday.

She had just enough time to dash to the store before dinner. The Beesleys bought many supplies in bulk. Neighboring farms provided milk, cream, eggs, meat, most vegetables. She and Robbie made the family soap, detergent and toothpaste. Toothpaste. Elaine had asked her why they didn't sell it, too. On the way to the store, across the street from Greyson's garage, Camille pondered the costs of the commercial manufacture of toothpaste.

Standing a short while later at the end of the line by the check-out counter, Camille chatted with Mrs.

Plumtree, another neighbor and the so-called farmer-who-kept-sheep. Her cheeks reddened as talk turned to her newspaper splash. Mrs. Plumtree informed her she was having the hand-kissing picture framed.

"I can point to it and say I've known you since you were so high!" the elderly woman beamed at her. She was short and plump—quite lovable, though she talked too much. "So handsome, the gentleman! So—"

"How's the arthritis in your knee?" Camille murmured quickly.

"Does anyone know if there's a sauna around here?" a voice queried from behind Camille, a soft velvety voice that was nevertheless loud enough for everyone in the line to hear.

Camille clutched her items to her breast—didn't move otherwise. She kept her back rigidly straight. Damn. She probably had cobwebs in her hair and at least one smudge on her nose!

"A sauna?" echoed the mob, and began to discuss where the nearest facility might be. Camille was scarlet with mortification.

"I particularly enjoy a sauna every now and then," the voice continued evenly. "So relaxing...."

She hated him—how she hated him!

"Well, sonny," said Mrs. Plumtree, "you'll have to go into Victoria for that."

"Isn't there one in Langford in that new hotel?" the neighbor suggested. Langford was a suburb between Metchosin and Victoria.

"I don't know. But they do have an indoor swimming pool, so that's your best bet,'' the farmer put in.

"You wouldn't know, would you, Camille?'' Jacob asked her rigid back.

"I'm sure there's one in Paris,'' she supplied sweetly, not turning around. "Why don't you go there?''

"Would you come with me?''

At her confused pause, the crowd began to smile and wink. Mrs. Plumtree nudged her neighbor, saying, "My, it is spring, isn't it?'' and gave a long romantic melodramatic sigh. Then, contrary to her wont, she was silent. How Camille wished she would yak-yak-yak away as usual.

"Saunas don't agree with my delicate constitution,'' she finally said lightly. The line moved up.

"Too hot?'' Jacob inquired pleasantly.

Camille gritted her teeth. "Among other things.''

"Betty said you sometimes give tours of the perfumery, if you're asked nicely enough,'' he continued. Betty was the cashier. "Would you give me a tour, Camille? Please....''

Betty treated them both to smiles—indeed, everybody seemed to be smiling expectantly at her, as if prompting her to say yes. What a damnable spot to be in. If she said no, all her friends and neighbors would think her ungracious—and well he knew it.

"I might be persuaded,'' she replied coolly, choking down a strident protest. Conversation seemed to be up to her and Jacob. She was sure everybody's ears were perked up so as not to miss anything. There were times when living in a small community had its negative side!

"When? Tomorrow?"

"I—I'm going to be busy all day...."

"Sunday, then?"

Rage surged within her. "Well, I have a date on Sunday, and—"

"Oh? All day?"

"Well...."

"Maybe I'll ask your mother?"

No way. There was no way she wanted her mother to show Jake the premises. She would be much too open, much too ready to answer sly questions. "Perhaps if you came early on Sunday I can squeeze you in." The mob smiled, and again Mrs. Plumtree nudged the lady in front of her. Camille thought she might die of pure aggravation.

"What time?"

Persistent devil. "Make it in the morning." Oh, no. Then mom would insist he stay for lunch! "Change that to one-thirty."

"One-thirty, Sunday."

"Very well," she agreed long-sufferingly.

"I would have thought you'd been already!" Mrs. Plumtree commented at last to Jacob. "You live right next door." Jacob was evidently better liked than his father—even if he did walk away abruptly in the middle of conversations. Mrs. Plumtree rattled on, oblivious....

On returning home, Camille reluctantly telephoned the gift-shop owner to ask him out for Sunday night. She had to produce him; she had no choice. He was gratified by her attention. While he was a nice enough fellow, Camille really didn't want to get too close to him. She wished she'd picked Greyson instead. At least he was uncomplicated fun to be with. Gloomily she contemplated the disaster Sunday was going to be as she began making a mushroom-and-cheese omelet for dinner.

By the time the omelet was almost done, Robbie, perpetually hungry, was already seated at the dinner table. Mother hadn't come downstairs yet. Under her breath Camille told her brother a portion of her contretemps in the store, ending with, "So he's coming on Sunday."

"Oh, damn, Camille!" he growled. "Couldn't you have got out of it?"

"How? Just tell me that! Luckily the lab's always been out of bounds, so at least he won't be able to stick his nose in there. You won't make me give him the tour all by myself, will you?"

"But—"

"Please, Robbie! I don't want to be alone with him!"

He looked at her, eyebrows rising. "What actually happened between you on that tour....?"

"N-nothing. Nothing. He took me out to dinner a couple of times—as mom asked him to," she finished caustically. "I'm just afraid of losing my temper, and you know that would never do."

"Oh, all right," he agreed morosely.

Fern appeared just then, obviously much more cheerful than she'd been at lunch. But when she discovered who was coming on Sunday, and for what purpose, she lighted right up and gazed at her daughter with such approval that Camille felt a twinge of guilt.

She had plenty of time to steel herself for this second meeting—God forbid she should act as tongue-tied and juvenile as at the first. She wanted to transmit a certain dignified reserve befitting a representative of Beesley Farm, an impenetrable front of all's-well-within-the-gates unity. There would no hint, no reference to any personal involvement.

She was outside and waiting for Jacob at twenty after one, so her mother wouldn't get the opportunity to invite him into the house. He wanted a tour—he was going to get a tour and not a smidgen more—certainly no cozy visit over coffee and cake.

He was punctual. The sleek little Mercedes Benz came to a neat halt underneath the flourishing grape arbor. "Good afternoon, Jacob," she greeted him impersonally, her pointed chin thrust slightly forward.

"Good afternoon, Camille," he replied equably after a fractional hesitation.

They stood in silence, eyeing each other. The last time they'd met, she'd never even turned to look at him. So childish, she thought now, wincing inwardly.

"Well! Are you ready?"

"What did you have in mind?" he countered.

Pursing her lips for an angry second, she suppressed her fiery antagonism and said in finely measured tones, "Your tour of the grounds, unless you've changed your mind?"

"No, no, lead on!" Smiling ever so faintly, he slid his hands into his pockets.

At that moment the poodles, Boogaloo and Razzmattaz, came bounding out of the house, Robbie following behind. Barking and capering around the professor, the dogs circled him several times before she had them under control and at her heels. They sat, looking up to her for guidance and, sensing her discomfort, pricked up their floppy ears to stare a little less welcomingly at the professor.

"Well, hello," Robbie greeted the visitor coolly. "Nice car, that."

"A '58."

"Don't know as I've seen any others on the Island."

"They're getting scarce. Most parts have to be shipped from Germany."

"Your dad's car?"

"No, I lend him the keys now and then."

"Six cylinders?"

"Four."

"Four! You're kidding! Does she go?"

"I've had her up to a hundred and twenty."

Robbie whistled in appreciation. Camille began tapping her foot against the worn tarmac. "A hundred twenty and only four cylinders!" her brother enthused, his earlier coolness forgotten.

"Well, she has four carburetors—two housings, two carbs each."

"Four carbs? Really? Hey, I'd like a look! A gas eater?"

"No, surprisingly good, actually." Opening the driver's door, Jacob reached in to pull something. There was an audible click, and the hood popped up an inch along the windshield, rather than lifting from the nose of the car. Both men bent over the exposed interior to poke around inside. With an impatient look at the heavens, Camille quit tapping her foot.

"If you two are going to tinker, I'll run along. Give me a yell when the tour's over." And she beat a hasty retreat to the one place Jacob couldn't go—the laboratory.

She sat down at the organ in front of the six *mouillettes* she had dipped yesterday. The first blotter represented Robbie's pure essential oil. The other five, in order, were representations of the oil plus one additive, plus two additives, et cetera. Five additives was as far as she'd come in this trial perfume, though she had already discarded six other trials. This process was part of plotting the type of perfume to create. Once she'd made a decision, the same procedure would be repeated but with a definite aim in mind.

She now tested the blotters in order for any breakdown in the aroma. Up until the fourth one she was satisfied, but beyond that...perhaps there was too much ilang-ilang oil, or maybe the wrong kind. Instead of using Manila ilang-ilang, maybe she should have used the Madagascar variety. Checking in the notebook where she recorded the precise amount of ingredients used in each mix, running her finger down her own recondite hieroglyphics, she decided first to try lessening the amount. She forced herself to concentrate on her work, though too often she found herself staring vacantly off into space....

Sometime later she heard the poodles in chorus outside the lab door—Robbie must have sent them to fetch her. Hastily tidying up, she went to say a courteous goodbye to Professor Darleah.

Fern joined them just after her daughter had added herself to the group. She asked conversationally, smiling around at everyone, "Did Camille give you a good tour, Jake?"

"I peered into every nook and cranny, I'm sure," Jacob replied easily, taking a sidelong look at Camille's rather red face. "Every nook allowed, that is."

"The lab is only insured for family," Robbie said a shade defensively, suggesting that Jacob pressed him about seeing it.

The professor continued. "Camille told me how everything bloomed here, even the grass, and I thought she was exaggerating because of all the snow we had. Victoria's one big flower show— But your farm is particularly beautiful. Robbie tells me the garage was the original distillery, and the garden shed the original lab."

"Yes," Camille put in crisply. "The old lab was gutted by fire in 1939 when an unwary visitor lighted a cigarette next to a vat of petroleum solvent. By pure luck no one was badly hurt. But since then. . . ." She paused, her silence eloquent.

"Won't you come inside for a cup of coffee?" Fern asked a trifle hurriedly. "I've just made a fresh pot, and Camille baked a cake yesterday."

"And what's more, the cake actually turned out!" Robbie grinned irrepressibly at his sister's black look.

"I'm sorry, but I'll have to sample Camille's baking another day," the professor declined smoothly.

She thought she detected a faint note of derision in

his calm tone, as if smirking to himself about local mamas and their eagerness to have him sample their daughters' cooking. Setting her jaw, Camille didn't trust herself to say anything more but smiled and smiled and smiled until at last he was gone, when her smile vanished.

"He really is very nice, isn't he?" Fern asked no one in particular, her hair a gilded wavy wreath in the sun.

Robbie grunted, saying neither yes nor no. Camille said shortly, "Oh, he's a real sweetheart!" and stalked off to the beach with the dogs in tow, feeling her mother's puzzled eyes following her.

That evening she went to dinner with the gift-shop owner, while her brother and mother went to dine with Charles and Jacob. Robbie unhappily reported to her later that night that Charles had been exceedingly interested in the results of her sales trip. He had seemed surprised at the magnitude of her success, as well. Fern hadn't spared the praise and had been inveigled into revealing, almost to the nickel, the total of Camille's gross sales. Among a bevy of questions, Charles had asked about the future of the perfumery—was expansion planned, new land, new machinery, new products? More sales trips? Any ideas about buying the cheaper chemical substitutes in lieu of the highly priced natural ingredients? Any new perfumes on the way? Money talks, he said. Money walks, and were they in the market for investors?

"I could have choked him!" Robbie spat vehemently. "Snooping and poking and prying! And mom, totally oblivious to what he was up to! Being flattered—flattered—by his interest!''

"What did Jake do during all this?'' Camille's cheeks were hot, remembering how she'd been flattered by Charles's son's interest.

"Just sat sort of quietly in the background soaking everything up. He.... I don't know what it is about him, but....'' Robbie twitched his shoulders in vague irritation. "I have this feeling he could repeat, verbatim, what was said tonight and by whom. Uncanny, that's the word I want. Seems to be just a harmless bump on a log until you notice the bump's got X-ray eyes. Then you start to wonder....''

THE SECOND WEEK IN APRIL flowed by smoothly enough, except that the bottling machine broke down again, in the midst of an operation, naturally. This time it was cologne that sprayed everywhere, making a hell of a mess. Harry chivied the monstrous machine back into working order with the aid of reels of black electricians' tape, a hose borrowed from the lab and various other last-minute magical tricks. The next time they might not be so lucky, he lugubriously predicted. The machine was simply worn out, replacement parts were hard to locate since it was long out of date. He did his best, commiserating with them over the outrageous price of a new machine.

Harry lived on the premises in a little log cabin down by the beach, the opposite direction from Damask, with his cat, Tom. Years ago Beesley had discovered him camping overnight in the unused hut. A vagrant, alone in the world but for his oversize pet,

Harry performed some small chores the next day in exchange for breakfast, lunch and supper—and never left. He had become indispensible, and Tom, grown long in the tooth, was still as fine a mouser as ever lived. The two huge standard poodles would only tease Tom until he hissed, and it only took one hiss. Harry didn't generally say much, but over the subject of the bottling machine he whipped himself into a downright lather.

Having said she was going to the Cannes film festival winner with Elaine Thursday night, Camille borrowed Robbie's Spider and drove into town. After the movie, on impulse, she and Elaine dropped in at a nightclub. Camille didn't return home until very late. She hoped her mother would be put in a better mood by this "time off."

And so she was, the next morning, when her daughter recreated the evening for her—or she was until Camille said she'd met a sailor. "A sailor?" she repeated dubiously.

"Why, yes, mom," replied Camille cheerfully. "You know, from the naval base."

"Y-yes, I know...."

Snickering, Robbie kept silent while Fern surveyed her daughter, a faint helpless frown between her brows.

After lunch, Camille headed, as usual, for Damask, this time with Tom purring fatly against her neck. The dogs, jealous, had been left behind. Letting the cat loose in the cellar, she set about washing the second-story windows and, after mopping and dusting and beating the many beds' eiderdown mattresses, went outside to care for the garden.

She was on her hands and knees in a flower bed, pulling weeds, when her peace and quiet was suddenly shattered by a calm, "Hello."

She felt as if she'd jumped about a foot off the ground. Sitting back on her heels, pressing a hand against her heart, she took one look at Jacob and spat, "What are you doing here?"

"Going for a walk," he said mildly. "Gorgeous day."

"Are you blind?" she stormed, outraged that he had the temerity to wander onto her property at will. "There are trespassing signs! Can't you read? I don't recall inviting you on yet another tour. Do you want to be prosecuted?" She couldn't even bear the sight of him, and here he was, on her hallowed ground. "I'd like to see your money talk you out of a trespassing charge. And more than anything I'd like to see your money walking you right off this property!"

In absolute silence, he considered her gravely. Camille trembled with rage.

"Get lost!" she hissed, as well as any cat.

Sighing in reply, he said nothing for the space of several taut seconds. Then, taking his pipe out of the pocket of his thick woolen lumberman's shirt, a bright red-and-green plaid, he tamped the tobacco contemplatively. Fishing for matches, he lighted the pipe in the breeze, shielding the flaring match with his hand.

"Are you mad because I didn't leave a message, as I'd promised?" he finally asked.

Startled anew, she stared a little wildly up at him

from her vantage point in among the tulips and pansies and violets and hyacinths, blowing a few curls out of her eyes.

"Please don't start boring me with excuses!" She could have bitten her tongue out as soon as the words escaped, for a part of her wanted to hear why he'd stood her up. "You can put your promises in your pipe and smoke them!"

Turning her back on him, she continued her weeding, putting an abrupt end to the interview—or so she thought. His galoshes didn't move. Galoshes were the best thing to wear on the beach besides bare feet. He had adapted quickly, she noticed, further annoyed. Her hope that he would be off abroad somewhere soon rather than acclimatizing himself and settling in, despite his father's wishes, was obviously futile.

As if no hard words had been said, he commented, "It seems, from what your mother said, your hard work has more or less put the company back on its feet. You must be delighted with your trip."

"It wasn't my hard work, it was *our* hard work," she retorted. "The perfumery is none of your business, nor is my state of mind. You've had your tour. What more do you want?"

"You really do know how to radiate, don't you, Camille...." So saying, he turned away and sauntered unhurriedly down to the beach and the breaking combers, where anyone was free to go for a stroll.

After he'd disappeared from sight, her fury turned inward. Why couldn't she be as cool as he was? Why couldn't she control her temper? Why couldn't she just act unconcerned, disinterested and refined, not stoop to flinging insults at him like a kid in a tantrum?

Robbie wasn't amused to hear Jacob had been snooping around. "Next thing he'll be roaming the compound!" he said.

"Just let him try! Boogaloo and Razzmattaz will have him for a snack! They know he's no friend!" Indeed, while the poodles hadn't been overtly threatening during the professor's Sunday visit, they had laid back their ears and curled their lips at all his overtures.

That evening, as Camille and Robbie were leaving the house to go down to the corner pub, Fern somewhat anxiously asked, "Are you meeting your new friend, Camille?" She looked at her daughter's dress and high heels.

"My new friend?" Camille echoed blankly.

"Yes. . . the sailor."

"Oh, him. No, I think he's on duty tonight."

Her answer should have soothed her mother, but it didn't appear to. She said, trying to sound very casual, "You've been talking to him?"

"Um-hm." Camille would volunteer no more. "See you later, mom."

When they arrived home much later, their mother was up, watching the late movie on television. When they came into the living room she said enthusiastically, nodding toward the screen, "It's just started, and is it ever good!" The movie didn't look particularly thrilling to either Robbie or Camille. They exchanged glances, wondering what was up, besides mother! They didn't have long to wait.

"I...have some good news..." she said uncertainly, as if she wasn't really sure it was good news but was trying to pave the way. She had their attention, but paused delicately, causing them to exchange another sideways glance. Their unease was heightened by her sudden determined smile. "Our new bottling machine arrives tomorrow morning! Isn't that wonderful?"

She couldn't have surprised them more had she tried. They sat gaping at her, not knowing at first what to say.

"Our new bottling machine?" Robbie croaked.

"What do you mean it arrives tomorrow?" Camille asked.

"Well, I ordered it several months ago, and it's finally here! It's being delivered tomorrow morning. Maybe it was a little precipitate of me," she hedged defensively at the stunned gazes confronting her, "but I—I simply couldn't bear to watch you two struggling with that old monster anymore!"

"But mom, they cost the earth!" Camille cried. "We haven't that kind of money, sales trip or no! And most of what I sold was on thirty- and sixty-day receivable. We won't see a dime for at least another three weeks, and most of it not for seven, eight, nine weeks! What if some of them default? In the meantime we've got to make loads of product. Where are we going to get the money to buy the ingredients? You know we have to pay cash on delivery—no sixty-day receivable for us! Oh, mom! Why didn't you say something about it before—before...." Camille was too distraught to continue.

"I didn't say anything because I knew you'd disagree, I suppose. But there's no need to worry about money, really. I took out a loan. We, er, pay back a little every month, and when things are better, we can pay it off at our own discretion."

"Oh," Robbie sighed, "thank God! I hate the thought of a loan over our heads, but it's better than being wiped out. I thought I was going to die for a minute."

"Whew!" Camille settled back in her chair. "But now our overhead is even more expensive, and we were trying so hard to keep costs down."

"I know, dear, and I'm sorry. But I thought I was helping. Our old machine—I mean, Harry told me how it was. What if it broke down next week for good? Then where would we be? We'd have to wait months for a new one to come, and how would we bottle things in the meantime? With a funnel, bottle by bottle? Licking every single solitary label?"

"Well, yes, I suppose you're right," Camille said hesitantly.

"It's done now. Let's just be happy we won't be wiping up puddles of shampoo or cologne," Robbie observed in his matter-of-fact way. "How much do we have pay back each month?"

"Two hundred dollars."

"Well, that's not so bad. We'll manage somehow. As long as the ferries don't go on strike again this summer...." Robbie frowned.

"And as long as we get lots of reorders," Camille prayed.

"Jake...sort of suggested a way out," Fern offered tentatively. "He had an idea that would put an end to our money worries—"

"He didn't mention anything to me when I saw him today," Camille said sharply.

"You saw him today?" A little smile lighted her mother's face. "At the pub?"

"No, at Damask. But maybe he didn't say anything because I told him he was trespassing and then told him to get lost!"

"Oh, Camille!" gasped Fern, aghast. "How could you? How rude! Why must you—"

"What was his big idea?" Robbie interrupted. "Don't get mad at her. After all, he *was* trespassing. The signs are clear enough."

"But I told him to go have a look. You see, he wants to buy Damask," she hurried on, not looking at her daughter's stricken face, "and he's prepared to pay a very good price for it. Just the house and the three acres of yard around it—we wouldn't lose any of our growing land. The house is empty, and it costs and costs to keep up. If we sell it we could pay off the loan immediately and save ourselves the interest payments, not to mention having a great deal of money left over to put in the bank. We'd have the funds for an advertising campaign and...and everything else we need around here and still have a comfortable margin left for savings. It makes sense, don't you see that? You do see that, don't you?"

Camille sat frozen in abject misery. Of course it made sense, but she couldn't force out a word. Precious Damask and its grounds were part of the original Beesley homestead. For it to pass into foreign hands, for it to go to an uncaring man who had deceived her and led her on for his own ends, only to unceremoniously dump her, then pretend nothing had happened.... She caught her breath on a barely audible sob.

"Now, mom—" Robbie stepped in "—there's no need for us to be in any sort of a rush, is there? I mean, we have a loan. We do have money coming in, and tourists will be arriving soon. Why sell the house if we don't absolutely have to?"

"But what if, when we do need to sell it, he's found something else?" Fern protested. "He offered us a lot of money! It seems he's serious about settling here."

"Mom," Robbie went on patiently, taking another glimpse at Camille's woebegone face. "You know we could sell Damask just like that." He snapped his fingers. "It's waterfront property. It's a beautiful historical house in excellent condition. We don't have to sell it to Mr. Darby—I mean, to Darleah—and there's no need to sell it this instant. Just the way it sits, it's like money in the bank."

"I don't want him to have it," Camille choked out in a small strangled voice.

Fern gazed at her, hardly surprised. "Very well. I can see your logic, but why do you feel such animosity toward Jake? Why? What's he done to you?"

The questioning was too close to home. Disgusted with herself—she'd always been too emotional for her own good—Camille wordlessly shook her head.

"Has he done something?" Fern pressed. "Is there something I don't know? Did he...? On your trip, did he...?"

In rising panic Camille knew she had to end the speculations. No one must ever know what had transpired while she was away. But, fearfully agitated, all she could do was shake her head vehemently. Tonight, for a while, she had managed to forget about him, but now the knowledge of her futile foolish lost love returned to torment her.

Once more Robbie helped her out. "I don't think he did, mom," he said slowly. "It's just that she's always been crazy about Damask, and they didn't get along very well, so.... He's always nice to you, and therefore you think he's always nice, period. He isn't. For instance, it wasn't really kosher of him to hide who he was from Camille."

"Oh, I see. Yes, I don't suppose it was. I just never gave it any thought.... It is curious, isn't it?" She eyed her children thoughtfully.

Robbie nodded his head. "Yes, isn't it. Makes one wonder...."

Camille gulped in quiet relief. Taking a superhuman grip on her quivering nerves, she muttered, "He didn't tell me because he wanted to worm information out of me, and they both—Charles and Jacob—want the perfumery, don't they?" There, at last it was out in the open—no beating around the bush about would-be investors.

"Well, yes," Fern replied. "They do. It's not such a bad idea, either. With Charles's backing and his know-how, our future would be assured. I know he's fed up with retirement and would like a little business to whip into shape. And Jake, well, he doesn't appear very interested in taking a teaching position at the university here, or anywhere for that matter. Of course, he is compiling a book of his studies. I guess a perfumery is at least vaguely in his line. Hmmm. Oh, dear, I do wish now I hadn't invited them over on Sunday! I mean, Charles has always been straightforward, but Jake...."

"What do you mean?" squeaked Camille. "Invited them both over on Sunday?"

"Mom!" Robbie cried.

"Didn't I tell you? Oh, well, I thought it would be lovely to have a dinner party, and I invited the Darbys and a few neighbors and Charles and...Jake." Fern squirmed under their combined stares. "After all, you've been working so hard, I thought you both deserved a little treat."

"That's, er, real nice of you, mom," murmured Robbie awkwardly.

"Yes, really nice," Camille repeated faintly.

"So if Jake asks me about Damask on Sunday I'll temporize, shall I? No point in burning our bridges with an absolute no."

THE BOTTLING MACHINE ARRIVED in splendor the next morning, with a technician to set it up and an operating manual the size of Webster's dictionary, or so it appeared to Camille. The technician explained the operating procedure for their benefit, and thereafter a trial run was put in motion. Despite her reservations, she was enthralled with the mechanical beast. It ran so quietly, so efficiently, so cleanly. Robbie's eyes were sparkling, while Harry kept walking round and round it, poking a finger in here, peering in there, scratching his balding head and muttering to himself about robots taking over the world.

Fern had to come out to remind them lunch was ready. She added her oohs and ahs. By the time they'd finished their meal, there were three hundred bottles of Island Rose bottled, labeled, corked, sealed with wax and packaged in boxes.

"Wow!" Camille announced reverently. "The robot even automatically cleaned itself! It's sorcery!"

The technician took himself off just as Rachael arrived to help Fern with the preparations for tomorrow's dinner party. Camille immediately began to edge away from her mother and Rachael—not because she didn't like her mother's friend. On the contrary, but the thought of being stuck in the kitchen when she had such a fabulous new toy to play with was abhorrent. For the sake of manners she suggested she might help them, but Fern demurred.

"No, dear, the party's your treat. Of course I'm not going to put you to work. But I want you and Robbie to go into town and buy yourselves some new clothes for tomorrow. Get yourself something pretty, and make sure he picks out a nice suit—a suit! Not jeans."

"But—"

"Will you for once listen to your mother? I want you both in something brand-new. Now not another argument about it." They could scarcely argue about the inadvisability of spending more money in front of Rachael, who was smiling so indulgently.

Left standing in the compound by themselves, Robbie and Camille turned glumly from the laboratory. "Damn!" Robbie grimaced. "A suit. Some treat!"

HE LOOKED QUITE outrageously handsome in his new suit the next day, but it took more than ten minutes of combined effort to neatly knot the tie Camille had picked out for him. He manned the bar; Camille, in an exquisite little summery shift—no hand-me-down—made sure glasses were filled, remembered what everyone was having and passed around the hors d'oeuvres.

Rachael, Wilson and Elaine were present, of course. So was Mrs. Plumtree, who could always be counted on to talk about anything to anyone, no matter how shy her victim. Harry was under her spell at the moment.

There were two couples there who had been long-standing friends of Camille's parents, as well as several of Robbie's and her own friends. Then there were Charles and Jake. Camille, counting heads, discovered that although the required twenty were present, one still had to be missing, for one of the couples had planned to bring along an extra guest. Another place had already been set at the dining-room table, which, with its six leaves, was plenty big enough for all.

Under cover of the babble, music and laughter, Camille asked her mother who hadn't yet arrived.

"Greyson. Since I asked that girl Robbie seems to be interested in, I thought it would be nice if you had someone, too. And since you seem so anti-Jake, I didn't know whether I should invite that gift-shop owner or your sailor, so I picked Greyson. Will you take these cheese sticks over to Jake? I saw him a moment ago standing all alone.''

Neither Camille nor Fern had noticed Jake coming up behind them. His sudden, "Good evening Mrs. Beesley," caused them both to start.

Turning, Camille was aware of a faint flush sweeping over her cheeks. She wondered how much he had overheard....

"Have you had time to consider my proposal, Mrs. Beesley?"

"Not really, Jake. Damask is sort of an heirloom...,"

"Of course I understand," he murmured quietly, his tawny eyes resting on Camille's bowed head. She was contemplating her shoes, the ones she'd bought in Montreal.

"If you'll excuse me?" she put in politely with her charming smile reserved for strangers, "I see Mrs. Plumtree has run out of cheese sticks...."

Making good her escape, she saw from across the living room that Jacob was still standing talking to her mother. What about? Trying to dig up information about the new bottling machine and how much it had cost? And where had they found the money to pay for it?

Greyson arrived then. He brought another unexpected guest, his older sister, Annette. Annette and Camille had never been the best of friends.

"She made me bring her—" Greyson pulled a face

"—when she found out the professor was going to be here."

"Oh, shut up, big mouth!" Annette snapped, smiling airily at Camille. "It's lies, all lies! How ever are you, darling! Is that a new dress? Don't you look wonderful!"

"The professor's right over there, talking to mom." Camille pointed him out helpfully, returning the smile. "I'm sure you can introduce yourself?"

"So sorry, Camille, but she said she'd 'drop in' if I didn't bring her along. Sometimes I could cheerfully belt her! See? There she goes, just like a homing pigeon! The guy's not safe with her around."

Smiling at Greyson's long face, Camille linked an arm through his and drew him into the party. She tried not to watch Annette chatting it up with Jacob. Feeling unwarrantedly relieved and pleased when Elaine drew Annette off, Camille began breathing again...but didn't stop watching the professor. Charles was mingling quite well, considering his unpopularity, but Jacob, well, he didn't seem to fit in exactly. Not with the older set and not with the younger crowd. Maybe it was because he seemed so perfectly content to be left on his own. Alone, but not lonely, absorbed in private thoughts.

Her eyes rested on the burnished sheen of his hair, on the wide cheekbones angling in to the narrow chin, on the careless grace of his shoulders, the long lean length of him in a superbly cut pale gray suit. Everybody had come dressed up, since Fern had issued the invitations and they knew she would prefer it. Annette was perhaps a little overdressed, but stunning nevertheless with her dark glossy hair and deep blue eyes. Elaine, swathed in voluminous silk, gave the impression of being older than her twenty-six years, while Mrs. Plumtree was decked out in her Sunday best. Charles looked like what he was—a wealthy, dynamic, hard-as-nails potentate. Over the heads and across the intervening space, Camille's eyes sought out the professor. Why, oh, why hadn't he left her a message? Because of some woman with long blond hair and a pert little hat? Camille tried to pay attention to what Greyson was telling her.

She and Robbie were unfailingly polite and hospitable to Charles and Jacob. It would never do to dampen the festive mood by slighting the guests. But brother and sister didn't extend themselves to those two particular guests beyond what would be considered proper form. Camille did her best to avoid them both without seeming to. She felt Charles's gimlet eye on her more than once, and caught him eyeing Robbie calculatingly. What was he doing? Sizing up his competition? She watched Charles in return, trying to fathom how mom could be attracted to him and just how far their relationship had progressed. She bridled at how often he touched Fern, a hand at her waist, on her arm, at her elbow.

At the same time, Camille circulated, kept glasses filled, made sure she talked to everyone—except Jacob. She even had a few words with Charles. Was he finding Vancouver Island too quiet after Toronto? Wasn't it a fine day? Yes, hadn't spring been absolutely glorious so far?

It was a fine day. The broad open expanse of sky

was a clear, peaceful cerulean blue. Far off to the south, mountains of ice-cream clouds were tinged with the colors of a very early sunset. A little to the east, Mount Baker rose across the shimmering dancing water of the strait like a perfect cone, white-capped, so far away it was more like a mirage. To the west, the rugged Olympics were a soft royal blue, ridged in white ice and snow. The cottage windows were thrown wide and the doors opening onto the front porch were wide, too, so in came the full pungence of a spring garden laden with the first evening dew. The window boxes spilled over with blooms. On the porch, strawberry pots sprouted forget-me-nots and begonias and freesias. The lawn swept long and shallow down and down to the beach, patterned with rose beds. Although only a few rosebuds were out, there were more than enough other blossoming beauties—from low borders to shrubs to bushes to trees—to cast before the eyes a feast of color.

Camille, seeing all this, passionately loving it—it was home—couldn't understand how her mother thought there was any security in selling out to strangers. Greyson nudged her then, had to repeat his question. To make up for her lack of attention, she smiled a little more warmly at him than he'd obviously expected. If Charles the financier got his clutches on this property, he would likely cram it full of concrete condominiums, raking in a fortune. After all, a perfumery didn't have to be on the waterfront, and a view didn't make the roses smell any better. The thought was sobering. She couldn't, really, have felt less like a party.

Jacob, she noticed, had gone out onto the porch, where he was leaning against a pillar smoking his pipe and gazing at the glory of the garden and the endless space beyond. Was he coveting what he saw? Wasn't his father's house enough? As if he felt her puzzled, searching gaze, he turned to look at her over his shoulder. She was quite unaware that her full lips were set in a decided pout, a very alluring, sad pout. Their eyes met across the large room before she could look away.

Using sheer will, he held her riveted to him with his cryptic gaze. She shivered inside, felt a tide of longing for what might have been surging up uncontrollably—and then, as his gaze held, a quiver of unexpected purely sexual heat. She had been convinced those feelings were long gone, only to find them more potent than ever. They had never truly gone, but had only been suppressed. One suddenly not-so-impersonal stare had bared them all.

Whatever she was suffering from, she had it bad. And it wasn't love, it couldn't be, but neither was it hate. Perhaps a deadly combination of the two? Shaken and all in pieces, Camille gazed abstractedly at Greyson when he nudged her again. Razzmattaz was out on the porch guarding Jacob. The dog was sitting close by, just sitting watching him, not moving an inch closer despite the encouragement offered by the professor. Giving up for the moment, Jacob turned again to look at her, and this time his level, rather accusing stare seemed to say, "What have you been telling this dog about me?"

Dinner began shortly afterward and since Jacob

was seated on the same side of the crowded table as Camille, she was spared having him in her sight. However, wonderful garrulous Mrs. Plumtree almost immediately vanquished Camille's peace of mind by asking the professor whether he'd found the sauna he'd been searching for.

"No, I discovered I didn't really want one that evening, after all," he replied smoothly.

"You don't like to sauna alone, eh?" Mrs. Plumtree chirruped with a teasing glance at Camille.

Annette, who had finagled the seat next to his, murmured insinuatingly, "Neither do I..." and went on, in an undertone, to tell the professor where the nearest facilities were located.

"I don't understand," Charles broke in vigorously, "why you should look elsewhere for a sauna when there's one at home!"

"Because it's spring!" Mrs. Plumtree clarified, causing greater confusion.

Camille felt as though her chair had turned into a bed of nails.

"Pardon me, but what has that to do with it?" Charles requested and Rachael laughingly echoed his question.

Camille, attempting to appear nonchalant and seriously interested in her clam chowder, swore to herself she would never, ever, set foot inside a sauna again.

"Well," explained Mrs. Plumtree, "it might not be proper at home."

"Not proper?" Charles's brow wrinkled. He stared at Mrs. Plumtree in astonishment. "Not proper to take a sauna at home? Whatever can you mean?"

Camille peeked at Jacob down the row of plates and cutlery. She marveled at his composure. He caught her eye for an instant, one corner of his mouth quivering as if he were having a hard time not laughing out loud.

"Young ladies might not be quite so averse to a public sauna. My dear Mr. Darby, in this day and age of appalling morals, I'm happy to say some of us don't lack propriety!" Mrs. Plumtree beamed at him.

"Young ladies?" he queried blankly. "Oh, young ladies! Er, I see."

Even though everyone at the table was now looking at Jacob, wondering which young lady he'd tried to interest in a sauna, he didn't appear perturbed. Smiling whimsically, he shrugged his shoulders and said, "It *is* spring." Everyone—except Camille, who breathed a silent relief, and Annette, who grimaced—chuckled in varying degrees. Yet glancing up from the appetizing creamy soup, Camille found her brother's gaze resting somewhat reflectively on her.

Not long after the five-course dinner was over and everyone, replete, was relaxing over coffee and liqueurs, Camille realized the professor had disappeared. And so had Razzmattaz.

CHAPTER SIX

THE PROFESSOR wasn't in the living room, or the dining room, or on the front porch. He wasn't in the kitchen or the study or the laundry room. Not in the basement, either, and she couldn't imagine any reason he would go up the stairs to the bedrooms. Both the poodles were missing now. An upwelling of suspicion had her slipping out the back door.

She didn't bother to check the front lawn or the surrounds of the house, but headed immediately along the tarmac of the drive back toward the compound. Noiselessly she unhinged the gate in the yew hedge and slid into the darkness beyond. Tiptoeing on the concrete pad fronting the workshop so that her high heels wouldn't make the least sound, she veered to the left after a second's hesitation, knowing instinctively that if he was nosing around, he would be nosing around the laboratory. Shivering a little in the chill of the night, clad only in the light dress, Camille rounded the corner—to see him standing by the lab door.

The poodles were with him, but not as friendly mates out on a lark. For a few taut seconds they stared at each other in the moonlit gloom. In the tense interval the dogs trotted to her side. Boogaloo whined.

"What the hell do you think you're doing?" she burst out.

"Going for a walk." He came toward her.

"You were snooping!"

"Well, yes, I suppose I was," he admitted placidly.

His agreement caught her by surprise. "Well!" She hesitated. "Aren't you ashamed of yourself?"

"Can't say that I am."

She stared at him in amazement. "But—but how dare you? What can you see now that you didn't see on your tour? Why do you find our provincial little perfume lab so fascinating?"

"Maybe because it's forbidden," he suggested with the hint of a smile.

"And it's going to stay that way! I've told you before, Professor Darleah, it's out of bounds! And I don't care if you are a chemist of sorts."

He sighed, looked up at the waning moon.

"Don't you think it's rather disgusting to presume upon our hospitality by snooping around like a thief?" she charged, her chin high, her dark eyes blazing. The fact that she was shivering ruined her warlike stance.

Sliding a keen glance down her supple shape, he removed his suit jacket and, even though she backed away, draped it around her shoulders. Its warmth enveloped her. The faint male scent of him clung to it, and she shivered again, for entirely different reasons.

"I stand reproved," he said softly, mocking her again with that irritatingly calm hint of a smile. He turned and went to the gate, opened it, waited for her to join him. Biting on her lip, she swept through ahead of him. The poodles hung back until he was out, then nipped past him just as he shut the gate. "Those dogs of yours. They're . . . well trained."

"What do you mean?" she said stiffly, knowing exactly what he meant.

"Top-caliber watchdogs. I suppose you know poodles are among the smartest breeds? Of course some of them, the smaller variety usually, tend to be overbred—but not these two. So innocent and fluffy-looking, aren't they? Like a pair of cuddly apricot sheep. I'm glad you don't have them cut like most poodles, with the pom-pom ears and tails. That over-all trim, what's that called?"

"A puppy cut!" Camille supplied through clenched teeth. She wished he wouldn't bother to make inane conversation with her. She longed to have this walk back to the house over with as quickly as possible. "Why do you ask?"

"It's rather like your haircut. Do you breed the dogs?"

"Boogaloo's pregnant now," she gritted.

"Would it be possible for me to have a look at the litter—with the aim of purchasing one? I imagine the pups would be expensive."

If he was considering getting himself a house and a dog, then surely he wasn't planning to go abroad. How ironic, to have thought she would never set eyes on him again! "Very expensive. Boo and Raz both have excellent kennel papers. However, we do take the best care to see that the puppies go only to good homes, and by that I don't necessarily mean wealthy homes.''

''Will I have to undergo an interview before you'll allow me a pup?''

Ignoring the openly taunting amusement in his tone, she snapped, ''You'll stand trial like anyone else!''

''I wonder. . .'' he retaliated dryly.

Hurrying up the back-porch steps ahead of him, she could barely control her fighting temper. She returned his jacket without so much as a thank-you.

Catching her wrist, he detained her a second more. ''Camille, when did you finally catch on to who I was? And why didn't you sooner?''

''I guess because I'm just a small-town girl. As you said, I'm not used to. . .traveling. Now please let me go. You're boring me again.''

When she arrived back at the party, it appeared at long, long last to be breaking up. Annette made a loud point of letting Greyson know Professor Darleah was seeing her home. Therefore, Wilson and Rachael were to drop Charles off on their way back into town. Camille prettily smiled Annette and the professor out the door, feeling as if she were tied into at least a million knots.

Greyson, the last to leave, drew Camille outside to see him off. ''Well, good night. Thanks for inviting me.''

Rather guiltily she murmured something appropriate.

He paused, looking down into her face in the moonlight. ''You're still the most beautiful dandelion I've ever seen." A quizzical smile lighted his features. His deep blue gaze lingered on her mouth. "I don't know whether to give you a hug and a pat on the back, or to grab you and kiss you."

"A hug will do, I think," she answered with a tremulous smile, feeling very edgy.

"You'll tell me to forget it, Camille, but I'm going to get more flowery here for a minute and tell you that you don't look like a dandelion at all...but like one of those wild roses down by the beach." He chuckled at his words. "That's pretty good for a garage mechanic, eh?"

"If I give you a bachelor button, will you go?" she said with a laugh, bending to pick one of the bright blue flowers.

"As long as I may come back?" He took it from her, his fingers brushing against hers.

"Of course you may, Greyson. You know you've always been welcome here."

Slanting an astute look at her, he did as she requested. He left and neither hugged nor kissed her, leaving the situation open for either eventuality.

Sighing slowly, Camille went back inside to help with the cleanup operations. Her mother was full of elation over a successful party where all the guests had enjoyed themselves. Camille wasn't about to let her think otherwise; however, when she and Robbie were stacking the multitude of glasses in the dishwasher, she told him rapidly about finding the professor snooping around the laboratory.

Her brother had some of his own snooping to relate. "I went over to Damask this morning—just to see how I felt about selling it—and he was there again. He's like a cold you can't get rid of!''

"That's it, exactly!" Fervently she nodded, and turned to find Robbie staring thoughtfully at her. "I wonder what we could use for medicine?" she added lightly, hastily.

"Well, I just hope we can squeak by without having to sell anything. How soon do you figure we can expect reorders to come, if any?''

TIRED AS SHE WAS, Camille couldn't sleep that night. She kept rolling from one side to the other, developed all sorts of restive itches. And the pillow would simply not cooperate. Finally she got up. There were too many worries circling round and round in her head. Too many things to sort out. Now on top of everything else, there was Annette. Cloying Annette. Camille reflected that she herself was in a classic dilemma—not wanting Jacob herself but not wanting anyone else to have him.

Slipping down the stairs in her pajamas, she wandered disconsolately around the darkened living room before deciding the only balm for her mood was a walk to Damask. She paused just long enough to slip on a pair of socks, then into her galoshes. Throwing a coat over her pajamas, she was off. The dogs protested, but she left them at home. After all, their job was to guard the perfumery, and what with all the nosy people around—

"You! Not again!" Camille gaped at Jacob, sitting at the top of the flight of marble stairs leading up from the beach. "Oh!" she stormed inarticulately.

He grinned. "You couldn't sleep, either?"

"Have you moved in here already?" she demanded, raking an impatient hand through her curls, sending them into greater disorder.

"Come up here and sit down. We'll count the stars together."

She retreated back down to the pebbles and sand. He came down the stairs after her.

Greyson hadn't grabbed and kissed her, but Jacob did. Too surprised to resist at first, she found herself swept into his iron-strong arms, his lips fusing with hers in a contact that was at once angry and wildly erotic. She was robbed of breath, and bending her head back over his arm, he expertly opened her mouth with his to admit the hungry thrust of his tongue. The fetters of civilization had dropped away from him in an instant, setting the carnal beast loose with a vengeance.

Twisting in his embrace, pushing against his shoulders, she tried to pull away from his ardent mouth...
but struggled more against the sensation of drowning within, drowning in consuming liquid fire...until at last her fingers clutched at the collar of his Windbreaker as if he were her life support.

When he raised his head to search her upturned face, she kept her eyes closed a moment longer, remaining dreamy in his arms, still panting softly. Then she blinked and sputtered, "Hey, just a damn minute!" She unfastened her fingers from his shoulders. "Let me go!"

"Why?"

"Why?" She gazed up at him, stupefied. "What do you mean, why?"

"I don't want to." His arms fastened yet more securely around her, all but lifting her off the sandy beach. Behind her, the waves gently swished against the shore.

"I don't care whether you want to or not!" She began pushing against him again, alarmed by his frightening intensity and her response. "You—"

"Caveman? Should I apologize for wrestling with you and winning? I won't."

"The inner man seems to have gotten the upper hand! A bookish misogynist, eh? How would you like it if I wiped that smug look off your face?"

"Go right ahead. I enjoy skirmishing with you."

"But I don't!"

"No?" There was a beguilingly hopeful note in the hushed word.

Camille froze as he lowered his head. Deliberately, exquisitely his mouth closed over hers, though she resolved to give him no satisfaction. No struggles, no response of any sort. Certainly no giving way to the molten yearning within, and most certainly not any revelation of the sweet pleasure she felt as his lean hard muscular frame intimately pressed against her, each contour of his masculine shape delineated, the fierce brand of his lips on her own. Most of his surprising anger—was he angry because all her insults had finally pierced his composure—had burned away but there was still an underlying threat of it in the urgent course of his mouth, and it was the hardest thing in the world to pretend she was unmoved, to lie still in his arms but not acquiescent.

She came quickly to life when a roaming hand slid inside her coat, up underneath the pajama shirt to glide along the bare flesh of her back. His hand was cool against the fever of her skin, and she discovered the full measure of their mutual desire. Her own reactions made a mockery of her resistance, so that through her wanton desire flared a sizzling rage directed as much at herself as him.

"I'll scream for help!" she snapped, wriggling and writhing, trying to bite the hand that lightly held her head imprisoned by a fistful of silvery gold curls.

Unkindly he laughed in his throat, a soft silky taunting laugh. "So scream away. It'll give me a chance to tell everyone how I feel about you. Mmm, Camille, you're too beautiful to be quite real. You make me do things I haven't done before...." He spoke thickly, as if he were drunk on strong wine, and looking up at his face in the moonlight, Camille knew both the greatest impetuous thirst and the greatest misgiving.

"I'm real, all right—" her nails dug into his wrist "—and if you went around doing things like this every day, they'd have to lock you up!" Her sharp nails forced him to let go of her hair, but in a deft transfer, he kept her close with an uncompromising arm while the other hand slid up over her ribs to find the firm swell of her breast. She gasped, and was silent.

"You see how it is with us?" Jacob murmured at the quiver in her body and the immediate hardening of the tip under his sensitive caress. "How can you expect me to stop wanting you? How can you pretend we're strangers, when we're closer to each other than we are to anyone else? What are we going to do about this?''

Dazedly Camille wondered how he could be so ruthless and so tender at the same time. While she knew she was infatuated with him still, while physically she was ready to make mad passionate love here on the sand, while, in some respects, he was more than she had ever wanted or dreamed of wanting in a mate, sometimes women couldn't help falling in love with bastards. No good ever came of it. Besides which, there was more to consider here than herself and her own suffocating desire. She didn't trust him—not an inch, not a millimeter. She couldn't trust him with anything, much less herself.

"We can't make our feelings go away, Camille, no matter how much we might want them to." Insidiously, his fingertips caressed and transmitted the promise of a sensual pleasure that denied cold hard reasoning. "You weren't in any of my plans. You're a complication I would rather do without. You waste my time. You stand in my way. You're adorable. And the worst of it is, the more I see you, the more delirious I get...." His hand closed over her breast, and his lips fastened over hers in a short hard kiss. "You can't go on ignoring me or insulting me—that won't work. So what are we going to do?"

"Not what you have in mind. We may react chemically, but chemical reactions are a dime a dozen. What's more, I don't even like you! I don't give a damn about you. So what would be the point?"

"If you don't give a damn, why are you so mad that I didn't leave that promised message?"

"I'm not!"

"You're madder than a wet hen, but I would tell you why I didn't, anyway...?"

"Please don't! Get off my land and get out of my pajamas!"

He released her entirely, but stood there with a faint discerning, reckoning smile that said he would persevere, that next time she might not be so lucky.... Next time, he might take greater advantage of the chemical reaction she'd scoffed at.

"Sleep well, my love," he mocked, and turned away from her to walk down the beach toward his father's house. She watched him until he was quite out of sight, until the night was filled only with the sound of little falling waves piling up on the sand— that, and the heavy, hollow beating of her heart. If only she could make up her mind whether she really hated or really loved him....

TUESDAY, hurrying along the covered walkway between the office and the shop with a case of dusting powder in her arms, Camille was surprised to hear the sound of hearty laughter through the shop door. Pushing the door ajar with her foot, she saw her mother behind the counter, leaning on it, Charles on the other side, leaning on it, too. They were both in stitches.

Camille stopped, feeling foolishly de trop and at the same time put out that he should be here, *and* laughing with mom. As they looked at her they sobered, making Camille feel even more the intruder.

Awkwardly she shifted the large box in her arms,

not knowing quite what to say. "H-hello, Mr. Darby." She tried to smile in what she hoped was a friendly manner. Why didn't they share the joke?

"Good afternoon, Camille," he returned, irreproachably polite, suavely correct. And very much on his guard. His gray eyes were flat and hard as he caught hers. Depositing the case without bothering to unpack it, she hurried away.

Late Wednesday afternoon, she parked the station wagon in the garage after a day of deliveries in downtown Victoria. Elated by her success, bounding up the back-porch steps and running into the kitchen, she stopped dead. Mom, Robbie and Jacob were sitting around the kitchen table having coffee and cookies. She had interrupted their conversation, and they all turned to stare at her.

"Looks like I'm just in time for the kaffeeklatsch!" she managed glibly despite a stab of irritation. Shedding her jacket and her soft leather boots, she poured herself a cup of coffee as the talk continued around her. To her brother's questions, she briefly replied that her day had been good. She tried mightily to ignore Jacob, his eyes, his soft deep serene voice that played havoc with her insides. Robbie, she couldn't help noticing, was being rather friendly. The foreign invasion, it seemed, had already begun.... Underneath her cool, contained veneer, Camille was a seething blend of indignation and unfulfilled yearning. Her big brown eyes were brimming with accusation every time she looked at the professor.

Nevertheless, things were going along smoothly

enough, when she felt Jacob's stockinged toes nudge her stockinged toes under the table.... She stiffened. He glided his toes up to capture her ankle while he explained to Fern some aspect of the book he was writing. "When they opened Tutankhamen's tomb in 1922, they found jars of unguents that still carried a faint but definite perfume, after more than three thousand—"

Camille hauled back and kicked him as hard as she was able, which wasn't very hard considering she hadn't shoes on, and considering it had to be done without Robbie's or mom's knowledge.

Jacob yelped in pain. "Camille!" he added in an injured tone, his sparkling amber eyes baiting her. "What did you do that for?"

"Oh, did I kick you?" she queried sweetly, sending him a hot glare of outrage. "I'm so sorry!"

Her mother cast her an embarrassed, reproachful glance—kicking visitors under the table, oh, really, darling—and even Robbie frowned at her in brotherly exasperation. Camille realized the tide of pink suffusing her cheeks made her look as if she felt guilty. When her victim decided to leave soon after, she knew her family was convinced it was her abuse that hurried him toward the door. Robbie went out with him and Camille, not wanting a lecture from a rather annoyed parent, hastily pulled on her galoshes and invented a chore needing immediate attention. Stomping across the back porch and down the stairs with her head bent, she didn't see Jacob until she bumped into him.

"Hi, angel." He grinned, his eyes dancing.

"You're just what I need to come home to after a hard day's work!" she grumbled, fighting an almost irresistible, inexplicable and sudden desire to laugh, too. Her peevishness had gone, yet she strove to hang on to all her various grudges as self-protection. Looking up into his face through the raindrops dribbling off the grape leaves above, she wondered what he had meant by saying they were closer to each other than to anyone else.

He took her momentary silence as encouragement. Before she knew what he was up to, he stepped dangerously close. Just then Fern came precipitately out of the house.

"Oh, Jake, I almost forgot—here's some cookies for your father." She held out a liberally filled brown paper bag.

"More of Camille's baking?" Jacob smiled, taking the bag, while his eyes still held Camille's, subtly enticing. She stood there, electrified by his sheer audacity.

"No." Fern smiled warmly back at him, trying to make up for her daughter's rash actions. "She prefers making perfume to making cookies. I'm just glad she didn't take a hankering to explosives as a career!" Giving her daughter another perturbed look, Fern retreated indoors.

Chuckling, Jacob murmured, "She's right, you know. But only because you're dynamite all on your own."

"Oh, go study a damn book about—about the remedial implications of preventative whatever-you-call-it!" She waved him away, quickly recovering from her momentary weakness.

"The longer you leave it, the worse it's going to get...." He turned and opened the door of his car. Not deigning to reply, Camille swiveled abruptly away in the direction of the compound. She had a few items to discuss with Robbie!

The laboratory door slammed behind her. "What was he doing here?" she demanded.

"You're a real brat sometimes, you know that?"

"Never mind that! What was he here for? All of you, so cozy in the kitchen!"

"Today I *was* happy to see him. That new kid I hired? I sent him to pick up a load of manure this morning. He managed okay until he turned into the field—" he jerked his head toward the field behind the compound "—too sharply, and the tractor, the trailer and all the manure—you know where it went?"

"Not in the ditch?" Camille winced.

"You bet in the ditch! The kid didn't have the sense to leave well enough alone—mired it in up to the rear axle. And of course Greyson had a call today, so he was away with his tow truck. I had to send the kid home. Harry and the boys were away at the lavender farm. Honestly, Jake looked like God's gift when he sauntered up and asked whether I could use a hand."

"He's got several to spare!" she muttered.

"What?"

"Oh, nothing!" Camille quickly added.

"You know he's as strong as a bear? Surprised the hell out of me! I mean, I didn't think he'd be much use, a bookish guy like him. Never a speck of dirt on him—but you should have seen him when we were finished!'' Robbie chortled, then went into great description about how the feat of unmiring the tractor had been accomplished. "And then, when I started shoveling the manure back into the trailer, he shoveled right alongside. Son of a gun. With him helping, we got the whole field done."

"You mean he helped spread the manure, too?" she said faintly.

"Yeah, sure. Said he didn't mind the chance to stretch his muscles. He sure stretched 'em today! You know, he's not so bad."

"Oh, Robbie! Maybe it was all a plot—coming across like a friend in need to get into our good graces!"

"Yeah, maybe. I thought of that. But, then, he could have quit after we got the tractor out. He didn't have to stay shoveling— Well, it's not a pretty job! Listen, I don't want to sell out to him and his father, not a chance. That doesn't mean we have to declare war, does it? Be reasonable. We had a lot of time to talk today. He's the first guy to really understand about my roses." Seeing Camille's doubtful shake of her head, he went on impatiently, "I don't mean he smiled and nodded and said, 'How nice.' I mean, he could talk intelligently about what I'm trying to do. Honestly, he's not so bad."

"Well, I don't know, Robbie. I still don't trust him."

"I didn't say I was all that keen on loading him down with trust. But I don't think we should go out of our way to tick him off—like kicking him under the table! You idiot! Who knows—we may yet need to sell Damask.''

"There's no way I'd agree to sell it!"

"It's not your house. It belongs to mom. If it's necessary to save the perfumery, we'll have no choice. What would you rather have? Nothing at all or the perfumery?"

"Oh, I know, Robbie, I know...." She sighed.

"Do you love Damask that much, or don't you want him to have it that much?"

Camille turned her back, fiddled with a few bottles on the counter. "The serpent in Eden," she said softly, remembering how she had once thought of the professor.

"Jake the snake?" Robbie laughed. "You always did overdo it, Calamity Camille." He paused for a moment, turning away from loading the bottling machine with Woodsmoke body oil. "Just what sort of a snake would you describe him as?"

"A—a boa constrictor!" she laughed in return, grinning impishly at her brother over her shoulder.

He pounced on her words. "Oh? You don't say? A squeezer, eh? What exactly has he been squeezing, kid?"

Camille drew a small shaky breath, her fingers stilled. "Don't tell me that after a day of chatting with the professor you've gone all learned and are going to accuse me of a Freudian slip!" she retorted breezily.

Her brother shot her a superior glance. "Something's fishy around here, that's all. You wouldn't know who it was, now would you, whom Jake invited to share a sauna...?"

"He might have invited half the ladies in Victoria, for all I know— I think I know what kind of perfume I'm going to make, Robbie." She faced him squarely now, knowing it was a change of subject he wouldn't be able to resist.

"Well?" His tone was eager.

Smiling fondly at him, she said, "Evening type. That oil is so deep, so rich, so musky and sexual, it should stand on its own. I want to heighten it, smooth it, round it out, give it a dash of sophistication and...I think we have the makings of a winner."

He was grinning from ear to ear.

Later that night, Fern wanted to talk about Jake, too. "Did you ask him why he didn't let on who he was?" she probed. When Camille shook her head, she went on, "Well, why not? Maybe he had a perfectly good reason. Well, maybe he did. I can't imagine what reason, but surely he can't be that bad. He does seem to be such a pleasant young man. I really can't think why you don't like him, dear. It's a shame you let Annette walk away with him."

Camille recognized the fluttering of butterflies in her stomach, a symptom of only-just-realized happiness over her secret: Jacob didn't want Annette; he wanted her. She did wish she didn't feel quite so ridiculously happy about that, though. It put everything out of perspective. "I hardly think Annette walked away with him," she replied lightly, as if totally unconcerned.

"You know her reputation as well as I do."

"Yeah," Robbie smirked. "She's like the

Mounties—always gets her man! She might have some unknown competition, though...."

"Who?" questioned Fern with interest. Camille chose that moment to exit the room.

On Sunday Charles came early to collect Fern in his white Cadillac. She was giving him a personal tour of the Island's sights. Both Camille and Robbie politely declined the offer to accompany them.

On Monday she found Jacob in the greenhouse with her brother, examining the trays of root stalks Robbie was going to use for grafting shoots of another variety. She left them before they were aware of her presence. Every time she turned around, she thought with a sinking sense of foreboding, either father or son, or both, were on the premises!

Jacob interrupted her later as she was wheeling a dolly of cases from the laboratory to the warehouse. "What exactly do you have against my father?" he asked without preamble, falling into step beside her.

"What do you mean?" Camille gaped at him, her hackles rising.

"That nose-up-in-the-air disapproval."

"For your information, professor, money might walk, as Charles says, but I don't want it walking all over us!" If he could be direct, then so could she.

"You're a snob, you know that?"

"I am not!" she gasped.

"You assume, just because he has more than you, that he must have obtained it through underhanded methods. The classic excuse for hating the rich."

She looked at him askance, wondering at the grimness of his tone while infuriated that he should sound so know-it-all. "I never—"

"You don't have to—you radiate, remember? I know he's abrasive and hard to get along with. You don't have to like him, but you *don't* have to be so god-awful contemptuous!"

Her fine dark eyes widened dramatically. "I—I wasn't aware I was so god-awful contemptuous."

"Maybe you're not, but everybody else is. And furthermore, you're making it damned hard on your mother."

"You leave my mother out of it. I won't discuss her with you. Just remember, too, that getting along with someone is a two-way street. You might ask your father what he has against me! If I can radiate, so can he! And you're assuming rather a lot, aren't you? It's not that your father isn't good enough—it's just that he might not be good for her! And *don't* you think you're getting a little too personal?" she added wrathfully.

"We *are* personal! Only you're too damn stubborn to admit it. As stubborn as your father, Fern says."

"My mother has been talking to you about him?" Camille's voice quavered. She didn't want to believe it, feeling curiously betrayed.

"Your mother and I happen to get along."

She swallowed, feeling like the foreign invasion had not only begun but was well under way, while she had been largely oblivious. She left him standing there while she pushed the dolly along, mad, confused and upset. She was trying to fight against

something that was intangible and, it seemed, inevitable.

Two days later, she caught Jacob red-handed, trying to sneak into the laboratory. Unfortunately, she
was the only one there to witness it, being on guard
more than her brother and being downright suspicious compared to her parent. He had Tom the cat
under his arm. His unruffled excuse was that the cat
had got stuck inside the lab, he had heard Tom
meowing piteously and come to his rescue.

All she said, shoving her hands into the pockets of
her narrow jeans and fixing him with a deadly eye,
was, "Su-ure you did." Brushing past Jacob and into
the lab, she slammed the door in his face.

She knew for an absolute certainty that Harry's cat
hadn't been inside the lab, and Jacob had been opening the door, not closing it. It would have done no
good to argue with him, though. The dogs had even
relaxed their watchfulness, because Robbie and Fern
had accepted his coming and going at will. But the
final straw came when she tried to tell Robbie about
the episode later. He told her she was exaggerating
again and was picking on the professor for "personal" reasons....

The question of why he should want to sneak into
their perfume laboratory still bewildered her. Even
she couldn't believe he wanted to steal their secret
formulas, but what else was there worth stealing? It
was clearer to her now what he'd meant by her standing in his way and being a complication, wasting his
time.... She might be falling in love with him, but
that didn't change the fact that he was dishonest and

a breaker of promises. Only two days ago she had
faintly admired him—albeit reluctantly—for standing up for his father. How could one man combine so
many diverse qualities?

That Friday, Camille took the path through the
woods to Damask rather than using the beach, for
from that vantage point she could ascertain whether
anyone else was there without being seen herself. She
didn't under any circumstances want to bump into
the professor while alone. Another wrestling match
could prove disastrous.

Not bothering to dust and mop the whole house
and finishing her few chores quickly, she puttered
around in the garden, pulling a weed here and there
but mostly admiring the climbing roses, sun-yellow
Alchemist and Champney's Pink Cluster among all
the others. If only the paint weren't peeling so badly,
Damask would have looked splendid amid the profusion of blooms.

Not wanting to go home yet, she relaxed in her
favorite spot underneath the weeping willow, whose
bright green leaves were almost full grown. But the
unmowed grass, scattered with tiny pink and white
daisies, was still too damp for her to sit long, so she
climbed up to a low and convenient bough, comfortably shaped for human bodies. Up higher she could
see the wooden apple crate she'd dragged their years
earlier, wedged into the crook of some branches. It
had been a secret treasure chest. It was half rotted
away now, full of dead leaves. Rolling up her shirt-
sleeves and kicking off her galoshes, she clambered
up higher to inspect it. Half-afraid of spiders and

other unmentionables, she quickly raked out the dead leaves with her fingers, to find an empty soggy worm-eaten cookie package, a rusty pen, some rope, a plastic doll....

She threw everything into the garbage but left the crate where it was. If Jacob, by mischance, bought the house, she didn't want to leave any of her old dolls lying around! At last she set off toward home, going down the stairs to the beach, unaware there had been someone with tiger's eyes watching her from the tower room the whole time.

She meandered along, going far out on the rocks that low tide had uncovered. The wind was brisk. Where the rock dropped down, the water coiled and surged around it, rising in sudden plumes, hissing and bubbling away through the layers of seaweed, encrusted barnacles and blue-shelled ridges of mussels. When it had foamed out, leaving behind trapped tidal pools, she could see starfish, many dark purple, a few pink, clinging to the rocky walls or tucked away in crevices. In higher, quieter pools, anemones pushed up their ruffled heads; tiny baby crabs scuttled sideways into hiding as soon as she dipped in her fingers. Long ribbons of kelp lay snagged and stranded. The cushion of seaweed was wet and slippery as she jumped from rock to rock, stopping to poke at something here and investigate something there.

Every time she stopped, someone else behind her stopped, too, and watched her discoveries from afar. She found a bright orange brittle star and an empty sea-urchin shell. Over her head the seagulls cried, ky, ky, ky. She arrived at the foot of the path to the cottage all too soon—still without noticing her shadow.

In the warehouse, taking a quick inventory before dinner of their gradually building stock, Camille heard Robbie and Jacob—here again—come into the office beyond. The door between was open. She could hear them plain as could be. Although she went on counting and marking, their topic of conversation soon had her in a fix. Jacob was trying to persuade Robbie to let him into the lab, and he was doing a very slick job of it!

"Just one minute!" She stood in the doorway, resolute. "Maybe you do know your way around a lab, but what happens if you slip and fall and break your neck?" She looked as though she might enjoy that eventuality. "What happens if you take some of our stock with you? Or some of the equipment? You could sue us, and the insurance company wouldn't pay for the damage."

Reluctantly Robbie agreed with her, but she could see he didn't think she had to be quite so adamant about it.

"I won't sue," Jacob said quietly, but the look in his vivid eyes told her that once more she was standing in his way, and he wasn't amused.

"See, Camille?"

"Dad was very definite about no one, *ever*, being allowed inside. If we let him in, we'd have to let the whole neighborhood in! Everybody's curious."

"Say that again," Jacob commanded abruptly, staring at her in a peculiar way.

The man must have lost his mind. "You want me to repeat that all again?"

"Just that part about your father."

"Well, he said definitely no one but family, and no one includes you, Jake." She gave up taking inventory and left the room.

Later she had an argument with Robbie over the professor, accusing her brother of going over to the enemy camp. He complained she was, as usual, grossly overreacting. The professor was a nice guy and he *was* a chemist. He had brains, too, which was more than he could say for her! In suffering silence, Camille gritted her teeth.

When Charles arrived to take Fern out for dinner Saturday night, Camille made sure she didn't eye him with contempt; she was carefully polite, but certainly not warm. On his side, he made no attempt to be anything less than cold.

He came again on Sunday morning to do more sight-seeing with Fern. Her mother didn't get home until very late that night. Camille saw him give Fern a quick light kiss—on the mouth—as he said goodnight at the back door. Her mother came in smiling, soft brown eyes sparkling, and Camille felt the dead weight of foreboding. If Charles let her mother down as Jacob had let her down...!

The payments for long-distance orders had started to arrive. These days when Camille went to collect their mail from the post-office box in Langford, she came home with a fistful of ever-so-beautiful money orders and checks. The cash was sweet indeed, for as the field work abounded, gardeners had to be hired.

A compelling love story of mystery and intrigue... conflicts and jealousies... and a forbidden love that threatens to shatter the lives of all involved with the aristocratic Lopez family.

☞ Mail this card today for your FREE gifts.

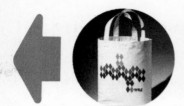

Apart from Harry, Robbie and her, their two steady gardeners and the three they'd just employed could handle the early-morning picking of the rosebuds for now, but fairly soon a full staff of pickers would have to be taken on. With the advent of the warmer sunnier days later in May, what the Beesleys paid out in salaries alone could be a staggering sum. From May to September, it would stay that way. Camille fervently prayed for reorders to start coming with the checks, but so far none had.

With Robbie hectically busy in the fields and the distillery, more of the laboratory work had fallen to Camille. Her days were consumed with incessant activity. It was up in the morning at dawn, down to the fields to pick the rosebuds before the sun's rays spent their fragrance, home for breakfast. Then, while Robbie was loading the still with rose petals, she tested aging vats of perfume, mixed master batches of shampoos, made soap, continued bottling the summer's requirements and tried, in intervals, to work on her new perfume. There never seemed to be a moment when she could say she had everything done. When, by chance, she stumbled across the professor and her brother enjoying a confab she swept past, muttering about loafers and layabouts.

The week following, the second in May, Fern went out twice more with Charles. Camille was to relieve her mother in the shop for the second time on the Thursday afternoon, because the couple were going "up Island," which basically meant anywhere north of Victoria. Since it was lunchtime, there were no customers in the shop, nor were any likely to come.

Camille was using this opportunity to hastily transfer cases of goods from the warehouse through the office to the store.

Generally Harry stacked cases in the warehouse. As Camille viewed the high, slightly askew rows she'd built herself, because the handyman had been flat out helping Robbie, she came to the conclusion he knew how to do it better than she did. He always made the rows of cases into stairs. His way took more room, yet one didn't need a ladder to retrieve a box. Sighing at her shortsightedness, Camille went to fetch the ladder—she was too short to reach the top of her towering wall. Trying to save time, she hoisted two boxes at once. In a sweat, fearing she would drop them and finding it a lot harder to get down the ladder with two cases than up it with one, she was teetering precariously halfway down when an exclamation behind her almost sent boxes and all flying.

"Give me those!" the professor demanded, snatching both away from her. He set them down, then lifted her bodily from the ladder. "If anyone's going to break their neck, it'll be you!"

She walked around him, picked up the cases and felt his hands resetting around her waist. Her forward movement was halted as he drew her back against him. "I have to get back to the shop!" she protested. In reply his arm slid between her and the boxes to anchor her firmly, while with his other hand he brushed aside a tangle of curls to kiss her nape.

"Jake!" she warned breathlessly, her heart beginning to hammer dizzily. Their mingled body heat formed a field of fire between them. "S-somebody could waltz into the shop and out with all the money in the till!''

He sighed exasperatedly, his warm breath against the sensitive skin of her nape sending a tremor through her slender form. In immediate response, his forearm across her waist tightened, and for a tantalizing moment longer his lips teased her. "Do you ever stand still long enough?" He took both cases from her.

"Long enough for what?" she asked mindlessly, going through the office ahead of him.

"Sweetheart, you are a little dim.''

"Don't 'sweetheart' me, Jake.''

"And don't you 'Jake' me! It means you're trying to keep me at arm's length. Call me Jacob, the way you used to, darling.''

Her temperature went up by several degrees. "Thank heavens your hands are full!" Opening the shop door wider for him to enter, she found she was in a terrible quandry, wavering dangerously on a razor's edge between doubt and desire.

"Not for long." He placed the cases on the counter and reached for her. "Come here, sweetie pie!" His cool reckoning smile and the rich glitter of challenge in his eyes belied the ridiculous inveigling endearment.

Her mouth trembled into an unbidden smile. Biting her bottom lip to stop the smile from spreading, she snapped, fending him off, "You're just trying to butter me up to get inside the lab.''

"That's right." He pursued her to the end of the walking space behind the counter. Neatly he lifted her to seat her on it, wedged his hips between her knees and slid his arms around her. "There now, isn't this nice?"

"Jake!" she pleaded impatiently, as warm as a toasted marshmallow, reveling in intimacy of his hips and torso snugly against her. "You can't simply go around manhandling me like this all the time. Didn't anybody ever teach you it takes two consenting adults? Two!"

"Don't wrestle in here." Unconcerned, he nuzzled her hair, his hands ranging all over her back. "We might break something."

"Smooching is not getting you inside that lab. You may have mom and Robbie in the palm of your hand, but—"

"Only you," and one hand sought the curve of her breast as his narrow hips pressed against the giving softness of her inner thighs, forcing her legs farther apart and affording him even closer, more suggestive contact. "Stop wriggling. You'll knock everything off the counter."

"Then stop groping!"

"I am not groping."

"What do you call it?"

"Do you want the exact scientific term? Some people would call it a part of the mating ritual, while others—"

"Jake, please—"

As soon as she brought her mouth within range, he possessed himself of it and administered such a long, thorough, potent kiss that when it was over she could only breathe, flushed, "I still won't let you in the lab."

"Why not? Because of rules that can't be broken, or simply because I'd like to see the inside?" One brown hand strayed into the sun-warmed cascade of curls against her cheek.

"All you want is to see the inside?"

"That's all."

"So you can take inventory of the stock and equipment? To give your father a better idea of how much we're worth?"

"But he already knows how much this perfumery is worth."

"Oh. Mother." She sighed in annoyance. "So it's just plain curiosity?" He nodded. "Well, your curiosity is practically criminal! Oh, Jacob, let me down—your father's coming!"

By the time Charles opened the shop door, Camille was still sitting on the counter. But she'd opened a case of moisturizing lotion and was placing a box on the shelf behind her head—where the lotion was never put. Jacob was leaning at his ease against the counter beside her.

"Jake, may I use your car?"

"Sure, dad." Fishing in his pocket, Jacob tossed the keys in his father's direction. "Take it easy, though. No wheelies."

Charles caught them, smiling thinly, and without acknowledging Camille, left.

She sighed gustily after he was gone, blowing tendrils off her forehead. "It's warm today!" she supplied waspishly when Jacob sent her a quizzical glance. Then she decided to get to the point. "Exactly what does your father want with mom?"

His eyebrows rose. The bright glitter in his tawny eyes should have warned her, but she'd already turned away to taking the boxes of lotion back off the shelf. "You mean you don't know?"

"Nobody's told me anything."

"It's no wonder I can't get you to cooperate if you don't even know that much! Well, I'll tell you all about everything if I may have your attention for a couple of minutes. It's really very simple, Camille. I could draw you some pictures.... No, I've never agreed with pure theory. It would be better if I explained it as I showed you...step by step." He put a finger over her lips to stop her impassioned speech. "Don't interrupt. Just try to concentrate. It's not difficult to understand about the birds and bees, but you don't want to miss anything. First thing is to get back as we were. That's as good a place to start as any—"

"If you won't give me a straight answer, then go write your book, why don't you! I should think working up a comprehensive study in your field would keep several people busy for several lifetimes—while you don't appear to do a lot of anything except hang around here getting in everybody's way!"

"I think he might want to marry her."

Camille felt as though she'd been kicked in the stomach. "But...but Elaine heard him saying he would never marry again." She gripped the edge of the counter with white-knuckled fingers.

"People change their minds."

She swallowed. "You...you think it's that bad?"

"Bad?"

"I mean—"

The little bell above the shop door rang. Elaine and a friend of hers came in, and Jacob left soon after. Relations between him and his cousin hadn't warmed any—he seemed hardly aware of her existence, and she seemed annoyed by his.

The next morning Camille found her brother alone in the office, sorting the paychecks Fern had just signed. She spoke to Robbie about Charles and his supposed intentions regarding their mother.

"Mom get married?" he responded incredulously.

"It could happen! You know how often they're out together. You've seen the way mom looks when she comes back. If only I felt sure he really cared for her.... If he marries her, he by rights will own half the perfumery, and he'll get it without spending one of his precious pennies!"

Her brother gazed at her in consternation. "I never thought of that." Raking a hand through his blond waves, he added a horrified, "Oh, no!"

"Oh, yes!" she could see the staff gathering outside for their pay, so hurried on quietly to finish what she had to say. "And that means Jake will probably have complete run of the place—no wonder he's so in favor of the marriage! D'you realize the codfish would be our stepfather, Jake our stepbrother? How would you like *that*!" Moving from her leaning position against the desk, Camille went to the door and continued, her vehemence carrying her away, "The very last thing on earth I'd want is Jacob Nathaniel Darleah for a brother!"

Turning around she bumped into the candidate in question, right behind her. She said nothing, just stared, arrested, into his face. Robbie said nothing, and the staff behind the professor, the lot of them gathered there now, were all very quiet, too.

"Why, Camille, for once we agree!" Planting his strong hands on her waist, the professor lifted her up and against him. He kissed her astonished mouth soundly, making it obvious to all and sundry the embrace was not of the sibling sort.

Clasping his shoulders, she pried herself away from him. In a whirl of tingling surprise and angry heat, she caught sight of all the intrigued stares beyond. "I'm not a rag doll to be picked up and put down," she whispered furiously. "And—and I'll slap you if you don't put me down this instant!" Her feet restored to solid ground, she added in a light sarcastic tone, for the benefit of the many ears, "I called you all to this meeting to discuss getting some work done around here!"

As she swept away she heard Robbie saying ruefully, "She's not big but she's mean. . ." and thought she might scream at the injustice of everything and everyone. She wished she were six feet tall and weighed three hundred pounds—then let the professor play around with her! Any other time she might have laughed, but today her anger prevailed.

That night, getting ready for bed, she was puzzling over Jacob Nathaniel and dissecting her various grudges, striving earnestly to determine the importance of each. This was developing into a full night's occupation, when she saw a thin sliver of light shining from the darkened lab's clerestory. It was the same sliver of light that she had become accustomed to seeing many years ago . . . hadn't seen for the past five, since her father had died. Overcome, she gulped in sheer and sudden terror, squeezed her eyes tightly shut and stood trembling for several agonized moments. When she cautiously opened her eyes again, the light was gone.

Sagging weakly onto her bed, Camille thought that light must, it *must* have been her imagination. . . .

CHAPTER SEVEN

As soon as Camille returned from picking roses Saturday morning, she went to the laboratory to check for signs of intruders. There were none. She remembered that she and her brother had spied on their father through a small hole in a drawn blind over a lab window, that they had been caught at it, and that Dr. Beesley had subsequently covered the hole with tape. She carefully removed the old, crumbling bit of tape and wiped the area clean with solvent. Now, should she by any remote chance see the light again, she could come down to investigate. A surprising amount could be seen through the tiny peephole, since the blind, when pulled down, ran close against the glass. Of course, it was silly even to think of intruders, but she felt better for removing the tape, anyway.

Some time later she was again in the laboratory, working this time, struggling to stir ten gallons of slowly solidifying Woodsmoke soap. Because it was a fabulous spring day, she had the door open wide. She was perspiring with the effort required to swing the paddle round and round the vat. The perfume satellites weren't the Beesleys' most sought-after items, and therefore they weren't as well equipped for production. Thinking about the professor and manfully attempting to beat the creamy soap before it became too hard to manipulate, she had a burst of energy and, panting, stopped to rest her chin on the handle of the wooden paddle. Jacob was standing in the doorway calmly observing her, puffing contentedly on his pipe.

"Writing a book doesn't seem to occupy much of your time!" She frowned reproachfully.

"Could you use a hand?" he queried, his mysteriously golden eyes holding her in warm regard. They slid contemplatively over her shorts and sleeveless T-shirt.

She felt the rise of an almost irrepressible yearning. "Oh, no! No hands, thank you." Her voice quavered conspicuously.

"I meant with whatever it is you're trying to mix," he reproved, smiling faintly at her. "Or would that be impossible, since I would then have to set foot inside your laboratory?"

"I...can manage." She thrust down the almost overpowering urge to ask him to kiss her instead.

"All right," he replied easily, turning away.

"Oh, wait, Jacob," she cried, not wanting him to go. When he reappeared at the door, she didn't know what to give as a reason for detaining him. "I, um... could sort of use some help."

She was a little disappointed when he simply took the paddle from her and started stirring. "What's the procedure? Fast, slow? Mmm, this smells good—and so do you."

"Steady and even," she instructed. "Not too slow

or too fast. That's it. Whew!'' She stretched her aching arms.

"You grow roses and lavender but no violets?"

"No. They're too delicate to have their oil extracted by distillation. We buy our violet essence, but our Island Violet perfume has our own rose and lavender oil in it, so it's still unique—besides the fact that nobody else has a violet formula quite like ours."

"You're wearing it, aren't you."

"Yes.... It is spring."

"Is it ever." He grinned back, the stirring task a simple matter for him. "This mixture must be Woodsmoke. Rachael presented me with some. Don't I smell wonderful, too? Did you know anointing the body with fragrance to attract the opposite sex is ancient pandemic custom? That the people of the Far East were the ones to start using it for that express purpose?"

"I had a faint idea, yes," she hedged.

"And did you know Cleopatra had the floor strewn with rose petals eighteen inches deep for her first meeting with Mark Anthony?"

"Er, no. Jacob?"

"Mm-hm?"

"When did your mother remarry?"

"When I was eleven."

"Did you like the idea?"

"I wasn't overjoyed."

"How did you get along with Charles?"

"Not too well—not at first. Not for quite a while. But he grows on you." He paused, caught her eyes and held them. "Why don't you give him a chance?"

Cautiously she replied, "How do you mean?"

"Well, you and Robbie could be standing in the way of our parents' happiness. What right do you have to do that?"

Contrarily, since she'd been the one to broach the topic, she retorted halfheartedly, "You should mind your own business."

"My father's happiness is my business. He and Fern are in love. Open your eyes. I think they want to get married but are waiting for you and your brother to accept him. Frankly, I'm for it. Dad's warmed right up. He actually seems to be enjoying himself these days, and I don't see Fern in tears."

"Are you so sure they want to get married, or do you just want them to?"

"Ask your mother if you don't trust my word. I know he...says the wrong thing sometimes and he's very opinionated, but then strong personalities usually are. He may be unsure of how to go about getting your approval—he's not terribly good at breaking the ice. After all this time that he's been alone, don't ruin his chance at happiness with your mother. You don't have to be afraid for her. My dad doesn't, er, fool around. He's the dedicated sort. If he loves Fern, and I think he does, then he'll take the best care of her. And what about when you and Robbie both get married? Do you want your mother all alone? Think about her future, not just your own. Don't they make an excellent pair?"

"Oh, heavens, the soap! Quick, Jacob—oh, hurry! We have to get it into the robot before it hardens too much!'' Disengaging the vat from its stand, she directed him to roll it to the bottling machine, where clamps lifted the vat off its rollers and eased it inside the bottler. Quickly pushing and pulling the required buttons, levers and gears, she set the mechanical wizard in motion. The trays of soap molds were already stacked inside. ''That was a close call! You see why visitors aren't encouraged? You distract me too much!''

''You're powerfully distracting yourself,'' he commented, but was absorbed in watching the robot perform. Camille wondered why, today, when she wanted him to, he didn't touch her. Her need for him hadn't diminished but had grown with each encounter, angry or otherwise. Yet she didn't quite have the nerve to reach out and touch him first. After all, what with all her denials and scoffing and defiance, to do an about-face would seem mighty peculiar.

Fervently she wished she hadn't so adamantly refused to discuss his unkept promise to her. Surely she couldn't reopen that old can of worms now. Why hadn't he clarified his identity? Why had those two men been following him around in Fredericton? Who was the lady with the hat? Why had his curiosity about the lab prompted him to try to sneak in? She stood there, a perplexed mass of longing and misgiving, totally absorbed in him, while he appeared totally captivated by the robot. At that moment he glanced around at her, and she immediately dropped her eyes. ''Since we're on the subject,'' he went on, ''why won't you sell me Damask? Is it because you in particular have something against me, or only because it's a family heirloom?''

''Wh-what has that to do with mom and Charles?''

''Darling, if they do get married I hardly think I would make desirable company. I'd like a place of my own, anyway, and Damask is perfect.''

''How do you know it's perfect? The inside might not suit you at all!''

''Fern let me have a key. I've looked the place over.''

''Mom gave you a key?'' she asked, dismayed.

''Uh-huh. I've noticed you don't go there as much as you used to. Anytime you want to sit under your willow, go right ahead—I'd hate to think I'd put you off.''

He had observed while she had thought herself alone! ''You sure don't act much like a professor, professor!'' Her voice was tart.

''How should professors behave? You think we're a breed apart?''

''I think you're a breed apart—maybe even downright weird!''

''Even a weird professor needs a place to live. Now I'll let you think about this first, and if you like the idea, you can pass it on to the rest of your family. Since Damask is an heirloom and not just a house, and you don't really want to sell it, why don't you rent it to me? As it is, it's a drain on your finances, but if I were living there I'd keep it up and pay rent on top. And don't put on that righteous we-don't-accept-charity look! It's an even trade.''

''How can you afford it?''

His expressive eyebrows rose. "What do you mean, how can I afford it?"

"Well, you don't *do* anything! How are you going to pay the rent? If you're a prospective tenant, I should at least have an idea that you can pay the rent! What if your father doesn't agree to cough up the money?"

"You think I live off my father?"

"Well...don't you?"

"No!" he exclaimed, staring at her incredulously.

"Well, then, what do you do?"

"I perform research for various organizations pertaining to my field of study."

"Jacob, that sounds a bit pat...."

"My, you're a suspicious little thing!" Camille eyed him warily, dubiously. He laughed at her pouting lips and knitted brow and said, "You know what you remind me of? An angel that lost its way, took the wrong turn and wound up on earth. You really are sweet—any moment you could sprout wings!"

"Balderdash and folderol!" Her eyes narrowed.

"Been brushing up on your English, have you?"

"Why are you never researching if you research?"

"I'm taking a deserved break."

"Why do you want to live here in Metchosin, where there's a marked dearth of ancient manuscripts?"

"I do more than read old books, darling."

"You need a lab?"

"It would be handy."

"Aha! And you want to use ours."

"Maybe, maybe not. In any case, you hardly have the sort of equipment I need."

"That's why you wanted in here? To see what sort of equipment we have?"

"Well, yes."

"If all you do is research, then how come you're so strong?"

He looked at her in quizzical surprise. "You ask the most peculiar questions! Is this all to decide whether I'd be a suitable tenant or a suitable...." Another taunting grin, and his eyes slid down to the outline of her bare breasts underneath her T-shirt. "Since my work requires a lot of sitting, I exercise. I lift weights, to be specific. What else do you want to know? Whether I smoke in bed? Whether I host wild parties? Whether I snore...?"

Smiling hugely at him, hopelessly in love, she took a hesitant step toward him—swiftly he closed the remaining distance. The next instant his mouth was urgently covering hers. Shivering in delight, she was about to wrap her arms around his neck when a, "Yoo-hoo! Where is everybody?" sounded outside amid a chorus of barking. Vexed, Camille decided she was seeing altogether too much of Elaine these days. Camille and Jacob went outside. He shut the door behind them.

"Hi!" Elaine beamed. "Oh, hi, Jake." Now she frowned. "You here again?"

Gravely and shortly greeting his cousin, he turned to Camille to say, "If you want me...just call." Such an ambiguous statement that her eyes widened on him. Smiling crookedly at her confusion, he took himself off down toward the beach.

"What did he mean by *that*?" Elaine sniffed.

"Why, he...he was giving me a hand with, er, some of the heavier work. Robbie's checking a drainage problem at the lavender farm, and everybody else is somewhere else."

"Oh, well, I brought you a blouse and a skirt and a couple of dresses—you usually like my old stuff. There are a couple of pairs of shoes, too. Isn't it lucky we have the same size feet? They are the only thing about me that's small!" she sighed.

Camille's forehead puckered. "Well, you could try exercise." Elaine groaned. "How about a dance class? I heard there's a new one starting down at the hall on Tuesday nights."

"Yes, but Annette's going, and can you see me standing beside her, both of us in tights?" Elaine shuddered.

"Then try a class in Victoria—it would be closer, anyway."

"It doesn't matter how much I spend on clothes anymore. Nothing looks good! I can't seem to stick to a diet, and I hate the thought of a prissy dance class. But I have to do something— Oh, I know! One of those fabulous fat farms opened on one of the Gulf Islands. I'll go there!"

"Aren't they awfully expensive?"

"Who cares?" Elaine shrugged, with a kindly condescending look at her. "You're lucky you're not heavy. You'd never be able to afford to go!"

Camille shoved down her annoyance. "We're not exactly destitute, Elaine."

"No...not exactly," she agreed generously. "The land you own is worth a fortune. But it's not like having ready cash, is it?"

"We also happen to own four perfume formulas that are worth a fortune each, and they're as good as ready cash. Better, because they keep making more money while holding their value."

"In that case, it's too bad they didn't make more cash a little faster, isn't it?" Elaine observed, while Camille gritted her teeth. "Say, did you know Jake's been taking Annette out?"

Camille came to a sudden stop.

"What's the matter?"

"Oh—oh, I stepped on a thorn...." Camille raised her bare foot to peer at the bottom, giving credence to her alarm. Her first feeling was one of desperate disbelief. But Elaine must know for certain, otherwise she would never say. Indignation welled up inside her. Taking Annette out, was he? Some misogynist! There had been the woman with the hat, too. Elaine went on to give details of where Annette and Jacob had been seen together. Camille pretended the utmost boredom in the professor's love life and listened with both ears.

On Sunday Fern and Charles were off again to another beautiful spot on the Island. With exquisite manners and a fairly warm smile, Camille waved them off, as did Robbie. She didn't want to harm her mother for the world—neither did she want her to marry Charles. She had to admit, though, that the widower appeared to be genuinely involved with mom.

From this point on, Jacob came as often to visit Beesley Farm as before, only to find Camille largely unresponsive to either jokes, taunts or plain conversation. She found his interest in the laboratory had waned. Now that he'd seen the inside, was it not to his specifications? With any luck, perhaps that meant Charles was no longer so interested in investing in the perfumery. Nothing more had been said about selling it, or even selling a part interest in it.... Camille wondered.

Rachael's visit toward the middle of that week brought more news about her nephew's interest in Annette Hill. Miserably hurrying away so she wouldn't have to listen to Annette's unsuitability for such a "nice boy" as Jake, Camille wondered whether the professor had tired of trying to persuade her into his arms and had found solace in another only-too-eager young woman.

That Friday night Fern told her children she was going salmon fishing with Charles tomorrow. What were they up to?

Robbie said he was going to the Butchart Gardens to discuss the sale of some of his new roses.

"I've a date with Greyson tomorrow, mom—a double date," Camille explained. She had accepted the date as a last desperate measure. Going out with other men was the fastest way to get one particular man out of her system—she hoped. "Rawly and Su were going to come with us, but his fishing trawler's going out a day early, so Greyson said he'd dig up another couple. Probably Bill and Jan." Greyson had wisely suggested a double date, as if he knew Camille would agree to that more quickly than just the two of them out together.

"Well, I'm glad you're going out, darling, and I always did like Greyson...." Fern watched Camille busily taking in the waistband of one of Elaine's skirts. "Jake was going to come fishing with us but he has a date with Annette tomorrow. You know, dear, I do think you had a chance with him, but your behavior hasn't been encouraging. Why is it you two don't get along? He's attractive, intelligent, charming. Honestly, why don't you like him?"

"I just don't, that's all," Camille muttered, clenching her teeth. Couldn't anybody talk about anything other than Jake, Jake and Annette!

But Fern didn't move away. She stood silently puzzling over her daughter's face, then bent down and put a hand on her arm. "Is anything wrong? You've seemed rather upset lately."

"I'll say!" Robbie grouched. "She's as touchy as a crab in a dinner pail!"

"What's bothering you, dear? And don't fob me off with the idea that you're fine. You're not. Did you ever ask Jake why he—"

"Mother!" cried Camille, throwing down the skirt, "please!" She jumped up from the couch to run out onto the front porch and down to the beach.

Crouched on a log, her knees drawn up to her chin, her arms around her knees, she watched the gulls, white against the darkening sky, circling and wheeling and crying...and felt like crying, too. Had she pushed him into Annette's arms? Had she? Had her stubborn pride and suspicion and doubt made him finally give up and go elsewhere? Instead of being so distant since she'd first heard about Annette, maybe she should have called him, after all. Needing him, she thought that tomorrow, while she would have to smile and laugh with Greyson, Bill and Jan, her darling professor would be somewhere, doing something, with gorgeous willing Annette. . . .

Sometime later, while the household slept and Camille prepared for bed, she saw the sliver of light shining from the clerestory of the lab. Yet the lab windows were dark as before; the blackout blinds must have been drawn just as her father had drawn them when he worked late.

This time the shock wasn't quite so great. Closing her eyes, she counted out a minute. But when she carefully opened them again, the light in the clerestory was still on. Still on! The hair on her nape prickled. Her father's ghost? Burglars? Flying down the stairs and out of the house, she wondered why the poodles hadn't sounded an alarm. They pranced beside her as she sped barefoot in her nightgown along the drive, through the gate and around to the back of the laboratory, where the hole in the blind would give her a view inside.

When she arrived at the window, all was in darkness; she could see nothing. And the dogs weren't acting as though trouble was afoot. Bewildered, she drew the spare lab key from its hiding place in the crook of a small arbutus tree and let herself in—the dogs, too, for she was thoroughly frightened and wanted them right beside her.

Everything was as it should be. The blinds weren't drawn. There was no burglar crouched under the counter or lurking behind the robot or secreted in between the library shelves of oils and essences. She must have been seeing things. Thank heavens she hadn't yanked Robbie out of bed! He would have thought she was cracking up. . . .

IN TIME FOR HER DOUBLE DATE the next day, fabulously dressed in a pale green watered silk blouse and skirt, Camille stepped outside to await Greyson. Her horror was unimaginable as she watched a big white Cadillac drive up under the grape arbor. Jacob was at the wheel, Annette sat beside him and Greyson was in the back seat. He hopped out, smiling happily.

"Bill and Jan couldn't make it. Step in, beautiful. You look fantastic!"

In a state approaching sleepwalking, Camille slid in the back seat and smiled at Jacob and Annette in the front, thinking, *I'm going to die. I know I'm going to die!*

Through the torturously long evening, every time Annette fondled Jacob's arm, or shoulder, or neck, or his lovely thick straight hair, Camille thought she would die all over again. How she managed to stay in one piece she had no idea. And when she heard Annette giggling in the dark quiet theater and whispering things in the professor's ear, she was convinced she was shortly going to go quite mad. Greyson couldn't have been nicer. She felt like a heel for not enjoying him more. If only she could transfer all her lusting after and yearning for to him, her problems would be over. But she sat in tense agony, not seeing or hearing the musical, conscious only of Annette beside her—and what was she doing with her hand on the professor's knee?

On returning home, she discovered the agony

didn't abate. She taunted herself by envisioning Jacob and Annette dropping Greyson off at home and then...and then.... She wouldn't have noticed a light in the clerestory that night had there been one! Oh, she'd been in love with the professor probably right at first sight—no, first sight had been in Vancouver. Since second sight, then, in Calgary, while he was eating his dinner roll. And what if she'd misjudged him all along? What if he hadn't taken her out in Toronto and Montreal only to "keep an eye on her"? What if he'd had no ulterior motives for asking all those questions about the perfumery and in particular the lab during her sales trip? And she might not like it, but it wasn't a crime that Charles was interested in the perfumery, as well as in her mother. Everybody—except Elaine—liked the professor. Even Robbie had completely revised his opinion. Also, surely any chemist would want to see the inside of somebody else's lab. All her misgivings now blew away like so much dust. Jacob had tried to reason with her, had tried to love her...and now he was out there in the night somewhere...with Annette.

The only place Camille could go in her consummate distress was to Damask. She didn't even bother to put a housecoat over her nightgown, for no one was ever out on their strip of beach this late, and it was a warm night. Picking her way carefully along the wet sand in her bare feet, she held up the trailing skirts of the gown that had belonged to her grandmother. Camille had rescued the pink cotton nightie, with the lace-edged sleeves and the lace-ruffled high neck, from one of the trunks in the cellar at Damask. Which provided even more proof that she was inextricably tied to this stretch of land and the ancestral home. At least she still had the beach, and Damask, to turn to. Thank goodness she hadn't told anyone about Jacob's offer to rent the house—what a disaster, to think of him living there and having Annette over of an evening!

When she came at last to the foot of the first flight of marble stairs, she couldn't believe her eyes. There was a light upstairs in Damask, in what had been her grandparents' bedroom. Only a faint glow, but her blinking didn't erase it. Was she indeed cracking up? Electricity to the house had been cut off years ago....

As she stood motionless, gazing helplessly up at the bedroom window, Jacob came into sight, walking down the stairs toward her. The full, leaf-fringed willow boughs had hidden him. Transfixed now, Camille wasn't altogether certain he was truly there.

But he came all the way down, and she felt the warmth of his hands as they ran ever so lightly down her arms. His voice was husky velvet. "I was waiting for you, Camille."

"Waiting for me?" she whispered, not understanding, still motionless, gazing up into his beloved face and the incredible intensity of his deep-set eyes. He had changed from his evening attire, now wore only a faded T-shirt with the arms cut off and jeans. He was barefoot, too.

"I can see the cottage from up there." He nodded back toward the house. "I was willing you to come for a long time. And then I saw you—" the deep velvet enwrapped her "—and I came down to meet my love."

"Oh, Jacob!" she uttered weakly, falling into ready arms that immediately closed tightly around her. "Jacob, Jacob, Jacob...."

He laughed softly, a hand sinking into the spun-gold fluff of her hair as he pressed her to him. "Wasn't tonight awful?"

"I thought I'd lost you, Jacob." She clung to him, arms circling his waist, uncaringly honest and artless.

"Never, baby...." The sensuous huskiness of his voice was heaven-sent balm. "Old Flypaper Jake, they call me...but you go right on calling me Jacob." A dizzy rapture had taken hold of her, and she smiled tremulously against his T-shirt. He was so ridiculous sometimes, perpetually unpredictable. Her whole world would be darker if she couldn't have him.

"But Annette...."

"Don't forget, I had not only a very admirable Greyson to compete with, but a gift-shop owner and a sailor, to boot. Given a mechanic, a professor, a gift-shop owner and a sailor to choose from, women invariably go for the sailor. I was worried."

Now she laughed outright, feeling like his lost angel that had at last found heaven. Rising on tiptoe in the sand, Camille wound her slender arms around Jacob's neck and touched her lips to his. He clasped his hands around her waist, bending her lissome body against him, imprinting her softness with his shape. The feather-light kiss awakened the insubstantial

gossamer of anticipation, the delicate touching barely touching at all, more evocative than any words,
more ephemeral than the stars above, more real than
the grains of sand beneath their feet.

A brief drawing apart only compelled closer contact, greater intimacy, impelled the full arousal of
ever-present desire. When their lips met again, it was
in a fusion of need; the need to give, the need to have
were inseparable, unrelenting and deliciously immediate.

As his mouth ravished the soft eagerness of hers,
their mingling blood heat spiraled slowly, urgently
into the burn of passion. The heat of his hands
through the thin pink cotton gave her at once a vast
peace and a tumultuous hunger. The taut sinewy
male body pressed against her, around her, melted
every fiber in her being. The hot increasing demands
of his mouth trailing slowly over her face sent her
senses reeling and her heart pounding, the pounding
echoing through her veins and echoing into his body
so close to hers, until she realized his heart was thudding against her breast with equal ferment.

Behind his neck her hands unlocked, one to curl
around his nape, luxuriating in the silkiness of his
hair, the other to meander down the length of his
shoulder, to run sensitized fingertips over his bared
flesh and the smooth warmth of his hard-muscled upper arm. She slid her hand inside the opening of the
shirt, across his back, slowly exploring...until his
lips again found hers to taste the nectar within. The
probing quest of his tongue ignited brighter flames
deeper within.

Again they drew apart, and as she gazed into his tiger eyes with a dizzy, sultry satisfaction, he placed his thin brown hands on either side of her face and kissed her once more, a short unmistakable statement of ultimate possession. "Come with me."

Taking both her hands, Jacob slid them down his chest beneath his own. Then, tightly clasping one, led her up the stairs. Gathering her flowing eyelet gown, Camille followed unhesitatingly. Across the dewy cushion of lawn and up the second set of stairs, a flick of the brass knob, and they were inside the dark house, the furniture ghostly white unrecognizable shapes under the dustcovers. Pressing herself closer against his side, she went up the broad fan of staircase with him.... The utter quiet and stillness of the night, the hushed aura of expectancy in Damask were vibrant, somehow surreal.

"Where are we going?" she asked in a breathless whisper, not daring to speak louder in case the walls should overhear.

His soft chuckle was as seductive and arousing as his tone. "You ask the darndest questions!"

They had gained the upper landing, and reaching out, he pushed the door of her grandparents' bedroom wider. He stopped on the threshold, holding her to him so that she could look inside, but not yet enter.

There were no dustcovers here; the room had the air of most abundant life. A small fire flickered in the grate, the south and west windows were flung wide and a coasting zephyr ruffled the old lace curtains. The swishing of waves upon the shore was a barely heard lullaby. Made up with crisp white sheets tucked over the plump feather mattress and turned back over the tasseled coverlet, the great antique bed occupied the center of the room. Fat pillows rested against the headboard. Candles inside the glass chimneys of shining brass lamps shed a soft glow of comfort. There was an uneven pile of books on the windowseat, Jacob's gold-rimmed glasses resting on top—that and his pipe and a small silver flask.

The room with its period furniture was lovely by any standards; to her, embellished by memories of bygone days and people she had loved, it had always been particularly lovely. But it had never seemed quite so welcoming before.

When she turned her head to look up at him, he explained, "I like camping out..." and released her hand, putting his fingers underneath her chin to keep her looking into the burn of his eyes, where a tender, very personal question lay.

He gazed into Camille's piquant face, the pointed chin, the full damask lips made redder and fuller from his kisses, the lustrous dark eyes and the creamy gold curls in characteristic disarray...the rest of her, swathed from the chin down in yards of pink cotton and fragile lace, bound by tiny buttons. His fingers moved lightly down the high neck of the gown, and the burn of the question intensified. Camille knew the answer was entirely up to her. She could go...or she could stay.

It was both the right time and the right place. Breaking away from him, she entered the master bedroom, made a dancing circuit, as at home as if it were her own room, and ended up by the bed. Glancing at him over her shoulder—he was leaning against the doorjamb—she raised her skirts a little to climb into the middle of the great bed. The eiderdown mattress sank accommodatingly, a pillowy cloud to cuddle around her. He came in and shut the door behind him... shutting out the remainder of the house and everything beyond. Her whole world was contained within the boundaries of shimmering candlelight. Bending to put more logs on the fire, he straightened and for a long exquisite shivery moment beheld her, awaiting him.

Her pulse was racing.... As he came slowly toward the bed, the tip of her tongue moved out to moisten her lips. He stripped off his T-shirt, and her pulse accelerated further at the sight of his sleek naked brown torso, tangled sandy curls in a drift across his chest. He opened his jeans, revealing a narrow column of waist and hips. He rested a knee on the bed, placing a hand on either side of her, and she sank acquiescent into the plumpness of the pillows.

"I love you, Camille." His voice was like the touch of raw silk. "I've loved you for a long time...."

Reaching up, she ran her fingers through the sweep of crisp hair so much lighter than his skin, and down, down his torso and around to glide over his bared hipbone... underneath the jeans, sliding them farther off, wanting to be rid of everything superfluous between them. At last, delighted by Jacob's slim nude body, she ran her hands back up to his shoulders, glorying in the warmth and texture of him. With a faint throaty laugh she murmured, "I've been wanting to take your clothes off for a long time, professor, darling— Oh, Jacob, I'm not an angel at all!''

"Too beautiful to be anything else. . . ." His hand slowly passed over the lace at her breast. "And whoever sewed all these endless buttons on did it in the mood of saintly chastity!" He lifted her arm to get at the row of tiny buttons leading upward from her wrist.

Laughing and tempting him with a slow delicious wriggle, she kissed and nibbled at his chin, "You know that I love you, too?"

He moved on to the other arm and another row of tiny pearl buttons. "Whatever's inside you shines through. I must be the best-loved man in the universe—and your grandmother must have done this to teach your grandfather patience!"

"But how do you know?"

"By how impatient I feel right now." His hand settled between her breasts as he kissed her mouth most impatiently, arching her against him, and as his lips savored the features of her face, kissing her eyes shut and tantalizing her lips, he began undoing button after button, moving from the neck slowly, slowly down and down, making many little side trips to roam over every delicate curve and contour. Finally he brought his hand to rest in the soft depression between the high curve of her hipbones. . . his fingers spreading out to reach from hip to hip, his palm seductively pressing into the yielding white satin skin.

And then he slid the old lace from her shoulders and the pink cotton from her arms, drawing the gown from her with total disregard for the time he took in doing so, when, only minutes ago, he had been impatient. His smoldering eyes, wandering over ever more bared flesh, made sure none of her was left to his imagination. This perusal was followed by the scorching trail of sensitive fingertips searching out the subtleties of her shape, lingering on the most responsive places, inciting pagan hunger in her every cell, right down to the pretty arch of a female foot and the electrified curl of pink toes. And all the while he bade her lie still and merely absorb his tangible adoration.... But finally the sweet greedy fever in her blood couldn't bear another second without more intimate contact. His desirous fingertips were no longer enough.

"Jacob," she pleaded softly, reaching out for him.

Leaning forward over her, he caught her tantalizing mouth beneath his, laying her back into the pillows. "No, baby." His voice was a throaty caress. "I've waited too long for you. I've loved you too well a thousand times over. I'm going to love you now the way no other man ever has or ever can, so that when you want loving you'll always come to me...."

The heat of his breath feathered over her skin. The heavenly shock of his lips and teeth and tongue was against her breast as he gently bit the hard raised tip, exploring the full rounded softness, wandering farther and farther, leaving no area untouched and unloved. A dreamy lassitude flowed through her. She felt like a crucible of passion, weightless, languorous, her ardor straining beyond bearable levels—until, with a strength born of consuming hunger and the entirety of her love, with a small husky triumphant laugh, she started a wrestling match, knowing he would win and wanting him to win quickly. Holding nothing back, giving freely of her endless store of desire and caring made it impossible for him to resist.

At long, long last the discarded nightgown wafted unnoticed from the bed onto the carpet. Entwined and surrounded by him, and he by her, the bronze skin and the white melting together, bodies in harmony and souls attuned, in passionate ecstasy and tender caress. . . the night was whiled away.

ACCUSTOMED TO WAKING at the crack of dawn, Camille opened her eyes as soon as the birds started singing. A spasm of panic gripped her—she should be up, already on her way to pick rosebuds! Robbie and mom would be frantic on discovering her bed unslept in. Then, with a soft sigh of pure pleasure, she nestled back into the eiderdown and back against the long lean length of the professor, who was still sound asleep. Robbie had hired eleven pickers only yesterday; she didn't have to go anywhere.

Turning her head on the pillow, she observed him in contemplative leisure. How sweet he looked in repose, like that "nice boy" mother was always touting him to be, hardly the erudite academic. His gold brown hair was ruffled across his wide forehead. What long lashes he had. . . and what a beautiful male mouth and chin, strong and resolute and yet so finely shaped, as if some master sculptor had taken a great deal of trouble to form every line. Utterly content, she stretched luxuriously between the white sheets and ran a light hand down his back, careful not to wake him and quite unable to love him better or more than she already did. He was hers. He was the most precious thing she'd ever known.

For an hour longer she dozed, warm and blissful, and eventually got up to pad barefoot over to the windows and look out on the morning, the wide glittering blue sweep of the Strait of Juan de Fuca. What a morning! The early sun couldn't have sparkled more brightly; the garden couldn't have been more magnificently fresh and vital in the fullness of spring. And the air—it was aquiver with tangy salt spray, the earthy sap smell of growth, the Fragrant Cloud roses beneath her window. In the glimmer of waves, seals splashed and rolled and dived, made brave by the absence of the killer whales. Farther to the left, Camille could see a school of porpoises performing water acrobatics. Far out, an ocean freighter was a blue gray smudge against the horizon.

The whole world seemed to share her happiness. She hadn't one regret. Jacob loved her—how he loved her—and instead of feeling beset by trials, as she had for the past months and months, she felt elated at the prospect of life before her. Problems. What problems? She'd been making mountains out of molehills and mysteries out of misunderstandings. There was nothing between her and the professor that one short talk wouldn't resolve. Given the new circumstances, everything had changed. Besides the past, they would have to discuss the future—"What are we going to do about this?" as Jacob had once asked her.

Strange, how one night could alter the world. Now

the idea of Jacob's sharing the lab was appealing. The idea of him, reasonable, capable and intelligent, helping in the running of the perfumery was like a godsend—three heads were better than two. And to share Damask with him? It would be her pleasure. Of course, since Jacob was now rather like one of the family, that meant Charles had to be numbered among the fold. Her brow wrinkled. Well, he would stand in the light of a father-in-law, so she would just have to get along with him, codfish or no.

She might have no choice in the matter, anyway, since mother might make him a close relative before long. Then her daughter would have to try her best, whether she wanted to or not. But even that, too, was no longer such a difficulty; it was merely a task that needed a cool head, a warm heart and, most likely, plenty of perseverence. If she really put her mind to winning Charles over, she could do it. First she would have to persuade him to like her, then she would have to persuade him that, no matter what his position, neither he nor his money was ever walking over the Beesleys. Jacob would be stuck with the ordeal of mediating, but he was equal to it.

But now she really had to get home or she would be missed, and she preferred to break the news that she and Jacob didn't spend all their time in argument in her own way, rather than to have a search party discover the secrets of the night. Donning her pink nightgown, she kissed the sleeping professor on the brow, meaning to simply slip away—but he caught her and tumbled her down into his arms.

"Where do you think you're going?" he murmured, brushing his face against her hair.

"I have to get home, Jacob." She laughed, trying to wriggle out of his clasp.

Slowly, roaming hands sought out the soft warmth beneath the pink cotton. "Not yet...." His teeth nibbled the shell of her ear. "What were you thinking about so seriously a minute ago?"

"Well, I...." She realized she'd been taking a lot for granted, but wasn't that allowed, since she was in love? The man holding her had had no change of mind with the coming of the morning.... She kissed his brown shoulder. "Oh, Jacob, I love you! But I have to get home soon."

"You mean your mother will have a fit if you don't turn up for breakfast." He trailed light kisses down her throat. "No doubt everybody would be a little surprised." He chuckled softly. "Meet me here for lunch. I'll bring a picnic basket...."

"THERE YOU ARE!" Fern exclaimed, leaning out the kitchen window. "I was just calling you to breakfast. Wonderful day, isn't it? You know, dear, you really should try to break your habit of wandering around in your nightclothes! What if somebody caught you? I must say you look positively happy this morning— did a full night's sleep make all that difference? I told Robbie he should have hired all fourteen of the applicants rather than just eleven, but at least now you're spared having to turn out of bed at the first hint of daylight. But he insists on being up to supervise, if nothing else, and...."

A little later, seeing her daughter help herself to three pancakes and three slices of bacon, Fern continued, "My, it's good to see your appetite has returned! You are feeling better, aren't you?"

"Mmm...." Camille swallowed a mouthful and beamed guilelessly at her mother. "A good night's rest really can work wonders!" Her eyes danced merrily, and Fern gazed at her in pleased perplexity. "If you want to take off somewhere with Charles," Camille went on, adroitly switching topics, "go ahead. I can give Phyllis a hand in the shop if she needs it this afternoon. I'm going to run into Langford to check our post-office box—there should be more checks and hopefully some reorders—then I'll be right back. Are you going somewhere with Charles today?"

"Well...." Her mother hesitated, and Camille, looking at her over a cup of freshly brewed coffee, wondered at the faint tinge of pink that washed over her mother's still youthful face. If she wasn't mistaken, there was also a glimmer of excitement in the soft brown eyes. She waited, but her parent was assiduously stirring sugar into her coffee, not meeting Camille's eyes.

Deciding to take an unprecedented plunge, Camille said very casually, "Has Charles been to Long Beach yet? I know it's quite a drive but I'm sure he'd like it. The western edge of all of Canada, miles of sand and unobstructed Pacific Ocean.... If you started out early enough...."

"We...we were...saving Long Beach," Fern delicately prevaricated, her blush a little more pronounced. She looked as though she had something to say but was stymied by how to phrase it. She added lamely, "No, we're not off anywhere today. Er, I'm going to do the laundry."

"But I just did it— Oh, well, I'd better dash. Where are the car keys?"

When she returned several hours later, after inspiration had overcome her and she'd splurged on having her hair trimmed and set, Camille was met by both her brother and mother. Their distraught expressions made her heart turn over in her breast.

"Where have you *been*?" cried Fern.

"Why is it you're never around when you're supposed to be?" Robbie accused, and looked at her with such uncomfortable dread that she could only stare from one to the other.

"Come into the house, dear," her mother said nervously, taking her arm and patting it. "And please, try not to get too upset, but there was nothing we could do!"

"Really, Camille, if you'd been here instead of galavanting around somewhere! It happened so fast and then we couldn't delay any longer." He argued on her other side. "In the end, we had no choice. We couldn't wait for you."

She stopped short on the back-porch stairs. *"What is it?"*

"It's all my fault!" Fern shook her head. "I never should have taken the loan from Rachael. I should have gone to our bank, but I've never borrowed from banks. They intimidate me, and I was afraid the manager wouldn't give me the money! You see, dear?"

"Not exactly," Camille murmured dryly.

Robbie interrupted impatiently, "The loan for the robot—it was from Rachael. You'd just left this morning when she called. Wilson got caught in some investment scheme and needs every penny he can scrape together. So he asked Rachael for her savings. Well, she'd loaned us all her savings. What could she do but ask for her money back? There's no way Wilson would go to his brother Charles for help! So we had to come up with a whole lot of money just like that!" He snapped his fingers. "There was nothing else we could do, honestly!"

"What is it you did?" Camille pressed.

"We...we...." Fern took a deep breath. "We sold Damask to Jake. You just missed him. He was here. He deposited a check for us and everything— the whole amount. I've phoned the bank, and the money's already been transferred to our account. Of course I told him why we had to sell Damask in such a hurry, but I swore him to secrecy because, as you can imagine, darling, Rachael and Wilson don't want anyone knowing they're in dire straits—in particular, not Charles. And the way banks work, we wouldn't have had the time to negotiate a loan and get Rachael her money in time. You do see, don't you, that there was nothing we could do? Jake had to go to Vancouver on some urgent business, so we couldn't even wait for you to get back home! He had a message for you, what was it now...something about an ultimatum? Oh, dear, it did sound a bit ominous to me—you two haven't been at each other's throats again, have you? What with everything going on at once, I just can't remember exactly what it was he said...."

Camille, still trying to absorb her mother's hurried speech, said, "You mean...Damask...."

"Yes, yes—I'm so sorry, darling!"

"Can't you remember what he said, mom? You mean he's already gone? But when is he coming back? Why did he have to go? What business in Vancouver?"

"He didn't say, dear. Urgent business that he couldn't put off. That's all we know. But he will be here Monday morning—I have to get the land deed as soon as our lawyer's office opens Monday to give to Jake. Really, dear, he couldn't have been nicer! He didn't have to give us the money until he had possession of the deed, but he didn't mind at all. Thank heavens for people like him! I know you don't care for him, but I truly can't think why! We'd be in a terrible spot but for him!"

"What was his message, mom? Try to remember!"

"What difference does it make?" Robbie broke in. "He'll be here Monday. Ask him then!"

Camille frowned at her brother. "Dammit! I wish I'd been here!"

"Frankly," Robbie added witheringly, "I'm glad you weren't. You'd have screeched at him or something!"

"Now, children, please! It's done. Let's be happy things worked out as well as they did. We've lost Damask, but now we're practically floating in the dough!" Fern giggled charmingly. "And Jake promised to keep Damask intact and as is—no hermetically sealed windows or atrocious renovations. He's very attached to the house. I could tell he was delighted to pay all that money for it—and he's one person who doesn't let his emotions show. Maybe that's why you two don't get along. You're so different!''

Camille suddenly smiled at her mother, a smile that took her family by complete surprise. ''Well,'' she said breezily, ''I'm sure he'll take good care of Damask—better than we could.'' They stared at her in uncertain amazement so that she started laughing, and with an impudent grin left them staring after her as she went into the house with the mail. No reorders yet, unfortunately.

They followed her in, watching as she sorted the envelopes.

''Well, I must say you're taking this decently!'' her mother commented, searching her face.

''You're not sick or anything, are you?'' Robbie queried, shoving his hands in his pockets. ''I mean, I'm happy the way things worked out, but you, you're such a fireball—''

''I am not.'' Camille grinned good-naturedly at her brother. What could Jacob have meant by ultimatums? What ultimatums? Oh, Monday seemed an age away—but this time he had left a message, and it didn't even matter that she hadn't got it. The urgent business might have something to do with providing the money to buy the house. Their house? She really did feel radiant.

In consequence, she missed some of the continuing

conversation, but tuned in again when her mother said in the curiously hesitant tone she'd used at breakfast, "With you both in one place and everybody in a good mood, I, er, have an announcement to make. But why don't I make a pot of coffee, and we can sit around the table and...."

"Come on, mom," Camille coaxed, "forget the coffee. You've been like a hen trying to lay an egg all morning!"

Fern raised an eyebrow. "I hardly think that's the case! But let's sit down." They sat. She looked from one to the other. She cleared her throat. Robbie and Camille unconsciously leaned forward, as if that would draw the news out of her. "Ahem.... On Monday, after Jake and I've finished our business, Charles and I are going to Toronto for a week. I've already arranged for Phyllis to take over for me in the shop."

There was the deepest silence.

Then Robbie slapped his hand down on the table explosively. "He's just going to take you away on... on, well, what amounts to an illicit weekend? My own mother? You're old enough to know better!"

Camille intervened, for her brother, as the only man in the family for some time, had always felt responsible for and protective of his womenfolk. "Now, Robbie! Who is ever old enough to know better? And what's illicit? They're both free. She doesn't have to ask our permission!"

"It's not right!" Robbie protested heatedly. "If he had any honorable intentions he would marry her! Our mother is no floozy to go here and there with strange men, and how dared he even ask it of her? How dared he?''

''It's their own affair—I mean,'' Camille amended hastily, ''their concern. All we have a right to say to mom is...is...oh, mom, be sure you really want to go away with him and that he's not just talked you into it!''

''I knew I didn't trust him!''

''Robbie, he didn't lie to her! They're both going into this with their eyes wide open.''

Fern was sitting back in her chair, holding in a smile as she watched the discussion raging back and forth.

''If he cared for her, he would marry her, and none of this hanky-panky!''

''Now you sound like Mrs. Plumtree!''

''What he does is his business, but mom—''

''Hanky-panky is okay for men but not for women? Double standard, Robbie!'' Camille observed. ''If mom's going to get hurt, then all we can do is be here to pick up the pieces.''

''But what would dad say?''

Fern finally entered the foray with a firm but quiet, ''I know your father would be happy I've found someone whom I can care about. Charles can't replace him—he never will—but Charles has also become very important to me. I am going to Toronto, and I am going because I want to. I do trust Charles, but if you're right, Robbie, and I'm wrong, then I am reassured to know you'll both be here to help me 'pick up the pieces.''' She smiled rather tenderly at them both.

Her last statement made both Camille and Robbie aware that mother was, in fact, in love with the codfish next door—otherwise she would not have any need for pickers-up-of-pieces. Consternated, Camille looked at her, fraught with anxieties, and Robbie was quiet, knowing there was no argument against love.

"Well, mom—" Camille broke the heavy silence "—I hope you have a wonderful time."

"And I hope he lives up to your expectations," sighed Robbie.

"How about that coffee now?" Fern beamed around, not the least worried, obviously. "It's lunchtime, anyway, and I'm hungry!"

After lunch, hardly the picnic at Damask Camille had been anticipating, she relieved Phyllis in the shop. Rachael popped in. Camille had been expecting her visit to collect the loan money.

"Hi, dear. Could you refill my bottle of Island Rose? And Wilson's Woodsmoke needs refilling, too. You should make another men's fragrance, you know. This one is so popular! Has your mother told you the exciting news?"

Camille smiled as she inserted a funnel into Rachael's little milk-glass bottle and poured out a measure of perfume from a large brown flask. "You mean about Charles and Toronto? Yes."

"Isn't it romantic? They make such a good couple! I'm simply delighted! Of course, I was hoping all along, you know...." She winked slyly, tucking a strand of dark hair behind one emerald earring.

"Oh, yes, all those candlelit dinners!" Camille chuckled. "Well, they worked. Oh, no, Rachael, no charge. Put your purse away. We've a lot to thank you for.''

''Nonsense, dear! I am sorry you had to sell Damask, though.... I just had lunch with Charles at his place—and he's positively a changed man! What with Jake settling down here and now Fern, well, I've never seen him so jolly. It's taken ten years off him. It would all be absolutely perfect if only you and Jake.... You know your mother and I were simply convinced you two would hit if off! It really is a shame that Annette's gotten her claws into him. Never did like that young lady. Too brash. When I got there, they were just leaving, and she was going on and on about how delighted she was that he'd bought Damask and how—''

''Who was just leaving? When?''

''Oh, well—'' Rachael flicked a glance at her gold watch ''—Jake and Annette. They were just driving off in his little car when I arrived. He told me they were going to Vancouver for the weekend. *Hmm,* I thought. *She already has him going away for weekends!* She works fast! She *is* fast. And you should have seen her outfit! Rather too much for a summer afternoon. I'm not blind. I know what men see in her. But Jake? I must say I was astonished—I always figured he had more class. Still, who knows with young folks these days. You, now, are just perfect for him, dear, and he's such a charmer I can't imagine why you don't like each other!''

As Rachael continued merrily on, Camille stoically finished refilling Wilson's bottle of Woodsmoke. Her eyes were a little glazed as she smiled the older woman out of the shop with instructions on where to find Fern—busily selecting her wardrobe to take to Toronto.

Once Camille was alone she stood staring frozenly at the beautiful garden beyond the shop windows, all abloom and sweet smelling, with the sun a warm golden glow over all, the loud heavy buzz of bumblebees vibrating in the air. It couldn't be true. It just couldn't be true that Jacob's urgent business was a weekend in Vancouver with Annette!

Had they made the arrangements to go last night, after dropping Greyson off at home...and before Jacob had met her at Damask? How could he go anywhere with Annette after last night? He'd said he loved her. Did he love Annette, too? She couldn't believe that words of love and physical unity meant nothing to him. Dammit. If only she hadn't chosen this morning to splurge on a hairdresser! Now he was gone, and there was nothing she could do. Maybe Rachael was mistaken....

Robbie thrust his head in the shop door at that moment. "There's a call for you from Greyson. Take it in the office. I'll watch the shop, but don't be long."

Automatically functioning, Camille went to the office to lift the telephone receiver. Greyson wanted to invite her to a barbecue that evening. In a daze, she agreed to go, then asked who was going to be there. Annette, maybe?

"Oh, no. She's off to Vancouver with her new heartthrob, your next-door neighbor, the professor."

CHAPTER EIGHT

IT WAS TRUE. Annette had told Greyson last night that she and the professor had planned a weekend together. Greyson had dropped her and her overnight cases off at Charles's this morning.

Camille felt as though the world had come to a sudden end. How could Jacob treat her this way—make use of her for a night and then toss her aside and go away with another woman. She was totally surprised. She had been so convinced of his sincerity...just as she'd been utterly convinced before Fredericton. If the weekend was aboveboard, why hadn't he written her a personal note explaining the situation, rather than giving mother a verbal message about ultimatums? Was the message, "You're okay, baby, but don't get any big ideas"? And now he owned Damask—what she had foolishly thought of as their house—and he could invite there whom he wished. One thing was clear. She was never going to set foot on that property again.

After having found heaven, Camille discovered a particular kind of hell. She went through all the mechanics of living, smiling when she was expected to smile, pretending everything was just fine, when she was made up of one big everlasting ache. Every part of her felt the pain of this second devastating rejection. She was totally baffled.

Jacob could be hesitant about getting too close to someone, so that when he did, he did a volte-face. Well, if he wasn't mature enough to know his own mind, if he changed his tune from one day to the next, if he couldn't bring himself to talk things out with her instead of administering these cruel unprovoked slaps, then she never wanted to see him again. Dear God, let Charles be different from his son!

Knowing Jacob would be back on Monday, at the barbecue Camille wheedled Greyson into agreeing to taking her fishing that day—all day. That way she would miss not only the professor's visit and the final signing over of Damask, but also Charles's coming to collect mother for their trip to Toronto. The less she saw of either father or son, the better. Her mother's anticipation only made her sick with worry.

Sunday evening she was in a haze of misery. Even Damask was no longer a place of refuge. She couldn't disappear down to the beach, either, to be soothed by the sound of the waves and the wide-flung space, having it all to herself. For Damask was only several hundred yards distant. She might bump into the new owner and Annette out for a stroll on the sands. Her misery was compounded by her feeling of being locked in; it was almost more than she could bear. She paced from one end of her bedroom to the other, knowing she had to get up early tomorrow morning to go fishing with Greyson, but was unable to sit still, much less lie down. She made yet another circuit, from the seaside windows back to those overlooking the compound.

If she leaned far out her window, Damask would come into partial view.... And as she leaned out she saw, through the trees, just barely discernible, a soft warm glow coming from the nearest second-floor room of the house—her grandparents' bedroom.

Camille's breath caught in her throat. Jacob was indeed back from Vancouver. For a wild moment, the urge to run all the way there to confront him was overpowering. She wanted to storm and rage and denounce him to his face. She wanted answers—and was already out on the landing when it struck her that, yes, Jacob was at Damask...but so might Annette be.

Camille returned to her room. One could screech at a man, but not while the other woman was present. And anyway, what was the point? He had made his choice. She would only make a bigger fool of herself by saying anything at all. He was home. He could come and talk to her—if he wanted to.

Leaning out her window again, she noticed the light in Damask was gone. He was probably sleeping blissfully right this minute, perhaps with Annette curled up at his side on the eiderdown, while she, the discarded lover, was in the midst of a nightmare. The uncaring wretch!

Pacing back to the far windows, she could not, for a moment, believe her eyes. The light in the clerestory was on. Again. Somebody was in there with the blinds drawn. Camille was out of her bedroom in a flash.

Racing along the uneven tarmac in her bare feet, holding up her pajama bottoms, she was not, really, even afraid. She was only bent on solving this mystery. The poodles, leaping along beside her, didn't seem to think there was any mystery, but only unending fun in a spree after dark.

Nearing the laboratory, Camille shushed them. There was no need for her to tiptoe, but she did anyway, around the corner of the lab, past the door, around to that one special pane of glass. Her heart was thudding. There, through that tiny hole in the blind, shone a wavering pencil-beam of light. She put her eye to the clear glass and peered through the tiny hole.

Until her eye adjusted to the change in light, everything inside was a blur of white and stainless steel. But out of the fog she could perceive a figure, and a few seconds later, she recognized the intruder. It was Jacob; her heart constricted at the mere sight of him. He was in his old T-shirt and jeans, supremely comfortable in this clinical environment. But it was the quiet careless elegance of him that captured her attention, that precipitated a rush of sensation she recognized only too well. It was the angle of his jaw narrowing from wide temples into his jutting chin that made her long to be cheek to cheek; it was the dull gleam of his straight, thick bronze hair under the lab lights that made her yearn to feel the texture beneath her fingers.

Somehow she wasn't all that surprised to learn Jacob was the mystery. No wonder he'd appeared to lose interest in the lab—he'd already been helping himself to it! The next instant, she felt very much like the fireball Robbie had described. Outraged that Jacob had the gall to appropriate their laboratory so cavalierly, she was set on wreaking vengeance on his head, when it occurred to her that it would be much wiser to let Robbie see this travesty of so-called friendship in action. No longer could he maintain she was picking on the professor!

But Camille stopped for a moment longer, too curious over what exactly Jacob was doing. The professor had a row of shallow trays arranged on the counter and, taking up a piece of what looked like letter paper—there was writing on it—cut three small pieces off the bottom before dipping each piece into one of the three trays. Now he had three small wet pieces of paper that he fished out with long tweezers. Letting the solutions drain off each, he pored intently over them, and appeared both dissatisfied and disgruntled by the results.

He was lighting a Bunsen burner. He could have the whole place going up in smoke! Tensely she watched as he turned down the flame until it was just a short blue glow. Lifting the first piece of paper, he wafted it to and fro above the concentrated heat, drying it slowly, evenly, carefully. Passing his hand over the flame, he turned it lower yet and held the piece of stationary over it. He was intent, absorbed. Just watching him, Camille sensed the paper was of the utmost importance.

When he stared in dawning joy at the heated scrap, his excitement was so acute she experienced a little of it vicariously. Her first thought was to find out what he was doing, not to rail at him for being there. But as if he felt he was no longer quite alone, he tilted his head to listen...and scanned the windows and the door. Camille jerked back guiltily. Then she considered just who should be feeling guilty and dashed away to pry Robbie from his bed.

Her brother called her a blighted lunatic and a raving insomniac—and those were his milder terms. His terms, when they arrived at back of the lab only to find all in darkness, were vitriolic. Snatching the key from the arbutus tree, he opened the lab and showed her that the blinds *weren't* drawn, adding that if she was determined to stay awake half the night, she was welcome to do it on her own. He stomped back to the house, sizzling mad.

Camille couldn't have been more irritated. If only Robbie hadn't taken so long to get out of bed! Now, after finding the lab exactly as they'd left it, he simply wouldn't listen to another word. She was rather astonished at Jacob's speed in covering up his tracks. The counter was bare, the trays gone—ah, the Bunsen burner! It was back in its clamp, but the spout was still warm. Robbie was convinced she was suffering from delusions, so that even if she thrust the warm spout at him, he wouldn't deem it proof. And where was Jacob? Probably halfway back to Damask.

But she was sure he would be using the lab again late at night. The sliver of light leaking past the clerestory blinds, visible only from the top floor of the cottage, would betray him. Camille was pretty certain the light could be seen from mother's bedroom as well as hers, but would mom have noticed it? Probably not, since it always came on so late. The next time it gave him away, she would set a trap for him. He had to be caught red-handed by both Robbie and mom. She had been completely discredited; no one would believe her idiotic-sounding stories. Stewing over the means of providing and triggering a trap, she closed up the lab, hid the key and rambled around the yard with the dogs.

What *was* Jacob using the lab for? Why the secrecy? What were those organizations under whose auspices he said he worked? Research...exactly what sort, she longed to know. Work with ancient ointments and unguents would scarcely prompt one to sneak around at night, surely. And for what express purpose had he been followed by that one spy from one end of the country to the other? Perhaps Jacob was involved in some politically motivated plot, or some Frankensteinian experiment. Oh, it was no wonder Robbie thought her absurd. She was! Nevertheless, something was going on, and she meant to find out what.

Maybe instead of apprehending the professor right away, she should observe him every time he used the lab. That way she was sure to get some clues, and once she had an idea what it was he was doing, she would have a better notion how to handle the situation, how to trap him. Having this new problem thus far solved, she went in to bed, finally tired out. Still she couldn't sleep.

She might have washed her hands of Jacob, but that didn't mean she could stop loving him. Now, on top of all her other concerns, there was his highly suspicious behavior! If she couldn't help falling in love with a bastard, neither could she help worrying about his actions. Frustrating though her reactions were, she couldn't simply be angry with him. She wanted to save him from doing himself harm by getting embroiled in questionable activities. Really, it was in her own best interests not to see him, not to go near him, except, of course, to perform spy duty at her peephole. At least she would be away fishing when he came tomorrow.

Setting off early in the morning after giving her mother a hug goodbye and entirely sincere wishes for an enjoyable trip, she climbed into Greyson's van. They began the drive to Port Renfrew. A fisherman friend of Greyson's lived there, so they were going to combine a visit with some angling. Port Renfrew marked the end of the West Coast Road. Beyond it was mile upon mile of fantastic coastal wilderness, the Pacific Rim, until about halfway up the island fishing villages of Ucluelet and Tofino interrupted the solitude. Between them stretched Long Beach.

The West Coast Road wasn't paved far past the tiny hamlet of River Jordan. Beyond, the gravel was rough with potholes from spring runoff, with twists and turns and all but perpendicular grades. Camille thought nothing of it. She was used to exploring the backwoods, and Vancouver Island was practically all backwoods but for a fringe of civilization along the south and east coasts. The road really did end abruptly in Port Renfrew. It ran through the town to the dock, and that was it.

On reaching their destination, Camille and Greyson enjoyed a relaxing day in the open air. By the time they set off for home, it was already late, and dark, for they had lingered so long—and so pleasantly—over a crackling fire by the shore, watching the sun sink into the Pacific, supplied with more fresh barbecued salmon than Camille could ever hope to eat—and she could put away a lot of salmon! When the fiery globe had completely disappeared behind the far waves, they had packed their impromptu camp back into the boat and chug-chugged down the inlet back to Port Renfrew. There they had lingered, too—over some very potent home brew. Greyson had only had half a glass, but she had finished her tumbler full...and was now feeling the effects of their long day. She could barely keep her eyes open.

She must have drifted off, for the first thing she noticed when she did open her eyes was that the van wasn't moving. Yawning and stretching and blinking she mumbled, "Where are we?"

There was no answer. Wide awake all of a sudden, she realized Greyson wasn't in the seat beside her, and turned to open her door just as it was opened for her. Greyson, smiling, handed her a steaming mug of coffee.

"You're up, eh, bright eyes?" He sipped from his own mug.

"Where are we?"

"Outside River Jordan."

"What time is it?"

"It's...midnight."

"What!" she gasped. "How long have we been here?"

"Half an hour."

"But why? Did something happen to the van?" She realized there was a small campfire just past him, beside the vehicle.

"Calamity Camille. No, it's simply a beautiful night. We've got a fire, an unlimited supply of coffee and—wait for it—marshmallows!"

"You idiot!" She giggled, sliding out of the seat. "But I'd love nothing better than to toast marshmallows by the light of the moon and watch the waves slide in!"

It was close to four in the morning when Greyson pulled up underneath the grape arbor. Feeling restored after a day of simply being herself—with someone who was not only a friend but, even better, a friend entirely uninvolved in her problems—had tilted her world back into some sort of focus. Waving goodbye, she was about to turn into the cottage when a thought stopped her, and she headed instead along the tarmac drive. When she realized there was indeed a pinpoint of light shining through that one window blind, she was glad she hadn't gone all the way upstairs first.

Leaning tiredly against the lab wall, she peeked through the hole. Jacob was seated on the far side of the counter. He didn't look too happy. He had his elbows on the counter and a hand at either temple, buried in his hair, and he appeared to be transfixed by the stainless steel of the counter top. A little farther down was a new contraption, what looked very much like a small portable sewing machine, closed up. It had a gray cover and snaps on either side to lock the top to the bottom.

When she glanced back at Jacob, he had his head up. He was seated directly underneath one of several lamps that hung down on long chains above the foot of the T-shaped counter. The planes of his face were cast in strong divisions of light and shadow. She stared, mesmerized, remembering that she had had a vague notion she'd seen him long before either Vancouver or Calgary. The notion was back, but strongly this time. Her attention was riveted on those distinctive features. Her whole being was concentrated on when...and how...and where....

Where! It was suddenly as clear as clear could be, and the revelation was staggering. She'd been seventeen—no, sixteen—so it was almost eight years ago. She had wanted to go to her boyfriend's high-school graduation dance. Her mother had vetoed the whole idea, declaring she was much too young to be present at what, she said, was sure to turn into a rowdy party. In protest, she had stormed out of the cottage to present her case to her father—and without warning had burst upon him in the laboratory before she realized he wasn't alone.

Then, as now, Jacob had been sitting at the counter, only on the other side. He'd been underneath the lamp. Eight years ago, but he still looked much the same. She'd been startled to find a visitor in the lab and had subsided in embarrassment. The men had both been surprised, too. In the interval of silence, Jacob had glanced from her tumbled curly locks to her father's white gold aureole, had looked back at her and smiled. "Your daughter, Dr. Beesley?"

"Er...yes." And hurrying her from the lab, Dr. Beesley had added, "Camille, this is a colleague of mine. Now, if you wanted to do something reasonable for a change, I'm sure your mother would be more reasonable, too! What is it this time?" He had walked with her back to the cottage, where her case had been settled so that, although she was allowed to go to the graduation dance, she had to be home by midnight. And because the dance had been a lot more important than a strange chemist in the lab, she had promptly forgotten all about her father's visitor.

Only now it occurred to her that dad hadn't introduced him, hadn't wanted her to linger in the laboratory. She hadn't set eyes on the stranger again until this March, when, in Vancouver, he'd seen her and Greyson coming out of the hotel room next to his. No wonder Jacob had stared after them as they walked to the elevator. He must have recognized her immediately—especially since mother had requested he "keep an eye on her." He knew all along she was his old colleague's daughter. And yet he'd told her he'd read the hotel register to discover her!

Jacob's interest in the lab and his presence here might well have something to do with her father. Perhaps they had been working on something together. Dad had spent an uncommon amount of time in the lab...and what, really, had he been doing?

Camille returned to the present to find Jacob look-

ing for an electrical outlet in which to plug his contraption—the cord came out of the top of the gray
box. There being no plug in his immediate vicinity,
he came around the counter closer to her, moved the
box so that it was dead center in front of her and
plugged the cord into a handy outlet just under the
counter top. Unsnapping the clasps on either side, he
lifted the high top of the box from the bottom and
laid it down flat. Puzzled, Camille nevertheless realized that whatever it was, it was *not* a sewing
machine.

Why, the bottom was a keyboard, and the top,
which he tilted up by resting its lower edge against the
keyboard, so that the interior was facing both him
and her, seemed solidly black. At that moment, a
flicker of light in the back caught her attention, and a
second later what appeared to be a miniature TV
screen blinked on it. Putting on his gold-rimmed
glasses, Jacob slid what looked like two records,
forty-fives still in their jackets, into the top on either
side of the TV screen. The pattern of light rapidly
changed, and little red lights on either side blinked on
and off. Camille thought, *it's a computer! A portable computer!*

Jacob was sitting in front of it, though a little to
one side, studying that letter paper again, which he'd
placed on the counter. She could see a portion of the
screen as he tapped the keys. Was he transferring the
writing into the computer? She was much too far
away to see the tiny type on the screen, but it didn't
seem to be in words, but rather in signs, symbols and
numerals. Mathematicians' language, if anything.

As he worked his blue mood faded; she could tell just by the set of his shoulders. He became intensely absorbed to the exclusion of everything but what that screen was telling him. She sensed his growing excitement. She simply couldn't tear herself away. Then, highly pleased with his results, he plugged another smaller box into the computer underneath the screen. As she watched, he picked up the lab telephone, dialed and placed the receiver onto the second smaller box, which was equipped with a telephone cradle. After he'd tapped several more keys, again the red lights blinked on and off; the screen flipped in rapid changes. Although she'd never seen anything like this before, it was clear what he was doing—transferring the information in his computer by telephone to some other computer waiting somewhere. Marveling at the miracles of modern science, Camille had to know what kind of information and where it was going.

After that operation was completed, when Camille was wishing he would finish for the night and go home to bed, he had yet another, greater surprise for her watching eye. He disappeared for a moment from her range of vision, coming very close to her window, then veering to her left. Straining to see him, she glimpsed only part of the case of bookshelves, filled with heavy perfumery tomes, next to the counter and against the wall of the lab that abutted the distillery. And then, right before her sleepy eyes, the bookcase swiveled open to form a doorway into—but it wasn't the distillery the swinging door led into.

She couldn't see much of what was beyond—what

she did see had her mouth sagging open: another brilliantly lighted laboratory. A veritable Disneyland of the most complex scientific equipment. A battery of machinery, rows and rows of colored lights and buttons, tubing and coils.... Camille rubbed her eyes, stretched her back and bent to peer some more.

All that equipment couldn't have been installed overnight, or in a couple of weeks. That secret lab must have been there all the time, with no one the wiser. Her father must have had it built when he'd renovated many, many years ago. Jacob certainly couldn't have conjured up a space between the lab and the distillery from the time he returned from Paris last December to now. Good heavens! Was that why he'd been so curious to know if any changes had been made to the lab? The secret lab...that wasn't for making perfume. That was for something altogether different. Her father must have been a lot more than a perfume chemist.

Jacob came briefly into sight before disappearing again into the secret lab. Camille stepped back a few paces to count the windows in the distillery. There were nine. Hurrying along the back of the building, she let herself into the office, through the warehouse and into the distillery, where she counted the windows again. Nine. Returning to her former position, she wondered why no one had ever noticed that while the lab wall should also be the wall of the distillery, there were a good many feet between the windows of the former and the latter. More feet than there appeared to be when one was inside one or the other, for the windows ran up against the walls.

Why had no one noticed? Probably because a person couldn't be in both rooms at once. And because the building was so familiar, she hadn't even thought to look for irregularities. It had always been there, and it always would be. The last, blasted place on earth she would have expected to find a sophisticated secret laboratory! Was that high barbed-wire fence hidden in the yew hedge not intended to protect their perfume formulas, then? Were the trained dogs doing more than guarding house and home? Because before Boogaloo and Razzmattaz, there had been two others. Perhaps only the safe was meant to hold the formulas secure, and all else was for. . . was for—Well, for whatever Dr. Darleah and Dr. Beesley were and had been involved in!

To say she was boggled would scarcely cover it. But surely her lovable father couldn't have had his fingers in either nefarious plots or Frankensteinian experiments. He must have been keeping something terribly important a secret for some good reason. With her whole heart she hoped that was it, for the idea that either the father she loved or the man she loved were—and had been—into something illegal or underhanded was abhorrent.

Jacob still hadn't reappeared. Watching myriad colored lights and dials and tape reels through the bookcase door was dull after only a minute. Camille gave up and trudged off toward the cottage and bed. The sun would be up soon; already the eastern sky was a pale shimmer of pearly gray. What should she do, she wondered, thoroughly bemused. Should she tell someone what she knew? Robbie would think she'd gone stark raving mad! Jacob would probably deny everything, and only he knew how to open that bookcase. Mom? She'd known how much time her husband had spent working—she must know a lot more than she had ever let on. "Puttering" was hardly plausible!

Yes, if she did tell anyone, mother would be the best bet. Maybe she already knew Jacob was making use of her husband's equipment. Maybe that was why she had wanted her offspring to accept the professor, so that access to the lab would be easier for him. And if her mother knew, then whatever was going on must be okay. Small wonder Jacob had been so angry at her own obstinacy.

CAMILLE GOT UP RATHER LATER than usual time Tuesday morning. She found her brother in the distillery, drawing off the end products of distillation. At the moment, it was rose water he was tapping from the condensers, which left the precious essential oil to be collected in the next step.

"Hi. Mom get away okay?" she said by way of greeting.

"You've finally turned up, have you?" He looked at her over his shoulder. "Yeah, I saw them off. So what happened to you? That's some fishing trip you went on! Greyson's reinstated, is he?"

"Not in the fashion you mean. I came home last night."

"The hell you did! Jake came over again last night, and we sat around waiting for you, getting drunk—"

"Drunk?"

"Well, not drunk, but we had a few. You sure weren't home when he left at two, and you weren't home when I got up at three-thirty to check! Why couldn't you have phoned or something? I was worried. I know it's stupid, but I was."

"I got home at four." Camille grinned cheekily. "We stopped and had a marshmallow roast on the way home. And it's none of your business, but I want you to know, anyway. We had a lovely time, but nothing happened and nothing's going to happen. What's past is past. Uh . . . Jake was over, eh?"

"He came over before mom left, of course, to pick up his deed. He said to tell you to make use of your willow any time you want. It's damn hard to tell with him, but I swear he was disappointed you weren't here. And as I said, he came again last night. He wasn't exactly flying high when he left, either." Robbie gave her a long shrewd look, which Camille didn't notice, for she was wondering somewhat grimly whether Jacob had the same view as Robbie—that hanky-panky was fine for men but not for women!

"Uh, what did you say, Robbie?"

"Why did you do it?"

"Do what?"

"Stay away all night, if nothing happened."

"It just turned out that way! And frankly, I wasn't in an all-fired hurry to get home. It felt nice to just sit on a log and stare at the moon and do absolutely nothing at all. D'you know how long it's been since we had a campfire on the beach? You know, in some ways mom's right. We sure don't have a lot of fun anymore."

"Fine, but how about the next time you decide to have some fun, you don't keep it all to yourself!"

"Aw, Robbie, you could have come fishing with us!"

"I didn't mean just me!"

Caught up short, Camille stared at him. "I—I don't know what you mean!" she retorted, and departed hastily.

She went directly to the office, locking herself in. Robbie would be busy for some time to come, and with mother away she was sure to remain undisturbed—she had some snooping of her own to do. Opening the safe, she riffled through the ledgers until she found the ones pertaining to years and years ago. Seven, six and five years, to be precise.

It wasn't long before she found what she was searching for. Monies, unexplained monies, deposited in the Beesley Farm bank account. Large amounts, too. And they were regularly deposited. Every month. So had her father been paid for his extra and secret work? It would seem that he had, for after his death, no more monthly deposits. That was why there had never been any shortage of cash while he was alive! They had sold less perfume than now, yet made four times the money.

Looking through more ledgers, Camille saw the bank balance had gradually dwindled and dwindled away during the past five years. The perfumery hadn't really been a paying proposition, as everyone supposed. Last fall, with father's savings all gone, that had become evident even to her and Robbie, though mom had known their true position all along.

That was probably why she'd tried to persuade them to let Charles buy a share of the perfumery, in hopes that he would not only keep them afloat, but also alter the running of their company to make it pay.

Now Camille dug into the recesses of the safe, pulling out all the old shoe boxes stuffed full of receipts. She was looking for canceled pay stubs, anything to give a hint about where those monthly deposits had come from. At last she found what looked like a company pay stub, the part employees retained when they deposited their checks. On it was the name Glendale Cosmetics, Ltd., Canada. That and the date and the amount, which matched the corresponding dated amount in the ledger.

With a little quiver of mingled fright and excitement, Camille dialed the registrar of companies in Victoria, not certain how much information was allowed to the general public. She asked the clerk for the address of Glendale Cosmetics, which she believed was a national company, but would they please check both the provincial and national listings? And it was urgent. Could they call her back as soon as possible? The rather bored young man said they might not call back until tomorrow or the next day. Very well, Camille replied. She was therefore astonished when hardly ten minutes later, she was informed no such company existed in Canada. And then the official—not the bored young man as before—wanted to know why she wanted to know. Making a hasty excuse, Camille hung up.

Dammit, she thought, *what am I prying into?* Why would that government official want to start asking her questions? She was a little shaken up. Should she tell Robbie everything right now? Or should she keep it under her hat a little longer and hope some good explanation would turn up? She decided to wait... and to keep her eyes and ears wide open.

Her brother was still occupied with collecting the essential oil from that morning's pickings, so Camille went to the lab next. There was no sign of its night visitor. She tried everything she could think of to make that bookcase swing open, but it simply would not budge. What she needed was another peephole, farther over to the left from the first one. Punching a small hole in the blind with a bodkin, she decided she had to be satisfied with that. *That* was when she remembered her father had kept a small handgun in the bottom drawer of the filing cabinet, the drawer that was never used. By accident she had discovered it. Her father had dismissed it casually by saying a friend had given it to him as it was supposed to be a collector's item, and while he hated guns, he didn't like to throw it away. It was still there under a mass of odds and ends. And it was loaded. Replacing it with trembling fingers, Camille didn't know what to think in the light of all these new facts.

Jacob didn't come around that day. She wasn't surprised—he'd been up all last night. She was glad, too, that she didn't see him. Coming face to face with him was not a prospect she relished. She fervently wished he would take his Annette and go back to Paris, and conduct his secret experiments there! Robbie must have been mistaken about his disappointment over her absence—Jacob could have been disappointed about anything. Maybe over his week-end. Maybe Annette hadn't lived up to her outward allure. Maybe his work in the lab Sunday night had been fruitless. And what did she care about his disappointment, when she knew only pain?

THAT NIGHT, she'd barely reached the back of the laboratory when the door suddenly opened and Jacob slipped out. He was whistling softly. Camille was annoyed to see how fast the poodles came to him. He patted them both and, issuing a quiet command for them to heel, glided away around to the front of the workshop. Her heart in her throat, Camille followed, being very careful to hang far enough back. Hoping the dogs wouldn't give her away by capering delightedly over to her, she tiptoed past the door and peeked around the corner. Jacob was opening not the small gate in the hedge, but the large one for farm traffic.

A covered truck—with no headlights on—rolled in. Camille shivered in her bare feet. At least she wasn't in her pajamas; she was properly attired for a night of lurking around in the dark—all in black, with a black scarf tied over her hair.

She had to make a sudden dash for the rear of the building when it became evident that Jacob, the poodles and the truck were all coming straight toward her. Hugging the rear wall of the building, she cautiously edged over to peek around. Her heart was thumping so loudly, she was terrified it would give her away. The truck backed up toward the lab door. Two men came out of the cab, and two more out of the covered box. She expected the dogs to bark at least, but superbly well behaved, they sat at Jacob's feet, panting. She ground her teeth.

"Dr. Jacob Darleah?" one man in the forefront said quietly, holding out his hand. As Jacob nodded and shook hands the fellow continued, "Sergeant Peterson, at your service. These are Corporals Eaburn, McIntyre and...." Camille didn't catch the last name.

Sergeant? Corporal? What were they? Soldiers? If so, they weren't in any sort of uniform, but dressed rather like herself, in dark unobstrusive colors. Her heart rate slowed a bit. At least they didn't appear to be murderous criminals. They could be soldiers gone bad, but she was relieved nonetheless.

"I appreciate your coming," Jacob murmured—she could barely hear him and had to strain her ears and hold her breath to be able to do so. "I realize Mounties don't usually act as delivery boys, but they're getting a little too close for comfort."

Who was getting too close for comfort? The spies who had been following him?

"We've got tabs on all of them," she heard the sergeant say. "Memorize my number. Call me anytime, day or night, the second you see or hear anything. We'd put surveillance on you, but that could give you away—"

"No, absolutely not!" Jacob agreed. "Too risky. My cover's tight, anyway."

Now she lost their conversation completely, for the three corporals had started to unload some big, obviously very heavy thing, swathed in dark material, from the back of the truck. Lowering it on a dolly, they wheeled it through the lab door Jacob opened. Slick and fast, everyone was inside the darkened room, the door shut. Camille raced to her peephole, the poodles at her heels now. She ordered them to be quiet as she saw two threads of light appear through the blind from both holes.

Unfortunately, she couldn't hear any more of what was said. As Jacob and the sergeant stood talking, the other three uncovered their burden, to reveal another piece of most peculiar-looking equipment. Then they left, going the way they'd come—no lights, very little sound, shutting the gate behind them, the operation accomplished. Returning to her peephole, Camille was vexed to see the bookcase was already open. Jacob and the thing were nowhere to be seen. He came into sight for a moment, moving around inside the secret lab. After a while she left her post. She might as well go to bed and get a good night's sleep, since the excitement seemed to be over for the night.

But she was a good deal relieved as she slipped silently back to the cottage. If the men in the truck were policemen—special detectives—then all must be okay. Provided they weren't cops on the take. But the conversation she'd overheard hadn't sounded threatening. No, it sounded as if Jacob was involved in something of import, and the RCMP would guard him, except that might betray that he wasn't a simple professor of ancient elixirs. And since the Mounties were involved, it probably meant he was working on some sort of government project. Could Glendale

Cosmetics be a government cover? Aha! No wonder the official who called back on behalf of the registrar of companies had pressed her for her name.

She hadn't realized until now quite how anxious she'd been over the goings-on in the lab. Jacob might still be a bastard, but at least he was a decent one! Her heart felt almost light as she slipped into the cottage and up the stairs to her room.

The following day, Robbie hired six more pickers and another gardener. Again, Jacob put in no appearance. Despite her earnest hope not to have to face him, Camille couldn't help feeling piqued. If possible, her hurt deepened. Obviously, he must have had a fine time with Annette, because he certainly displayed not the slightest interest in her anymore! Even Robbie remarked on his absence.

"You haven't gone over there and fought with him, have you?"

"That doesn't even deserve an answer!"

"Knowing you! What's the matter with you, anyway?"

"Now what do you mean?" she snapped.

"You've been damn hard to live with lately! One minute you're pie in the sky, the next you're moping around or staring off into space. Any more bad dreams?"

"Bad dreams?"

"You know, seeing lights! Imagining dad's back in the lab."

"No more bad dreams, Robbie," Camille replied mildly, then started laughing. And laughed and laughed, struck by the ridiculousness of the whole thing. What would Robbie say if only he knew what went on in the lab late at night! He gave her a disgusted look.

"You've flipped your blooming lid, I swear!" He stalked away from her, impatient with her obtuseness.

Now that they had more staff, the pressure on them was lifted a bit. Robbie once more took over making the master batches of perfume formulas that very afternoon, which left Camille time to work at her organ. They were both in the lab when they heard an ominous rumble, a loud sheering hiss, and a split second later, a compressed pop. They'd both heard that string of sounds before.

"Oh, hell!" Robbie cried. "The boiler!"

Dropping what they were doing, they ran pell-mell to view the disaster. Camille was first out the lab door, and she crashed into Elaine.

"Hi! I'm back! Don't—"

"Not now, Elaine!" Camille gasped, charging past her, Robbie behind. They didn't even pause to close the lab door behind them.

The huge old boiler, which produced steam to mingle with the fresh rose petals, had overheated, rupturing itself. Not only were there inches of scalding water all over the distillery floor, but also a little fire was flickering underneath the apparatus. While Robbie grabbed an extinguisher and splashed through the water in his sandals, Camille snatched up another cylinder to follow. Luckily the water cooled rapidly. Hopping from one foot to the other, she managed to administer a telling blast of white foam to her side of the boiler. The fire was out in moments.

Robbie, wiping the perspiration off his brow, rolling his eyes at her, exclaimed, "What next, eh?"

"And people are convinced making perfume is romantic!" Camille blew some curls out of her eyes.

While Robbie attended to the extinguishers, making sure they were prepped for another emergency, she flung wide the heavy double doors and, taking a long broom, began sweeping the water out.

"I'll have to call for a new boiler—let's hope we can get one by tomorrow morning. Thank heavens we've got the money to buy it!" Robbie was already at the telephone as he spoke.

Camille agreed, but since the money to pay for a new boiler came from selling Damask, she didn't agree too heartily. She'd forgotten all about Elaine until the other woman appeared in the doorway, stepping between the runnels of steaming water pouring out.

"Lord!" she exclaimed.

"Hi. Sorry, but, er. . . ." Camille stared. Elaine looked simply marvelous! Svelte and slender and very pleased with herself. "Wow! Don't you look good!"

"Oh, you think so?" Elaine asked rhetorically, preening, and glanced at Robbie to judge his reaction. But he was busily arguing on the phone. "I've just come back from you-know-where—that place I was telling you about in the Gulf Islands. Fabulous place! Much better than any dance class! Whatever happened?"

"Oh, nothing much," said Camille. "The boiler burst."

"Well, he promised me something by tomorrow morning, but I'm not sure exactly what!" Robbie hung up, adding most unflatteringly to Elaine, "Yikes! What happened to you?"

That night Camille was back at her post in her slinking-around-at-night getup. Jacob was keying information into his little computer again, then feeding that data into the telephone, as he'd done the night before last. Next he started to search the perfume lab—the secret room was locked away behind the bookcase. He meticulously checked each heavy tome in the bookcase. He checked the library shelves jammed with jugs of essences and tinctures. He checked the filing cabinet . . . and came upon the gun. Gingerly he replaced it. He went through all the drawers, looked underneath them, poked through the glass-fronted cupboards. At last he gave up and, frowning, stood in the middle of the lab, gazing around as if he thought he might have missed looking in the magic spot. Ultimately, in frustration, he raked his hands through his hair, ruffling it very attractively.

Camille, cold and stiff and cramped, watched him snapping his computer back together. Switching off the lab lights, he plunged the place into darkness. She barely had the presence of mind to drop down on the ground when she realized he was rolling up the blinds. She lay there for some time, but at last daring to get up, she carefully circled the building, to see him vanishing down the driveway past the yew-hedge enclosure.

Her throat felt constricted. She swallowed hard to ease the overwhelming urge to run after him. To ask him not about his secretive work but why—why he preferred Annette to her. To beg him to hold her and kiss her and make love to her for the remainder of the night. She was so lovesick, she saw no hope of recovery. Why didn't he drop by to visit anymore? Robbie had gone to see him earlier that evening, so if, by any chance, the professor was curious about her fishing trip—if he even knew about it—Robbie would have been only too happy to tell him what had happened. Or that nothing had happened. But he didn't care.... Camille bit down on her lip and took herself off to her lonely cold bed.

Thursday morning she found the first reorder in their mailbox, and that truly gave her pleasure. She wafted it under Robbie's nose on returning home, finding him and a pipe fitter occupied with the new boiler.

"Whoopee!" She laughed. "Look what I found! It's from Winnipeg, of all places!"

He clapped her on the back after he'd read it and seen the amount of cases wanted. "You must have charmed 'em, kid! And this is only the start! I feel it!" In a mood of great elation, he swept her into his arms and waltzed her around the concrete pad, while the pipe fitter, crouched underneath the boiler, stared at them. "We've done it! Hot diggety! Charles—go to hell!"

After they'd both calmed down a bit and had thoroughly discussed the implications of this first bona fide reorder, he added as an afterthought, while he was on his way back to the boiler and she was on her way to prepare lunch, "Oh, Jake came by while you were gone."

Camille gripped the closest thing to hand, the veranda post. She schooled her voice to coolness, "Oh...? What did he want?"

Robbie shrugged. "Nothing in particular, I guess," and strode away. "Hey! Please don't make another omelet!"

After an inspired lunch of a huge chef's salad and garlic toast, Camille squarely faced the thought that had tempted her ever since her brother had told her about the professor's morning visit. Hadn't he said, on getting his deed, that she should feel free to make use of her willow? Well, what if she went and sat under it for a while...? Really, it was craven of her to want him so much. But maybe if they could talk... and she could always say she'd only come to find out what he was doing in the lab at night—which was, of course, a major concern....

Dashing upstairs to change into a more becoming ensemble than jeans and T-shirt, she paused long enough to run lip gloss over her mouth and dab on the fresh clean fragrance of Lavender Mist. She had to hurry. She was in danger of losing her conviction and remaining, cowardlike, at home.

Once on the beach she dallied, overturning clam and abalone shells. She found some limpets and collected a handful of tellens, only to throw the tiny pink shells away again. She looked for white quartz and red jasper and greeny chert along the edge of sand, picked around in the driftwood, watched some mallards glide by and saw a blue heron standing motionless on one long stilt of a leg. What, exactly, should she say to the professor? Lovely day, what? How was your weekend in Vancouver? Camille sighed ruefully. She wished she'd never set eyes on him.

In spite of all her procrastinating, she arrived at the foot of the first flight of marble stairs before she had any sort of speech rehearsed. With an inward quiver of apprehension, she gazed up at the house. Peeling paint and all, it looked so pretty with the roses rambling up the veranda, against the backdrop of Gary oaks and pines and arbutus trees, wild broom and tangled rose briars, bracken and sword fern....

She started up the stairs. As soon as she reached the willow in the bend, she saw Jacob coming down the steps toward her. Her throat closed, and it seemed her heart stopped beating—in his tawny eyes was no welcome. Automatically her chin went up. She stared levelly back at him until he stopped in front of her.

"I came to take you up on your offer." She ran a long slender wand of the willow through her fingers. "I've been neglecting my tree."

"It's my tree, and the offer's canceled."

Stung, Camille stared at him, wide-eyed. She could scarcely believe his cold calculating tone. What right had he to be angry with her? What damnable right did he have! Her chin went up several more degrees, and her coffee-dark eyes snapped with indignation. "Oh, I see." Her voice was icy. "Now that you have the deed and the sale is final, you renege. I should have known better than to take you at your word."

"What the hell did you come here for?" The un-welcoming gaze blazed into a tigerish yellow fire.

She stared at him for a startled moment longer, then turned her face from him. She couldn't flee. For a long terrible moment she could do nothing and, in further distress, felt the dreadful prickle of tears behind her eyes. Never in her wildest imaginings had she considered he would treat her like this.

"Answer me!" Wrapping his hand around her upper arm, he spun her to face him. Gazing up at his set face, she detected yet another new side to the professor, enraged and reckless besides.

She wrenched her arm free and slipped quickly out of reach underneath the sun-spangled green tent of the weeping willow, meaning to make good her escape by a shortcut slither down to the beach. She couldn't believe how he'd taken her in, made her think he was the most wonderful person on earth. From the most tender overflow of love to this utter callousness! His attitude was a complete reversal, by God, and she was having no more of him!

She cried out as he caught her. Pulling her back from the bank, he yanked her farther underneath the shelter of the willow boughs and into his arms. As her lips opened to unleash a spate of outrage, his mouth closed down upon them, impassioned, desirous, searing the rose-petal softness with heat. His hands and arms strained her against him so that every male contour was pressed into her supple form, bringing the clearest memories of intimacy back to her in an inward incandescent rush. Sweet lassitude followed. She couldn't pretend not to love him, neither did she want to. Her taut body molded against the sinewy hardness of his thighs, and hips and torso melted into a sudden and seductive invitation.

His chin was raspy against the smooth creamy skin of her throat. His mouth pursued its hungry, devastating course inch by luscious inch, at his leisure. Hands hugging her hips, he held her against the sensuous swaying of his, imbuing the very air around them with such sheer sexuality that Camille felt afloat in it. Their green-and-gold-dappled bower was a secluded haven, and even if there had been strollers on the beach, the two would have remained unnoticed. Brushing his face into the tousle of her hair, he nibbled and teased her earlobe, ran his tongue along the pale pink shell, and while holding her still, added a line of kisses up underneath her jaw, tipping her head farther back until his lips hovered over hers. Then one of his hands slid between their bodies. Nimble fingers had three of her buttons undone, before she stopped him with a hand like a vise around his wrist.

His fingers tightened in mute reply, pulling the flimsy material taut across one breast, revealing the perfection of its round comely shape...and his glance flickered up. The amber eyes were aglow, but not with a warm burn, and hers mutely met his challenge with a deadly smoldering I-dare-you-to-go-one-step-further look.

His fingers relaxed. He dropped his hands away

and stepped back from her. The hot sleepy summer afternoon felt cold against her skin where he had touched her. She felt the pain of withdrawal—but she didn't want what he had to offer. She felt a little like the waves below them. He was the rock upon which she had hurled herself, dispersing in a million teardrops. She shouldn't have come, she knew now. In the midst of her tempestuous feelings, his eyes, now cool, and his calm, contained demeanor were brought even more sharply into contrast.

With a goading half smirk, he said offhandedly, "Why don't you get lost?"

And her temper, already teetering in dangerous imbalance, bounded right out of control. She'd never met anyone who could so profoundly antagonize her. "You abject toad!" she snapped.

"Ah... but toads turn into princes."

"That'll be the day! And it'll be a cold day in hell before you lay another finger on me!"

"I won't apologize for taking what was offered."

Camille raised her hands in disgust. "You may be some sort of a genius, but as far as I'm concerned you're about as swift as a dinosaur!"

"I've never had time to waste on women, and as pleasant as it is to play with you, Camille, I don't have time for you, either. I have much too much to do. My work has always been a lot more interesting than dealing with endless frivolity."

Her hands clenched into fists at her sides at his disdainful tone. "Am I to take it I'm a frivolous doll you picked up to play with, to entertain yourself for a few hours? Thank you for being so graphic! So very concise! Suddenly everything is clear—why you didn't tell me who you were and why you shoveled manure and why you wrapped mom around your little finger! Why you want her to marry Charles and why you wasted your precious time escorting me around Montreal. Why you had to have Damask...and why you told me you loved me! It was all for your crummy work, whatever the hell it is! You, professor, are a stinker. A real honest-to-God, down-in-the-dirt stinker!'' She whirled away from him.

"You come back here!"

She turned to face him like a cornered animal, a slinky cat, tooth and claw primed under the velvet, her torment burning through to flush her skin and render her eyes a depthless lambent black. "I'm getting lost! And as far as you're concerned, professor, *I am lost!*''

She was gone in a flash. And she didn't stop running for some distance. Then she slowed, panting, stopped and glanced over her shoulder to ascertain that she was alone on the beach. She buttoned up her blouse right to the very top with trembling fingers. Pressing her hands over her palpitating heart, she gulped in the summery salty air, trying to get a grip on herself. She was burning up. She could never return home in this state. Kneeling on the sand, Camille scooped up handfuls of cool crystal water to bathe her face.

Robbie, when she found him about an hour later in the lab, looked about as bad as she felt. Catching her breath in alarm, she asked directly, "What's happened now?''

His face was ashen. "The formula for Island Rose.... It's gone.''

CHAPTER NINE

CAMILLE GAZED AT HER BROTHER uncomprehendingly, her brow wrinkling. "What do you mean, it's gone?"

"It's gone! Disappeared. Vanished. And, yes, I've looked everywhere. I was working on it yesterday afternoon—when the boiler blew up. I thought I'd left it on the counter.... I don't remember putting it back in the safe. And today, when I went to finish the master batch after lunch, no formula. It's gone. The goldarned thing is gone! I think I'm going to be sick."

"Oh," Camille whispered, closing her eyes. "The first time mom leaves home for more than two days, and we lose the most important perfume formula we have! I think I'm going to be sick, too. Without that formula...."

Robbie nodded. "Without that formula we're bust. We've got the packaged stock, the aging vats and that's all, and no way to make more." He raised desperate eyes to her stricken face. "I must have misplaced the thing, but I'll be damned if I can find it! And wouldn't you know it, now the reorders start. If we can't deliver...."

"Oh," she moaned again. The world was coming

apart at the seams; she was convinced of it. Things just kept going from bad to worse and worse. "You've looked everywhere?"

"Everywhere! I've turned the place upside down! It's gone, gone, gone! What could I have possibly done with the thing?"

Her brother was shouldering the responsibility, yet she wasn't so sure it was his fault at all. "Maybe it was stolen."

"What? Don't be crazy! There was nobody around the place to steal it!"

Oh, no? She thought, *what about the professor?* Camille pulled up a stool to the counter and sat down beside Robbie, placing her chin in her hands and staring fixedly at some point in space. If Robbie had left the formula in the lab rather than returning it to the safe, then the formula would have been on the counter when Jacob came to work here last night. And today, it was gone.

But why would he want to steal it? Camille pondered the situation. Fact: Jacob wanted, and needed, the perfumery because of the secret lab. Fact: he was helping Fern and Charles on the road to matrimony to ensure that if he didn't get the perfumery one way, he would get it another. Fact: with the sale of Damask, the Beesleys were no longer in dire need of funds, so buying into the perfumery was no longer quite so viable for Charles and Jacob. But he needed Damask, for it was so close by, and he could easily come and go unnoticed. So with Charles cozying up to Fern in the forefront, maybe stealing the formula was meant to bring a little selling pressure to bear on them from the rear. Jacob knew how fundamental the formulas were, especially Island Rose, to the success of the family business.

Well, it did sound somewhat farfetched, but these days nothing would surprise her.

And she still had one matter to clear up with the professor—his unorthodox and unsanctioned use of their lab. He wasn't getting away with that scot-free, even if he was halfway to discovering the cure for cancer! He had just better be working on something damnably important, or else she would kick him out of the lab altogether, and change the lock—he must know about the spare key in the arbutus tree. This missing formula was just the sort of thing she'd been waiting for to trigger the confrontation. She wouldn't confront him on his property, where he had the advantage. She would wait until he ventured onto hers, then she would catch him at a double disadvantage. If she could string him high, she would! He was inhuman, using people left, right and center for his god—his work!

Robbie shifted on his stool. "What are we going to do, Camille?"

"A piece of paper covered in plastic doesn't vanish into thin air. I have my suspicions.... I'll let you know what I turn up. In the meantime, keep your eyes peeled, don't say anything to anybody—you haven't, have you?" He shook his head dismally. "Good. And whatever you do, don't let anyone in or near the lab. Handle the other three formulas as if they were gold bars. If one was stolen—and it might have been—the thief could be on the lookout for the others. If he got them, we'd really be in a fine pickle!''

Two seconds later, having gone to her organ, she exclaimed, "What's this?" holding up a sheet of paper encased in clear plastic.

"I don't know. Isn't it yours? I couldn't figure out what it was, so I put it there. I thought maybe it was the new perfume you're working on.''

She stared perplexed at the heading, Formula. Reading down, she could make no sense of what seemed to be a code of some sort, a strange mixture of letters, numbers and symbols, arranged rather like their perfume formulas were, items listed one below the other. "It's not mine. I've never seen it before, but this is the type of plastic page cover we use—and look. The plastic's worn and scratched, just as it was on the Island Rose formula. Do...do you suppose the formula was in here, and somebody slipped it out and put this in instead?''

"Why would anyone do that? C'mon!" protested her brother impatiently.

He was too concerned about the missing formula to worry about this document or why it was in their lab. Camille, however, wondered whether it belonged to Jacob. Maybe it was some of his work that he'd inadvertently left behind last night. Aha! Another thing she could use against him—and it must be his. Who else skulked around inside their lab? Or had he meant to leave it behind in place of the Island Rose formula, meaning to confound them? She slipped it in her drawer underneath her other notes.

Camille tried to will evening and night to come

faster than usual. But the late-spring twilight took its own sweet time, lingering on and on in a gorgeous panoply of mauve and violet and pink and fuschia threaded through with vivid gold. It seemed to take forever for the sky to turn from apple green to peacock to soft royal blue, and from there to fade to India ink. Tonight the stars seemed to want to appear one at a time.... At last the moon coasted into sight, a mother-of-pearl sickle.

The closer the time came for her confrontation with Jacob the more tense Camille became, until it seemed every nerve in her body was tightly wound into compacted coils. She sat with her brother on the front-porch steps discussing, from every possible angle—except her own—the disappearance of the formula and what they would do about it, what they could do about it. Robbie tentatively observed, "Well, if it doesn't turn up, if it was stolen—after all, it is worth a lot of money—should we bring in the police?"

"Er, let's wait and see.... Come on, Robbie, no point in sitting here stewing. We'll think better after a good night's sleep."

As soon as her brother was in bed, Camille went to her room to change into her lurking attire. Last on was the black silk scarf tied over her hair—she meant to surprise the professor, pounce upon him unsuspected. Then she waited for the light to appear in the clerestory of the lab.

The second the light flashed on, she was heading for her door. Out of the house and through the soft warm freshness of the night she hurried, along the tarmac, into the compound, around to the back of the workshop building. There were two tiny pinpoints of light shining out into the darkness. She'd just managed to wiggle between the rhododendron shrubs and put her eye to one of her peepholes, when the lights inside went out. *Oh, no,* she thought, annoyed. She specifically wanted to walk in on him while he was busy in the lab.

A shiver chased over her skin. The lilac bush five or six feet to her right began to tremble and shake. Was there someone else spying on Jacob? Was it *the* spy? He would have seen her coming. Was he coming now to pounce on her?

Biting down on her lip to stop from screaming or making any noise at all, Camille eased down to sit on her heels, hidden in among the lush leaves and flowers of the shrubs, her terror overwhelming. Her skin was frozen into goose bumps; she didn't even dare breathe. Straining to see through her leafy covering, straining to see into the deep shadowy gloom, she saw nothing at first...but heard a stealthy rustle—could it be a raccoon? A deer? There were many deer on the island, though those that inhabited the fringes of civilization were fairly tame.

The professor, brushing lilac blossoms from his hair, disengaged himself from the bush and, looking first left then right, began to tread lightly toward where she crouched.

Camille was too astonished to move. So that was how he got in and out of the lab—there was a secret entrance! Flabbergasted by yet another unknown aspect of their modest lab, she held herself absolutely rigid as he passed her by and continued along the back of the building. What was he up to? Was he leaving for the night? She began to uncurl from her position. When he had disappeared around the corner of the warehouse, she stepped out after him, her bare feet making no sound over the cushion of grass. At the corner she cautiously peered around.

He was standing underneath the walkway by the office door with the poodles happily watching him. He had taken a ring of keys out of his pocket and was trying key after key in the office door. Was he about to return the Island Rose formula? Why? Ah, but she could catch him at it—better and better!

At last one of his keys clicked open the door. He slid inside, shut and locked it behind him. Camille slunk back to the office's rear window. Grasping the window ledge, she raised herself to peek inside. What she saw had her eyes widening in protest. He had the medicine cabinet open, and with the aid of his pencil-beam flashlight, the light further shaded by his hand, he was spinning the dial of the safe as if he knew the combination. Anger bubbled within her. Before her eyes he hit the trick switch, swung open the first door and went on to unlock the second. How could he know how to open their safe unless he'd been informed...by Robbie? No, Robbie wouldn't go that far in trusting their neighbors. Neither would mom give out such details. It must have been her father who had, years ago, passed on the combination. But why?

That was what she meant to discover, and very shortly. To pounce on him with his hands in their safe was just as good as pouncing on him in the lab. But he'd locked the outside door behind him—which meant she would have to enter the office through the warehouse. She crept around the corner, through the walkway and down the front of the building. They had a spare distillery key wedged in the sill of the distillery's seventh window across. Retrieving it, she let herself into the huge room, shivering a little at its hushed spooky darkness. Any number of spies could be sheltered behind the tanks, the condensers, the brand-new and gleaming boiler.... Out of habit she tiptoed toward the inner warehouse door. Opening it slowly to prevent its telltale squeak, she slipped inside and tiptoed on toward the connecting office door.

She had her fingers on the knob when a hand clamped over her mouth and a steely arm whipped around her, pinning her arms to her sides, crushing her ribs and forcing the breath from her body. The attack was so sudden that for an instant she could do nothing. But then self-preservation took the upper hand, and she wriggled and squirmed like a wild thing, biting the palm pressing her lips into her teeth, clawing and scratching at whatever came to hand, kicking and twisting and wrenching against her assailant. He, ten times stronger, had all he could do to keep her silent and within his determined grasp.

A hand accidentally came in contact with her breast, stopped to settle in surprise around the firm upthrusted swell...moved across to find the other and test its soft curves. She saw her opportunity, and while he was still occupied, she viciously bit the hand across her mouth, doubly incensed that not only was she being assaulted, but now her female shape was being intimately checked out! If only she could scream. Jacob was just on the other side of the door!

The intruder swore in pain, yanking his hand away to free her mouth. As he did so the scarf was tugged off her head, and all her creamy curls spilled out. She, panting and gasping, gathered breath to scream.

"Camille!" came the professor's stunned voice from above her head. "What the hell are you doing here?"

She stopped all movement abruptly, then went limp once more, collapsing weakly against him. A ragged whimper left her lips. "Oh," she panted, "I thought I was going to be dead in two minutes, and it's *you*! Only you!" She gulped long energizing drafts of sweet night air.

Now the arms that had imprisoned her imprisoned her in another fashion, gathering her against him as if he meant to absorb her into his very being, protective and cuddling and gentle. "Dammit, I hope I didn't hurt you!" he murmured anxiously. "I thought you were...were— What the devil are you doing here?"

"Don't you think *I* should be asking that question?" she asked tartly, her equilibrium somewhat restored. "What the devil are *you* doing here, Jacob?" She denied herself the comfort of his body, recognizing the instantaneous tangible chemistry between them as a dire warning. The scene under the weeping willow that afternoon was too clearly and harshly engraved in her mind for her to be that close to him without flinching away. For the second time she attempted to wriggle out of his clasp. Her futile love was a supreme physical agony while his arms were around her. And how could she have a proper confrontation, wrapped in his embrace, his mouth within kissing distance? Planting her hands on his chest, she pushed firmly. "Let me go!" Her low tone was vehement.

"Camille—" He attempted to retain her.

"Blast you, Jake!" His hard body against her had her bones dissolving.

"Just one quick kiss..." he whispered, capturing her mouth with his. A lean brown hand sought her breast. Sensitive and tantalizing, the fingers molded the rounded swell. Her anger burning into passion, she curled her hands into fists against his chest, not to punch but to keep them from clasping him and caressing him and holding him to her. But he could feel the response in her, the sweet heat of desire conveyed on lips that tried not to kiss him back. He took immediate advantage, forcing her arms from between them and pressing her more intimately against him. The urgent contact weakened her resolve further. She was trembling within, her need a conflagration—if she just loved him enough, would he begin to love her? Surely there was some hope if he could hunger for her as he now did, his hot mouth teasing a reply from her lips, his searching touch removing the barriers her mind had flung up. Memories of divine physical satisfaction in his arms robbed her of cool judgment. Her being craved fulfillment. She wanted loving and only he could satisfy that want.

Whereas this afternoon she'd had the willpower to

refuse him, now, after the initial shock and relief of their meeting in the stillness of the night, with hope taking the place of caution, there was no hand to stop his pursuit. Loosening every button of her shirt, he brushed the black material away, to run his lips and tongue along the line of an exposed white shoulder. His sharp teeth nibbled at the curve of her throat. Her toes curled on the cold concrete floor.

"But Jacob," she whispered.

Sliding his hands underneath the shirt, around her bare waist and up her back, he held her tautly to him. His mouth covered hers again, putting an abrupt halt to any protests. The ardent demands of that ravishing mouth seduced all rational thought from her head. Her fingers entwined in the tawny hair; her body clung to him. Then he started another long, slow journey down her throat, again taking advantage of her response. His stimulating desirous mouth continued over her silky flesh to harden the tips of her breasts, and as he sank down in front of her, his lips burned a downward path to the waistband of her jeans.

"Oh, Jacob. . . ." Her faint voice quavered as his fingers searched out her belt buckle. "Yes, Jacob. . . ." The distillery was in deepest quiet; her shortened breath was loud in her ears. Already he had the buckle unfastened, and his fingers slid inside her waistband to open the button.

"Stop!" Her hands clutched at his. "No! Not here. We can't! I won't!" She scarcely knew what she was saying. "I'll scream if you don't stop. I swear I will!" It had suddenly occurred to her that perhaps he was using her once more. Perhaps it wasn't only desire that prompted him, but the need to distract her. He shouldn't even be here, let alone be making love to her! "You'll be sorry!" she warned, angry with herself, trying to pry his fingers away, her breast heaving in distress.

Groaning, he rose, removing his hands to place them on his waist. "Now why—"

"I'm asking the questions!" she snapped, fully remembering the afternoon's bitter words. She clutched at her shirt, attempting to close the buttons. "Just what were you doing with your hands in our safe?" An avenging angel, she faced him squarely, the light of battle shining from the dark pools of her eyes.

"Well, I . . . . Well, I . . . ."

"Yes?" she mocked. "You'd better start talking, Jacob—and fast!"

He brushed a hand through his hair, sighing exasperatedly. "I was looking for your Island Rose formula."

"Don't give me that! You took it last night. Were you returning it? Why did you take it in the first place? What were you intending to do with it?"

He stared. "Why would I break into your safe to look for it if I already had it?"

"You mean you . . . don't have it?" She swallowed, feeling an upsurge of dismay.

"No. Why would you think I have it?"

"But you must! You're the only one who could have it! It's gone! Don't you understand? Our only copy of the formula has vanished, and if you didn't steal it—'' she was trembling, horrified, her hurrying fingers stilled ''—who did?''

''What do you mean it's gone?'' He appeared to be as upset as she felt, Camille noticed dejectedly. ''It can't be!''

''Oh, yes, it can, and it is.'' She explained as much about its disappearance as she and Robbie knew, ending with, ''So you must have it!''

''I don't, Camille. I looked for it last night. I turned your lab inside out. That's why I opened the safe tonight, thinking you must keep all your formulas in there. I found the other three, but not Island Rose.''

''Oh,'' she moaned softly, her disappointment falling on her hopes like a ton of bricks. ''Oh, I was sure you'd stolen it and put the fake in it's place!''

''Well, thanks! On top of all my other sins, now I'm a thief!'' Abruptly he grasped her arm. ''The fake? What fake? What are you talking about?''

She told him about the plastic page cover she was certain had protected the Island Rose formula, adding sarcastically, ''You mean you didn't see the fake lying in plain view in your search last night?''

''Yes, I did, but....'' He paused, frowning, and when he spoke again his tone was very tense. ''Show it to me, Camille! Where is it now?''

''I'm not showing you a thing until you come clean, professor! I want to know all about your— your covert activities in our lab! I want to know about that bookcase and secret laboratory between the lab and distillery! And what is it you send off through that little computer of yours? And to whom do you send that information? And who were those men Tuesday night, and what did they bring you? Were you and my father working together? What's Glendale Cosmetics?''

He gazed at her in growing astonishment and consternation.

"Either you tell me now, Jake, or I'm phoning the cops! Plain ordinary cops, not the kind that sneak around at night without headlights on!''

"How do you know all this?''

"Never mind. Start talking!''

But he kept on staring at her in unhappy astonishment. "You mean to tell me you've been watching me? How? You knew I was using your lab all this time?''

"Yes! And I swear you have something to do with that missing formula and the fake! Unless you give me one damn good reason for not calling the police. . . .''

"There's no point in talking here—let's go back to the lab. You're sure that formula isn't in the safe somewhere?''

"It's not.'' Camille opened the office door to check that everything was as it should be, locked up tight, then on impulse, she reopened the safe to be certain the other three formulas were still there. They were. Sending him an I-don't-trust-you-anyway look, she shut it in sequence, shut the medicine cabinet on it and was ready to follow him back to the lab. "Don't you lay another finger on me, Jake,'' she warned. "You may have those dogs eating out of your hand, but I can still order them to attack you, and they will if I say the word." They were outside once more. The poodles pattered up to them, frisky, tails wagging.

Jacob sent her an impatient appalled glance. "I wouldn't harm you, Camille," he replied very quietly.

"Oh?" was her scornful disbelieving comment. He already had, more than he would ever know. "Let's go in through the secret door."

He swore softly. "Is there nothing you haven't discovered? When I said you were a complication, I didn't know how right I was!"

"Quit the small talk and let's go!"

He slid in behind the lilac bush first; she followed. Releasing a catch at the bottom of the small half door, he easily swung it open, bent to enter and held it open for her. Once they and the dogs were all in and the professor had put on the light, Camille saw how well the door vanished into the wall of white laboratory tiles. Now that she knew where the seam was, she could barely discern a hairline crack in the grout between the tiles. She turned to see the professor leaning against the counter, eyeing her slender figure encased in black and denim.

To the dogs she commanded, "Heel. Sit." With one on either side of her she added, in the same tone to Jacob, hooking her thumbs into her black belt, "Start."

"Nine Western countries have pooled their resources to form a consortium. Each has contributed one scientist or, in some cases, two, making thirteen altogether. I'm the Canadian representative. As a matter of fact, your father recruited me, so for a while there were two Canadian scientists on the team. We were brought together to crack a . . . certain problem we've been working on for the past fourteen years. Your father was working on it independently long before the consortium was formed. I was brought in eight years ago.''

"I had a suspicion you had worked with dad. . . . I remembered, finally, seeing you here almost eight years ago.''

"Ah, yes. . . . You wanted to go to some dance, didn't you? Did you get to go?''

"Yes, I did, and I had a lovely time, and don't change the subject. What I want to know is, what's this project? Why is it so secret? If you're making some sort of dreadful weapon, some sort of bomb, forget it—not in my lab! I want people to smell nice—I don't want to blow them up!''

A faint smile appeared as he surveyed her. "I can't tell you, Camille.''

"You either tell me, or you tell the police I'm going to call.''

"They won't come.''

"Why not?'' It was her turn to be astonished. "The police always come!''

"Because they'll be instructed not to by their superiors.''

Camille glared back at him. "Well, then, you tell me, or I'll tell the whole neighborhood you're doing something underhanded here after dark. You know your father isn't liked. They'd be only too happy to find some reason to dislike you, too. I mean it, Jake.''

Jacob took the measure of his opposition, and deep in his level gaze flickered acute annoyance.

"You tell me, or else I'll spread everything I know. You wouldn't like that, would you?"

"You!" He bit his lip, and she smiled thinly. Taking a deep breath, he began wearily, "You know, I suppose, that to make plastic one needs petroleum products. Plastic is an extensively used material, practical for much more than dish racks and automobile interiors. But one difficulty with it is that once the expensive petroleum goes in, it doesn't come out. It's irretrieveable. More and more needs to be found to supply an endless market. Petroleum—oil—is a finite energy source, as you know.

"What we're trying to do is find the means to recover it from used plastic material—of which there is an unlimited and cheap supply." As he talked, his annoyance gradually evanesced into quiet but infectious enthusiasm. His eyes, fixed on hers, held an eager intensity that again made her think there were unrealized depths to the professor. . . .

"It's a form of recycling—a particularly important form. Energy and a constant supply of it means security and power to any nation. Tremendous power. Wielding power. Power to effect changes across the globe. With a constant and cheap energy supply, the whole world could take a great step forward. Poverty can be eased, hungry children fed, there'll be more funds to research sickness and disease. All that can be done, and more—or the wealth and power can be used to make war. That's the reason for the secrecy at this stage of the game. Naturally, the consortium wants to control this priceless information. These countries aren't warmongers. They realize how small the world really is, how much we all have to work together for the common good."

"You mean you've solved the problem of how to recycle plastic?"

"Not quite, but we're getting close. Very close. After fourteen years! Camille, I've put eight years of my life into this...and your father put in a lot more. The miraculous thing is, we've come so far without detection. No security leaks, nothing. Er...except for a minor irritation that we're aware of." He frowned for an instant, looking away from her, and went on to speak.

But she interrupted. "Minor irritation? You mean me? Or do you mean that spy supposedly after the perfume formulas? That guy who kept on following you around—two of them, in fact."

"Well, the second one is actually our man, keeping tabs on the first." Jacob looked faintly apologetic, as if this sort of cat-and-mouse ploy was a bit embarrassing for him to admit to being involved in. "As I was saying, it was perfect—everyone's cover, I mean—until just recently. Your father's cover, this perfumery, was—is ideal. So wonderfully innocent. So pretty and peaceful and out of the way. No one ever suspected—and it's vital that no one ever does."

"And you as a professor of archaeology, a disciple of archaic remedies and potions, a dispenser of lectures—that's your cover?"

"I had to have one. It's certainly an entertaining subject to study on the side. The stories I could tell you! Did you know one aristocratic Frenchwoman desired beauty so much she had her whole face plated in gold, but she couldn't peel all of it away from her nose, and so she had a gold-plated nose for the rest of her life!''

She eyed him in amazement. How could he be so cool about a situation of such magnitude? ''But, Jacob—they suspect you! Why else would they be following you? And *who* are they?'' Her hostility had ebbed away. She was only intrigued, eager to know more.

''But they only suspect. They're not sure. What I had to do was convince them they were on the wrong track. By the time I came back here after the lecture tour, they'd lost interest. Now they figure I'm just a dull history professor moldering away in the country. You see?''

''Well, yes, but who's 'they'?'' she persisted worriedly.

''As far as we know, a small independent group that is hoping to annex the project—once it's completed, of course—to sell to the highest bidder. I hate to disappoint you, but it's ordinary mercenary gain they're after. They're not foreign spies out for patriotic glory.''

''But—but,'' she choked, gazing at him wide-eyed, ''they must really want to get it. Otherwise why would they follow you right across Canada on a hunch?''

''Oh, they want it, all right. Money is a wonderful incentive. Especially when we're talking round about the fifty-million-dollar mark. Oh, the project's long-range financial benefits to one nation would amount to a lot—a vast, an illimitable—sum. But fifty million is about the highest an independent group is going to ask for. If it asks for fifty, it might get, oh, twenty-five, thirty—if the members aren't double-crossed. Who knows, they might wind up with eighty, ninety, if the bidding gets hot. After all, if we're talking international markets, ninety million is a drop in the bucket.''

Camille swallowed. He really didn't care about anything except his precious project. Only that brought the sparkle to his eyes. The danger was all just so much bother. "Well, I...I'm glad they stopped following you,'' she muttered weakly.

"I'm really sorry you had to find out. In this case, what you don't know can't hurt you. How did you find out?''

Camille nodded upward. "That clerestory. It's used for ventillation—the perfume smell can get pretty thick. The blinds don't quite cover. Even with them drawn, I can see a sliver of light. I used to know whenever dad was working late. When I first saw the light several weeks ago, it scared me silly. Does mom know about you?''

"She knows I used to work with your father.''

"Then even if she had noticed the clerestory light, she wouldn't interfere.'' Camille sighed. "She probably doesn't want to know.''

"No, and I wish you didn't, either. That still doesn't explain how you do know exactly what I've been doing each night.''

"I have a peephole in the blind.'' She grinned. "It

worked with dad, too—until he found out. But how can I believe what you say is true? And why, if there are thirteen scientists supposed to be working together, are you working alone?''

"We work together, independently. Safer that way. This project was broken down into parts. We each took a section of particular interest to the individual. For instance, your father was working on the beginning. I'm working on the end, if that makes any sense.''

"Not much.''

"You know rudimentary chemistry. You realize there are principles, laws, in any science. For every action there's an equal reaction, et cetera. Roughly speaking, we're working it in stages. If we can turn a into b and b into c, and so on and so forth, eventually we get to z. But though we now know how to turn b all the way into y, we haven't yet discovered how to turn a into b. That's the part your father was working on. I think I have the answer to turn y into z, but the z is only of use if we can get the a solved.''

"You mean you have every part of the equation between b and y solved? You're that close?''

"That close!'' His eyes were sparkling again. "I can show you a letter your father wrote to the consortium shortly before his death. That's proof. If you insist further... well, I suppose I'll have to try to arrange a meeting between you and the sergeant. Would that convince you? It's very risky. The more fuss, the more likelihood of being discovered.''

"Okay, show me the letter.''

He pulled two sheets of paper out of the breast

pocket of his dark veridian shirt. She noticed, as he unfolded the paper reverently, that the top page had had three pieces cut off the bottom and taped back on. "This is the paper you were dunking in solutions and holding over the Bunsen burner?" she asked excitedly.

"Camille, if you ever get tired of perfume, I know where you could get a job," he murmured dryly, handing her the pages. "And Glendale Cosmetics is one of the Canadian pseudonyms for our energy board." She scanned the writing, the date, the addressee. It was her father's handwriting, of that she was certain, and the letter had been sent to Glendale Cosmetics. "For five years that sat in our vaults," Jacob continued. "Read it. You might notice something that none of us noticed for five long years." He waited while she read the two sheets, enthralled that her own father had written them. "What's your impression?" he asked as soon as she was finished.

"Well. . . ." She looked up, puzzled. "He doesn't say much, does he? I mean, he goes the long way around to say he's not sure whether he's found something or not. This doesn't really prove anything."

"Talking with you on the tour made me remember this letter and decide to have another look at it. Nobody had paid much attention to it. It was put away, filed. While you were in Montreal, I went to Ottawa and dug it out and read it for myself, but I couldn't put my finger on what it was that bothered me about it. Everyone assumed he'd hit a dead end. Yet he doesn't come right out and say so. And *that's* the clue! I didn't figure it out until you said one day—the day I almost had Robbie talked into letting me see the lab—that your father had always been very definite. That letter is the most indefinite piece of writing I've ever come across.''

''Well, so?''

''So I had copies sent to me through my computer, and I tried to decode it. No luck. I tried every means. No luck. Then it struck me—maybe I needed the original letter! I had it—'' he pointed to the sheets in her hand ''—sent to me by special courier. That's why I had to go to Vancouver suddenly last weekend.''

''Oh? Oh, it is?'' So he hadn't gone just to be with Annette....

''But I didn't have much more luck with the original, until I thought perhaps he'd hidden the real letter within the letter. That's why I was messing around with the solutions. Your father's method turned out to be very simple—invisible ink!'' He grinned, delighted by the trick. ''Only not quite so simple, since it disappears over and over again.''

''You mean,'' she faltered, ''there's another letter between the lines?''

''Exactly! Heat brings it out. That ink must be your father's own invention. It's marvelous!'' Anything to do with recondite chemistry, she was certain, Jacob would think was marvelous. ''Now for the proof. Hand me the Bunsen burner, will you?'' He fished his gold-rimmed glasses from his pocket.

Camille watched spellbound as faint writing appeared between the lines of the ordinary ink scrawl. The letter was very much to the point, revealing that

Dr. Beesley had cracked his part of the plastics experiment. Her father had wasted no words on even a greeting. Farther down, she recognized one or two of the symbols in the string, and nothing more.

"Isn't it beautiful?" the professor asked happily, gazing down at the sheet.

"Um...lovely, I'm sure...."

"Even parts of the invisible ink are in code. It took me the better part of the week to break each and every cipher! And then he threw in another twister, a reference to your Island Rose formula. I couldn't make head or tail of it, until it occurred to me that he meant the last part of the puzzle was hidden in the formula itself! And that's why I was looking for it."

"Oh, no!" she breathed. "And now it's gone!"

"Show me that fake. It's a long shot, but maybe he slipped the information in behind the Rose formula, where it remained undetected all these years. Whoever took the perfume formula was probably in a hurry, might have thought the fake a duplicate—I thought it was a perfume or lotion recipe of some sort when I saw it lying here on the counter last night. And you know, if the thief thought you had a duplicate, he or she wouldn't feel so quilty about taking it. Why in heaven's name don't you have a copy." He took his glasses off.

"Well, company policy. Only four papers to worry about instead of eight."

"I suppose that does have a sort of logic. Please, Camille, will you show me the fake?"

She went to get it, surmising, "So...whoever stole the formula must have taken it between the time the boiler burst and the time you came to work last night...."

When she had given him the fake, he sat down at the counter and asked, putting on his glasses again, "Is this your father's writing?"

"It could be.... It's hard to tell, though, since it's printed. But he did put slashes through his zeros and sevens and he used to dot the *i*'s with tiny circles just like this." She pointed to an example. Standing beside him, she pondered his strong profile while he perused the fake.

Now, of course, she understood why his work was paramount to him, to the exclusion of all else. It was now clear why he often had that unworldly, introverted air, seeming to be miles away in thought. He *was* miles away, locked into chemical equations of incredible complexity. Being a virile male, of course, sometimes he digressed for diversion with handy females who made themselves available... and she'd been both handy and available. Annette, too. He had used Camille's own gullibility to further his work, convincing her he truly cared, when in fact all he wanted was to get past her into the lab. She might not even be present at this moment, Camille thought, unbidden tears beginning to swim in her eyes. Oh, she foolishly adored him, every last inch of him and every last blasted hair on his head! Now that he needed her, now that it was vital she keep quiet, he was no longer telling her to get lost.

"Jacob—one thing I don't understand. If the secret door was there all the time, and it must have been, why didn't you get into the lab that way right from the beginning?"

"What?" He looked up blankly. She repeated her question, keeping her back to him so that he wouldn't notice the suspicious shine in her eyes.

"It wouldn't open. I had to get in to find out why. Your library shelves of stock were the culprits. One shelf was a mere half inch over the edge of the door. The sergeant came out to bring me some skeleton keys, and I finally got in that way. I used them on the office, too." He bent back to the fake.

"He and his corporals are...special detectives?"

"Well, they're in a separate squad, sort of the Canadian version of the CIA." Again he turned back to the curious fake. While he'd answered patiently enough, she could sense his annoyance at her interruptions. She sighed and wandered disconsolately around the lab.

"Jacob, why didn't you tell me who you really were?" She couldn't stop the question. "Was it to find out about the lab?"

"Not at first. I thought you would catch on any second—" he didn't even look up this time "—and even before that I didn't introduce myself because I didn't want 'keeping an eye on you' to become too active a part of my cover. But then...and then you didn't catch on, so, well, yes, I did sort of make use of the opportunity." He spoke almost brusquely. Certainly there was no apology in his tone. She gazed at his back with big injured eyes.

Naturally she was glad to get to the bottom of the goings-on. But her status with the professor, which he had made plain that afternoon, was even plainer now. Perversely, she wished he hadn't such a good reason for using the lab. She would like to kick him out and tell him not to come back! She wiped a single spilled-over tear off her cheek with the back of her hand. Where there was love, one could overcome anything. How could one fight disinterest?

"Oh, my God," Jacob breathed quietly. Camille swung around to stare, signaled by his tone. "Oh, my God," he said again, and she saw a shiver ripple across his shoulders. "I don't believe it...."

"What?" She hurried to his side, leaning over his shoulder to look at the fake, infused with his intensity despite herself. "What is it?"

Slowly, dazedly, he turned and tipped his head to gaze up at her, pulling his glasses down his nose to look over them. "I...I'm a little afraid to get too happy too soon, but I think this is it."

"The last part of dad's puzzle?"

He nodded in the same stunned sort of way. "I can't believe it. After all this time...after years and years and years.... I—I can't find the right words...." He put his spectacles down on the plastic cover.

"Eureka. How about eureka? Isn't that reserved for great discoveries?"

He blinked at her. Then his mouth eased into a smile, then a grin. And then he was laughing. "Eureka! *Eureka!*" He stood up and, grasping her by the shoulders, pressed his lips to hers in a wildly exultant, wildly erotic kiss.

"Hey!" Camille sputtered, her mood far from romantic. "Lay off!"

But he folded her tightly into his arms. Laughing softly into her wide indignant big brown eyes, he murmured, "Double eureka!" Recklessly he kissed and kissed and kissed her again, short hard kisses, a rainstorm of kisses, each more seductive than the last, each more sweetly undermining, each more provoking, intimate, desirous. Her skin flushed with blood heat. Caught in the raging fire running free between them, she couldn't make up her mind whether to put her arms around his neck or to slap him. And while she couldn't help but absorb some of his excited happiness, that afternoon's put-down pulled her in the opposite direction. She was still undecided, when suddenly he broke off his kisses with a throaty sigh. His hand brushed up her cheek, entangled in a few stray curls, touched a lilac blossom caught in the corn silk.

"Will you do me a favor?" he muttered, his tone not quite even.

"What now?" she asked warily. The careful fingertips moved ever so softly down to outline the tempting curve of her moist bottom lip.

"Will you go to bed so I can get some work done? I have this sinking suspicion each and every line of that fake is in a different code. And I don't think I could concentrate knowing you were here...." The fingertips continued on down her throat, down the opening of her black blouse.

She moved quickly out of his embrace. "I'd be only too happy to leave!" Camille retorted shortly, trying to gather her scattered wits. Without pause she went toward the door, the usual one, trembling inside with hurt, longing and frustration.

"Camille?"

"What?" She kept walking.

"You won't give me away? If you're still not satisfied, I'll arrange a meeting between you and whomever you want to explain further."

With her back to him, she tipped her head back, raking both hands through the blond tousle. Then she sighed, feeling at the end of her rope. "I'll keep quiet. I haven't told anyone, not even Robbie. So don't worry. But why don't you give me the sergeant's telephone number, the one you memorized. Just in case. I'd feel safer if. . .if I knew somebody was within reach."

He gave her the number, adding that she dare not commit it to paper but must memorize it.

"Okay, I have it now."

"Wait a second. I'll turn the lights off while you go out. I know it sounds silly, but we can't be too careful." He started flipping down the row of switches controlling all the various lamps and light fixtures.

"Oh!" Camille exclaimed. "I hate to bother you with trivial details, professor, but what about our missing perfume formula? As I said, if you didn't take it, who did?"

"Oh, hell! I'd forgotten all about that. Can it wait till morning? I'll come around then." The last light went off. Camille turned the knob and slipped into the night, repeating silently to herself, *Five, five, five, forty-one, forty-nine. Triple five, forty-one, forty-nine; triple. . . .*

SHE SAW THE PROFESSOR AGAIN late the next morning. He poked his head in the kitchen window, smiled very faintly at her and said, "Hi!"

Her heart turned a giddy somersault. "Hi," she returned, at lot cooler. Then her curiosity and excitement won over, and lowering her voice she asked, "Did you decipher the fake?"

He leaned against the sill, keenly considering her heart-shaped face in the brilliant summery sunshine. Something deep in the tawny depths was troubled as he seemed to search her gaze for some elusive answer. Then he replied in a soft tone that wouldn't carry, "A good portion of it. And your father's signature was at the bottom." A quick grin flashed over his face as he saw her pleasure. "It is without a doubt the final piece in his puzzle, the last touch to turn *a* into *b*."

"Oh, Jacob!" Her smile was radiant; her eyes shone. "Oh!" was all she could say. And perversely now—all morning the feeling had been growing—she was elated by the whole drama taking place under Metchosin's nose without anyone's being the wiser. It was fabulous, the idea of scientific history taking shape in the precinct of Beesley Farm! The more she really thought about it, all personal feelings for the professor aside, the more she was struck by the sheer excitement of another great human discovery.

But the professor's attention had wandered. He was staring abstractedly at the pitcher of fresh lemonade in her hands.

"What's wrong, Jacob?"

"Oh, nothing's wrong." He blinked. "It's just that . . . well, the *a* isn't anything like what I expected it to be. Of course, I'm not exactly sure how it's going to turn out yet—but the way it's shaping up! It's bloody ingenious. Nobody's ever thought of taking that route before.... Your dad was downright mean when it came to codes, you know. I tried every damn configuration on the computer—saves time—but, no, he had to devise his own! His name—it took me an hour to figure out his signature!''

''Why didn't you work on a different line?''

''The right signature's important. It verifies the work. Sort of like a stamp or an artist's signature on a painting.''

''Here comes Robbie.''

All conversation ceased as her brother bounded up the back-porch steps. Then it resumed in greetings and the usual sort of questions and answers. Aggravated, Robbie announced that the new boiler wasn't living up to expectations.

''Brand spanking new!'' he protested. ''What's the world coming to, to foist a boiler like that on me! Harry will be in later. He's trying to guess why we can't get an even steam pressure out of the jets. Let me tell you, I just hope you didn't make an omelet!'' Robbie's mood hadn't improved from yesterday.

''No—eggs Benedict.'' Camille felt relatively safe with eggs. ''And salad. Have you had breakfast yet, Jacob? There's plenty.''

''You mean has he had lunch yet. Jake, has Camille told you about—no, I don't suppose she would.'' Her brother turned to her placatingly, ''Now just hold onto your hat. I'm going to tell him. Maybe he'll have some ideas. It is Friday—mom's going to be home tomorrow!'' And turning back to the professor, he went on, "One of our perfume formulas is missing."

"I know, Camille told me."

"She did? She did! Well, what do you know! I'm beginning to believe your theory, Camille, that it was stolen. Did your lead come to anything?" As she shook her head, Jacob took a sidelong look at her, one corner of his mouth quirking up in a rather sarcastic smile. Robbie continued, "But I've been over and over it, everyone who was here yesterday morning and the day before."

"Who came?" Jacob queried keenly, sitting down beside Robbie at the table on the veranda. Camille was just inside the window, a party to the discussion. She passed out tall glasses of icy lemonade with a sprig of mint in each.

"Well, let's see. Our glassware delivery man with a shipment, the pipe fitter for the new boiler, Canadian National Express with some crates of oil. . . ."

"Don't forget Herb brought over some milk and cream. Elaine dropped in, too," Camille added.

"A flow of customers in the shop, but none of them entered the compound. Then Mrs. Plumtree came right after lunch yesterday. But we've known all the deliverymen for years! Only the pipe fitter was new to us, and I was beside him practically every second." Robbie shook his head. "What I can't figure is, why didn't the dogs do anything? It couldn't have been anyone we know. I'm. . . ."

"Bamboozled?" Camille supplied. "Me, too! It doesn't make any sense." Passing out the tossed salad of lettuce, alfalfa sprouts and sweet red peppers, she had to dash to catch the telephone on its third ring. Two minutes later she was listening to her mother telling her she and Charles weren't coming home until Sunday, and that they'd been married earlier that afternoon. It was already three o'clock Toronto time.

"Married?" Camille whispered. She cleared her throat and tried again. "You got married? You mean you're married to Charles?"

"Yes, dear. I told him what a fuss you two made—" she chuckled "—and he insisted on making a decent woman out of me. There, are you happy now?"

"Are... are you happy?" Camille asked a little dubiously, wondering if Charles had pushed or rushed her into it.

"Yes, darling—otherwise I wouldn't have married him!" Fern laughed, and Camille knew from the sound of her voice that her mother was indeed, without any reservations, very happy.

Camille swallowed. "Oh, mom, that's grand! That's wonderful! What a surprise!" Passing a hand over her forehead she added, "I'll call Robbie. Oh, mom, where did you get married? When did you decide? Do you realize you practically eloped? What did you wear? Did you have flowers?"

"Of course I had flowers, darling! The most lovely roses." And Mrs. Fern Darby went on to answer all her daughter's many questions. Before Camille passed the receiver on to Robbie, she pressed her hand over the mouthpiece to warn him, "Mom and Charles got married. Now *you'd* better hold on to *your* hat!"

Complete dismay registered on Robbie's face for a moment before he had himself in hand. She stood beside him, listening to his expressions of slightly uncertain joy and congratulations. Looking through the kitchen toward the professor, she thought he would be unreservedly happy, too. Jacob now had all he wanted: the perfumery, the lab, Damask....

She realized by her brother's change of tone and comment that he was talking to Charles, offering his congratulations to his new stepfather. Camille shrank from the word. For an agonized instant, hopeless tears flooded her eyes. Oh, yes, Jacob had all he wanted, while she and Robbie were left with nothing. And just when they'd started to reverse the tide of the perfumery's fortunes! Now they'd never get the chance to find out if they could have made it on their own. God only knew what changes Charles would bring about.

"Don't say anything about the missing formula!" she whispered to Robbie. "We can't spoil their day." He shook his head, trying to conduct two conversations at once. Then he passed the receiver back to her. While she was doing her level best to talk to Charles and sound enthusiastic, Robbie went out to fetch Jacob to the telephone. It was while he was talking to their parents that Camille pulled herself together behind a serene front. Robbie, as well, had no wish to expose his true feelings toward Charles in front of the professor, whom he'd grown to like. Robbie and Camille had a hasty consultation.

"Well, at least they're not arriving until Sunday," Robbie was saying when Jacob rejoined the table.

"That gives us an extra day to try to find that formula."

Jacob was still smiling. He looked from one to the other. "Do you think we're related now?" he asked whimsically. "Let's see. He's my stepfather and your stepfather. What does that make us?"

Camille looked at him in helpless irritation. What did he care about Beesley Farm as long as he had his secret laboratory? What did he care about missing formulas? Nevertheless, Robbie was glad to have an additional head to help with the unexplainable disappearance. Camille was none too talkative for the remainder of the meal.

"If all else fails," Jacob mused as he and Robbie were preparing to go to the greenhouse, "I suppose I could try breaking down the formula from a sample of perfume. You have a vague idea of the mixing order, Robbie, and what with Camille's Nose, we could come up with something close.... Let's put off telling anyone, even if nothing's turned up by Sunday."

"Not let mom in on it?" Robbie frowned.

"She'll have all sorts of other things to think about," Jacob pointed out, glancing at Camille, who quickly looked away.

That night, when the light in the clerestory winked on and Camille went out, she found both her peepholes taped up. She could have gone in, but instead, in her gloom, she went for a long, lonely walk on the beach, leaving the poodles behind with strict orders to guard the professor while he was at work.

JUST AFTER Camille returned from the post office on Saturday, with four more reorders, Jacob dropped by again. He had all but one line of the fake deciphered. By this time, Camille had her conflicting emotions firmly and securely bottled up inside. She showed only a cursory interest in the professor or his work or the fact that they might now be related in some obscure fashion. Not that he seemed to notice her standoffishness. The happy, exultant kisses of the night before last were entirely forgotten, or so it seemed to her. He displayed only the most casual friendliness—since he needed her cooperation he couldn't afford to be rude, obviously.

There was still no sign of the missing perfume formula, let alone one single clue as to who could have snatched it in broad daylight, considering all the activity around the lab. There just didn't seem to be any way the formula could have been stolen, yet there was no other possible explanation. Robbie was in a pother about it; Camille was morose. Only the professor, she noticed in fierce irritation, seemed tranquil. Not lingering long after imparting his news, he took himself off home to Damask, whistling in thoughtful complacency. It was his whistling that almost convinced her to pick up a rock and throw it at him.

No sooner had he disappeared down the beach than there was another long-distance telephone call to the farm. Camille was astonished to hear Pierre's charming French accent as he inquired after her health.

"I am bored, *ma petite*, and I knew talking to you would cheer me up."

"You old smoothie, you!" She smiled wryly.

"But I am serious! I *am* bored! How is my good friend Jacob Nathaniel? Is the passion in full bloom? Or is there now a chance for me?"

He made her laugh, and that was quite an accomplishment these days. She could have caught Jacob to pass along Pierre's inquiries, but she much preferred to see as little of him as possible. Anyway, he would be coming again tomorrow in the big white Cadillac to drive them all down to the Victoria Harbour to meet the newlyweds.

Robbie's mouth dropped open when she told him Pierre had called. He stared at her in vague apprehension. He didn't say much more than, "Oh?"

THEY WERE GATHERED waiting for the float plane at the lovely harbor front. Robbie had wandered off to buy a lottery ticket, leaving them alone for the first time that day, and Jacob announced, "I've cracked the code." He glanced down at her, while she gazed at the intricate stonework of the huge regal Empress Hotel. "It's a mighty unusual *a*, but it'll work!"

"And you've got the *z* to finish the whole business," she added evenly, denying the jump of joy inside. "Congratulations, professor. What happens now?"

He eyed her quizzically, trying to probe her closed expression, but she kept on staring at the Empress, watching the flow of people leaving after afternoon tea, an English tradition in Victoria among tourists and locals alike, enjoyed every afternoon in the elegant lobby of the hotel. "Your congratulations are premature. Empirical data must.... This a alters a few things. I must first go through the actual experiment from front to back, to be absolutely certain there are no bugs."

"How long will that take?"

"Maybe a week, working every night. I've been expecting you to drop in on me...."

She shrugged and lied, "I've been too tired. Oh. Pierre called yesterday. He asked how you were." She stole an upward glance at him through her dark lashes. Normally a calm still person, he had positively turned to stone.

"Oh? Er, how nice. Listen, Camille, I know it's none of my concern—" he spoke hurriedly, for Robbie was approaching from one direction and the Twin Otter plane from the other "—but I know Pierre, and believe me, I love him like a brother. But he really is the world's worst playboy."

Now she stared at him outright, her carefully held temper exploding. "Pierre is the world's worst? Oh, now I've heard everything! What does that make *you*?"

"Me?" His eyebrows rose in astonishment. "Me?"

"Yes, you! Jake the rake! How dare you malign Pierre! And I'll tell you something else! Your father might not be quite so smug when he learns he's married for a perfumery that's missing its biggest moneymaker!"

"You...you little monster!" he growled, his eyes flaring into hers. "You awful little fiend!"

Robbie, sauntering up, groaned, "A fine reception committee we're going to make, with you two at each other's throats again! Can't you quit for an hour? As if there wasn't enough to worry about already!"

CHAPTER TEN

It was not an auspicious beginning to the wedding supper they had planned for their parents, especially added to the dreadful weight of guilt burdening two of the three children whenever they thought of a certain perfume formula they had managed to lose.

Sitting between her brother and Jacob, Camille utterly ignored the professor through the toasts and the champagne and the six long courses; Jacob smoothly retaliated by continually drawing her into conversation. Robbie attempted to keep the peace between them *and* tried to cover up for them, while all three pretended to be merry for the parents' sake. At least Jacob didn't have to pretend to be happy about the reason for the celebration. Robbie and Camille avoided addressing Charles directly, not knowing what to call him. Every time she had to look at her new stepfather, which was often, Camille's heart sank a little further.

Fern, flushed and excited, and appearing much too young and charming to be the mother of two grown children, picked up on the thick atmosphere between her daughter and her stepson. Placing her hand on her husband's arm and laughing, she said, ''To think

I tried to matchmake between these two! I do wish I'd never started it!''

Charles added, his thin lips twitching into a sudden smile, ''Perhaps they'll get along better as brother and sister. Camille, Robbie, I realize you're both too old to start calling me dad. Please feel free to use Charles.''

Camille met his slate-gray eyes, didn't back down and drop her gaze before his forthright stare, even though she was still blushing after her mother's comment. Why did parents invariably say the most embarrassing thing at the most inopportune time? To her stepfather she replied levelly, ''I believe I will, thank you, Charles. And mom, I'm going to make a request from the bottom of my heart—please don't ever matchmake for me again!''

Charles actually chuckled. He put his hand over his wife's and said, ''You see how it's had the opposite of the intended effect? Now if you had told Camille to stay away from Jake at all costs, she would have searched him out instantaneously! I have a confession to make, though. It wasn't all Fern's fault. I had a hand in it, too. Very well, from now on no more matchmaking, and if you two want to have a row, go right ahead. It might help to clear the air.''

Camille turned a slightly darker shade of pink. Still, she said in the same light, even tone, almost breezily, ''Oh, but Jake and I understand each other perfectly...don't we, stepbrother, dear?'' She turned to Jacob, smiling sweetly, a subtle baring of teeth.

His curious tiger-yellow eyes held torrid flames

when she met them, but she boldly held that shriveling glance, condemning him in return. She could have shrieked when he suddenly reached out to tauntingly tug at a blond curl. It was all she could do not to slap his hand away. The professor could be very physical when he had a mind to be.... "In some ways, yes, perfectly!" he gibed softly.

Seeing his sister's hands clenching in her lap, Robbie hastily intervened with a non sequitur about having to purchase a new boiler. Camille was glad when Charles took up the topic, but her relief faded moments later.

"Can't stand for that sort of nonsense when purchasing a piece of equipment. You should have insisted on either another new boiler, or at least snappy service in setting the defective one right. Fern and I will be staying at my house tonight, but for the rest of the week I think we'll be at the farm. I want to look into a few things, and it will be handier to be right on the spot. Might as well not waste any time in making a few changes."

Camille, even though she'd been expecting just this sort of attitude, was dumbfounded. Charles couldn't wait to get his hands on the perfumery. He was so eager, he had to discuss it at his wedding supper! He wasn't even taking mom on a short honeymoon first! She gazed down at her hands, not saying anything, and beside her, Robbie shifted uneasily in his chair. It wasn't her place to say anything, she considered. After all, the perfumery belonged to mother, lock, stock and boiler. If she wanted to hand it over to Charles on a platter, that was her right. Her despair complete, Camille raised her head to determinedly smile and smile and smile. . . .

She had to sit in the front seat of the Cadillac between Jacob, who was driving, and Robbie, while her mother and Charles shared the back. Even though the car was huge, there didn't seem to be enough room on that front seat. She tried not to scrunch up against Robbie, but Jacob was driving with supreme ease, one-handed, while his other rested on the seat between them. Every time he turned left, she felt his fingers underneath her thigh as the motion made her lean toward him. Finally she couldn't restrain herself any longer. She picked up his hand and placed it on his thigh and Robbie, in the middle of a sentence, stopped to raise his eyebrows at her. Camille boiled in stoic silence.

They had prepared Charles's house with fresh-cut flowers that afternoon to welcome the couple home, and set out the wedding presents. But they didn't stay once they'd dropped the newlyweds off.

Now complete silence reigned in the car. The three in the front were busy with their own thoughts, morbid and otherwise. Camille sensed Robbie was feeling rather torn—while he greatly admired Jacob, he wasn't keen on the father and was made vastly uncomfortable by the whole situation. She was busy telling herself she didn't care about anything anymore. Not to care, that was the best way, for then one couldn't be hurt.

When the Cadillac slipped under the grape arbor, Robbie slid out. Camille, right behind him, suddenly found the professor's hand anchored around her wrist. Her brother, sensing unfinished business, closed the car door behind him and quickly made himself scarce. Camille swiveled to glower pointedly at Jacob's unrelenting hand and said not a word.

He didn't ease up, instead yanked her purse out of her other hand and availed himself of that one, too. "Look at me, damn you!" he warned dangerously.

"If I look at you, I'll spit in your eye!" She stared blindly away from him. "It's not fair, the way you see fit to manhandle me! I may be small compared to you, but what gives you the right!"

"You gave it to me."

"I gave you nothing!"

"You gave me everything."

"If you're referring to that one night, forget it. I have!"

He said, "I'll let you go *if* you promise to sit here and talk."

"Okay, then!" As he released her, she slid still farther away until she was up against the door. "Just what do we have to talk about? I think everything's been said."

He sighed explosively, then seemed to be making an effort to control his exasperation. When he spoke again, it was in a calm reasoning tone. "Why must you think the worst of Charles? Even if you don't like him, can't you see the marriage could be of advantage to you?"

"What advantage can it possibly have?" she retorted bitterly. So this was what he wanted to talk about!

"Well, for one thing, you'll never want for anything again. And you certainly won't have to wear Elaine's cast-offs.''

"I happen to like Elaine's cast-offs. I see no reason to throw perfectly good clothes away! I don't want your father's money! Not one red cent!''

He leaned back against the seat, surveying her, and as he did a reflective smile slowly transformed his face. His voice grew velvety. "Camille, that's one of the many things I like about you. Wealth doesn't impress you, doesn't even make a dint. But he can help you. In more ways than one. Instead of fighting him, try to live with him—he's not so bad once you get to know him. And, Camille...I haven't forgotten that night...not for a minute. We can't talk properly here, like this. Will you—''

She clicked open the door and slipped out, then leaned down to talk through the open door, unaware that her pose offered an enticing view of shadowy cleavage, that what was visible to him was a sizzling mad, unthinking beauty. "Come on, professor! There's no need to be nice to me now that I can't kick you out of the lab. There's no need to pour on the sentiment now that you have everything you always wanted. Take it. Take everything with my blessing—'' his eyes drank her in ''—take the lab, the perfumery, Damask, even my mother. Take every last thing in the name of your precious work, but leave me alone!''

His suffocating gaze seemed to melt her dress away. She took a deep breath; her breasts swelled against the décolletage...and he began to slide across the seat toward her. She slammed the door, adding, "You don't have to sweet-talk me into keeping quiet for you, either! I'll keep quiet, but for the sake of what you're doing—not for you!" And she ran away up the porch stairs, slamming the kitchen door behind her, too.

Coming out of the living room when he heard the second slam, Robbie took one look at her face and said wearily, "You didn't make up."

"Make up?" she queried, gazing at her brother as if he were demented. She was a mass of nerves.

"Why the dickens do you have to spat with him all the time? What is it about him that drives you insane? Don't you see he could help us fight Charles? Charles will listen to Jake!"

"But your wonderful professor doesn't want us to fight Charles. He wants us to 'try to live with him,' and that's a quote! Now do *you* see? I wouldn't be nice to Jake if my life depended on it!"

"Well, then, it looks as if we're sunk."

"Enjoy tonight, Robbie. Charles will be under this roof tomorrow—with all his changes! He'd just better make mom happy is all I can say!" her voice quavered.

"Please, Camille. Now don't start crying! C'mon! If it gets unbearable we'll ship out and find jobs elsewhere."

"Doing what? All we know how to do is wrapped up in this place!" She took a shuddering breath, refusing the release of tears.

"I'll grow roses somewhere else, and you can still make perfume. . . . What did Jake want to talk to you about?"

"Thanks for running out on me the way you did!"

"It hardly looked as though he wanted my company!"

"He. . .he was only trying to smooth the way for his father."

"We should have told them." Camille didn't need to ask whom they should have told what; she knew only too well. Filling the kettle for coffee, Robbie went on, "I think we should call the police in, but Jake keeps saying not to, says he's working on an angle of his own—did he tell you?"

Camille passed Robbie the coffee cannister, biting on her lip. "No. What angle?"

"Wouldn't say. I gave him all the ingredients I could remember, and he's started breaking down the sample of perfume I gave him. So maybe he's not so sure of his angle, either. Anyway, to tell you the truth, I'd feel like a fool telling the cops to investigate Mrs. Plumtree! Fine way for us to treat our friends!"

"Let's just hope it doesn't take him too long to break down that sample," she replied wearily. "You realize we might not end up with anything close to Island Rose, even so?"

"But if we know the ingredients, and I roughly remember the mixing order, you could work out the rest, couldn't you?"

"With time, yes—I could probably get damn close, anyway. But do we have the time? We've received five reorders so far, shops in Victoria are selling briskly and so is our shop. We could run out of Island Rose before we know it. I never thought I'd ever say this—but let's just hope no more reorders come! At least, not for the time being...."

MONDAY MORNING she found three more reorders in their post-office box, and when she returned home her mother and Charles were already there. Charles immediately set to perusing the company books, all of them. But not in the office. He had the dining-room table heaped high with papers and ledgers and catalogs of all their various suppliers. Camille was glad about only one small thing—mother was doing the cooking again. Robbie and Camille avoided the house; therefore, their mother came out to find them in the lab.

"I know you don't want Charles involved here," she said gently, getting right down to facts, "but he can help, and he will. He's a very good businessman. If nothing else, you can learn from him. Now I want you both to promise you'll try to cooperate with him. Please, for me?"

What could they say? "Very well, mom, I'll try. But I can't promise more than that," Camille sighed, and Robbie nodded, echoing her words. "Mom... do you really love him?" she asked.

"Yes, darling. Is that so strange?"

"Well... does he love you?" Camille persisted.

"Yes, darlings, he does!"

"Well, then, cross my heart, I'll try!"

"We could have waited, but what was the point? You two and Jake are all grown up. You have your own lives to lead." Fern suddenly smiled. "And as Charles said, you might never have given your blessings. So we just went ahead and pleased ourselves."

They watched their mother, her step light, return to the cottage. Then they went back into the lab. "Okay," muttered Camille, "now we give it a try."

"Yeah...."

Charles was busy with the books all afternoon, and that night Rachael and Wilson and Mrs. Plumtree came over for another celebration dinner. For some obscure reason Elaine didn't come; her mother made excuses for her. Of course Jacob was present. Camille studiously avoided having more to do with him than was necessary for the maintenance of the festive occasion. He didn't attempt to draw her into conversation. He left her alone, as she had requested, except she couldn't help noticing every time she looked up or turned around that he was watching her. It made her terribly edgy. Through it all she smiled until she thought her face might crack right in half. Later, when the house was quiet and the light in the clerestory came on, she sat by the window of her bedroom watching it, unmoving.

The following day, Charles adhered himself to her. Everywhere she went, he went. Everything she did, he wanted explained. A painter also came to give an estimate for painting every building on the premises. A roofer came to give an estimate for red tile roofs for the lot. A road-construction company salesman came to give an estimate for repaving the tarmac drive.

Camille had a first-hand opportunity to watch Charles in action. He harrassed each representative as much as he harrassed her. If ever they hadn't a ready answer, he demanded to know why.

"What do you mean you don't know how much clay tiles cost per square foot? What's your guarantee for materials and labor? What if your workmen go on strike? Can you guarantee my deadline? What do you mean you can't?" He was relentless, thorough, exact. He left nothing to chance. He wanted estimates in detail, written and signed.

"I don't care," he said to her once, sharply, "how long you've known that fellow! If he's not prepared to give good work for good pay, then he's not getting any work from me! You are not a charity organization! You have to stand behind your product—why shouldn't he? And if he has a wife and five children, all the more reason for him to pull up his socks!"

Camille wondered whether they'd have any friends left in the neighborhood after Charles got through with them.

"How long has it been since this warehouse was cleaned out?"

"It's perfectly clean." She forced herself not to shout.

"I can see it's clean!" her stepfather snapped brusquely. "What I want to know is, where is your stock list?" Camille tapped her head in reply, not daring to trust her powers of speech.

"I admire your intelligence, dear girl, but Great Scott! You mean to tell me your whole inventory is memorized? Are you really so inefficient, or what is your excuse? How many cases of Island Violet Body Oil do you have?" he barked.

"Ah, um, I think about thirty."

"You think? About thirty? What does that mean?"

On and on and on. By suppertime Camille felt as if she'd been flattened by a steamroller.

Robbie got him the next day. That day, representatives of painting companies, pavers, roofers and carpenters, a whole new flock, came to give more estimates. Camille stumbled across an unexplained someone on the front lawn, staring at the view. The woman turned out to be a real-estate agent, there to assess the property value. Camille's breath choked in her throat on learning this. But still she smiled and left the woman to her work. Another new boiler arrived; the defective one was taken away. And that evening, Robbie told her he'd barely restrained himself from throttling their stepfather, that he had seen surveyors in the rose fields....

Her brother was, however, more worried about when Jake planned to finish breaking down the perfume sample. He didn't know the professor was in the lab every night, as Camille did. She, too, wondered how he was doing with the sample, as well as the final going-over of the plastics experiment to check for bugs. She could have punched another hole in the blind with the bodkin, but if she could spy on him through it, so could others. Even a pinpoint of light shining out of the lab in the wee hours of the morning would be like a neon advertisement to somebody spying on the professor. Repeating the sergeant's telephone number gave her a measure of reassurance. Triple five, forty-one, forty-nine.

On Thursday, Charles attached himself to her again, following her everywhere. On Thursday a team of painters swarmed over the cottage, roofers attacked the garage. Pavers came in the afternoon to repair the tarmac. Camille was doubly careful to lock the lab every time she left it, since it struck her that any one of the tradespeople could in reality be a cutthroat mercenary. She kept all of them as much under her surveillance as she could, earning Charles's praise.

"Very wise, to keep an eye on outside workers. Prevents pilfering and lagging on the job. An hour's pay is worth an hour's work."

Next he wanted the warehouse emptied and every last case counted, marked and tallied on a sheet. "We're getting a little low on Island Rose perfume," her stepfather observed, frowning—while Camille felt temporarily elated because they'd found twenty-nine cases she didn't know they had.

That evening, feeling an escape was necessary, she went into town to catch a movie with Elaine. She was hoping Elaine would cheer her up, but instead her snobby friend seemed overly bright, setting Camille's teeth on edge. One thing Elaine happened to toss out, however, made her perk up her ears. Apparently Annette had found a new flame. Had the professor tired of her? Had he also told Annette he was too involved with his work to have more than a few hours to spare for women?

Jacob still hadn't come around to the farm in the daytime. Robbie, in a dither, had announced to Camille earlier that he was going to Damask that evening to find out what the professor was doing about his supposed "angle" and the perfume sample.

Friday, Camille came home with a fistful of re-orders. Charles was pleased, Fern was delighted, she and Robbie were pale with guilt and anxiety.

"What did Jake say last night?" Camille asked her brother when they were alone for a second—Charles was mostly hounding Robbie that day.

"He's still breaking down the sample. And—" Robbie brightened "—he's still working on some other angle he said he preferred to keep quiet. He's okay, you know that? If only his father wasn't such a royal pain. . . ."

Beesley Farm was a hotbed of activity everywhere one looked. Carpenters were also busy in the store, adding more shelf space. "Can't sell product if it's not there to be seen!" Charles had said.

Next he was off to the lavender farm with Robbie. Jacob dropped in just before he and Robbie returned. Camille had met Jacob in the yard, on the curve of brand-new tarmac and had asked him how he was progressing with the perfume sample.

"Well, I'm getting there," he'd replied nonchalantly, his thoughts seemingly miles away as he stared down into her face.

"Jake—" Camille held on to flighty emotions with a will "—Jake, I realize you're busy with your work and that it's of primary importance to you, and I realize that you want to get that experiment finished as quickly as possible—but! Dammit, what the hell are we going to tell our parents when we run out of Island Rose? What are we going to tell our customers? What are we going to send in reply to all those reorders? Jacob, can't you tell me more than, 'I'm getting there'?'' She was furious. She was upset, and lovesick, too. She didn't hear the farm truck parking behind them. "You make me so...so mad I could scream!''

"You don't exactly bring a song to my heart, either! My time—''

"You egotistical, self-centered, rotten genius! Why can't you concern yourself with plain everyday facts for two minutes! You—''

"If you kept still long enough to get anything through that thick head of yours—'' He broke off abruptly.

Charles, Fern and Robbie were all standing behind them, gazing at them in alarm. Camille looked at them, horrified. Sighing shakily, she shuffled her feet. "Er—'' she glanced at Jacob "—you were saying?''

There was a pool of silence as he stared down into her eyes a moment longer. Then his mouth turned up in a gibing half-smile as he murmured, "I hope the rest of my family is more welcoming than you, Camille, dear.'' Which made everyone think he was staying away because of her. Camille had never been so certain that life was completely unfair as at that moment.

Saturday Charles once more reigned at the dining-room table among a welter of ledgers. At dinner he announced that everyone was requested to be present for a "big meeting'' early Monday morning. Jake, too, would be there, had already been informed. Camille and Robbie exchanged despairing glances. The sword over their heads was now primed, timed to fall.

She left right after dinner to go to Greyson's garage, hoping he would be free that night so that they could have another marshmallow roast—Jacob was coming over that evening, and she wanted to be out of the way. She drove into the parking space beside the garage, got out of the car, walked to the corner—and stopped in her tracks.

Quickly she ducked back around the corner before Greyson, or the man he was talking to, noticed her. The fellow was dressed in a clergyman's white collar, but she recognized him, anyway. He was the spy who had followed Jacob from Vancouver to Fredericton. Her heart in her throat, she leaned against the cold concrete wall of the garage, trying to catch some of their conversation.

Her panic mushroomed into terror as she heard Greyson saying, very helpfully, "Oh, yes. No end of sights to see right around here. Beesley Farm, for instance. They make perfume there. Beautiful spot—you should stop to see it. What's that? A lab? Naturally, they make the perfume on the premises. Yes, it's unusual. A Canadian perfumery. Have you been to Fort Rodd Hill? Or Hatley Castle? Or...."

Fearfully agitated, Camille raced back to Robbie's Spider convertible, didn't even stop to open the door, but swung herself over it and into the seat. She was off like blazes. Luckily there was no highway patrol on her route.

She found her mother and Charles sitting on the

front-porch swing. "Where's Jacob?" she demanded peremptorily.

"You're back already, dear?"

"Please, mom, where is he?" She was trembling.

"In the greenhouse with Robbie, I think. Camille—" But she was gone.

"Robbie—I have to talk to Jacob alone."

"What now?" he groused, turning with a root stalk in one hand and a grafting slip in the other. "Pick on him some other time, why don't you?"

"I'll only be a minute, Robbie," the professor placated, taking her arm and leading her outside.

"Oh, Jacob," she quavered the second they were alone, "the spy! He's here!" She told him all she'd heard. She was quite happy he had his hands on her shoulders, for she felt terribly cold and his hands were warm and tight and helped to hold her up.

He swore softly under his breath, then added, "Sometimes you Islanders are a bit too friendly and helpful!"

"What are we going to do?" She hung on to his supportive arms.

"I'll call Sergeant Peterson. Our clergyman is probably already being followed, but just in case.... If he shows up here in the next few days, call the sergeant immediately, but other than that, handle him just like any other customer. Stay out of his way. You hear me? Do you remember the number?" She nodded. "Repeat it." She did. "Promise me you'll stay out of the way!"

"Okay, okay. Jacob, I'm so scared. Are you almost finished with the experiment?"

"I ran into a slight fix, but I should have it finished by tonight or tomorrow."

"Can't you put if off until he goes away?"

"The sooner it's done, the better. Who knows how long he plans to hang around."

"Well, then. . . will you tell me the second you're done? The very second?"

"If you want. Camille, please don't worry. I'll be all right. Those Mounties will be watching him like hawks."

"Why do they let him run around loose? Why don't they lock him up?"

"If they take him, they lose the chance of catching the whole group. That must be done so that no hint of this project leaks out. You see, the gang won't contact potential buyers until they actually have what they want in their hands—otherwise, one of those buyers could beat them to the mark. Don't you set foot out of the house at night. For any reason. All they want is that equation, so the farther you stay away from it the better, you understand? Just go about business as usual. And in case you see something funny going on, call the sergeant at the number—don't you do anything else!" His hands tightened on her shoulders, and he shook her slightly. "Nothing else! You understand?"

"Hey!" Robbie obviously objected to seeing his sister being jostled, even if it was by her stepbrother. "Quit that! Listen, I don't mind if you two want to spat, but keep it in line, eh?"

"Er. . . ." The professor quickly dropped his hands.

"I know she's aggravating, but—"

"I am not!"

"Oh, yeah?" Jacob mocked, sounding so utterly sincere that Camille bridled in the midst of her fear and worry.

She turned on Robbie, pointing at Jacob. "You like him—then you're taking a big risk! I've had it. I've just bloody well had it!" She turned again, and bumped into Charles and Fern. One look at their startled expressions and she sobbed a fed-up, "Oh, damn!" and took off at a run. Sliding into Robbie's Spider, she lelt with a telling squeal of tires.

When she returned home much, much later, everyone was already in bed...except her mother. Fern was sitting at the kitchen table with a freshly brewed pot of coffee.

"Sit down, dear," she said as soon as Camille came in the back door. "Where have you been?" she started conversationally after her daughter, with a weary sigh, had poured herself a cup.

"Oh, here and there," Camille answered glumly.

"What *is* the matter between you and Jake, dear? Won't you tell me what's eating you up? It's getting worse and worse! Now surely if you could just calm down and have a heart-to-heart talk instead of...of yelling at each other all the time—"

"I am never speaking to him again."

"But, Camille!" exclaimed her mother, gazing at her in amazement. "You have to talk to him! He's your brother now!"

"He is not! I loathe and despise him, do you hear me? If you try to cram him down my throat any more than you've already done, then...then I'm leaving home! It's bad enough around here already—be nice to Jake, talk to Jake, sit with Jake, smile at Jake, dance with Jake, take Jake another piece of cake. Well! I'm sick and tired of Jake, Jake, Jake! I wish he'd take his brains and go back to Paris!''

They talked for some time after that, but Jacob wasn't mentioned again.

On Sunday the parents were bound for a sailing regatta. Robbie and Camille wouldn't have gone even if they'd been invited. He had the weight of guilt sitting uneasily on his shoulders, and she wasn't about to leave the farm while there was a spy in the neighborhood.

Once Charles and Fern had left, Robbie wanted to have a very serious discussion with her about the missing formula.

"Tomorrow, at the scheduled 'big meeting—'" he scowled "—I'm going to tell them. I can't stand it any longer. And I've told Jake I'm going to tell them.''

"What did he say?''

Robbie shrugged. "He said if I had to, then I had to. But he did ask me to keep it quiet until tomorrow morning. I guess he's still working on his angle, whatever it is.''

"It makes me squeamish just thinking about admitting to Charles that the formula is gone. After what we went through this week with him, how do you think he's going to take it?'' She shuddered. She was wondering why Jacob wanted it kept quiet until Monday. Because by tomorrow morning, after one more night's work, he'd be finished with the experiment? In that case, he wouldn't mind if the police were brought in. Charles would likely have the whole Victoria constabulary over here by noon, dusting for fingerprints—and worse, interrogating Mrs. Plumtree, and Herb at the corner, who supplied all their milk and cream! Why wouldn't Jacob tell them what this angle was?

"You know, I sure wish you'd cool it with Jake. It would be a lot easier for us tomorrow if we had him on our side!"

"He's on his father's side. You're too blinded by him to see that!" Camille retorted sourly. "Right from the start Jacob wanted the perfumery. He used every one of us to get it! There are a dozen little floundering businesses around, so why did Charles zero in on us? Just because of mom? Don't you believe it!"

"But even you have to admit they're in love with each other. After seeing them together for a whole week! And why would Jake want the perfumery? Because of the lab? Both he and his father are loaded. Why not build their own lab? Be reasonable, Camille!" Robbie raked a hand through his wavy mane. "Because of some personal pique, you're trying to poison me against Jake, and I think that stinks! Furthermore, I agree with him about Pierre. That guy's old enough to be your father. A playboy like that, with women panting after him on all sides, and you try to tell me he's a buddy of yours? Ha, ha!"

With that humorless comment, Robbie took himself off to a baseball tournament. He couldn't understand why she didn't want to come, since Greyson was going to be there. Camille stayed where she was, sitting on the front-porch steps, staring out over the strait and patting Boogaloo. The bitch was due any day now, and bets had been placed as to how many pups she would have. Razzmattaz, jealous, stuck a cold wet nose against his mistress's neck.

That night as soon as the clerestroy light went on, Camille went to bed. But she turned, and she tossed, and she rolled first on one side, then the other, until her grandmother's pink cotton nightgown was twisted around her. She straightened out the gown, but the yards and yards soon entangled her limbs again. In frustration she pulled it off entirely. It reminded her too much of the professor, anyway....

A faint sound had her springing suddenly upright in bed. There it was again. Ping, ping. What was it? She reached her window just as another little pebble bounced off the glass. Peeking down, she saw the professor standing on the lawn below, aiming another small stone.

Waving to stop him, she grabbed a short wrap Elaine had given her—a terry-cloth leopard-skin one. Hastily pulling it on, she opened her bedroom door and tiptoed down stairs. Moments later she was closing the kitchen door behind her, tying the wrap's sash.

"You shouldn't have come down!" Jacob whispered, taking her hands. "I just wanted you to lean out the window."

"What do you want? Why did you get me out of

bed?'' she whispered back crossly, quickly pulling her hands out of his hard warm clasp.

"You wanted to know the second I was finished. Well, I'm finished! Now hurry up and get back to bed!''

"You're finished?'' She saw the bright gleam of victory in his tiger eyes. "Oh! And...and...it worked?'' It was the hardest thing in the world not to show her own excitement. She remembered she'd decided never to speak to him again, while here she was, ready to throw her arms around his neck in joy. To stop herself, she looked away from him, shoved her hands in the pockets of the wrap and remarked peevishly, "Big deal! Couldn't you have told me in the morning? Do you realize it's almost one-thirty?''

His disappointment in her response was palpable. He said nothing for a moment, then muttered distantly, "I'm sorry I took you literally. I know we have our differences, but I did think you were interested. Well, go on, what are you waiting for? Get inside!'' and he turned away from her to walk toward the lab, not looking back.

She watched him go, his straight shoulders a little slumped...and felt mean and contemptible for raining on his parade. Jacob had worked so hard, up all night with both the experiment and the perfume sample on his mind.... She bit her lip. He might be a louse, but did she have to be one, too? He may have shamefully used her, but was that a good enough excuse for denying him earned pleasure? After all, he wasn't just working for himself. What it boiled down to was that she loved him, and while she went out of her way to hurt him, once she'd succeeded, she wished she hadn't. She ran after him, hoping to catch him before he disappeared inside the hidden door.

She was rounding the front of the workshop when it struck her as odd that the dogs weren't around. Striding faster, anxiety stabbing at her, she was just about to circle the rear corner, when she heard a grunt and a muffled exclamation. Instantly, she froze. Her whole body felt dipped in ice. Placing her hands against the brick wall, she inched cautiously forward to peer around the corner.

A shaft of light spilled out through the lilac bush. The brilliant beam highlighted two men crouched over a third inert figure. They were pulling the body across the threshold. One of the two was the spy; Camille could see his features clearly in the light. She'd never seen the other before, but it was Jacob who was as limp as a sack of flour.

"Quick—watch that door doesn't close!" her spy muttered to the other. "I don't want to spend half the night trying to figure out how it opens!" Lifting Jacob's arms, grunting, he heaved him clear of the lilac bush, while his companion held the door, then closed it carefully, slipping what looked like a charge card between it and the catch so that the lock wouldn't hold.

"We've got to get rid of him now!"

She failed to catch the other man's reply.

"Get a move on! Take his feet. Can't leave tracks...."

Cursing and muttering to each other in undertones, they hoisted the professor and bore him off.

Camille was terrified—she didn't know what to do. Call the sergeant. Yes, but she couldn't let them take Jacob only God knew where! And where were the dogs? What had they done to the dogs? She followed the men, staying far behind, cautiously sneaking from bush to tree to shrub. But then she thought, *if they're going to throw Jacob in the ocean, how can I stop them, one small woman against two men!* Was Jacob still alive? Panic threatened to overwhelm her.

She knew she had to pull herself together. She had to stop them. Her mind raced. First she would see where they meant to take her professor, then she would run back to call the sergeant and get her father's gun. With the gun, she would return to rescue Jacob. With a gun, one small woman could do a great deal.

They knew the territory—without hesitation they took the track through the woods to Damask after crossing the public road. It was peculiar that when it was necessary cold cunning took over. Camille realized she had evolved into woman the hunter, stalking prey. All her senses were alive. Adrenaline pumped through her veins. Emotion was gone, fright was gone. She was bent on one purpose, and she dared not fail.

And so it was that she slithered behind a clump of bracken to watch the two dump the professor on the ground behind the American Queen Anne house. They fumbled around in the dark for a second. Then a flashlight beam illuminated the coal-shute hatch, partially covered over with blackberry briars. One man opened the hatch, while the other heaved Jacob up, and feet first, pushed and shoved him over the lip and down. Camille didn't stay to watch any longer. She ran back to the lab as she'd never run before.

Behind the lilac bush, open the door, grab the card and put it in her pocket, shut the door firmly, run to the phone, dial triple five, forty-one, forty-nine.... The call was answered in the middle of the first ring. Sergeant Peterson's blessed voice was on the other end. Camille wasted no words. She had the whole situation explained in less than a minute.

"We're on our way. You, you go straight to bed and stay the hell there!" He hung up.

Go to bed? Was he crazy? Camille dashed to the filing cabinet. Snatching up the ornate gun, she thrust it through her sash and was already running for the door when it occurred to her that the mercenaries were coming back for the equation. She wasn't about to let them grab eight years of the professor's life—and fourteen years or more of her father's!

The computer was open on the counter, still on. She knew now that the equation was stored on diskettes. It was easy enough to snap open the flaps on either side of the TV screen and pull the two out that were in the machine. Underneath the two ports were small storage spaces, both crammed with more diskettes. She took them all. A quick check to make sure she'd missed none, then she rolled one library shelf over the secret door and left by the regular door, locking it behind her.

With her arms full—there must have been twenty of them—she stood motionless for a second, straining her ears for any sound...and heard the low mur-

mur of the mens' voices as they approached on the rear side of the workshop. In five seconds they would discover the secret door was locked! She tore off in front of the workshop and back to Damask, while the conspirators were hopefully still busy trying to figure out what had happened to their charge card.

Breaking into the clearing, the Damask lawn, she wondered where to hide her priceless burden. She couldn't take it with her to the professor, because the men might come back to him when they broke into the lab and found nothing. They must have knocked Jacob out before he could close the secret door behind him. She'd caught them right at that point and hadn't seen them even looking inside. So they probably hadn't seen that the diskettes were actually in plain view. Which meant they wouldn't realize somebody had seized them in the meantime. Did they even know how the equation had been stored? Better if they didn't, for then they would search until the sergeant came—"

Of course! Her old treasure chest in the weeping willow. The apple crate. The diskettes would be safe there. Not hesitating a moment longer, Camille ran to the tree, and clutching the armful of thin, pliable squares against her breast, clambered up the boughs in her bare feet, one-handed. She tossed the works into the crate with the greatest relief. Back down lickety-split, she jumped the last several feet to the ground and crouched there, checking to make sure the coast was clear. With a touch at the gun to reassure herself, Camille dashed to the coal shute.

The shute door yawned in the darkness. She leaned

in, and the thick stench of whiskey assailed her nostrils. What had they done? Poured a whole bottle over him? Casting a swift backward glance down the path, seeing no one yet, she swung her bare legs over the lip and slid down, breaking her slide with her feet and hands so that she wouldn't land on top of Jacob. In the pitch black she groped her way over his body, sprawled at the bottom.

With trembling hands she touched him. He was warm. Beneath her fingers, the vein below his ear throbbed with life. She gulped in shattered relief and uncontainable joy. She couldn't go on for a moment, just crouched there in the blackness, holding on to him. But he was all wet—was it blood or was it whiskey? And he was so ominously still.... She ran her hands along his neck, his limbs. Nothing appeared to be broken. She slid her hands over his head. There was no sticky warm wetness in his hair, but there was a lump forming on his skull. Shaking him by the shoulders, Camille urgently repeated his name over and over again. He didn't stir. She shook him harder, but he remained limp and lifeless.

Now was not the time to hold back. Biting her lip, she slapped him. Anxiously peering upward through the shute, to see only stars, she slapped him again, harder, and again, harder yet. He didn't move.

What to do now, she asked herself, agonized. Cold water? In the terrible and complete dark, she felt her way through the cellar, arms out in front. There was a cold-water tap by the laundry tubs. And there was that pail of ammonia solution. She would empty it, rinse it out and.... She had just emptied the pail into one of the tubs when a beam of light fell down the shute onto Jacob's body. Terror struck anew. Were they back already? She fled to duck behind one of her grandfather's wine racks.

Not a moment too soon. Her spy slid down the shute, swearing under his breath. At the bottom he stepped over the professor and, setting down his flashlight so the beam shot upward, began to grope in Jacob's vest pocket. Camille's fingers tightened around the handle of the revolver.... Slowly she withdrew it from her sash, and even more slowly, holding her breath, eased off the safety catch so that it didn't make the slightest sound.

"So sorry to have to wake you up, Darleah," she could hear the spy muttering away to himself. "Especially after putting you to sleep so nicely. But business is business. Damned inconsiderate of you not to leave those diskettes where we could find 'em." He had a small, narrow black case in his hands now. Holding it under the light, he snapped it open, and before her horror-struck eyes, lifted out a hypodermic needle. Her insides turned to jelly.

He put down the case, lifted out a tiny glass bottle, jammed the needle into the top of it. "This'll not only have you staring and wide awake, but singing like a bird. And what's more, you won't remember anything in the morning."

Camille thought she would forever remember the man's curiously nondescript features, the pale hair flopping forward, lighted from beneath in grotesque fashion. In the eerie light, the man looked utterly evil. Trying to lick her lips, her mouth as dry as the

Sahara, she raised the gun, resting it on the edge of
the wine rack to hold it steady. But she might hit
Jacob, she fretted. Her position was bad.

Suddenly Jacob moaned. The sound was very clear
in the quiet. The man stopped in the process of pulling the needle from the little vial. As Jacob moaned
again and stirred slightly, the man raised the needle,
point in the air and pressed in the plunger. In the
light, tiny droplets sprayed up. Camille saw her opportunity; aiming for the center of the malevolent
hand, she pulled the trigger.

The hypodermic shattered into a thousand frag-
ments. In the confines of the rock-walled cellar, the
report of the gun roared around the stone like a trapped locomotive. The spy rolled out of the immediate
circle of light. Jacob, violently jerked awake by the
noise, lifted himself up on one elbow. Camille remained crouched behind the wine rack, revolver
aimed—while in a flash her target had not only
reached inside his jacket to produce a small automatic, but was on his feet facing her. His weapon was
sweeping the air as he advanced, step by step. Camille watched him in fascinated frozen fear.

She was, in fact, so fixed on him that when Jacob
hurled himself on the spy's back, she was almost as
astonished as Jacob's victim. The men went down in
a flying crash, taking some oaken barrels with them;
the automatic clattered across the granite floor. Camille darted out to snatch it up, and now she had a
gun in each hand. She turned to see Jacob, sprawled
on top of the spy, being throttled, while with two fist-
fuls of hair, Jacob lifted the man's head to smack the

crown soundly back against the stone. Camille saw the spy go limp as he passed out. The professor staggered to his feet, rubbing his throat... and they looked at each other.

She grinned. A great beatific smile all over her face as she stood there, armed cap-a-pie, her leopard-skin wrap cinched at the waist, her long legs bare and black streaked. But her elation was short-lived. The creak of a boot against the cellar stairs had her leaping toward Jacob. Snatching the automatic, he thrust her behind him and raised his arm. Sheltered, she raised her arm, too. Both guns were leveled at the stairs. She slid her other arm around his waist.

"Whoaah!" the sergeant exclaimed, seeing two weapons trained on him. The coal shute was suddenly full of light and noise. One after another, corporals appeared, more weapons at the ready. Camille started giggling. The cellar was alive with Mounties.

Hero and heroine gladly handed the guns to the sergeant while he was issuing orders, after which Jacob promptly wrapped his arms very tightly around her.

"We've got the other one," Sergeant Peterson reassured them. "I see you got this one! Our men staked around the lab? All out cold. They're too damned efficient, these boys. We've rounded up the whole lot except somehow, one we didn't know about slipped through our fingers with the diskettes. Unless you hid them, Dr. Darleah?"

"What?" Camille felt the shudder of Jacob's body so close to hers and opened her eyes. "What?" he repeated, aghast. "They have them?"

"No," she said. "I do."

"What?" Both Jacob and the sergeant cried in unison.

"Well, I do."

The sergeant wrinkled his brow at her. "I thought I told you to go to bed."

"Camille," Jacob protested, "you could have been killed! It's not worth it!"

They were ringed by Mounties. The spy had already been carried away up the stairs. "It's too late to get mad at me now. They're in the willow. Let's go get them."

"Camille, I don't think there are words to describe you— No, darling, I meant that as a compliment, believe me!" Jacob laughed, burying a hand in her curls to plant a swift speaking kiss on her lips. She was pink with embarrassment when the kiss was over . . . and somewhat dazed.

Up the stairs they went and through the house. It looked very different with all the dustcovers gone. Different and lived in. Some pieces moved, some new pieces added—she hadn't enough time for a really good look.

Soon they were all gathered beneath the willow. As Camille prepared to swing herself up to the first bough, she stopped. "Um, how about shining the light somewhere else?" she requested, suddenly aware that she wasn't overdressed, certainly not dressed enough to have flashlights spotlighting her upward climb. She saw a few grins as the beams dropped to the ground.

"Ugh!" she shrieked a few minutes later, her hand

in the apple crate. She had the presence of mind to
tuck the wrap around her legs just as all the beams
flashed upward. "Never mind, never mind!" she
hastened to shout. "I—it's only a spider, I think!"
She shivered nevertheless.

"You're afraid of a little spider, and yet you're
willing to tackle—"

"You don't understand," she snapped at Jacob.
"Spiders have eight legs; they only had four!" That
raised a chuckle down below, and once more all the
beams lowered. "Should I drop them down one at a
time?" Hearing the affirmative, she dropped all
nineteen diskettes, one after another, into the professor's waiting hands. He caught them gingerly,
careful not to bend them or let them fall into the
dewy grass. She was back down on the ground in seconds flat, in time to watch the diskettes disappear into a slender black attaché case that one of his men
handed the sergeant.

No sooner had she touched ground than Jacob,
with an astute look at all the admiring glances being
showered his stepsister, cleared his throat slightly and
tugged her wrap a little closer together in the front,
pulled it a little farther down her thighs, and ended
by placing a rather possessive arm around her shoulders.

CHAPTER ELEVEN

CAMILLE WALKED BACK to the farm between the professor and Sergeant Peterson, the rest of the Mounties behind. Those who had apprehended the mercenaries were long gone. She told her side of events. All Jacob could remember was a stunning blow on the back of his head; he now had a full-fledged headache as a souvenir. The sergeant told her they'd found the dogs, drugged but alive, dragged out of sight underneath the yew hedge. The conspirators hadn't damaged the lab, either entering it or searching it. They had been frighteningly efficient.

The farm was quiet and dark. As the squad behind them left in an unmarked truck parked on the public road, Camille, the professor and the sergeant returned to the lab, where three detectives were waiting in the darkness. One, who had medical training, was checking the dogs. He reassured Camille they would be right as rain once they revived. Boogaloo and her unborn pups shouldn't suffer any ill effects. To the professor's annoyance, the man insisted on checking him out, too.

"They obviously wanted a clean job," Sergeant Peterson said. "No trace of them having been here. Shows the caliber of the gang we were dealing with.

That's why they treated you the way they did, Jacob—and you smell terrible! They had everything planned perfectly, although they should have sent three men to handle this job, not two. They didn't bargain for a certain Camille Beesley!" His stern face with the incongruous freckles dissolved into a quick grin as he looked at her, and at Jacob's arm firmly planted around her shoulders. "What I can't figure, Jacob, is why they didn't search the lab, interrogate you before disposing of you. Oh, well, I guess no one's perfect! The important thing is, we owe you a great deal, Miss—"

"Camille," she said, and shook his hand. "Think nothing of it."

He chuckled in reply.

Jacob gave him a small metal case, which apparently contained samples of the experiment in all its stages from start to finish. Her father's letter and more papers went inside the attaché case, as well as the charge card Camille had taken from the secret door. Then all the night visitors were gone, and it was as though no one had ever been. In the cottage, everyone still slept.

Kneeling between the sleeping dogs, running her fingers through their fleecy apricot coats, Camille breathed deeply of the clean night air, fragrant with blossoms and ozone and sea spume...feeling the wonderful release from fear that had haunted her ever since Fredericton, when she'd realized a strange man was following Jacob. She watched the professor at the outdoor tap by the distillery door, stripping off his shirt and dousing himself, holding the hose over his head to let the tingling cold water stream down his sleek virile torso.... She looked quickly away, recognizing those fluttering butterflies within. But a moment later, she was watching him again. He had rinsed his shirt and was using it as a towel.

"I'll get you a towel." She stood up.

"Don't bother. This feels great." Turning off the tap, he came toward her, drops trailing from his hair. He wiped them away with the shirt. His jeans were wet. He was all wet, but smelling considerably sweeter. "Oh—" he flexed his shoulders, rubbing his nape "—does it feel good to be finished with it! It feels like a load just fell off my back!"

"I was just thinking.... My dad started at the *a*, and you finished with the *z*...quite symbolic in a way. It started here and it ended here. How's your head?" she added anxiously. "Is the lump any bigger?"

"Don't fuss, darling. The water helped. I feel brand-new." He stopped. "You're some lady, you know that?"

Suddenly she felt incredibly nervous, shaky inside. "I...." She rubbed one bare foot on the other. "I'm just ever so glad you're alive!" Her light voice quavered slightly.

"I guess there's no point in saying you shouldn't have."

"No, no point at all."

"I'm ever so glad you're alive, too. I...I don't know what I'd do without you...."

Now all of her was trembling, and she could feel the pounding of her heart throughout her body. She stared at her feet, afraid to look into his amber eyes, afraid to trust the disarming velvety tone that she'd heard before but hadn't heard enough.

"We're a dirty pair." He chuckled softly, surprising her by sitting down on his heels to run his shirt over her coal-dusty legs. She gazed down at his bent head...and then couldn't resist. One hand reached out to tentatively slide through his wet hair, brushing it off his forehead. "I'm afraid you need a bath," he said, giving up his efforts with the shirt. Tipping his head back, he looked up at her. When she would have withdrawn her hand, he caught it and, turning it over, kissed the palm. His lips, the soft flick of his tongue against the sensitive skin had shock waves reverberating through her. She tried to tug her hand away. He held on, suddenly frowning at the spot he'd kissed, as if an unpleasant memory had assailed him. "Camille, about Pierre—"

"Oh!" This time she managed to free her hand, then flung both up in the air. "You're not on about him again, are you?" She forgot to speak quietly. Turning, she hurried toward the cottage, calling over her shoulder, "You have a bone to pick with Pierre? Take it up with him!"

"Camille!" Jacob started after her.

"Pierre has done absolutely nothing to merit your abuse!"

"Camille!"

She reached the house, passed it and headed for the front lawn.

"Camille, dammit, will you stay in one spot for a damn second!"

She swiveled, placing her hands on her hips. "I like Pierre, and if you so much as start in about him being a lecherous old man...! It's disgusting! Your friend!"

He flung his shirt down. "One of these days I'm going to tie you down to a chair! Pierre is not a lecherous old man—I never said he was! I only...I only want to know how you feel about him."

"I just told you! I keep telling and telling everybody, and everybody insists on not believing me! You want to know how I feel about Pierre? Very well, then, stand right there!" She pointed adamantly to the other side of a sawn-off tree trunk, which had been used as a low garden seat for as long as she could remember. She was standing on the other side of it.

"Why?"

"Never mind. Just stand there!"

"Camille, you make me downright uneasy sometimes!" But Jacob complied, eyeing her warily.

Once he was in exactly the right place, she stepped up on the trunk, and with him comfortably nose to nose and within her easy reach, she slid her arms around his bare shoulders. Pressing her body against him, she kissed him. Her soft pink lips melted into his with beguiling conviction, evocatively tender lips that kissed each corner, lingering on the lovely masculine curves of his mouth. The tip of her tongue slid slowly along the lower curve of his bottom lip, and more slowly yet, delicately sensual, inside his mouth to touch the tip of his tongue. In heady abandonment she kissed him, while his hands came to rest on her hips and he began to return her kiss.

Longingly he kissed her, hungrily tasting the sweet promise of her mouth, his hands molding her pliant body against him in a way that told her how much he wanted her, yet how uncertain he was. His tactile seduction transformed her elation into a fluid yearning ache for him. Every nerve in her body unwound.

"Do you see now how I feel about Pierre?" she whispered against his lips.

"But Camille—" his fingers bit urgently into her soft flesh "—I won't have you feeling this way about two men at once! It's not fair play!"

"Oh!" She fell against him, locking her arm around his neck. "You darling idiotic dinosaur!"

"Only me?"

"Unfortunately, yes."

"You're going to take back that 'unfortunately.'"

"We'll see."

"Indeed you will...." He held her mesmerized with his eyes, his fingers trailing up her cheek and temple in tender caress. "Starting right now, love." His fingers spread into her wayward curls, firmly entangling themselves in the lustrous creamy gold. His other hand moved in slow circles down the curve of her back.

"Jacob," she murmured, "don't say that unless—"

"Shh, my love." His lips fastened over hers in an exquisite simmer of passion, sending shivers of delight racing over her skin. Trembling within his embrace, she threaded her fingers into the drenched hair at his nape, glorying in the touch and the feel

and the male scent of his body, his skin damp and
cool under her wandering fingers.

As his lips imprinted his desire on her upturned
face and roamed slowly, delectably down the length
of her throat, his arms held her with infinite care.
The terry-cloth leopard skin cushioned the hard
planes and angles of his thighs and hips and chest,
fitted to her yielding curves. But it was no protec-
tion against his searching hands as they caressed and
pulled loose the sash.

Then his touch against her bared flesh as he savored the swell of her breast, the smooth curve into
the indent of her waist, following the outline of
her hipbone and moving to the trim roundness
of her petite derriere, the softness of her upper
thigh, exploring all lovingly.... Camille was
wanton, delirious with the potency of his lovemaking. She could do nothing but cling to him
or else, she knew, she might float right away. His
naked skin against hers was an ardent scorching in-
ducement. She felt light as air, suffused with happiness that he felt precisely this way about her in
return.

"My, my, my! And what have we here?"

Unceremoniously jerked from her trance, Camille
couldn't at first tell where her brother's laughing
drawl was coming from. Jacob's arms tightened
around her, holding her wrap closed. But he needn't
have worried, for she saw Robbie then as she looked
over Jacob's shoulder. Her brother was leaning out
his bedroom window, grinning hugely.

"I thought I heard voices. I went outside to check
but couldn't see hide nor hair of anybody. So I come

back up here to fall back into bed—and look what I see down below! You fight in the daytime and make up at night, eh? D'you two realize just exactly what time of night it is?''

"Shh, Robbie! You'll wake up the parents!"

"Oh, and wouldn't they just love to see this!" he chortled. "I knew something was fishy!"

"Robbie," Jacob growled softly, "go to bed!"

"Oh, hell, and I was just going to get my violin! Well, carry on without the serenade, then, but just remember—the 'big meeting' happens in four hours! In four little hours you two are going to have to look bright-eyed and bushy-tailed around the dining-room table. And what's the objection to admitting that you don't fight all the time?"

"Beat it, Robbie!" Camille warned. "Your big-brother act is wearing thin."

Jacob tied her sask, suddenly laughing under his breath. He put his hands on either side of her waist and murmured to her, "We'll continue this tomorrow, or later on today, without our serenade. I get the notion he's not going back to bed until you're in yours. Maybe tomorrow—today—I can persuade him to let me take you off his hands." His grin was wide and white in the fading darkness. His eyes danced brilliantly into hers.

"That's it—I'm going for my violin!" Robbie ducked his head back inside his window.

"Off you go, baby. I'll see you in four hours." He captured her mouth in a soft, sweet kiss. "In just four hours, darling...."

She met her brother at the kitchen door. "Really, Robbie, I'm not six years old!"

"What's going on around here?" He followed her through the kitchen.

"Go stick your head under your pillow." She smiled radiantly at him, standing there in his pajamas, arms akimbo.

"Why won't anybody tell me anything," he complained as she shut the downstairs bathroom door in his face. She meant to take a shower, and she wasn't going to wake the whole household by using the one upstairs.

CAMILLE REALIZED, when she was taking another shower some three hours later, that she'd forgotten all about the still-missing perfume formula. Her happy spirits sank as she contemplated the ordeal in store. But she couldn't wait to see her professor again; even the morbid thought of facing Charles couldn't ruin her mood. What exactly had Jacob meant by taking her off Robbie's hands?

It was obvious to her, the second she saw Robbie, that he, too, had remembered the formula was missing. Fidgety, he was trying to eat breakfast with his mother and stepfather. His worried brown eyes latched on to her as soon as she appeared. With a sunny smile and a greeting, she poured herself a cup of coffee, but declined more, feeling too excited to do something so mundane as eat. Her smile was so sunny, in fact, that both Fern and Charles gazed after her in faint puzzlement when, excusing herself, she went out to the back porch to wait for Jacob. Robbie joined her minutes later.

"Did Jake—"

"No, he didn't."

"Oh, honestly! You could have stopped smooching long enough to ask him about it!"

"Ask him yourself—here he comes."

Jacob caught her eyes first, and the look in the tawny depths made her heart turn over. A slow tide of warm rosy pink seemed to sweep over her whole body, and she clasped her coffee cup tighter.

"I have it right here," was his opening comment. He tapped his breast pocket.

"What?" Robbie exclaimed, while Camille's brown eyes widened on Jacob in astonishment.

"But how? Where? Who?" Dazed, Robbie took the folded piece of paper to kiss it fervently.

The professor smiled from one to the other. "Deductive reasoning. Elaine."

"No!" Camille cried.

"Er...it's eight!" Charles stuck his head out the door. "Time for the meeting."

"We'll be right there, dad." Charles disappeared back inside after greeting his son. "Yes, Elaine! She took it when the boiler burst. She saw it lying on the counter, slipped it out of the plastic cover, thinking the fake was an exact duplicate and that the copy she had wouldn't be missed."

"But why?" Camille shook her head in disbelief.

"Well, she'd racked up a mountain of bills, not to mention her visit to the fat farm, and was afraid to face her father—Wilson's not the easiest nut to crack when it comes to money. Then he got hit by his investments. She knew he didn't have the money to give her. She was running scared. She came to me for a loan—that's how desperate she was! But I was tired of bailing her out and told her to confess to her father. Instead, she took the formula and—''

''Three minutes past eight!'' affirmed Charles testily from inside.

''And then didn't know how to go about turning it into cash. And then began to feel the pangs of guilt. I've been baiting her, suspecting she had the formula. Last night I hinted that if she gave it to me, I'd help her out. She couldn't give it to me fast enough. But this is the last time, the very last time she's ever sponging a loan out of me!''

''That rotten so-and-so!'' Robbie snarled.

''Five minutes past!'' their stepfather curtly qualified.

Robbie, rolling his eyes, went in, and as Camille went to leave, Jacob stopped her with a touch on her cheek. ''Camille, tell me again about Pierre. Those ringing wedding bells have me worried. What happened in Montreal after I left? I do know Pierre, and he doesn't casually ask ladies to marry him!''

''Are you doubting me?'' Her delicate eyebrows rose.

''Not exactly. I'm just worried.''

''You're worried? What about me? You're not Mr. Reliable himself!''

''Six minutes!'' Charles roared. ''Will you two quit this constant arguing!''

''What do you mean? When wasn't I reliable?'' Jacob asked, injured, holding open the screen door for her to precede him.

''How about Fredericton for starters?'' They went

through the kitchen to the dining room, where Charles was glowering at the head of the six-leaves-long table. Fern sat next to him on his left, Robbie on his right. Camille and Jacob took chairs at the other end, close to the door. "You promised to leave a message, and you didn't!" she tacked on in a quick whisper.

"Finally!" Charles frowned at them down the length of the table. "I've spent this past week studying the function and the...."

"Aha!" Jacob muttered in an undertone. "So you aren't bored, after all! I didn't call you because... because, well, I suppose I was sulking."

"Sulking?" she whispered, gaping at him.

Charles's voice rose a trifle; Camille glanced disconcertedly toward him. While the meeting was important to her, this little private meeting with Jacob was much more so. She tried, studiously, to pay attention to Charles's measured deliberate tone. "Fern and I have decided the best policy would be to turn the perfumery over to you, Camille, and you, Robbie. I've had all the legal papers prepared. It's now entirely in your names. The only thing required is your signatures." In shock, Camille stared at her stepfather. "I don't usually believe in fifty-fifty partnerships. There should be one decision maker in most cases, but I've watched you two, and you work as an equal team. Therefore, I trust you will continue to do so. The land, the buildings, everything is signed over...."

"Okay, I admit it was stupid of me. But how do you think I felt?" Jacob continued very quietly.

"I'm hundreds of miles away from you in Quebec City. I pick up a Montreal paper, and there you are, splashed across the front page, getting married to a friend of mine!"

"It was not the front page!" she said under her breath. "And Pierre only said all that nonsense for advertising! He explained it all to me the next morning—"

"Advertising? Men don't get married for advertising!"

"He didn't say he was; he said he *hoped* to. Those pictures might have looked incriminating, but the kiss that was photographed was the only kiss I got from him! And I only went out to dinner with him because he said you told him to take care of me while I was in Montreal."

The professor gazed at her in amazement. "I'll kill him!" he protested vigorously.

"*Can't* you control yourselves?" Charles stared at them in aggravated bewilderment.

"Who are you going to kill?" asked Fern curiously.

"Please!" Charles begged. Everyone subsided. Glancing around, Charles picked up another sheaf of papers from the neat piles before him. "You've sorted the duties between you already. Robbie's in charge of the fields, the plants, the production of the oil. Camille, you're already acting in the capacity of general manager without knowing it, and with Jake to take over the lab work—and that includes the warehouse—that'll leave you more time for your roses, Robbie, and you more time for your organ, Camille."

"But...." Camille paused. "What are *you* going to do?"

"I'll act as consultant. And here are some suggestions. First, I think you should invest in more land to plant Robbie's new rose. Later you can think of growing other things. Second, advertising!" Camille took a sideways peek at Jacob, he caught her eye. "Advertising can either cost a fortune or be dirt cheap, depending on whether it works for you or not...."

"Pierre lied," the professor whispered to her.

"But he had me home by midnight!" she whispered back.

"Okay.... But what about Greyson? The very first damn night of your trip, he's coming out of your hotel room—your boyfriend."

"He hasn't been my boyfriend for years. He had to go to Vancouver to pick up parts. He took me out for dinner! That's all."

"Okay.... But what about that fishing trip? That was some fishing trip!"

"*Can't* you be in the same room without starting a fight?" Charles appealed. "What is it with you two?"

Camille squirmed. "I—I'm sorry, Charles. I'm listening, honestly I am. You were discussing the advertising, and you were saying...you were saying...."

"I was saying," he sighed, glaring at his son but speaking to her, "that I think we should continue to use your face. We should try to get the rights to that picture of Pierre kissing your hand—a marvelous promo, that. As to the firm to use, I know a...."

"What exactly were you fishing for?" Jacob shot at her in a vehement undertone.

"If you wondered about it then, why didn't you ask then?" she simply couldn't resist asking.

Jacob frowned at her. "I'm not used to asking these kinds of questions!"

"You're doing pretty well at it now!" Her lips quivered into a faint smile as she pretended to listen to their stepfather.

"I can't stand it a second longer," he murmured back.

"Did you tell me to get lost because of my fishing trip with Greyson?" she whispered carefully.

"I'd barely left town, and you're out with him for a barbecue. The day I get back—where were you? Fishing!" he accused wrathfully.

"And what about Annette? How did you think I felt—one night with me, the weekend with her?"

Jacob's eyebrows rose. "All I did was give her a ride to Vancouver and back. And actually, her needing a ride was handy. It was a great cover."

"Well!" she exclaimed, somewhat louder than was wise, "couldn't you have told me that?"

"I would have, except the night before we were otherwise occupied.... I missed you the next morning, and when I came back, you'd the hell and gone fishing!"

"Why didn't you take me?"

"And just what do you think mother's and father's—not to mention brother's—opinion would have been of *that*?"

Camille giggled, then realized they had a silent and

intrigued audience at the far end of the table. How long had everyone been tuned in to their private conversation? She turned a delightful shade of scarlet.

"Oh, please, continue!" Charles instructed suavely. "Only speak up, so we can all get in on it! I must admit, I'm dying of curiosity!"

"Well, at least they're talking to each other. That's something," Fern put in a little anxiously.

"I only have one more thing...." Camille leaned toward Jacob and whispered, to their audience's supreme annoyance, "Who was that lady in Fredericton?"

"Dr. Marilyn Davies, U.S.A. representative of the consortium," he whispered back.

"Carry on, Charles. You have my undivided attention," Camille said, settling back in her chair.

"No! Really?" he remarked sarcastically. "Four. Your mother and I could handle some of your sales. We're planning on doing some traveling, anyway. Five. Here are the revamped plans for changes to the store—" he shot Camille a glance "—and this is the plan for the new greenhouse, Robbie. Look it over to make sure I have it right. I'd like to see you begin to sell your roses as a sideline. Six. I noticed none of you is very good at keeping orderly books. I'll set up a system and find a good accountant. Seven...."

On the front porch after the meeting, Camille, Robbie and Jacob were discussing Elaine when Charles came out of the house.

Jacob said he was homeward bound, adding to her, "I'll be waiting. Don't be long. We'll have that picnic...."

She looked back at him, her heart unknowingly revealed in her deep brown eyes, and wondered where all this in-depth talk was going to end. Remembering Charles, she glanced at him. It was clear he wanted another chat. Biting her lip, she considered she owed him one. She turned to him as Jacob left.

Looking from her to Robbie, he said bluntly, "You didn't have many suggestions to make."

"Well, no," Robbie agreed. "I...liked everything I heard."

"I think I...owe you an apology, Charles." Camille steeled herself to look him in the eye, feeling rather ashamed of herself.

"That feeling is mutual. You misjudged me, and I misjudged both of you. I mistook tenacity for stubbornness, loyalty for selfishness. I think you'll both do very well."

"You do? Oh!" She beamed up at his austere face after a startled second. "But I'm sure we could do with some sound business advice. Robbie and I are a little short on management skills."

"You learn fast. Er...Camille...is the situation between you and Jake beyond hope?"

She blinked at her stepfather. "I'll let you know," she replied, turning away down the steps.

Taking the path through the woods to Damask to be there all the sooner, she maintained a sedate pace until she was out of sight of the cottage, then broke into a run. Jacob was indeed waiting for her. He caught her as she ran to him and swept her up into a hug that all but damaged her ribs.

"So what did you do, fishing all day and all night? Camille, I was in hell!"

"We had a marshamllow roast. Have you never had a marshmallow roast?"

"No!"

"We'll have one tonight—initiate you and Charles. Greyson really is awfully nice, you know."

"I know, I know! Too nice."

"Not nice enough."

"Why didn't I just ask? I could have saved myself so much—"

"That'll teach you not to sulk in the future." She smiled, wrapping her arms around his neck and kissing his chin.

"You could have asked about Annette!" he reminded her, spilling her down into the sun-warmed grass and stretching out beside her.

"I hardly think you gave me a chance, what with your abominable 'get lost'!"

Propping himself up on one elbow, he fitted her closer against him. "Camille, I don't have everything I want...." Bending his head, he brushed his lips over hers. When he would have kissed her fully she turned her head, although she slid a hand up to his shoulder.

"Wait a minute, professor," she stalled cautiously. "Your work—"

"Before I met you all I did was work. I meant what I said about having little time for women—until I met you. And since I met you I've wanted to spend all my time with you. I don't know what I'd do without you, Camille.... I love you."

"But," she protested still, while joy bubbled inside her, "Jacob, you won't be happy just mixing shampoo. It'll hardly keep you busy, anyway."

"There are only about a dozen other projects I've had in mind, but never had the time to pursue. I have yet to finish my book, too. But, Camille, my life doesn't count for much if I can't have you with me." The hushed velvet of his deep voice enwrapped her.

"I can't cook."

"Neither can I," he laughed, kissing the tip of her nose. He slid a long thin hand around her throat, holding her very still. "I bought Damask for you, Camille—here is one dinosaur begging you to marry him!"

"I hope you like eggs, darling!" She sighed huskily. "Oh, Jacob, I love you, I love you, I—" Their lips met in a shimmering blend of sunshine and unquenchable happiness, their feather-soft touching fragile, yet of boundless strength. When he raised his head slightly, she ran her fingers down his temple and cheekbone and the narrowing line of his jaw, her lambent gaze shining up into the jeweled sparkle of tiger eyes.

"Camille—"

"See?" broke in an unexpected voice.

"If you brought your violin, Robbie," Jacob threatened, sitting up and bringing Camille with him, resting her against his chest, "you're going to be wearing it around your neck!"

"Don't blame me," Robbie averred cheerfully. "Blame Boogaloo—she had five puppies while we had our meeting! You won the bet, Jake."

"Er, we all thought we'd tag along to give you the news..." Charles commented, eyeing them as if he was unsure of the evidence before his eyes.

"And all this time," Fern remonstrated, starting to laugh. "I was convinced you didn't even like him! Oh, go on. Kiss Jake, dear!"

ABOUT THE AUTHOR

In trying to choose a profession, Vancouver author Christine Hella Cott found she wanted to do practically everything. She decided on writing as the perfect outlet for her "rampant imagination," since it allows her to delve into a range of subjects—from Peruvian gem dealing in *Dangerous Delight* to the creation of perfume on Vancouver Island.

Perfume and Lace chronicles the comic trials of heroine Camille on her small rose-and-lavender farm. The setting, a recreation of a defunct Island perfumery, struck the author as a natural for romance, deftly employed to uncover chemical reactions both human and scientific....

Christine is a regular contributor to Superromance. Her other novels for the line include *Midnight Magic* and *A Tender Wilderness*.

Yours FREE, with a home subscription to SUPERROMANCE™

Now you never have to miss reading the newest **SUPERROMANCES**... because they'll be delivered right to your door.

Start with your **FREE** LOVE BEYOND DESIRE. You'll be enthralled by this powerful love story ..from the moment Robin meets the dark, handsome Carlos and finds herself involved in the jealousies, bitterness and secret passions of the Lopez family. Where her own forbidden love threatens to shatter her life

Your **FREE** LOVE BEYOND DESIRE is only the beginning. A subscription to **SUPERROMANCE** lets you look forward to a long love affair Month after month, you'll receive four love stories of heroic dimension Novels that will involve you in spellbinding intrigue, forbidden love and fiery passions

You'll begin this series of sensuous, exciting contemporary novels written by some of the top romance novelists of the day with four every month

And this big value each novel, almost 400 pages of compelling reading is yours for only $2 50 a book Hours of entertainment every month for so little. Far less than a first-run movie or pay-TV Newly published novels, with beautifully illustrated covers, filled with page after page of delicious escape into a world of romantic love delivered right to your home

Begin a long love affair with

SUPER?OMANCE.

Accept LOVE BEYOND DESIRE **FREE.**

Complete and mail the coupon below today!

- -

FREE! Mail to: SUPER?OMANCE

In the U S
2504 West Southern Avenue
Tempe, AZ 85282

In Canada
649 Ontario St
Stratford, Ontario N5A 6W2

YES, please send me FREE and without any obligation, my
SUPER?OMANCE novel, LOVE BEYOND DESIRE If you do not hear
from me after I have examined my FREE book, please send me the
4 new **SUPER?OMANCE** books every month as soon as they come
off the press. I understand that I will be billed only $2 50 for each book
(total $10.00). There are no shipping and handling or any other hidden
charges. There is no minimum number of books that I have to
purchase. In fact, I may cancel this arrangement at any time
LOVE BEYOND DESIRE is mine to keep as a FREE gift, even if
I do not buy any additional books.

NAME _____ (Please Print) _____

ADDRESS _____ APT NO ____

CITY _____

STATE/PROV _____ ZIP/POSTAL CODE _____

SIGNATURE (If under 18, parent or guardian must sign) _____ 134-BPS-KA

SUP-SU